NORTH

OF THE

NOTCH

A LEGAL THRILLER

LOIS WOOCHER KARFUNKEL

"I wanted you to see what real courage is, instead of getting the idea that courage is a man with a gun in his hand. It's when you know you're licked before you begin but you begin anyway and you see it through no matter what." —Atticus, *To Kill a Mockingbird*

"The truth is rarely pure and never simple."
Oscar Wilde, "The Importance of Being Earnest"

"The beginning is always today."
Mary Wollstonecraft Shelly, *The Short Stories of MaryShelley, Volume 2*

CHAPTER ONE

How did a thirtysomething kid from Queens, a Columbia Law Honors grad, find herself arguing a deer case in rural New Hampshire – where mosquitoes and moose outnumbered residents?

"Trust me, it's not a winner, Joe."

"My client said two large deer jumped over the fence and ran across the highway. He had to swerve to avoid them."

Gwen Wilson listened and almost laughed. "Joe, that story won't play. No jury in Middleton, or anywhere North of the Notch, will buy it. You're claiming two big deer no one else saw walked out of the woods, passed Macy's windows in the mall, pranced through the parking lot, leaped over a fence onto the four-lane highway, thereby distracting your client so he missed the yield sign and plowed into my client's car? And somehow the deer after another Olympic leap then magically disappeared into the wilderness? All at mid-day? Come on, counselor. Wait 'til I tell the jury that your kid's alcohol level was higher than his IQ."

"I don't see that, Gwen."

"Joe, I know the juries here. Maybe that could sell in New Jersey where you are, but as an ex-New Yorker I've learned that folks up here, where 'Live Free or Die' is printed on every license plate, they know their wildlife, especially during hunting season. And they don't take kindly to rich ski bums not coming clean with the law. Make a reasonable offer by Monday or I'll file suit. And then, Joe, you can look forward to ice cold winter days staying at the Middleton Motel bundled in your winter coat and lined L.L. Bean hat while you defend deposition after deposition."

Gwen swiveled in her executive chair, a find as promised at 'Josephs' Used Furniture Finds' along with her beautiful well-worn banker's desk. Joe, the insurance carrier's lawyer, continued blowing smoke and piling up more billable hours. While Gwen's patience was thin after a long week of lawyering, she knew Joe needed to make his case before settlement talks would begin.

Leaning back in her chair, she used the time to play with strands of her hair, thankfully still 'sassy auburn' according to her stylist Roberto. She again vowed to stop pulling out the unwelcome gray hairs that kept coming like ghosts in the night. Not so many at her age, almost thirty-four, but who knew how long before baldness beckoned if she continued this habit.

Yawning, Gwen still had one more client to see. Glancing out the picture window behind her desk, she watched the snow-covered mountains pull the setting sun down until its golden light almost disappeared. Done with her hair, Gwen took up doodling on her legal pad. Joe, like a puppy was stopping to smell every bush. He continued meandering through his notes. Gwen's eyes began to close.

Bang! The loud sudden knock on her office door startled Gwen so much she almost fell off her chair. The door flung open as Judy, her secretary and office manager extraordinaire, shouted, "Gwen, come quickly. Your new client's having a heart attack!"

Gwen shouted to Joe she'd have to call him back, and then ran into her office reception area. Her heart pounding in *her* chest, she saw a small man sitting with his head bent down and arms folded over his knees. Encased in a huge red ski parka, he groaned softly. Flummoxed as to what to do – she hadn't learned first-aid in law school -- Gwen settled for, "Judy, get a cold towel." Then, turning back to the distressed man, Gwen stammered, "Should I call an ambulance?"

The man shook his head no. With effort, he sat up slightly. "You no worry. I be okay soon, need to breathe slow like doctor say."

Relieved, Gwen sat down in the client chair next to him and watched as he began inhaling deeply, and then exhaling slowly. Shortly Judy returned carrying several wet paper towels and together both women removed the man's puffy jacket. Then they placed cold wet paper towels around his neck. The effect was positive and immediate; the man's brown face no longer resembled the color of the tan towels.

Gwen asked again, "Are you feeling better, sir? Should I call an ambulance?"

"No, I better. Be good. No worry, it not heart. Doctor, he say I get 'panic attack' when I nervous." Reaching into his jacket pocket the man added, "See, I take white pill he give me, then I be okay."

With the help of a cup of water Judy had retrieved, Gwen's potential client, his hands still shaking, swallowed his pills.

Then the trio sat and waited. After several minutes the man announced, "I better now. I sit here please 'til I talk with Attorney Wilson."

Judy, her back now turned to the maybe client, explained to Gwen that the man's name was Sammy Perez, and he was her last appointment. "He wants to talk about problems with buying stocks. Says it's urgent."

"Guess it's clear I chose the right profession -- law instead of medicine."

Judy smiled. "I was so nervous, Gwennie, I was going to grab more wet towels for me!

"Judy, why don't you bring Mr. Perez in soon -- so I can call it a day. After all this hoopla, I'm curious to find out what his story is, what's caused him so much harm he had to get medical help. Returning to her desk, Gwen placed a yellow legal pad on her blotter and checked her watch. Six o'clock already, too late to call Joe back. While waiting for Mr. Perez, she took the moment to study her office to see if it appeared intimidating for a nervous client. The green walls and maroon carpet conveyed to her boring rather than decorated expensive. At the same time, the framed achievements and row of mahogany bookcases filled with dowdy law books hopefully expressed 'experienced professional'. Maybe she'd add some flowers next week, to affirm New Hampshire welcoming.

She began reviewing the two-page file Judy had placed on her desk. The intake form showed this was, as Judy had said, a stock trading case and, thankfully, not another nasty divorce. Maybe a potentially good paying case, Gwen thought, like the Carpenter case she was now close to settling for good money. That matter also dealt with claims of broker negligence and investment misrepresentations. Gwen began to look forward to speaking with this possible new client.

Judy's soft knock this time brought her to attention. Judy led Mr. Perez into her office and he took a seat on one of her client chairs.

"Gwen, do you need anything before I leave?"

"No thanks Judy, you're sufficiently late already. See you tomorrow."

As Judy left, Gwen had her usual reaction when observing her secretary. How did she deserve this classy, super competent, Mrs. America -- who had the organizational skills and smarts to be a CEO somewhere a lot warmer? Yet here she was running Gwen's small law office in Middleton, New Hampshire, a once upon a time mill town. Located above the granite Notch that separated the state's hard–nosed mountain Up Country communities from the prosperous and populated towns below. Gwen figured the job clincher for Judy had been the great office coffee -- and easy commute. Plus maybe the fact that Judy's husband ran both the area's Chamber of Commerce and the town's championship little league team. And, then again, there was their friendship, which mattered much to them both.

Turning her attention to Mr. Perez, Gwen saw an older Hispanic man, neatly if casually dressed, small nondescript features except for his slightly flying ears, and thinning dark wavy hair combed straight back. It was his eyes that pulled her in, they were intensely deep brown and framed by delicate long black eye lashes. Gwen began the interview with her usual sales pitch. She extolled her legal credentials: honors from an Ivy League Law School, experience at a Big Firm in New York, and, after quitting the urban life for Middleton, where she now ran her solo general practice.

Gwen paused, aware that she'd omitted a few pertinent facts, such as her increasing dislike of the Big Firm's pressures, the unwelcome partner tirades and sexual advances, the never-ending associate's hours, and, thanks to not being a possible rainmaker, well... and also her gender, that she wasn't a likely candidate for the 'partnership' promotion. All contributed to her readiness to leave the city where she'd grown up and come to love. And, yes, there was the overwhelming Brian factor and the grief that blackened her life. When she found it increasingly painful to be surrounded by 'their' special places, she knew it was time to find a different locale, one that was absent her Brian memories. One day while grabbing lunch at her desk, she read an ad in *The Law Journal* for an associate position with a small firm in Middleton, a town that bordered the White Mountains and near where her family had spent happy vacations when she was a child. Gwen had jumped at the opportunity. Fortuitous, she told herself, meant to be. She quickly sent a letter of interest to the Senior Partner, well solo lawyer, Chris, whom she'd adored from the minute they'd connected. The feeling had been mutual and soon she found herself surrounded by woods and granite.

"Do you have any questions Mr. Perez?"

The man shook his head no, so Gwen went on to describe in a few sentences the work she did in her practice, pointing out that she'd had some experience with securities matters including stock fraud.

With the background narrative done, Gwen finally asked, "Mr. Perez, why don't you tell me why you came here today?"

In a low voice that, like a symphonic crescendo, lilted upwards in tone, Mr. Perez began his story.

CHAPTER TWO

"Attorney, my name Sammy. Sammy Perez. I here because I need good lawyer to help me." Sammy stopped to blow his nose, using a cloth handkerchief retrieved from his pants back pocket.

Looking up from writing down notes, Gwen said, "Sammy, I appreciate that this is difficult for you. Just tell me as best you can why you're here today."

"I here 'cause I lost all money I gave to broker. He not do what I tell him I want."

"That's a good start, Sammy. Please tell me more what happened, okay?"

Sammy's gaze shifted from the carpet to Gwen. He nodded his head, blew bubbles with his lips, then answered, "Sí. I do my best. You tell me if no good. Attorney, I work at company in Dortman many years. As tester. I get pay and stock, thanks to union. I put stock in bank. Keep safe. Then, friends at my plant say stock market, it do good. They tell me they use their stock from company and make lots of money, pay for nice car, college. See, I want to do what they do, be smart like them so money grow. Big, like tree." Sammy stopped and raised his arms as if in the shape of a tree. "My friend, Al, he give me name of broker he use, he say broker good, make him lots of money. After work I go to see broker. He at Stanley, ...what it called? It in town. You know company?"

Gwen looked up from her notes. "Yes, I think so, Mr. Perez. I believe you mean Stanley, Howe. They have a branch financial office in Middleton. Go on."

"Attorney, my name Sammy. You call me Sammy, okay?"
Gwen smiled and nodded yes.

"See, I listen to Al, after work I take bus and go to Stanley. But lady at desk give me different broker, a Mr. Murphy. He seem nice, he tell me if I on his team I make good money. He say it good time as market up, and he promise he good at his job. Say his clients, they happy. I think he broker at big firm, he help me be smart, so I give him money." Sammy rubbed his knees, and, with eyes facing down at his red sneakers, he added, "But he not do good for me, lost all my money." With tears welling in his eyes, Sammy spit out, "He bad man, not tell me truth. He ruin my life. I no money left. I borrow money from family and friends to give Mr. Murphy so I don't lose all, what he call for margerine..."

"I think you mean 'margin'."

"Yes, that it, but I lose more money. He say all gone."

After a deep cleansing breath, Sammy explained that Murphy had not invested in good quality stock as Sammy had instructed. "I say again and again I want only quality stock, you know, I think IBM, Ford, like that. He buy stock I no can even say name. Then he say I need give him more, and again more money. And now I no money left."

Gwen nodded in sympathy and passed Sammy a glass of water from the pitcher on her credenza. "So then what happened?"

Sammy went through the nose-blowing process again and, after a sip of water, he continued. "I so stupid. Family angry at me, wife Olanda go to court and push me out of house. Can't see children – we have three boys – like before. No money left so I can retire. All my dreams, now they no good. Each morning I pray on Bible for the Good Lord help me so can be like before, with family, live in house. I need lawyer so can get back what Mr. Murphy stole from me." Hitting his thighs with his fists, his eyes looking at Gwen, Sammy added, "It not right, not here in America."

Gwen nodded, then waited while Sammy composed himself. She didn't know what to make of this troubled man's story. Looking again at the intake form she asked a less painful question, "Sammy, I see on your client form that you were referred to my office by José Sanchez, a former client of mine?"

"Yes, Attorney. He cousin. Say you help him win money after he lose his job. He say you smart, you good lawyer." Sammy fiddled with his jacket zipper and then added, "Josè say you honest, and not, you know, scary. And you listen nice, no yell." Gwen smiled. Nothing like affirmation that she wasn't frightening. "That's good to hear. I liked José. I hope he's managing all right?"

Sammy at last smiled back. "Sí. He good. Got new, better job."

"That's great." Watching Sammy start to relax, sitting up straighter in the chair, Gwen went on. "Tell me more about yourself, Sammy. Where do you work?"

"As I say, I work at big plant in Dortman, LCD company. I Level 1 Quality Tester. You know it, company?"

"Yes, Sammy. Big plant." Gwen knew Dortman; a once thriving mill city, it bordered the canals along the Amoosking River across from Middleton. In the last decade Dortman had been experiencing an economic turn-around, thanks to government subsidies that helped update the old industrial mills and the new dam upriver that connected these industrial parks to cheap electricity and water. This had attracted hi-tech companies like Sammy's employer. "As I recall, LCD makes parts for computer equipment. Go on."

"At lunch, my friends sit at table. Like I say, they talk about stocks and selling LCD shares. They drive new cars now, give money to wives, help kids pay for college. All what I want for my family."

Gwen watched Sammy's face and body language as he told her about his problem. He seemed sincere, but there wasn't much eye contact. Assessing truthfulness, Gwen had learned, was a difficult skill, even for residents of New Hampshire where every four years Presidential primary candidates campaigned for votes. More than once she'd been taken in by a Presidential candidate's smooth-talking jabber, only to discover later that the spoken grandiose promises lacked substance. At least Sammy, with his limited English, couldn't be called 'smooth'.

Sammy then described in more detail his meetings with Murphy, which he thought began around March of 1999. "Sorry. No good with time. Think happen at end of winter year my first son, Marcus, start high school."

"So three years ago?" Smiling, Gwen added, "Although that's optimistic for the end of a New Hampshire winter." Weather was a major topic of discussion in New Hampshire, especially above the Notch where the mountains formed their own ever-changing unpredictable weather pattern. "We can check the account statements for the dates. But from what you say, it was before 9/11. Many investment houses, as well as regulators, were impacted tragically by that disaster. So obtaining records if we need to might be difficult. Sammy, let's go back a little. Tell me more about your first meeting with Mr. Murphy. What promises did he make?"

"Mr. Murphy as I say was company what she call broker for day. He seem nice, like you. Shake my hand, talk like he know what he do. He say he like captain of team, like, you know, baseball team. He say he take care of his players. All I need do is give him check and he put me on his team. He say market good, getting better -- it good time buy stock. He show me pictures with black lines go up hill. He say my money, you know, safe since market strong like bull." Sammy thrust his hands out, imitating a charging bull. "Strong," Sammy repeated.

Gwen was leaning forward now, as the facts so far appeared to lay out a promising case of wrongful actions by a broker. "Sammy, how old are you?"

"I soon turn fifty-eight. At company can retire when sixty."

"You are fortunate. Did you tell Mr. Murphy that is what you were planning to do?"

"Sí. For sure. I tell him that, want money so can retire. He say that what he do best for his team."

"Sammy, what is your education level?"

Proudly Sammy said, "When come to this country as young man, work as cleaner, and to be smarter, went to school at night. After many years I get GED. Then go to LCD and rose to be Tester."

"You mentioned your wife, are you married?"

"Yes, to Olanda, many years now. We have three boys, Marcos senior in high school, others are younger. With wife I did own house in Dortman, before divorce. Wife own beauty place... work there."

"Do you have any prior experience investing in the market, Sammy?" This was an important question to establish Sammy's level of market sophistication. A sophisticated client requires has less regulatory protection as he's assumed to be familiar with how the industry works.

"Sí, but just little. Bad time. Years ago, wife's nephew José, he work at big stock company. He tell Olanda he know stock, his company charge low fee, and he make us money. Wife say we should do for college for our three boys. So I give him family money."

"What happened?"

"He do good for time, then not so good, then he get sick and move back to Island. Dominican Republic. He not be captain of account then. So I have to do, as no broker there to help. I talk to friends, listen at work. You know." Sammy became more agitated again. He began wringing his hands. "But I stupid. I make mistakes. Buy no quality stock -- lose money. Why I tell Mr. Murphy I want him do different, not like me. I want good broker who know how choose quality stock. I pay money for help. Why I go to Stanley office, they rich company, big broker, see ads on television."

Gwen glanced at her watch and knew she needed to speed up. She'd already heard the front door slam when Judy had left. "Sammy, tell me more how your account did with Mr. Murphy, how much did you invest? How much did you lose?"

"Account no good. He tell me money be safe. Grow money like plant grow in his office. He feed it, water it so it grow good, big."

Sammy rubbed his eyes – which Gwen thought had again started to glisten. "Sorry, I hurt, like if I fall down stairs. I think Mr. Murphy he honest with me. I think this my chance. Be man who help boys, have money so can stop work in few years. I happy, give Mr. Murphy $48,000 in my savings to open account, be on his team. I say to him again, you know, so he hear, that I want only stock that keep money safe, good quality, not like before."

"Sammy, how much did you give him over all?

In a low voice, Sammy said, "Maybe I give Mr. Murphy, I don't count you know, but maybe, let me think..." Sammy counted on his fingers. "I not good with numbers but think more than $100,000, like almost $150,000." He paused and then used his fingers to count again as he listed the funds he gave to Murphy. "I use pension money, wife money, we take loan on house, and money I borrow from Mariah, aunt on island, and family. And my stock from company. He lose all."

Gwen sat up, surprised at the amount of the loss. "I know this is hard to relive, Sammy and we're both tired. We'll need to meet again should we go forward with your case." Gwen looked again at her watch face. It was even later this time. "Sammy, why don't we go on for another ten minutes and then I'll send you on your way. Can you discuss your experience a little longer?"

"Yes. I try."

"Good." Gwen poured herself some water and filled Sammy's glass on her desk. They both drank. Gwen continued the interview, focusing on specific information legally important in terms of a claim for wrongful investment, at least those issues she could remember from the Carpenter case.

"Did Mr. Murphy ask you about your financial assets, your education?"

"When I give him check first time he ask me about my job, what I make, he fill out form."

Gwen interjected, her curiosity high. "How much do you make?" "When I work I make $53,000. He also ask what wife make. As I say, she own business but take home only little after pay all workers. Mr. Murphy had me sign lots of papers, like I say.

Then he told me I now his client, on his company's best team. He shook my hand and we smile."

"You said 'when you work'. Sammy, are you working now?"

"No, after all with Mr. Murphy I problem in head, feel tired all time and anxious. Why I take pill. And at work I hurt back. So nephew help me fill out form for disability. It approved and I on disability now."

"Was your wife with you at any time when you met with Mr. Murphy?"

"No, she work in afternoon, but I sign paper for her like he ask. She not want to get involved with this, she angry at me for hurting family, why we divorce. She say it my problem, I one who stupid, play with money. But she know I come see you and it okay with her."

Gwen leaned on her desk with her elbows. "Sammy, this is important. Did you read and understand the papers you signed for Mr. Murphy?"

"No time. I sign where he say. He ask me question, I give answer and he put on paper. I not read big words good. He say all company clients need sign to have account, so I do. Like at bank, he say."

"Do you have copies of these papers?"

"Have at wife's house."

"I'll need them, Sammy, if we proceed with your case."

"I get. No problem."

Doodling on her paper, Gwen focused on what else she needed to know. She noticed again what a small-featured man her possible new client was, from his small size sneakers to his small hands. 'Small', a word not applied to her since she was, maybe, ... never. She'd learned to live and like her curves, as had Brian. She decided that while not charismatic, Sammy exuded an earnestness that was appealing.

From her window she could see the moon rising above the trees. It was almost totally dark outside and her stomach was rumbling. It said it wanted white wine and leftover mushroom tartlets. Twisting in her chair, Gwen moved on. "Tell me about the margin calls, and how you decided to buy stocks on margin. As you've learned, you're essentially borrowing against your assets. This can be quite risky if your stocks' value goes down. Most investment firms require that margin customers maintain a certain level of assets in an account."

"Mr. Murphy call me and say I need give him more or I could lose all money in account. I call family on island and I borrow from Aunt Mariah who own store, and my sisters. Again, Mr. Murphy call and say need more or may lose everything. At night I up with worry. I call him to talk, but lady say he busy. When we talk, he give me his word my account will be good, not to worry. That his job." Sammy stopped, then leaned over and hit Gwen's desk with his fist. "His job, no? He not do his job. All got more bad, I no good sleep, no can eat, no good in head. I not use care and like I say hurt back at work." Raising his hands, Sammy added, "All go wrong."

"I understand how hard this is for you, Sammy. Did you close the account?"

"Mr. Murphy tell me he sell my stock to pay off call, what it? Margin." Sammy's shoulders slumped and in a barely audible voice he said, "I tell Mr. Murphy I unhappy. He get angry. Yell at me." In a louder voice, his hands moving up and down, Sammy added, "Tell me he work hard for me. Say he put in many hours. He say my loss not due to him. He tell me way it is, market have up and down. I need work with him better." Sammy stared at his hands and in a rising voice, added, "He ruin my life. I pray to my Lord, read Bible every day, but no help. I angry in heart."

Gwen leaned back in her chair and while doodling geometric figures next to her notes, she considered Sammy's story. Her small law firm had limited resources. Sammy wouldn't be a paying client so she'd be working for nothing if she lost his case. Could she rely on Sammy's version of what happened? What should she do?

"That's a bad outcome, Sammy. But from what you say, this

may be a big, expensive case to bring. And in an area of law that's not my expertise. Let me do some research on the issues you've raised, okay, get those papers from you, and then I'll know better whether I may be able to help you."

"Yes. I like you help me. I get for you papers."

Gwen stood up and walked Sammy to her front office door. She confirmed with him that it was not too late for him to catch the bus to Dortman. Then Gwen watched Sammy disappear into the dark, his red coat reminding her of a traffic light, turning from 'on' under the streetlamp to 'off' as he walked down the unlit Main Street.

Gwen had always been a sucker for helping the little guy. Was this a case where she could both bring justice for a harmed small investor like Sammy and also help her firm's bottom line? From what he'd said, Sammy had a decent claim that Murphy traded unsuitably in risky stocks and even used margin, a broker 'no no' for a client with limited assets. As to the truthfulness of Sammy's tale, Gwen decided that her possible new client appeared honest, at least at first blush.

She'd been trying to get by on small cases, but they just weren't paying the bills anymore. Did she need to step up to bigger matters? Sure, the case could take over her life if the opposition played nasty. Would that be so bad? Maybe a jolt would be good -- both for her life and her practice. Fighting the big law firms below the Notch might open up new horizons -- legal, social, who knows what.

Big risks versus big rewards? Was she ready to be David taking on Goliath? Was it time to lean in? Was she confident she could handle this complex case? Or was she, like Sammy, betting on margin and its high risk?

CHAPTER THREE

Gwen sat in her parked car waiting for Sammy so they could collect the Stanley, Howe documents at his former house. Tired, shivering and a little afraid, she waited near Dortman's industrial park, an area with a reputation for borderline sketchy. Once the adjacent block-long brick factory buildings lining the canals had been the City's thriving center, home to prosperous cotton mills. But the mills had long since moved South where they could operate more cheaply, leaving behind boarded up buildings covered in graffiti. Dortman's economy remained depressed for decades as it experienced the waves of migrant communities. Once established, the workers moved on to more prosperous neighborhoods, like Middleton, to be replaced by the next immigrant arrivals.

Thankfully, the past decade of government programs, business investment, and progressive politics was already producing positive economic and social results. The City, most agreed, was getting its *mojo* back. Newly refurbished specialty mills and technology plants had put down roots and were attracting Latino immigrants seeking good blue-collar jobs. Dortman's main street now sported Hispanic furniture rental companies, barber shops where Spanish was the chosen language, and ethnic *pastelerias* offering rich puddings and deserts. When the weather was warm, men played chess outside the grocery stores, the sidewalks were busy with shoppers, and commerce thrived.

Gwen turned up the heat in her car. *Where is Sammy?* Finally, through the half-moon clearing created by the car's defogger, Gwen saw Sammy walking towards the car, waving hello in his red parka with red hat.

"Hi, Sammy. Cold out there. I was starting to worry you wouldn't be coming."

"Sorry late, have no car and my cousin, Julio, he away so I walk."

"Give me directions to your family's house, okay?" said Gwen as she shifted to face him.

"Si, not far." Sammy then gave her 'point of interest' directions and once past the Chinese restaurant Gwen saw three houses floating on a sea of black asphalt.

Pointing at them Sammy said in his high-pitched voice, "There, that my house, white with fence."

"Here we go," said Gwen as she put her turn signal on. She'd decided to use this time with Sammy to ask him more questions, hoping he'd feel less intimidated outside her office and she'd be able to get a better feel for his story – and his integrity.

"Good. Sammy, some background questions, okay?"

"Okay."

"When did you move to Dortman?"

"I from Dominican Republic, you know. As young man, no jobs. Cousin in Dortman, told me good jobs here. I save money and come, want make better life. He sponsor me."

"How old were you?"

"Eighteen."

"Then what happened?"

"Work at wool mill and, like I tell you, go to school at night. I earn GED. But I work too hard, long hours, and get sick." Sammy paused as if to gather his memories. Gwen stopped at the red octagon sign and then continued towards the lighted area.

"Went on unemployment, you know, welfare. They train me and I get new job cleaning machines. When I start work at LCD plant. Big company."

"Yes, I remember that," Gwen said.

"I want do better, have family, so take class at company and get better job, as tester." Pointing to the intersection ahead, Sammy went on, "Turn left at light."

Gwen followed his directions and pulled up to the curb in front of a compact two-story white house that sat on an oasis of green. Streetlights lit up the front yard and the smell of Chinese food from the nearby restaurant reminded her she'd missed dinner, so far.

"This my house. You meet wife, Olanda. We married thirty years." In a throaty voice, Sammy added, "But then I lose her money and she much angry. She talk to mean lawyer who push her to divorce me. Now house hers and I don't see boys like before." Sammy adds with pride in his voice, "They good boys, no drugs, no trouble."

Gwen followed Sammy through the unlocked front door. She found herself in a small but comfortable looking living room and she again trailed behind Sammy as he entered a brightly lit kitchen. A small and slight woman with reddish hair neatly pinned up stood over the sink. Three teen-age boys seated at the Formica table were finishing their dinner. The aroma of hot spices and warmed cornbread wafted through the room; Gwen hoped no one heard her growling stomach.

"*Hola,* Olanda," Sammy said from the doorway. "It me, Sammy."

Olanda, with her back to Sammy, jumped in place. "Saints be to God, Sammy Perez, do you have to scare me to death?" She made the sign of the cross. "Can't you call or knock first? And what are you doing here tonight? It's a school night."

"Olanda, this my nice attorney I tell you 'bout. This Attorney Wilson. You remember, I tell you what José told me? She one help him when he hurt back at work and they fire him. She now help *me*. I stop to get files in basement on stock account. I maybe can fight bad man who stole family's money. Okay you speak to her?"

Olanda turned, glared at Sammy, and then gave Gwen a hard stare as well. "Sammy, you know you are to call ahead before you come here. That written in divorce paper."

"Si. Sorry. But it important I get papers for my case. Need them now."

One of the boys joined in the discussion, animatedly saying, "Hey Dad, you should see the new video game I got from Pedro. It's cool. I'm up to the* eighth level of destruction. New computer's so fast, hard to keep up. Can we play after dinner?"

Before Sammy could respond Olanda broke in, saying to Sammy, "See what you done? They need to do their homework, not play with you. It's a school night." Olanda then twisted her body around and said to Gwen, "Lawyer, I told him, now I tell you. I want no part of this law case. It's nothing to do with me. He lost our money by himself. This is Sammy's stupid idea to be rich guy, make easy money, no risk he says. If I listened to him and his big promises I would be out on the street with no house." Olanda turned to face Sammy. "Sammy, this your mess. You do what you do, but don't come here and pester me no more 'bout it."

Sammy returned her stare. "Jesus, Mary, and Joseph, Olanda. I know was bad at end. But he cheat me, not do what I say, and that not right. This lawyer say I can sue because he break law. Then we have money and I can stay at house again."

Gwen broke in, "Wait a minute Sammy. I haven't said that I am prepared to sue on your behalf. Remember, we are here because I need to review the investment documents you told me about so I can understand your case better *before* deciding what we will do."

Olanda also joined in, saying, "Sammy, even if the good Lord smile down on you and help you get our money back that you lost, it is *not* going to happen – your moving back in. We divorced now and you're on your own. Now I have to get to work as it is my late night at the shop."

As she was hanging up her apron, Olanda stated to Gwen, "Not to be rude, attorney, but I have to clean up and go to work. You can wait in the living room." And before Gwen was able to ask Olanda questions about the Murphy meeting, Olanda had shooed the boys into their rooms, cleared the table, rinsed the dishes, put on her coat and exited the front door. Sammy soon disappeared down the kitchen door into the basement leaving Gwen alone.

Sitting on the gold and blue flowered couch in the living room, Gwen looked around. Framed pictures of the family were everywhere. A younger Olanda holding smiling children giggling in their bathing suits as they slid down a high curved slide at a water park. All five of them attired in Red Sox gear waiving from bleacher seats at Fenway Park. And there was a picture of Sammy and his boys playing basketball. School class pictures lined one wall, portraying the children's growth over the years, and change in dental status. One bookshelf held sports trophies, another featured framed school art projects, and there were original school–made Mother's Day cards taped to the wall. Gwen smiled at the happy detritus of family life.

She sat and waited, checking her watch to decide whether she'd be home in time for the re-run of Masterpiece Theater. As she passed the moment in her mind she compared this family's living room and its aura of love with her Middleton cape house and its visual reminders of her life experiences. The photographs she displayed in her living room comprised a picture of her brother Artie when he was still a kid and one of her as a cute smiling child in a pink frilly party dress, her head topped by a plastic tiara. That one was taken before the Mark accident – the event that no family member talked about, but that all these years later still haunted all of them.

She'd hung no pictures of her parents taken after the accident – of her dad who'd fled to California and found his new family, or her mom. Except for the recent one of her mother at the nursing home, nicely coifed and smiling but with eyes not all mentally there. No family scenes of sharing popcorn at a ballgame or blowing out birthday candles. She did place on her bookshelf one framed picture of her and Brian laughing and wearing silly shiny New Year's Eve party hats. They were the image of the happy young professional couple, confident, the bright world waiting in a straight line ahead of them. Gwen had placed this Brian picture on a high shelf so it was out of her casual sight line. Even a brief revisit to that moment in time still allowed in grief.

Absorbing Sammy's living room, heaviness weighed on Gwen

as if a dark, rain-soaked cloud had entered the house and enveloped her, causing her surprisingly to fight back tears. *Maybe, Gwennie, it is okay to personalize the house more, maybe place in the living room some of the souvenirs I've gathered over the years.* She had a chest in the basement filled with old camp awards, canoeing medals, stuffed animals bearing her college's logo, samples of her shot glass collection purchased at too many bars during her college travels... and her carved wood box containing Brian's letters and cards. Tomorrow maybe she'd look into it.

At last, Sammy appeared holding two big bags filled with papers. They walked together back to Gwen's car and put the bags in the trunk. Sammy declined the offer of a lift to his cousin's and he soon disappeared down the dark street.

But before she went to bed Gwen couldn't help but checkout Sammy's haul. She reviewed statements of trades made in his account over two months, and was taken aback by the high number of transactions. Many stocks were held for less than a day. She found a letter on Stanley, Howe stationary informing Sammy that he needed to come up with more money to meet a margin call. The letter bore Murphy's initials. And then there were the fancy colored graphs with lines by category of stock, all going downward, showing the repeated decline in the value of Sammy's holdings. She was confident this initial document check confirmed the basics of Sammy's story.

Gwen then spent the next few hours tossing and turning in bed trying to decide, *Gwennie, what's my next step?*

CHAPTER FOUR

Today Gwen wanted to decide on the Perez case. Should she commit to take it, yes or no? She updated her finger logic procedure, raising one finger for each argument made. First was the "accept the case" position: 1) she'd be helping a brave man fight a greedy cheating Wall Street investment firm; 2) the potential financial reward would help her stay in business and fight another day; and 3) the case presented important racial and other social issues on top of its legal challenges. Gwen had taken on contingency cases before when she thought 'doing good' was reason enough. Only last year she'd settled a case on behalf of the town's public housing tenants who according to the law had paid more rent than allowed thanks to the method used for calculating electricity charges. It had been a small win, but it helped finance the tenant's union going forward. Handling such cases she'd believed was part of the *tithe* – using the old-fashioned payment in kind rather than cash – that lawyers should pay as their contribution to the legal system. *Should Sammy be my current tithe?* And, a possible number four – it might open up new avenues for professional development and growth.

All reasons seemed important, especially at the moment the potential pot of gold outcome. Gwen sighed. She'd expected that making a buck practicing law would be easier, especially in the 'we're one legal family' environment still prevalent above the Notch.. As Chris told her, during his day it used to be that way. But her ongoing expenses – for malpractice insurance, bar dues, license fees, legal research expenses, plus of course rent, staff... the list, which went on and on, was increasing far faster than her earnings, despite having a very busy practice. With the economy's continued downturn – it was 2002, and post-9/11 – the prospects for cash improvement did not appear great. She'd noticed that quick settlements weren't happening. Even her deer case with Joe, despite the clear liability of his clients and available resources of the insurance carrier, was still crawling along, near settlement he's said – just not there yet. More and more clients, good people struggling to make a living, were behind on their bills. Maybe Mr. Perez's case would be the one to save her practice.

On the other side of the equation: contingency cases could lead directly to bankruptcy. She'd only get paid if she won, a shaky proposition these days. Not only did she risk unpaid hours and expenses on the case, but the 'unknowns' were just that – would her client stay around to the end – which could be years away? Was he reliable, honest, telling her the good and the bad? Would the other side fight hard – they surely would have the funds to do so? As a single practitioner without an 'endowment' like a fancy college – or a sugar daddy, these risks could shut her firm's door.

Rubbing her shoulders to relieve her tension, Gwen walked over to the coffee maker for a morning caffeine fix. She saw that Mary Dunkin, her paralegal and 'best' friend, had beaten her into the office and was already sitting at the conference table and surrounded by law books.

"Hey Mary, you're working early. Want some coffee?"

Mary looked up, greeting her with a smile that lit up her round, wide-set face and gave a sparkle to her blue eyes. As usual, Gwen instantly felt happier with Mary around.

"Tired, huh? Must be all that bar trawling you did last night," Mary joked. "No thanks to the coffee; another run to you-know-where will only delay me from getting this memo done for you."

"Right. Ah, the young and swinging single life in Middleton. Sorry, I had a date last night with the Stonehearts, that's the zoning board application hearing I told you about. And it looks like I'll be seeing them again tonight. My playtime these days consists of watching the evening weather report. Ha. When the current wind speed on Mt. Washington gets your heart pumping, you know there's some balance issues in your life. Hey, Mares, did you have a chance to read that SEC case about unsuitable investments just decided by the DC Circuit? I think it may be helpful for the Perez case, if I take it."

"Yup. I think it may be helpful if I understood it, but the court I think narrowed the advisor's fiduciary obligations, so maybe not so much. I left my notes in your inbox."

"Thanks. I'm thinking I may want to take Sammy's case, one reason being I could use a financial windfall. The other being the public interest thing. And, you know, I've been thinking also maybe it will be a family thing as well. As I recall, my mom's grandfather was taken to the cleaners in the heyday of the 1920's stock market crash, so maybe it will be karma, what goes around comes around."

"'As you sow, so shall you reap'. As you can see, I studied my *Bhagavad-Gita* when recovering from Tony."

"Nice to think it has some personal connection. You do bad to my family, and watch out buddy, my great granddaughter will get you. What's your sense, Mary, is a settlement likely? That was the case with the Carpenters, so.... "

"Gwen, they were rich, had political and bank connections, and they were good investment clients. Mr. Perez is not in that position. And the investment firm knows that. Maybe a little riskier."

"All true. Sure, Mary, I don't want money needs to decide my work. Yet bottom line business realities won't go away. Just gets tighter."

"Sorry, Gwennie, but I can't be much help here. I've never played the market – that requires actual money, unless that is you're playing Monopoly. Sadly, I know as much about securities law as I know about baseball – which is that there are nine players on a team. Oh, yes, and there are two teams. Ergo, eighteen players."

"Nice math. About my level. But you're right. If I take the matter we'll all probably be burning the midnight oil learning about such exciting subjects as turnover ratios."

"Does it help that I know lots about Apple Turnovers?"

Gwen smiled, always glad for one of Mary's efforts at humor. "Here, Mary, why don't you read this brief summary, a Securities Law 101 that I copied from a continuing legal ed. book, and then maybe talking about the issues will help me decide."

While Mary read, Gwen sat down at the table and began reviewing her Stoneheart notes for the hearing tomorrow. While reading the requirements for a Special Permit, she found herself instead back in New York City. It was 1997 and she was still a lowly unhappy associate with a multi-national law firm with no long-term future partnership potential and stuck in personal grief. So when she saw a want-ad for an associate position in New Hampshire, she'd applied – on a whim. When Christopher Lynden offered her the job, she'd accepted on the spot. A sensible personal and career decision she told herself, despite the serious cut in pay. It felt right in her gut, and she denied internally that it was a grab at an escape from her past. She'd liked her new boss a lot – warm, welcoming, smart, and mentoring, and courageous for bringing in the first female lawyer in active practice, and an outsider at that. When she joined the business, she'd expected all major practice worries to be dealt with by Chris. He'd had his own firm for years and was highly regarded by the profession – and, he assured her, financially doing fine. Enough so he was ready to expand and bring her on board.

But two and a half years ago seemingly robust, fly-fishing addict Chris experienced an early heart attack. His doctor encouraged retirement to Florida and its warm weather, walking paths, and no stress lifestyle. Smartly, Chris listened to his doctor's advice – and to his wife Arlene's ultimatum. Generously, as he was a truly nice guy, Chris "sold" the practice to Gwen in exchange for a small brief consultant's fee. It had all seemed so prudent. But increasingly she'd been wondering if that were still the case.

"Hey, you okay?"

Gwen dropped her pen and was back in her conference room with Mary who explained, "I'm done reading, but perhaps we can go over the issues more as, to be frank, it is a little confusing."

"That's why they pay me the big bucks, Mary – or is it because I shelled out all that money for law school? Let me see if I can explain the basics of our claims in a five-minute lecture if you can put up with that. If nothing else, you'll be more familiar with the concepts and some of the basic terms, and ready to invest your millions."

And so Gwen began. "Essentially the case is similar to a claim that the house you bought on the beach from a builder didn't come with the promised ocean view, had a roof that leaked, an electric system that shorted out regularly, and required a sump pump in the basement. You had given the builder money in good faith, relying on his expertise and representations. But you found out after he was paid that there was no water view other than from the attic, the house had so many building problems it wasn't habitable, and the builder, rather than paying you for his mistakes, kept demanding more money to make it right, including money for his increased expenses in buying wood from his dad's business. Now you can claim fraud based on the builder's lies, misrepresentations, and self-serving nature. Got it so far?"

Mary nodded, but hesitantly.

"Similarly, the sales representative at an investment firm, in this case a salesman, takes your money to invest. Because he works at a full-service firm, he supposedly gives expert advice to help you make good trades and he and the firm earn a fee to carry out the trades. Remember, all you're expecting is that the people you hired will make a reasonable effort to use your money to make money. And there's always some risk involved. But this salesman works your account to benefit him and his employer, not so much to make money for you. He puts you in a high-risk position – although you're not rich, and you end up losing all your money.

You want to sue to make yourself whole."

"Okay, a little like a consumer claim that your car seller lied to you and cheated."

"Yes, you're getting the idea. Except if you claim foul, the persons who decide on what's allowed, and often this is not a judge, also likely play in the trading game. In some cases it can be a little like the fox is designated to guard the hen house."

"Sounds not so fair."

"Exactly. Mary, some of the claims we would make use special securities terms. And these are defined in case law, statutes, and agency rules of the securities industry itself."

"Sounds more and more one-sided..."

"Now it is important to remember that if you lose money, well that doesn't mean there was fraud, just expected market risks, normal part of investment process. I'm almost done. The typical investment fraud claims an investor like Sammy may bring are: one, the investments weren't 'suitable' for that person's reasonable risk level, his risk tolerance. The broker needs to consider that customer's assets, income, age, and other factors affecting risk, to 'know' his customer, when recommending trades.

The second major claim would be for 'churning', a form of fraud. This happens when a broker buys and sells stock shares often – in order to increase the broker's commission, not the value of the customer's account."

At this point in the 'lecture', Mary yawned and Gwen followed suit. And then Baby Ben, the town name for the brick and metal tower clock that stood atop the Abington Mill buildings – one of the largest mill clocks in the world and Middleton's crown jewel, rang its bell twelve times signaling it was noon.

"Let's do lunch, Mary. My treat today."

As Mary put away the case books in the space designated for each volume, Gwen stared out the conference room's windows, watching the water, once ripping with the power of the Ammonoosuc River, enough power to run the mills, now casually meandering between the rocks on its downward journey. In the process the river languidly turned the large wooden paddles that moved the historic gristmill's grinding stone – which still ground wheat flour for bread. As the clock stopped its song, Gwen grabbed some cash in Judy's 'all- things' drawer and she and Mary jawed about life on their way out the door.

But in the back of her mind, Gwen was still debating the pros and cons of taking on a contingency suit. Would she be betting her practice with this roll of the dice? Or pursuing justice for the 'little guy' taking on a powerful company?

CHAPTER FIVE

Gwen and Mary walked from Gwen's office down Middleton's Main Street to Peaches for lunch. Once a water-powered mill town and thriving county seat, historic Middleton – almost as old as the state – struggled to find a source of income for its residents after shoe manufacturing moved to the South. Then in the early 1950's a group of the area's business owners got together and, with assurances of tax benefits, low-cost hydroelectric power, a modern hospital, and the addition of an exit off the nearby highway, they pooled their resources and built several industrial parks. Over the years manufacturing plants and tech businesses moved into these spaces, offering good jobs and tax support. Middleton began again to prosper; the tourist business came to life thanks to the new motels, nearby ski resorts, historic covered bridges, wilderness trails, numerous streams for recreation, and a developing arts center along the riverfront. The town reached 8,000 residents and it became a vibrant place to live, at least for North of the Notch.

The two women paraded past the rows of red brick buildings towards Peaches, Gwen in her power navy pants suit and handy sneakers and Mary, almost a head taller than Gwen, walking as if on a Dior runway with auburn red hair flying. Men in her path stopped what they were doing to watch her pass. Mary, however, ignored these attentive glances. She was not ready yet, Gwen knew, to focus on the world of men and dating since her messy divorce from Dr. Tony.

Gwen could relate to Mary's hesitation. For to be truthful, since she'd lost Brian now some five years ago, she'd not been ready to think about another serious relationship, or even casual dating – that is, to move on with her personal life. Was it the lingering grief for what she'd lost? Or her lost confidence that the 'Love Deity' would be good to her? Her inability to forgive herself for feeling that she'd hurt the men in her life? *Am I living in*

Middleton, where the 'thirty-something' dating scene isn't great, and maybe offers me an easy way to avoid relationships?

Pausing in front of one store's front window, Gwen looked with awe at the shelves of colorful plastic bobble-heads bouncing up and down. She wasn't certain which one of the large collection was her favorite – the pink bear, green elephant, maybe the hula dancer? Not exactly a scene she would behold on Fifth Avenue, but, then again, wasn't that the specialness of smalltown life? Moving onwards, Gwen reluctantly passed the general store promising the longest line of penny candy this side of the North Pole.

After almost half a decade in Middleton, Gwen was pretty confident she loved living in this town. Any lingering need she might have for the excitement of the Big Apple would be more than satisfied by a two-week vacation at a hotel in Midtown. While Rockefeller Center had its big holiday tree and parading skaters, Downtown Middleton offered its own special displays. In fact, Gwen loved the downtown area with its panoply of Americana. An historic somewhat ramshackle New England Inn that had expanded by additions over the years – welcomed the Rotary Club for lunch. The Inn faced the county's Grecian columned U.S. District Court House. Adjacent to that was a once upon a time millionaire's mansion, now converted into the town library.

Recently added to the mix of bookstores and delis were fringe "hippie" apparel shops offering handmade cotton frocks and dangling beads. Hunting and fishing gear were displayed in the local hardware store's window, next to the snow blowers. Corners at the intersection of business and residential streets were home to various denominational churches, many with white tall wood steeples. Piles of carefully placed firewood stood like towers outside the small supermarket abutting Main St. And Gwen enjoyed the friendliness, sense of community. This was a place where the town's residents were pleased they'd settled in a village where jobs were plenty, middle-class life affordable, and that offered clean rivers and mountains, plentiful for outdoor adventures in all seasons.

Peaches' exterior was covered in red, white and blue bunting, fitting for this town that prided itself on being part of the political center of the nation every four years during the Presidential primaries. Two outside benches -- one marked 'Democrats' and the other 'Republicans' reminded visitors of the town's patriotic role.

Gwen and Mary entered the restaurant and sat in a back booth. Their waitress, Viv, ambled over to them and handed them two menus – each thick enough to pass as a novella. Gwen didn't need to flip through hers, however, as she knew what she wanted and duly ordered her turkey Reuben with lots of warm sauerkraut. Mary ordered a tuna sandwich and fries.

"So, Mary, how are the kids?"

"Got a post-card from Jason. He's a barista in some small town in Spain. Thinking of trying out for Dunkin' Donuts when he returns to the States. Glad to know he graduated high school cum laude before taking a year off -- to experience life he says. More likely, it's to recover from his parents' mess. Jonah's working after school, doing something with computers I can't explain. Janice is developing a bad case of 'teenitis'. At least Jon's still adorable, for another year or so."

"And the dogs, anything new?"

"Now you're talking. Tiger almost pulled a good one this morning. Thought he could go with me to work if he hid behind the front seat of my car, but he made a mistake by sitting up too soon. There he was in my rearview mirror with – I swear – a grin on his mug. 'No luck, buster' I told him and turned around and brought him home. Can you believe? He may be smarter than my kids. Certainly he's smarter than Dr. Phony."

Dr. Phony, Gwen knew, was Mary's former spouse, Tony Lattimore. In the dark days of Mary's divorce, Mary had spilled out to Gwen her marriage history. She and Tony had met when he was in dental school in Pittsburgh and Mary was pursuing a master's degree there. They'd moved to Middleton when Tony became the new Associate at the local dental practice. Mary took on the role of stay-at-home mom and animal caretaker for the family's three dogs, guinea pig, and parakeet. Thanks to Tony's good looks, gentle hands, and million-dollar charm, women quickly flocked to his practice. In short order he became a partner. All seemed good.

But one day when collecting Tony's suits to take to the cleaners, Mary went through all the pockets, including the hidden inner one inside the jacket to make sure all was safe for pressing. That's when she found a long blond hair stuck to a slightly sticky fifty-dollar bill. And so Mary discovered that her beloved Dr. Tony was in reality Philandering Phony. Turned out, Mary explained to Gwen, as she learned on the grapevine, Tony's gentle hands had wandered far from teeth. On many occasions. But it got worse. Tony's dental partners discovered that her charming hubby had been stealing from the till to support his growing lustful and lascivious lifestyle. They divorced. Presently, Mary said, Tony was fighting extradition from Brazil.

And so smart and savvy Mary, still credits short of her Master's degree, had taken a job as a paralegal at Gwen's firm to support her family. Since then, the two women had become fast friends. Mary and her children anointed Gwen 'Auntie' with the responsibility of bringing the pumpkin pie at Thanksgiving and on other holiday occasions. Gwen happily obliged, not mentioning that the pies were bought at a nearby farm store.

While waiting for their meals, the women talked shop.

"Mary, did you find out anything helpful on Sammy or his family when researching at the Middleton library, or anything scandalous that might help me with the Perez case if I take it, something I can use at a hearing, or to persuade them that settlement makes sense?"

"Gwen, I did a thorough microfiche review for the past ten years. Do my eyes look crossed from all that intensive reading on those machines?"

"Ha. No. So what did you find?"

"One article which might be helpful. I printed up a copy. See, that's a picture of your broker, Larry Murphy. It shows him winning an all-paid vacation to Hawaii from Stanley, Howe for being one of the firm's branch top trading brokers. I guess that indicates lots of commission income?"

"Well, that might be handy to show churning. Otherwise, how would he be so ahead of his peers? Anything else?"

"I checked some business magazines using the microfiche and did find a few articles talking about how the stock market was holding its own during the past five years and that the Dow Jones had been going up modestly. So, it seems, Sammy's account should have made money. I also made a quick stop at the law library in the District Court building and did a Westlaw search for decisions involving Stanley, Howe. Here, I've printed up the findings. You'll notice that they've entered into a number of SEC settlements agreeing to stop certain trading activities, including failing to supervise their salespeople for excessive trading. But nothing I could find involving claims in New Hampshire, maybe the local cases were too small."

"Both might be helpful. Can you see if you could contact the SEC's office in Washington to get copies of these agreements? I'm sure they all contain language that the company's not admitting any wrongdoing, but still, it is something."

"Got it. Almost forgot. I did find one picture of Sammy's wife in the local paper at some charity event, and one of his sons on the High School's basketball team, but none of Sammy. And I checked the Bankruptcy Court's dockets. As you said, Sammy might be a gambler -- but I found nothing there. And that's about it."

"Good job, Mary. Helpful maybe, but, sadly, far from a smoking gun. Anyhow, I'm sure that the lawyers for the other side will be carefully examining Sammy's life for ammunition. This PI stuff's become pretty routine I gather with the big guys."

"Gwen, I've been thinking. Seeing as you're not getting paid on cases where you work at an hourly rate, maybe taking a risk on a big payout case makes sense?"

Gwen laughed. "A little jaundiced perspective, but maybe right."

Their sandwiches arrived. Gwen and Mary immediately exchanged Gwen's potato chips for Mary's pickle. Both women opened their mouths and dug in.

But Gwen was beginning to feel exasperated with herself, another day and another non-decision. Nevertheless, she began to write down and organize those steps she'd need to take if she were going forward with 'Sammy'.

CHAPTER SIX

Seemingly overnight the forsythias' buds had burst into flower, the first sign that mud season was soon to be in the past. Soon, thankfully, color and bird songs would replace Middleton's drab winter world. After grabbing strong coffee, still attired in winter gear but for her hot-looking 'shades', Gwen drove off to another workday – one that would include moving the Perez case forward. Gwen had started the preliminary steps to bring the case, reaching out to Martha Stoneham, her own financial advisor, and Linda DeNardi, her accountant to see if they might be willing to be her 'experts' if she took on Sammy's case. Both had been surprisingly available for a working lunch today at the nearby family-run Chinese/Thai/Japanese restaurant. Hot Chinese tea and plastic chopsticks might provide the proper atmosphere to persuade her friends to get on board the Sammy train if it left the station – at a fee she could afford.

Entering the restaurant, Gwen admired the large fish tank and then sat down at the only empty booth. Martha arrived first, looking as usual competent and confident in a designer suit and with her blond hair carefully coifed. Around her neck hung statement eyeglasses, dark blue with rhinestones circling the lenses. Martha wanted to make sure you remembered her, Gwen suspected. Gwen had known and bonded with Martha since they both had volunteered at the local Y years back to help newly arrived immigrant students in Dortman learn the logistics to get into college. Gwen had immediately recognized that Martha was savvy, sophisticated, smart, and had a blistering wit.

Linda finally joined them, apologizing for her delay. Linda was Martha's opposite: quiet, unobtrusive in her black polyester business suit. But Linda spoke comfortably with numbers and Gwen was confident she could assist in the Perez case.

After they ordered and briefly shared updates of their lives, Gwen began the 'meeting'.

"Okay, guys, I want to talk with you about helping me out on a securities case, one where I think we're doing good, you know, helping the little guy fight the big investment firm in Middleton for securities fraud. Up front, I don't have much money to pay you for your time if things get nasty, but the potential recovery could be good, at least by my smalltown standards. So if we win it won't necessarily be viewed as pro bono by your firms. You will be advising me on the appropriateness of the financial trades and assessing damage estimates. Hopefully not testifying at any hearing -- as I think the case will settle if the facts are as my client claims. Worst case scenario is we file for arbitration, thanks to the mandatory arbitration clause in the firm's standard client agreement. No court delays, endless discovery fights. Should be short and sweet, and hopefully affordable.

Linda's mouth instantly descended into a pout. "Testifying would be a deal-breaker for me. I'm not one for public speaking."

"I'm pretty hopeful for an early settlement, Linda, as my brief understanding of the facts is that my client was taken for a ride by a greedy broker. You know, the standard overreaching of an unsophisticated investor. In this case a Hispanic man with not a great grasp of English, certainly of securities concepts. He's a family man from Dortman, was a blue-collar worker until he hurt his back, now on disability, and near retirement age. Appealing plaintiff. He got nice stock options when working at the tech company LCD. But his broker put him in risky stock. When they went kaput, more shares were bought on margin, leading to margin calls. Records so far show an awful lot of quick trades. Bottom line – in a gently up market, he lost it all – including family loans, he claims well over $100,000. Could be an experience to put on your resume, but since it's on contingency, who knows about whether it will pay any of us."

Both women sat in silence.

Gwen, sounding she hoped enthusiastic, added, "I know it is a reach. But there's the plus that we'll be working together, presenting a powerful women's team."

Martha paused while eating her raw fish and washing it down with her umbrella drink. "Is the client reliable?"

"All I can say at this point is – I think so. I'm meeting with him again this week."

Linda, playing with her noodles, asked, "Gwen, what's the role of an expert in such a case? What would you need from me?"

"Yes, I'd like to know that also," chimed in Martha.

"Good question." Gwen explained that in a legal case an expert is someone who has special skills resulting from education, training or experience that enables them to give an opinion in a legal proceeding, not just state a fact. In this case, your main job likely is to help me prepare the case. Admittedly, if things go really sour, there's the possibility of a day or so hearing at some hotel before people in the industry and you may have to tell them how the company broke the law.

Linda stopped spearing her food and looked down at her small rice bowl. "Well, I've never done anything like this, you know." She hemmed and hesitated. "Testifying sounds pretty scary. Gwen, I have trouble when my firm asks me to give a speech at Rotary." Her voice faded as she took off her glasses, wiped them, then put them back on. "Are you sure you want me, Gwen?"

"Hey Linda. You're my accountant and I have faith in your being able to do this. Most small cases settle – and that's been my experience to the extent I have any. This case raises lots of social, maybe racial issues otherwise. And if the shit hits the fan and we have to go to a hearing, experience as an expert witness can be a pretty lucrative field for a CPA, maybe be a leg up for partnership."

Linda played more with her utensils, still not quite getting the two wood sticks to meet together long enough to carry food the distance to her mouth. Sighing, she picked up her fork. "Okay, I get the message. I guess ... I say, maybe, it's not tax season so may have time, um... maybe yes." Linda wiped her glasses again, drank some tea, and looked at Martha. "What do you think, Martha?"

Brushing back her hair and opening and closing the paper umbrella in her cocktail, Martha stared at Gwen for untold seconds. "Gwen, I've reviewed the documents you faxed me and I do think your client was taken for a ride. But, as you say, any case has its uncertainties and we're making a commitment." After sipping the last of her cocktail, Martha laughed and then said, "What the hell. Maybe it is time for 'I am woman, hear me roar'. Good opportunity to go after some of the jerks in my business, address the greed. And we did have fun when we worked for a good cause before. So, Gwen, I'm in, at least for now."

Smiling broadly, Gwen said, "You guys are the best. I knew you had the mojo and wouldn't let me down. But as to pay, what I was thinking was a percentage when we win, depending on the stage we're at. Linda can run the options and suggest what's fair. Does that work?"

Martha and Linda in unison gave the thumbs up sign. All three raised their teacups and clicked them together. As the women were putting their papers away, the waiter came over and placed three fortune cookies on the table. Each woman took one and opened it.

Gwen read hers aloud: "You will meet tall, handsome stranger who will bring mystery and excitement to life. But beware of hidden danger." Secretly Gwen placed this missive in her handbag, just in case it might be more than print on cheap paper. The other women's sayings were the usual assurances that good luck and happy life would follow. These were left on the table.

Gwen was pleased that things so far had fallen into place. She now had her experts committed, and they were people she'd enjoy working with. Plus their upfront expense demands were minimal. The case was developing and the more she learned, the more convinced she was that Stanley, Howe's actions didn't pass the smell test. The stars seemed aligned, the legal fairies in place, and the case ripe to pursue justice and financial recompense for Sammy, his family – and her law firm.

As for the tall stranger who would be arriving in her life... she'd just have to wait and see.

CHAPTER SEVEN

Another Friday afternoon had arrived seemingly on the sly, like Sandburg's fog on little silent feet. It was time to close up shop for the week. Gwen filed her time sheets, put together work to take home, and prepared emotionally for her weekly 'mom' visit.

"Judy, off to see my mom. Leave any messages on my desk please, and go home early. I'll probably stop in tomorrow morning as I want to revise the draft motion in the Kowalsky case."

Judy smiled; being a mom several times over she was pleased when children of any age looked after their parents. "Okay. Give your mom a hug for me."

"Will do. Not sure if this will be a visit where she'll notice my presence."

"Hey Gwen, after mom any fun plans?"

"Catch up on sleep, and maybe buy a new garden shovel at Morrisons. Going to plant some tomatoes this year. Oh, and if my opponent in Kowalsky asks for one more continuance, I may plant some local lawyers next to my herbs."

"Wow, sounds exciting, both options. You know, I hear – from my son – there's a local band playing at the Tavern tonight. Expecting a big crowd."

Gwen squirmed. "Thanks but don't know if my ears can handle the volume anymore. And excitement. Truth be told, I'm ready to crash; its been a long week. And you and John, week-end plans?"

"Spring cleanup. I'm planning on cleaning out my attic. Time to donate all the clothes and sports stuff the boys grew out of before I could remove the tags. And we may go to the movies Saturday night. John said there's a good action film about a British spy hunk who's lost his memory and doesn't know he's undercover M12 or something. Want to join us? I'll buy the popcorn."

Gwen placed a finger on her lips as if thinking hard, then said,

"While two hours with a hunk sounds promising, and you know I love popcorn, but I've agreed to baby sit my neighbor's dog while they're away. So I think highlight will be pooch walk. Say hi to John for me." And with that, Gwen was out the door.

Coward.. It would be another weekend with no frivolity – other than playing fetch with the pooch. Way past time to put a note in her Lawyer's Diary: 'Commit to doing something fun'. It was time for her to meet people her age, even if they were coupled. *Otherwise I'll become one of those crotchety old ladies found months later, alone and dead in my ramshackle house by the FedEx deliveryman.* What in heavens was holding her back? She missed Brian, sure, but still? While she was approaching her mid-thirties, in today's world, wasn't thirty the new twenty? Gwen grimaced. She knew it was past time to put herself on her 'to do' list, somewhere above 'the cleaners' and 'caring for neighbor's pet'. Gwen vowed to prioritize taking care of herself. That had been the take-home lesson from her Big Apple support group she'd joined when she was recovering from Brian's death. Yes, it was time to practice 'me-ism' and get some better life balance. Maybe not just this weekend.

Throwing her overflowing briefcase in the back seat Gwen drove up the winding mountain road to her mother Sylvia's nursing home. The ride was beautiful at this time of day as the sun was diving down towards the horizon, splashing long shadows over the valley. During the drive Gwen thought again about the ironic state of her relationship with her mother. As Sylvia's Alzheimer's slowly progressed, mom and daughter had been enjoying their time together more than at any time in Gwen's life. The irony was that the illness had made her mom less inhibited, released her irreverent sense of humor and revealed even moments of emotional warmth. These were qualities hidden for so many years behind Sylvia's lingering depression and withdrawal from family life following Gwen's younger brother Mark's tragic 'accident'. After that trauma, there had followed many years when Sylvia had not been a part of Gwen's world. But then, while Gwen was in law school, came the call from the hospital that her mom had fallen, appeared to have early dementia, and Gwen had been appointed, by default, her mother's caregiver. While her brother Artie, living the high life in California, contributed money towards Sylvia's expenses, her mom's care had become her responsibility. Lately Gwen had noticed her mom's mental decline was advancing more rapidly and the welcomed affectionate person more and more was retreating into silence. This was making each weekly visit even harder.

Pulling into the Mount Pleasant Nursing Home parking lot, Gwen grabbed the paper bag filled with cleaned and new clothes from the back seat. At the entrance desk, Gwen paused, gathering courage to enter the difficult world of dementia. Putting on a friendly smile, she greeted the large woman in a crisp white uniform behind the front desk.

"Hi Dolores, here to see my mother, Sylvia Wilson."

In a friendly Southern drawl, delightful but unusual to hear in New Hampshire, Dolores answered, "Well, then, Ms. Wilson, it must be Friday. Your mom had a good week and is resting in the movie room. You know where that is, right? You may find her a little tired today."

"Yes. Thanks."

Gwen followed the yellow painted line to the large lounge. Looking around the row of patients lined up in their wheelchairs, she found her mother, head down and apparently sleeping. As usual, Gwen felt a sharp stab of pain watching Sylvia slowly slip away into the world of memory loss. Walking around the darkened lounge, Gwen approached Sylvia, who was softly snoring, unlocked the wheelchair's brakes, and pushed her mom through the halls into the 'garden room', an oval space filled with large potted green plants and raised beds of real flowers. Light shone through the ceiling skylights, creating a cheerful atmosphere. Sylvia remained, however, in her private world and so Gwen spent the next hour carrying on a monologue about her week, and life.

Even though her mom wasn't really there, Gwen found it was still comforting to share her life with Sylvia.

As the end of visitor's hours approached, Gwen wheeled her mother into her private room. Gwen sat down on the plastic covered chair -- not dissimilar to those found in her dentist's waiting room. After catching her breath from the wheeling exercise, Gwen emptied the large paper bag onto her mother's bed and folded and placed the clothes neatly into her mother's dresser. Gwen then carefully placed the newly purchased small stuffed green frog on Sylvia's lap for her to hold. Sylvia suddenly opened her eyes and, looking up at Gwen, smiled and said, "Hello, darling." Then, the moment gone and Sylvia's eyes again shut, Gwen smiled as her mother gently rubbed the frog's green belly with both her thumbs. Gwen leaned over and kissed Sylvia on her warm cheek, then said, "See you next week, Mom. Love ya'."

CHAPTER EIGHT

Her desk had been invaded overnight by a paper intruder. It was now covered in five large piles labeled: sign, comment, discard, review, and, in capital letters, URGENT. As Gwen was tackling the urgent pile, Judy entered, announcing that Sammy and a young man were in the waiting room for their appointment. Gwen was nonplussed at this news; Sammy had promised to bring his ex-wife Olanda.

Both men followed Judy in and sat down on Gwen's two client chairs – black lacquered wood chairs bearing her law school's name and logo, sort of a professional's version of the 'old college tie', but one that stayed put. Sammy was wearing a large gray sweatshirt that blared in crimson letters 'Dortman High'. Next to him sat a tall young man. Gwen marveled at what she thought must be his size 15 sneakers.

"Sammy, who's your friend and where's Olanda?"

Sammy squirmed in his seat. "Sí, this is my nephew, Carlos, Carl. He speaks English good and help me say my story."

Carl smiled at her and didn't seem at all intimidated at meeting a lawyer. Gwen repeated her question about the absent Olanda.

Sammy, eyes staring at the carpet, in a low disappearing voice said, "She say won't come, we divorced and this my mess. I say important to my case, but she say she no can help as she do nothing in case."

"So she didn't meet with Mr. Murphy?"

"No, she working as I say. Attorney, no be angry with me. I bring Carl; he help."

"Sammy, as I said in my email, I need to look at the language in your divorce's Separation Agreement. Make sure you own your case. Do you have it with you?"

Sammy slid lower in his chair. "I not find, look at all papers. Maybe I leave at friend to keep safe. Don't remember. I ask

Olanda tomorrow and bring, I promise."

"You know, Sammy, as we've discussed, you need to work with me. Can you do that, be there to help me when I need you? Even if this case goes on for many months? Can you give me your word, make me a promise, that you will stay and fight to the very end?"

Sammy nodded. Then he crossed himself and said, "Attorney, I promise – on my Bible."

Gwen continued, "And you must tell me everything, even if you think it is not good for your case. And that means finding documents I ask to see and bringing them to me. Do you understand?"

Turning towards Carl, Gwen asked him to tell this to Sammy in Spanish. Carl did so and Sammy vigorously nodded his head, then sitting up straight added, "Attorney, I be good client, do what you say, you trust. You my Savior. I pray every day to the good Lord, ask that he look over you."

Gwen smiled, accepting all help offered with this case, before asking Carl for his input. Carl hesitated, and then added, "My uncle, he's an honest guy, but maybe easy mark. Uncle Sammy told me his problem, how he went to a big company to invest his savings, and he met this smooth talking sales guy who showed him fancy charts, pictures. You know the kind. Lots of 'everything'll be great' promises. And my Uncle Sammy, he told me he believed this bull. What did he know, you understand? He didn't know anything about the stock market. He didn't study finance in school like me – I'm set to start community college this Fall. No, he worked his way through high school at night. You ask him what is *Standard & Poor's*? He's no idea. Family all sick that this pendenjo, this greedy asshole, took my uncle's and aunt's money, made pretty promises but then lost it all. My Uncle Sammy now has nothing left, no more even his home. He's ready to fight and get back what they stole from him."

"Well said, Carl." Gwen wondered if she could put Carl on the stand if it came to a hearing.

Gwen rose and left the room, soon coming back holding a document. "Sammy, and Carl, please review my standard contingency fee agreement meaning I don't get paid unless we win, and that I can drop the case if I believe I'm not getting cooperation. Please review and let me know if you have any questions."

Fifteen minutes later Sammy marked his name on the last page of the contingency fee agreement, and Gwen signed under him. And so it happened at last. Gwen was now formally in the game. Gwen wasn't sure what finally sealed the deal in her mind, moved the chains. And whether it was a smart decision, or desperate one. Only time would tell whether she'd made the right choice. *Maybe by then I'll also have encountered this tall, dark, and handsome stranger who will lay claim to my heart.*

CHAPTER NINE

Ugh, today's the Middleton Bar Association Annual June Meeting, thought Gwen. And this year she'd promised John Seduka, her best lawyer friend, she'd show up. At least she'd be able to get his feedback and maybe some help on the Sammy case. As she dressed more carefully than usual, Gwen couldn't remember whether she'd checked off the savory chicken or filet of fish for lunch on the invitation, and hoped she'd be able to tell which meal once the plates were served.

Gwen heard her name over the tumult, "Gwen, over here."

She saw John waving his arms above the fray, trying to get her attention as she walked around the large meeting room. The place was already packed with lawyers sitting at large tables covered with pressed white tablecloths. Gwen waived back and then walked through the tight maze of chairs to his table. Sitting down next to John she gave him a friendly peck on the cheek.

She'd known John Seduka since she had set up shop working for her former boss Chris, and she liked him. He was friendly, outgoing, and looked like a billboard's version of a lawyer at 6' 2," blond, blue-eyed, with a smile that charmed and a runner's physique. John had been leasing an office in Chris's suite when she'd arrived, and was the first lawyer in town to invite her out for lunch. And refer a paying case to her. About the same age, Gwen and John soon became professional friends. Unlike Judy and Mary, though, he was the person she would talk with about the foibles of practice, who gave her confidence that her legal ideas made sense, who understood her malpractice concerns, who made her feel less isolated as a woman in practice. John in fact was the only lawyer she actually knew on a 'you have time for a quick lunch?' social level in Middleton.

Since her start with Chris, John had served as her confidant and sound board on many a sticky legal and practice issue. On occasions she'd been second chair on his litigation cases. In turn, John had partnered with her on some of her bigger cases. While Gwen knew that John was not the smartest lawyer in town, he had good intuition on how judges saw issues plus helpful insight on opposing counsel's motives. He made sure her Big Apple practice impulses were grounded in Middleton's small-town bar approach -- we're all trying to make a living, I'll help you this time and you'll reciprocate down the road.

Squeezing between the tables, Gwen said to John as she twisted into her seat, "I'm amazed! I didn't expect such a large turnout. Did I miss the Filet Mignon lunch option?"

"Not to my knowledge. I think the throngs are here because Judge Madden will be the speaker."

"She's on the Family bench, in Concord, right?"

"Yeah. Somehow I think the attraction is less the substance of her speech, unless you're really into the finer tax implications of business expenses as marital assets. It's more likely the tightness of her dress, usually hidden under her robes except at bar meetings."

"My god, what a bunch of adolescents. I keep forgetting men wearing three piece suits, rayon ties, and gold cufflinks aren't necessarily actually grownups." Alas, Gwen had learned over her brief career as a woman in a man's world that testosterone was not a recessive hormone. And, like with birds, it seemed more pronounced during spring.

Gwen poured herself a glass of water, started digging into her once warm onion soup that had magically appeared thanks to the numerous women serving the luncheon, and surveyed the scene. She'd gone to a handful of these 'training' luncheons held at the historic one-hundred-year-old Middleton Inn, mostly to earn easy continuing ed credits to meet the state's annual requirement. Arranged by the Bar's education committee, each luncheon had been mostly dreadfully boring. Still, who knew whether this might be the time that one of the attending brethren, due to a conflict, vacation, or golf obligation might be looking for a friendly local lawyer to take on a case. As the sole female attorney doing litigation in town, and an outsider – made more foreign by being also an ex- New Yorker and Ivy Leaguer, Gwen thought it helpful to be physically in eyeball range in case that event should occur. Otherwise the male buddy network would not select her to be the recipient of manna from heaven, a paying referral.

Surveying the tables, Gwen was surprised that she knew most of the faces. Some of the lawyers smiled at her and waived. The lawyer on her right, Jim, who specialized in DUI cases, in fact became chatty as the meal progressed. She wondered if his loud voice might be due to his second cocktail. As he began to tell her a joke, the remaining attendees at her table and those nearby stopped talking and listened in.

Jim said, "So Gwen, did you hear the one about how many lawyers it took to change a light-bulb?"

Smiling, Gwen warily said, "No, not that one Jim."

Already laughing before the punch line, Jim said, "Four: one partner, one secretary to prepare the invoice, and two paralegals."

This was followed by a slow rolling chuckle across the table. Gwen said with an attempt at cheeriness, "Got me on that one, Jim."

John interjected, "I thought you were going to say 'how many can you afford'."

That also brought a guffaw from those round the table.

And, not to be outdone, Brad the town counsel guy, chimed in, "And Gwen, if it were a female lawyer, the answer would be none, as she'd have to call her husband to do the job."

This effort got the biggest laugh of all the answers. By the time the dessert course came around — yellow sugar in the form of lemon meringue pie, she was feeling a little shell-shocked. This confirmed her long-standing premise that the scarcity of other practicing women lawyers left her talking shop only with John and, via phone, Chris at his lake-front home in Florida, when he wasn't out golfing, and provided he hadn't yet been eaten by one of the 8' sunning alligators floating in his complex's lake. She knew there were others like Chris at the event, smart and responsible lawyers, just maybe not at her table.

Before the judge, wearing a demure navy blue pants suit that covered up her legs – and chest, started her after-lunch talk, Gwen told John that she'd taken on the Perez case. She summarized briefly the facts she knew so far and legal issues.

"John, if the case doesn't settle quickly, I'm expecting the investment house's lawyers to try to overwhelm me with paper during discovery. Are you still teaching a class at Granite State Law?" The last Gwen knew, John, who's family donated each year to the school's building fund, had been hired as an adjunct to teach real estate law at the school's branch campus near Middleton. The school prided itself on accepting students who'd learned skills from real life, not necessarily in college classrooms. And no exam scores needed to be submitted. As she recalled, its mission was to allow 'motivated' adults, no matter their age or income, to pursue accredited and affordable higher education. Gwen thought this a great equalizer, one needed to ensure more diversity in the bar.

"Gwen, teaching's become my favorite lawyer time, although, ha, I can't complain about being overpaid."

"Do you have any students who might be interested in the role of 'associate for the day' and could help me out? I'll pay them for their time, but sorry not too much."

"Sure Gwen, I'll put out the word. I think I can get a few. Just let me know how many you need and the dates. But they won't know much about securities law."

"Great. No problem, they just have to look like lawyers and create the impression I have more resources than I really do. Hopefully, I won't need them. You know I've been thinking lately that I'd like to give teaching a try. If anything comes up and they're looking to take on adjuncts, let me know. Might be fun to be a professor. That is, of course, in priority after 'your honor'. But

I hear judging has its own issues. Isolation, poor pay, and politics. At least you can dress casual under the robes and they get August vacations."

"Yeah, and you're in control, regular hours I hear, fixed income, and you make the decisions. By the way, heard on the grapevine, actually from my uncle who's on the Town's planning board, that they're looking for someone practicing above the Notch to fill a judge seat sometime soon. They were hoping for a person of color to add diversity, but no one like that I know, so a woman might be next choice."

"Actually, I think judging would be a meaningful way to practice law. You get to make law, bring about justice, not just argue with other lawyers and draft paperwork. To be frank, I've been thinking lately that with my money stress, not sure that lawyering is a healthy way to make a living." Gwen didn't add that she'd already been looking at want ads for auto mechanics.

"I know what you mean," John sighed aloud. "In this economy, it's becoming increasingly tough, not like the old days. When I started, Middleton was a nice small bar. Lawyers looked out for each other, all while taking care of their clients of course. That was the North of the Notch way. Like a men's drinking club. But those days appear gone, what with law schools like Granite State chugging out more competition every year. No more chumminess." John leaned over towards Gwen and lowered his voice. "Between us, I find myself worrying so much these days. I have a pretty secure practice, what with my family connections. Last week my dentist fit me with a night retainer 'cause I'm grinding down my teeth at night from anxiety. You understand the problems. We have a big overhead; it's become harder to support my family, pay the mortgage. Make it."

"Yes, too much stress these days. And you haven't even mentioned malpractice. Let alone the constant concern that some crazy client will sue you."

"I thought we were supposed to be made, Gwennie, like in the

Mafia, once we became members of the bar." Touching her hand with his fingers, John added, "Gwennie, that's confidential, okay?"

Gwen nodded, hoping she was exuding empathy. John changed the subject. "Doing anything fun lately?"

"You bet. I've been trying out a new running routine. So far, however, it's more of a routine in its absence. How do you get your run in?"

"Mostly the pressure from being anxious, so I wake up when everyone's asleep. And I've been doing it long enough I need the high. My junk fix."

Gwen had been worried about John the past year. She'd watched him more than once down with water small white capsules that he said took the edge off and eased his anxiety. She wondered if they were the same as Sammy's. And at times, when his pills weren't available, he'd check out the booze. Now there was a dental retainer. Not good signs going forward. *Damn it. Is lawyering dangerous to your health?*

The sound of a spoon knocking against a water glass brought the room to silence. All counsel applauded as Judge Madden stood up to share her wisdom on family court law.

CHAPTER TEN

The start gun was about to sound. Gwen reviewed again her draft representation letter to Stanley, Howe that set out Sammy's fraud and negligence claims against the firm and Larry. Gwen hoped a convincing presentation of her client's strong legal position would lead to a quick end of the case. She'd decided to ask for damages on the high side, $215,000, a figure that would get their attention but also allow plenty of room for compromise. In support, she'd thrown in the kitchen sink in terms of statutory and common law claims, even citing in a footnote the important 1978 case, Leib v. Merrill, Lynch. She included lots of legal jargon to establish that, while a smalltown lawyer, she had some expertise in securities law. At the end of the letter she stated her availability to meet to discuss the matter -- code she hoped for 'make me a fair offer and we can put this baby to sleep'.

Gwen walked into the conference room where Mary, as usual, was hard at work. "Mary, do you have a minute. I've decided to take on the Perez case and have drafted a Notice of Representation letter. I'd appreciate a second set of eyes and feedback."

"Sure, Gwen, I'll be happy to try. But remember my knowledge of securities law's pretty much limited to the primer you gave me." Mary read the papers quickly. "Seems fine, firm yet the last lines imply your availability to settle."

"Good. I was worried I might appear overeager. My inclination – unlike that of my male colleagues -- can be too conciliatory, press for settlement too early."

"I know. I started compromising at an early age, allowing my twin brother to come out first."

Gwen laughed. "You weren't weak, you were girl smart. That way you're always the younger child. Anything else?"

Mary, scrunching up her eyes, hesitated, then said, "Gwen, if I'm going to work on this case more, maybe now that you know the facts you can go over again Sammy's legal claims with me. And this time I'll take notes."

"Sure but let's be clear, my securities law expertise isn't great – yet. I did take one course in law school, but I barely recall the color of the case book, let alone the substance inside."

"Gwen, Columbia is blue, Harvard case books are red."

Gwen nodded. "However, funny thing is that I do recall that the Professor was a named senior partner with a Wall Street firm. He'd show up in his chauffeured limousine for the class each week. The limo would be parked illegally outside in front of the law school while he taught the class. This fact made a great impression on my fellow male students who all wanted to be like him -- stinking rich."

Gwen looked at her nails, which appeared as if she'd nibbled them for breakfast, and then began a brief review of Sammy's claims. "Now, a broker of course should work to have his client's money earn more money, and he's entitled to a fair fee for this service. It's when the broker puts his financial interest in front of his clients that we may enter the realm of investment fraud. You may remember adhesion contracts from contract law —where the more powerful party writes the contract and then offers it as a take it or leave it deal? Sammy signed the firm's boilerplate account agreement. It requires all disputes be arbitrated. So Sammy can't sue in a court of law. The NASD, National Association of Securities Dealers, the self-regulatory agency in this field, handles most cases like ours, and applies its rules as well as federal law. With this background, Sammy's first claim is that Murphy hadn't invested in 'suitable' stocks *for him*."

"Meaning?"

"The NASD's Rule 2310 says in pertinent part,...and as I quote in my letter:

In recommending...the purchase...of any security, a member...shall have reasonable grounds for believing that the recommendation is suitable for such customer... upon the basis of facts... disclosed as to... his financial situation and needs.

In other words, Larry should have made reasonable efforts to assess Sammy's appropriate trading risk, his risk tolerance, and to recommend only those stocks that met this risk standard, that were suitable. We contend that Larry failed to do this, to learn about Sammy's net worth, his assets, financial position, assess background info on age, family obligations, and such, and to apply this to trade decisions. It makes sense. A broker should not treat the account of a rich client, like your ex – Dr. Tony before he became Dr. Phony – who can accept more financial risk of a stock going South, the same was as he handles a Sammy – an investor with minimal assets and who's set to retire soon."

"If that's the standard, trading for me should be limited to my son's old baseball cards down in the basement."

"Yeah, I know. Me too. Anyhow, our next claim is based on Linda's summary showing what we say is excessive trading, a/k/a 'churning' if you remember the securities lingo. Brokers can't make trades for the primary purpose of earning more commission. This covers, for example, excessive in and out sales to make the broker more profit – and win him a Hawaiian trip."

Mary doodled on her legal pad, and then said, "Duh. If I went to a broker, it seems *ipso facto* he'd be obligated to put my interests first. They need a rule for this?"

"Our claim against the investment company, Stanley, Howe, is that they failed to meet their duty to supervise their broker – Larry."

"Yeah, babe, like you supervise me."

Gwen nodded. "Expertly I may add. And there's one more issue, margin abuse. As you know, at Larry's suggestion, Sammy borrowed funds from Stanley, Howe so he could purchase more stock. This loan incurs interest; so it costs money, and it's secured, now get this, by the assets in Sammy's two accounts. If his margin account goes below the firm's set amount, Sammy has to sell assets to fill up the larder, or the firm will sell any of the assets held in either account, even if at a loss. As such, while margin increases Sammy's purchasing power, it also greatly increases his risk. And margin trading is profitable for both Larry who earns fees on both the margin interest paid and the amount of the loan, and Stanley, Howe which charges account fees as well.

Turning towards Gwen, Mary added, "This is helpful, Gwen, but going back to basics. I keep wondering how a blue-collar worker like Sammy decided to play the market. It's one thing for your wealthy clients like the Carpenters to get involved, but, I mean, Sammy doesn't make a lot of money – nor likely read *The Wall Street Journal*. Um... Unless, you know, he does because he got into playing the market."

"Good question, and one I went into with Sammy. Yes, he had limited assets, and his friends were goading him on, but why shouldn't a blue-collar worker, especially a person of color, be able to take advantage of what's offered to the rest of us, to make his money work for him. He should be able to benefit from people like Martha, or at least more affordable versions. The problem here is that he was a patsy for unfair practices by both Respondents."

"Gwen, are you sure you aren't stepping into quicksand? Even I know that Stanley, Howe is one of the big guys with unlimited resources should they elect to fight this case. You'll be the solo practitioner against a shitload of lawyers if for some reason they won't settle."

Gwen sat back in her chair and found herself pulling on her knuckles. She could already feel her stomach curling into knots, thanks to the prospect Mary presented of being way in over her head, and budget. But she'd committed. And part of her whispered in her ear that she needed this case, to have something to believe in again, to take on the usurpers and hold them accountable. She had the skills, the legal acumen. If not her, then who would be the one to stand up?

"Mary, you did a check on Sammy right, when you were at the library? No legal actions, I don't know, such as collection cases or police involvement?"

"None that I found, but I only checked the Middleton papers. And not knowing Spanish I didn't have access to that type of information for Dortman. Remember, Gwen, when you took on Middleton's Public Housing Tenants group as a contingency case, you were right on the law but your clients as the case dragged on began to disappear."

"I know. They were good people, but one family moved from town, and one of the senior tenants passed away. Without plaintiffs you can be in trouble. But we did settle and I did 'good' for the justice thing, and it came out all right financially. You think Sammy will disappear?"

"The law moves slowly, you know, like they say, with glacial speed."

"True, but this is arbitration, a much quicker process, or so they promise. So, you know, I'm only committing a little time and effort, not enough to break the bank." Gwen looked at her yellow pad and noticed that her doodles were looking more and more like scary creatures. "Here are the questions we need to be prepared to answer: Why did Sammy play the market with his family's security at stake? Is he a gambler? Even though a bull market, why didn't he appreciate the risk? We could argue that his co-workers were making good money and no one wants to think the market will go down, still... And who am I to say that a hard-working Hispanic man with a GED near retirement, earning very modest income, shouldn't benefit from the American way of getting rich? Besides, the fault lays with Respondents, surely. We should not be blaming the victim for the crime."

Gwen returned to her desk and twirled her hair, knowing that once she mailed the letter of representation she would be, in her mind, finally committed to the case. Despite her lingering unease, she believed her instinct to trust Sammy was correct. And the law, if it's to be respected, must serve a fairness purpose, to protect investors like Sammy.

Gwen made a few final pencil changes to the draft letter and walked it over to Judy's desk to retype and mail. Judy was already wearing her travel home boots.

"Will do tomorrow Gwen. Got to run, have a dinner date with my man."

Gwen, back at her desk, her toes happily in her sneakers, paused and watched the sun set through her window. *Is it normal for a highly educated person to be anxious about whether the disappearing sun will visit China tonight and then rise on the other side of town tomorrow morning?*

Thinking of China and the leftover Chinese food waiting for her, Gwen remembered her saved fortune cookie. It had said she would meet a handsome stranger. Yet it had been lots of weeks with no such visitor in sight. Was that a less likely event than the sun getting stuck on the other side of the planet?

CHAPTER ELEVEN

The weeks followed quickly after the initial formal contact with Stanley, Howe. Yet Gwen hadn't received any response from Bill Wadford, the firm's New England in-house Counsel. She knew many companies didn't take claims seriously until legal action had been filed, but she'd hoped that in this highly regulated area there'd be more interest in giving input at the start. Maybe all it meant was that Wadford was away on vacation with his family during August.

Otherwise, for Gwen life was pretty much same old. She continued to visit with her mom on Fridays. As daylight still lingered, she'd been able to catch a few runs after work and was enjoying the novel sensation of increasing strength in her legs. Sadly, though now stronger, they'd not become longer. She'd been impatiently watching the handful of tomatoes growing on her three tomato plants as they slowly switched from green to red, but somehow the animals didn't understand that red meant stop and some four-legged creatures had happily been helping them disappear before she could pick them. Next year she decided to install netting or hang up a plastic hawk.

On the social scene, Gwen's batting average remained pretty much in the cellar. She did occasionally dog sit for Bud, her neighbor's cuddly Golden Retriever. A few weeks ago she'd attended a meet and greet with a lawyer friend of John's. Not exactly a success. On the rebound from a broken marriage, he couldn't stop talking about his ex-wife. All in all, her social time with eligible members of the opposite sex remained below the dating horizon. She was thinking of joining a rock-climbing club to see if that might change her luck. She'd gotten a letter from a friend who'd met her now spouse at such a club. Gwen was concerned, however, that she'd never been good at pulling her body up anything taller than an SUV seat, and, besides, she suffered from acrophobia. Maybe joining a chess club made more sense.

And where was that dark handsome stranger, the one promised by the fortune cookie still tucked in her wallet?

Occasionally even these many years later she'd find an image or comment that would bring Gwen back to her troubling early days in Middleton, before she'd settled in and found friendship and support with her office team. There had been a brief period when, still traumatized by losing Brian, and so lonely, she'd acted stupidly, visiting raunchy bars after work and making risky self-destructive decisions, including even a few quickie motel visits with strangers. Then, thankfully, one night, fighting a cold and chilled to the bone while drinking frozen daiquiris at a dingy tavern, she found she'd lost interest in living on the edge. Instead she took up as an evening pastime the far less dangerous practice of gobbling pints of Ben & Jerry's Moose Track ice cream; that is, until her pants started becoming tight. Gwen chalked this time up to passing through her seven levels of grieving. She was now open, at least theoretically, to getting a life, maybe even finding a soul mate. She knew Brian would have wanted that.

On the work scene, while handling her normal busy caseload, even over the beautiful summer months when the grass was green and mountain lakes demanded a visit, Gwen had been working on the Perez case. As so far there'd been no interest in exploring settlement, Gwen did her due diligence and prepared for the litigation route, although still believing this course unlikely. She drafted a six page Statement of Claims to file with the NASD to begin the litigation, and to let the investment firm know she was serious. Faced with the nuisance expense of defending the case, they'd realize surely that it made more sense to explore settlement.

Then, one early September day as the trees were beginning their fall display, mail arrived from Stanley, Howe's Concord office. It was a one-page form letter informing Gwen that the company and Mr. Murphy had received her representation letter and that they were reviewing the matter. It was signed by Wadford, except the actual signature was by a computer. Gwen was furious.

Heaven help me. It took them how many weeks to spit this out? At this rate I, maybe more likely Sammy as he's older, will be dead before we even get to a hearing.

Gritting her teeth, Gwen vowed to finish revising Sammy's complaint within the week

So much for being a pushover, Wadford.

The case had begun. The wheels were now rolling.

Upon completing the paperwork, she gave it, along with the pleading and supporting documents, to Judy to mail to the NASD, certified, and to the two named respondents.

Within a few days she received official notice from the agency that Sammy's action had been filed and was now designated, 'Case No. 2103528C, Perez v. Stanley, Howe *et. al*' on the NASD's docket.

The formal settlement game had begun, or so Gwen hoped.

Every few days she'd check her phone messages to learn if Stanley's counsel had left a voicemail. But days, then weeks passed – and there was no such missive. Nor was there a letter to the tune of 'let's meet and see if we can settle,' as had happened in Carpenter.

Gwen wondered to Judy, "What gives?"

Judy shrugged since she had no clue.

Finally, frustrated with the non-action, Gwen filed a Motion with the NASD demanding a decision in her favor as the Respondents had failed to file an Answer within the time allotted. She served her Motion on the firm and on Murphy by express mail to Wadford. No response from anyone. Her next move was to submit a discovery request for all related documents to Sammy's claims. This also was greeted with silence. If this case had been in federal court, Gwen would have marched down to the courthouse and demanded sanctions from a Judge. But there was no Judge, or even law clerk, to appeal to in Sammy's case.

With no sign of a meaningful response in sight, let alone interest in settlement, and no recourse she could think of, Gwen began worrying more and more about her lack of expertise in this area and with the logistics of arbitration. She understood that after 9/11's impact on Wall Street, many securities firms and their regulators had been dysfunctional for a time and were just catching up. But surely that wasn't impacting this case. Increasingly, Gwen worried that she was setting herself up for a malpractice claim, always a lawyer's scary dark shadow. At night in bed, she'd find the "malpractice ghost" leaning over and whispering into her ear, *Gwen, you could mess up big time, causing an expensive malpractice meltdown.* After these visits Gwen woke in cold sweats – her subconscious wrestling with the wisdom of the poltergeist's warnings.

At last, with increasingly cold feet, Gwen decided it was time to protect herself. She'd explore referring the case to a lawyer specializing in this law, someone who would protect Sammy's interest, and maybe pay her firm a small referral fee.

She knew just the person, a former law school friend, Todd Jameson. Todd practiced securities law with a big Portsmouth firm. Maybe it didn't matter that they'd briefly dated while in school before he'd walked down the aisle with his current firm's senior partner's daughter. Todd answered his phone on the first ring.

"Todd, Gwen Wilson here. Long time no speak. I've missed you. I hear on the Columbia grapevine that your practice is doing great. Hope I'm not interrupting something?"

"Hello, Gwen, what a nice surprise. Great to hear from you. It must be months since I saw you at the last CLE meeting in Concord. I've been meaning to catch up. Maybe now that ski season's approaching we can connect up your end. Is this phone call social or can I help you with some case?"

"Sharp as usual, Todd." Gwen explained her concerns to him, summarizing Sammy's case. She said that it had been many weeks since she filed her initial claim with no response from the company, other than a one page 'we're looking into it' letter. She added that she'd filed motions with the NASD as well, and no response. Finally, she offered to fax over Sammy's Statement of Claims. In short, she was worried that she had gotten in over her head. "Todd, any chance you might be interested in taking on the case, or, if not, can you recommend another lawyer with experience in this area whom I could contact?" She ended with the sales pitch that she believed Sammy's case likely would be a winner.

"Gwen, what's the damage amount you think?"

"We're asking for $215,000, but I think considerably less would be more probable."

There was a pause in the line. Gwen's throat tightened.

"Gwen, I'd like to help you out, and it seems like a promising case, but, well, my firm is too big now to take on this case. Not enough money involved to justify the expense, the burden for us. We might do it for an established client as a favor. Also, I'm concerned that, let me see how to express this...your client presents issues concerning...I guess things like long-term reliability."

Gwen paused. "Yes, Todd, not too surprised to hear all that. Still, Mr. Perez seems quite committed to me, and the little guy needs to have some representation in our system."

"Wish I could suggest someone else, but lawyers in my field will have the same concerns I do. Really sorry, Gwen. But call me if I can help down the road if you pursue it. I just checked; I have no client conflict. I'm confident you'll do fine, you were top quarter of our class as I recall, but I'll be happy to help."

Gwen understood Todd's decision. Her optimal bottom line wasn't sufficient even with his firm's 40% contingency rate, considering expected expert fees and travel costs and all. Sadly, the price of justice came high these days. Gwen's commitment to Sammy was firm, she would push forward with the case, whether a practice killer or lottery winner – it was now hers.

Finally, after almost two months past the time set in the rules for a responsive pleading, Judy placed a large envelope from the NASD on Gwen's desk. Gwen stared at it, trying to discern from the envelope whether it contained good news. Unable to read the contents through the yellow paper, despite her laser like focus, she opened it up. Inside was a five-page filing titled 'Respondents' Responsive Pleading'. In it Stanley, Howe and Murphy, the two named Respondents, stated they were filing an Answer while requesting more time to prepare a revised Supplemental Answer.

Reading the rest of the response, it was evident that the firm's lawyers had dashed out a quick filing. To each of her numbered claims, Wadford had merely replied 'Denied'. The final paragraph, parroting the samples in Gwen's securities pleadings book, stated that "on information and belief, any losses in Mr. Perez's accounts were due primarily to stock purchases made at his behest and under his direction." Her client, it further claimed, was a sophisticated investor who had previously traded. The response concluded with the malpractice preventing catchall that Sammy's case was "totally frivolous, without substance, and not filed in good faith."

Gwen focused on the pleading's last affirmative claim. Laying out specific facts applicable to Sammy's case, Wadford asserted that Sammy not only was a sophisticated investor, but he controlled his accounts and repeatedly had taken funds from them for his own personal use. This, it was asserted, was a primary factor in reducing his account assets.

Gwen's heart raced as if she were driving at the Indianapolis 500. *Did I read that right?* She read the claim again. *What the shit? Did I miss something? Did Linda mess up? Did Sammy pull one over on me? Was this the reason no settlement call?*

She sat down and caught her breath while trying to think it through. She cracked her knuckles, listening for the popping sound for each finger. Slowly, her anger and trepidation dissipated into the office air.

She called out, "Judy, please come in for a moment."

Judy rushed in, notebook and pen in hand. She saw the unsmiling look on Gwen's face. "Not good news, huh, boss?"

"No. Not good news. We may be spending nights on this case after all. Would you please contact Sammy and make an appointment for him to come in as soon as possible. I need to get some facts straight, and make sure he's been on the up and up with us."

"Ah. It seems the client sometimes is more of a problem than the opposing side."

"You can say that again. You know I told him again and again I needed to know all that happened, including the bad facts. He assured me he had."

Her hopes of a quick resolution were smashed. *Damn, no settlement interest, just the beginning of a delay campaign.* As Gwen knew, continuing delays did not favor Sammy. Walking around her office, Gwen considered her options while playing 'trash basketball' with her junk mail and her trash can. Her floor soon was covered with paper representing missed baskets. She wasn't sure whether to play along with Wadford's request for more time, or to act tough and file motions for sanctions. If this ball went in, she told herself, she'd give them more time. She bunched up another piece of paper into a ball and, pretending she was shooting a three-point shot in the Boston Garden, let loose the paper and listened for the crowd's roar.

More time. Good idea, she decided. Why not wait to see if Respondents' cross more non-compliance bridges before resorting to the big guns. As she was putting the package aside, she noticed included were papers from the agency as well. These provided biographies of ten persons who were possible Panel members should the matter go to a hearing. Gwen put them aside to review the next day, although her curiosity was certainly awake.

Driving home Gwen began to relax as she tried to place work pressures in a healthier place. *Look around Gwen, all is beautiful.* The spectacle of Fall in New England had arrived. Soon October's splendor would be marked by the parade of tourist buses, leaf peeping photographers, and maple syrup stands selling last spring's sap. The baby sparrows had already flown from the nest above her porch, and her tomato plants had recently joined the compost heap. Leaf detritus had been raked into the road where the town's special trucks would vacuum them up, then crunch the lot into town mulch. The landscape was getting ready for the white stuff to arrive.

And so was Gwen, except her 'white stuff' was Respondents revised pleadings.

CHAPTER TWELVE

The phone rang, beeped, and went into answer mode, and a friendly male voice stated, "Law Firm of Attorney John Seduka. Your call is important to me. Kindly leave a message."

Gwen liked John's message, warm and personal. But then again, based on her years of working with John, that's who he was.

John suddenly started to speak into her ear. "Hello, John Seduka. Can I help you?"

"Hi John. Gwen here. Glad I caught you. No secretary?"

"Hello, Gwennie. No, Rachelle's left for the day, something to do with her mother. I'm just on my way out to meet a client. Love to talk but in a bit of a rush. Still I have a few minutes as traffic's likely to be light."

"Thanks, won't take long. Following up on our talk about my Perez case, weeks ago, well months I guess, at the Bar meeting." Gwen then updated John on the status of the case including the NASD's inaction in appointing a Panel and no interest in settling. "John, I'm dealing with the big guys now. Bill Wadford's hired outside counsel to help him, an established Concord law firm, Stearns, Foster. Have you dealt with them?"

"No. They're supposed to be good, but tough."

"That's the name of the game these days. I've been dealing with an associate at the firm and so far it's been one delay after another, mostly claiming they need time to get up to snuff on the case. I'm finally going to be able to review the documents I've requested."

"Sounds like they're giving you the runaround Gwen, but what else's new when playing with the big firms."

"No surprise I guess. Anyhow, I'm expecting I'll need more eyes than mine and Mary's to get this done, unless I want to camp out at their offices. So, wondering if you've had any interest from your law students, I'm thinking four, who might be available to help me, for some pay of course? The dates are Tuesday and if really needed, Wednesday, that's October 15th and 16th. It will mean their missing maybe one day of class, possibly two if they're available."

"Sure, don't think there'll be an issue as most of my students would welcome a chance for some income. And it's before they'll be studying for midterms. I did get lots of interest when I mentioned this before and I'll find out tonight who's available those days as I'm actually teaching my class. But, Gwennie, some may be first L's, so really babes in the wood in terms of legal skills."

"No problem. As I said, they just have to look like lawyers. You know the saying, if it walks like a duck, and talks...."

"Yes, got it."

"So that would be great. Just select four and have them come to my office by 8 a.m. on that Tuesday. I know you're in a rush but just need to vent that already arbitration sucks. Very limited discovery tools, minimal enforcement. Slow, still haven't decided on Panel that will sit -- and I promise you the potential panelists would be welcome at the investment industry's trade group meeting. All this delay and such, gives them the upper hand. So, not surprisingly, arbitration's the business world's rage. Soon you won't be able to sue a company in court for any claim. There goes our judicial system. The hell with trial by jury."

"Yeah, Gwennie, but the judges love it, saves money and reduces pressure on the court system. And has the appearance of fairness. Anyhow, I'll call tomorrow with those names and their phone numbers in case you need to reach them.

"Thanks, John. Have I told you lately you are a sweetie?"

"Compliments always welcome. Now if I weren't married with two kids and a big mortgage, I might have insisted on hearing that in person."

Laughing, Gwen retorted, "Sure, you'll always be my one that got away. Speak with you." Gwen enjoyed her repartees with John

– which she couldn't do with any other male in her life at the moment, except maybe Bud the dog. But it reminded her also how much she was the minority gender in her profession, especially above the Notch.

The following weeks passed with the Perez case moving slowly along. Gwen had had another meeting with Sammy and he assured her he was telling her what happened, that the company had gotten it wrong – or 'they lie' as he said. And Martha and Linda's preliminary analysis of Sammy's records confirmed the gist of his story. As Gwen found herself busy with her other cases, she didn't have time to fret more about her Sammy commitment.

Early on October15th, four tired students, dressed in interview attire, showed up at Gwen's office, eager to experience a day as a practicing lawyer. She arranged them in chairs around the conference table and began to prepare them for their day. After introducing herself, she described their 'discovery' task. "Okay, my 'associates', welcome to the world of Perez v. Stanley, Howe, *et. al.* Before discussing the case I thought we'd go around the room and you can tell me about yourself. After all, we'll be spending the next day or two in close contact." Gwen leaned in, interested to learn about the type of North of the Notch person attending the local law school. Especially as she was still considering teaching a class there, and who knows -- it might be securities law.

The student on her immediate left -- who apparently had gone directly from middle school to law school -- began. "Hi Attorney Wilson. I'm Jimmy Sauer, Junior, but people call me Junior."

"Right, Junior. What year are you in?"

"I'm I guess a 1L, first year that is. Almost halfway through first term."

"And what's your goal in law school?" Gwen wasn't sure why she asked this question, but she was trying to make small talk to get everyone relaxed about the job ahead.

"Oh, my dad's a partner with a firm in Dortman, does criminal law, and, Granite State's the law school I got into. I'm planning to join his firm after I graduate."

Gwen smiled. "It's always good to have a criminal law expert with me when I work on a case, Junior, to protect my back." The next student, the only other female in the room, wore a blouse, plaid skirt, and a string of pearls around her neck. Gwen wondered whether she was going on a date after the discovery work. "Hi. I'm Serena, second year, but I'm going to law school only part-time, have three kids at home." Gwen secretly hit her arm in penance for her prior mean thought and decided Serena must be Wonder Woman in disguise. "Wow, that's a heavy load. Are you finding the time to do all the reading?"

"Most of the time, unless one of the kids gets sick. They're all in school now."

"And why'd you decide to join us today?"

"Really, I thought it might be fun, you know, to play like a real lawyer and all. But, I guess, basically, it's for the money. My kids could use new shoes for the holidays, so this will help a lot."

Bam! Gwen bent over as if she'd been punched in the stomach. How had she forgotten that this was above the Notch where the median income was probably $50,000, or so? Gwen realized that 'outsiders' like her didn't think of rural poverty here, so close to ski country and the fancy second homes and luxury Inns. She couldn't imagine her mom worrying about money for an extra pair of shoes for her. But, perhaps she had. Gwen promised to give her mother a special hug when she next visited the nursing home.

"Thanks Serena. I'm very glad you're able to join us today."

Gwen turned to the tall man on her right. He was the first student who actually looked old enough to be in graduate school. On closer inspection, and Gwen was glad she had put on her eyeglasses, he looked with his slightly graying hair at the temples, older than her. Gwen wondered how George Clooney with his dark, sexy eyes had somehow found his way to her office.

"Good morning, Attorney Wilson. Adam Webber, and I'm also

a first year. Although, as I'm sure you've noticed, I'm more seasoned."

Gwen liked seasonings, and even had an herb garden on her windowsill. "Adam, it's a relief to know that the world hasn't done away with the over 30 crowd. They say with age comes wisdom. So there's hope for us yet."

"I agree. As to why I'm here, well, law school's my second career. I thought after my first career I'd try something closer to the land, a career less about money, more about meaning."

Gwen stared, longer perhaps than was polite, into Adam's deer eyes -- that she noticed fluttered underneath thick dark bushy eyebrows. *Had a tiny earthquake hit the ground under her chair?* Despite feeling swoony, as if she were back in middle school watching the 'cool kid' walk towards *her* for a dance, Gwen stammered, "Adam, yes. Nice. And interesting not to connect practicing law with money." Swallowing hard, she continued in a more lawyerly fashion, "What preceded this adventure with justice?"

"Little complicated. Short version. After Stanford I stayed and worked in high-tech, founded a company with friends, was lucky, and after a few years of hard work we got a buy-out offer we couldn't refuse. Decided I was at a good place in my life to take time off. Spent a year traveling. I saw some beautiful places that, to be honest, the human race is not taking good care of. That's when I realized what I wanted to do. Spend my energies on behalf of the planet. So, law school made sense. Granite State, well, they don't require all those prerequisites, including law boards. So they could take me for this term. It seemed like a good fit. And here I am."

Gwen's gaze lingered at this member of her 'associates for a day,' then, after an awkward pause, she piped up, "Glad you could join us today, Adam. Hopefully, you'll learn something."

Addressing the group she added, "And all of you, we're now colleagues, so please call me Gwen."

Seated to the right of Adam was another young man, who also was seemingly not too long out of diapers. *Does he shave yet? At least he's not lily white like the rest.* Smiling, she asked, "What's your name?"

"Topper."

"Topper, that's an unusual name. What year are you in?"

"I'm a 2L, but I'm not sure I'll be able to continue next term unless I can find some way of getting the money for tuition. Yeah, Topper was my dad's name. Don't know how he got it; something to do with when he was overseas in the Army. Anyhow, the work today will help me out."

"Great. We definitely have a varied group here. As of now, please consider yourselves 'associates' of the Law Firm of Gwen Wilson! Now let me tell you a little about the specifics of the case – the basic facts and legal issues – and what I'd like you to do. And be forewarned, I think we may be in for a long and tense day ahead of us." Gwen gave a quick outline of the characters and the main legal issues, not wanting to overwhelm them. "Any questions?"

"I'm not sure exactly what we'll be looking for?" Junior said.

"Good question. Use your smarts -- and gut – to see if there is anything that might be damaging or explanatory about what the investment firm and broker were doing, about trading policies, stock selection, how to make money. Like the Supreme Court said about pornography, you'll know it when you see it. Anything that smells, set it aside so we can make a copy. Err on the side of being expansive, as we'll likely have only one bite of this apple.

"Now I'm expecting that when we get to the law firm's offices, they're going to try to overwhelm us with a room full of documents to review. Just one of those fun legal games of, 'I have lots of big money to spend on this case and you don't.' Don't be surprised if you find lots of duplicates, irrelevant papers, basically garbage. I'll be there as will my paralegal, Mary, so if you have any questions, just ask one of us. And remember, a top-notch Concord law firm now represents the Respondents, so get ready to be impressed with the furnishings, but not too much. Issues anyone? One final thought. Remember, we may be David and they're Goliath, but..." smiling, Gwen added, "we know who won that fight."

The "associates" arranged themselves in carpools with Gwen and Mary. Gwen was pleasantly aware that her heart speeded up when Adam got into the passenger seat of her car. *Had he pushed to do that?* Once through the Notch, they parked in a nearby lot, and Gwen and her 'firm' entered the high-rise office building. Inside, she noticed that the ornate granite pillars ascended to a painted ceiling showing floating angels, cute cherubs, singing nymphs, and clouds. She wondered if one of the heavenly angels represented Justice, and hoped it was not the one seemingly peeing behind the bushes.

After being granted permission by the security guards at the reception desk in the lobby, they all rode the elevator to the 23rd floor to meet Attorney Patman at the Stearns, Foster law firm.

When the elevator door opened Gwen found herself in a waiting area richly decorated with thick crimson carpeting, large expansive chintz armchairs flanked by colorful Tiffany lamps, and a big mahogany inlaid coffee table on which were neatly stacked piles of *The Wall Street Journal* and *Barons*. No *People* magazine here. Gwen thought she might ask Judy to stack up the local Middleton paper and Bar Journal Quarterly in similar fashion in her waiting room, next to *Hunting & Fishing Digest*, and *Outdoor Life*.

Walking up to the young female receptionist in sleeveless blouse behind the large, polished desk – and in front of the foot high silver letters that announced "Law Firm of Stearns, Foster, LLP.," Gwen stated, "Attorney Wilson here to see Attorney Patman."

Gwen and her "associates" were directed to take seats in the waiting area while the receptionist let Ms. Patman know of their arrival. The minutes ticked by. Gwen, sitting in the big client chair, began to feel so comfortable she worried about nodding off – as she'd been up since 6 a.m. that morning. Instead, she decided to use the time to catch up on legal developments, and scanned the New Hampshire Bar Journal. At last, a tall, slim woman, in blue-striped suit attire, walked up to Adam – who pointed her to Gwen.

"You must be Attorney Wilson?"

"Yes."

The woman held out her hand and with her skinny fingers squeezed Gwen's right hand so tightly that Gwen worried if she could hold a pen again.

In a friendly manner, the woman said, "Hi, glad you got here okay. I understand the traffic's tough today. I'm Anna Patman. Sorry to have kept you waiting; I was trying to make sure all the documents are organized and the boxes ready for you. I think I have the room set so you can begin. Once we get upstairs, Gwen, we can discuss the process for the day."

Anna stepped back and looked around the room, her eyes momentarily stopping on Adam. Her voice rising, she asked, "And are all these people your associates?"

"They are, along with my paralegal Mary Dunkin. Anna, I expected there might be a large volume of documents to review. So I figured that rather than my taking up your office space for the week, I'd bring my associates and we can try to finish our review today."

"How considerate. Please follow me." Anna's friendly tone had already changed to combative. Gwen wondered if Anna had expected a lone lowly lawyer from above the Notch and so was surprised to see her troops ready to work. She and Mary, the associates trailing like ducklings, marched behind Anna down the long, carpeted hallway, past the secretaries in their cubicles busily typing all the words of legal wisdom that $350 an hour will buy. Anna finally made a right turn and started walking up a steep circular staircase.

"We're going to the twenty-sixth floor, Gwen. I hope you don't mind walking. There is an elevator we could use if you like."

"No problem," Gwen said, glad she'd left her five-inch heels in Never-Never-Land.

With Gwen in the rear, like a good parent, they climbed, and climbed some more, going round and round on the staircase. Gwen held the banister tightly as she was feeling dizzy from the close turning. The staircase began to spin. Her legs wobbly, she resorted to using her arms to pull herself up to the next higher step. Almost there! At last Gwen stepped onto the twenty-sixth floor. Trying not to pant too loudly, she realized that her current running program perhaps left room for stamina improvement. At the same time, Anna had seemingly pranced up the stairs. Gwen speculated that she'd recently spent time in Kenya training at high altitude and that that had accounted for her alacrity.

At the top of the stairs, Anna took Gwen aside.

Gwen's stomach- tightened; she prepared for the first volley off the bow. Yes, as she had suspected, it was going to be a trying day.

CHAPTER THIRTEEN

Anna led Gwen to the conference room, explaining, "Just want to show you where it is. And how to get to my office if you need to."

Gwen traipsed behind Anna down the hallway and they entered a bright room where the row of windows along two walls displayed the golden Capital dome. In the center stood a walnut table large enough for a meeting of the U.N.'s Security Counsel, or at least the permanent members and their staff. Matching dark red leather chairs surrounded the long table. Lining the walls of the room were rows of neatly stacked white legal boxes, all marked with labels stating "Perez" followed by numbers and dates. Gwen quickly estimated that there were almost 40 legal boxes of documents. She couldn't imagine how the paperwork had mushroomed into this enormous stack in the brief time Sammy had had his trading account. At this rate, by the end of two years if the case continued that long there'd be enough filled boxes to de-forest Middleton.

Of course, big expensive law firms were experts at padding, whether time sheets or discovery responses. The bottom line was that each of her crew would need to review some seven boxes. Not impossible in a day, but surely a challenge. Fortunately, she expected the boxes full of duplicates, unrelated and outdated material, and maybe even the complete works of Shakespeare. Despite the excessive warmth of the room, Gwen felt goose bumps up and down her arms. The job certainly – as it was intended -- looked intimidating. *Buckle up, Gwennie. I've learned legal gamesmanship from New York's finest and the battle has just begun.*

"Anna, seems pretty straightforward. Now if you can just give me directions to the coffee and copy machines, I can get my team started. I'll try to have my associates periodically make the copies we need so that we don't monopolize the firm's machine – or is it machines?"

"Gwen, that's not…"

"If it's easier, I guess we can take a box of originals with us for copying at my office and then I'll FedEx them back to you next week."

Anna stood up straight, buttoned her suit jacket, and firmly announced, "No, Gwen. Neither is acceptable." Almost a foot taller, thanks to her five-inch heels, Anna leaned in towards Gwen. With an icy stare that Gwen thought might fight global warming, Anna added, "While you have the right to review relevant documents under NASD's arbitration rules, if you wish copies, I'll make them once I assure myself that the requested material is responsive and includes nothing confidential. If you like, after I've done my review, I'll overnight the copies to your office." Anna paused, then commented, "Sorry, Gwen, but at the moment I'm really tied up with another case. I should be able to complete this process end of next week."

Gwen thought about climbing up on one of the leather chairs to respond eyeball to eyeball, but put that idea aside as perhaps too dramatic, and demanding more gymnastic talent than she likely could muster. Instead, her eyebrows raised as if in surprise, she said, "Anna, come now. That's not the way I read the NASD's rules on discovery, which is supposed to be generous. You've already determined – and it took you way over the time provided to do this – that these materials are responsive. So producing them is required now. It's settled law that discovery does not allow your client *two* bites of the apple."

"Gwen, my instructions are to proceed this way. If you disagree, you have the option to file a motion for relief with the agency." Anna folded her arms in front of her like armor, then continued, "In which case you won't be allowed access today, and may end up waiting more weeks, maybe months, for a ruling. Or you can proceed as I've outlined. Really, Gwen, we're only talking about a few days wait."

Gwen had expected difficulties, but not this. Were they

concerned there might be something damaging in these materials? Sometimes overkill could yield the unexpected bonus of a misplaced document being turned over by mistake. Gwen knew she was being jerked around, but what were her realistic choices? *Okay, Gwennie, is one bite today better than no bites until who knows when? Yeah, a chicken in the basket is worth two in the bush.* Score one for Anna. Gwen hoped that at least the size of her extensive team, all looking busy and officious, would give Sammy's case more importance, earning higher marks in the litigation department's pecking order. Gwen put on a smile and using her sweetest voice agreed to Anna's plan.

"Fine Gwen, but two more things before you begin. First, I want to let you know that we've had some difficulty in getting all of the documents together. Some storage issues with the Middleton office. And locating papers involving the NASD. Lots of chaos still since 9/11. So a heads-up that we may need to supplement this production. Sorry for that. Second, I need you to initial this form." Anna handed Gwen a one-page letter. "It says you agree to comply with our firm's policy that our client documents are not to be removed without explicit consent. And, again, Gwen, we need this signed before we can release anything."

"Come on, Anna, what are we dealing with, nuclear secrets? Of course my team shall work within your questionable parameters – for now. And remember, what works for the goose also applies to the gander." After preserving her position, Gwen hesitated, and then added her initials.

"Fine. You should be all set. My secretary will come by within the hour to see if there are any coffee requests. Sorry, we don't have a coffee machine available to you. In the meantime, I'll be in my office at the end of this corridor -- where I showed you, although I'll be in and out thanks to a deposition." Anna pointed with her long index finger and lovely red painted nail down the hallway on the right. "You can ring my secretary, Patty, using the phone on the table. Just press zero and her extension number, 22.

And, of course, let me know when you're done and I'll make arrangements for the copying and delivery."

With that, Anna smiled, turned, and Gwen watched her sashay in her lawyer's suit of dark gray past the typing secretaries back towards her office. Suddenly, she pivoted and again walked back to Gwen.

"Oh, I almost forgot. We've been having some security issues lately, equipment missing, who knows. The firm's hired some private guards to keep an eye on the goings on, and upgraded our cameras. Just didn't want you to be surprised if you see big burly guys in blue uniform walking around. They keep a pretty close eye on things, thank goodness. And even have guns, ha, should there be a coup attempt by us associates.

No, just kidding, about the coup that is. Sorry for the humor, heard that from another associate."

Gwen watched as Anna turned around, and while sashaying again towards her office, paused as she approached where Adam was standing, glanced quickly at him and smiled, and then disappeared into her office.

Having already spent almost an unexpected hour dealing with Anna's demands, Gwen rushed her waiting contingent of students and Mary into the conference room and organized the search logistics. Setting herself up at the table's head, the senior partner's chair, Gwen opened her first box. As expected, she encountered numerous duplicates, totally unrelated documents, and even manuals long out of date and marked in red 'EXPIRED'. All were intended to make the task as onerous as possible while providing the barest of meaningful material. Gwen appreciated that the more costly discovery became, the greater the pressure on her to settle cheaply. *First round to Anna maybe, but Sammy's time is just around the corner.*

The review continued in silence, each attorney wannabe engrossed in getting through the paper search as quickly as possible, but without missing anything that might be helpful. A needle in a haystack, Gwen knew, but this process needed to be completed before she could move on with the next step in the case. After about an hour, Anna's secretary, Patty, arrived, introduced herself to Gwen, and took coffee requests. And so the day progressed. Gwen took orders for lunch -- her treat -- from the deli downstairs, the menu having been left on the table next to extra yellow legal pads, paper clips, and Mont Blanc pens imprinted with the firm's name to impress. Good pens, Gwen thought as she openly pocketed a few. Soon the smell of chicken curry and warm chocolate chip cookies filled the room and the pile of reviewed boxes began to rise in the corner.

Gwen reviewed the papers for copying placed in the lone box on the table. At first glance none appeared to be significant. Missing so far were many categories of requested documents, including specifics as to her client's trading experience, Larry's compensation, the firm's sales incentives, stock analysis for purchases, Larry's analysis for the account's stated risk goals and margin trades, any supervisor notes.

Reviewing her fifth box midway through the afternoon, Gwen, while sifting through duplicates of duplicates of NASD correspondence about broker supervision compliance, realized she'd cut her index finger. Blood had dripped onto several documents resting on her lap. *Blood, sweat and tears – what I do for my clients.*

Checking to assess the damage, she noticed that one page had attached to it several more pages via staples. Sure enough, one staple was partially open and probably the culprit for her cut. That document now bore a partial bloody fingerprint of hers, evidence should she elect to pursue a tort claim for damages.

Wiping the blood spots off with a tissue and about to put the pages back in the box, Gwen noticed a handwritten red-penciled comment in the upper right-hand corner of the cover page. It stated a recent date and the words, 'RED CONFIDENTIAL! Code Blue; Limited Circulation Only'. Underneath, were the initials 'ATD.'

Gwen recognized them to be those of Stanley, Howe's current CEO, Arthur T. Dement. Curious, Gwen began reading the cover page.

Her heart speeding up, she glanced at the attachments. At first blush the document appeared to be just another internal Executive memorandum. But then the room turned silent and a tingle spread up her back as she realized that what she held in her hands might be potentially, legally, lethal.

The cover memo was from the Senior Investment Manager to the company's Executive Committee, including Dement. It stated that the attached 2000 document, as revised, was for immediate implementation. Gwen then read the rest of the cover page. It described a 'Pinehills Investment Program, a/k/a 'PIP'," and included a three-page report from the company's management executive, L. Girard which was attached.

The second page was entitled, 'Diverse Asset Management Firm Assessment: Study results.' Gwen read on:

A cornerstone of the global economy, and our firm's industry strength, is the asset management industry, with assets valued in the many trillions of dollars. Our firm's asset managers and branch staff including brokers and traders, serve to facilitate the movement of capital from our investors to growth companies, and particularly to companies where S/H acts as market maker. But as has been pointed out by outsiders, like with other firms, our study concludes that the firm's small investors lack racial/ethnic diversity, especially those of Latino and African American background. These small investors are dramatically underrepresented in our programs, owning on average less than 3% of all firm trade division assets. Moreover, the performance of said diverse-owned assets significantly lag behind that of the firm's investors at large. Experimental evidence suggests that implicit bias on the part of firm representatives distorts performance metrics and may partially explain the reluctance to invest more affectively, and aggressively, resulting in the underperformance of results based on market share and performance.

Very interesting, Gwen thought. She continued her reading:

Our study relies on a number of public, commercial, and hand- compiled datasets that represent the most comprehensive data sources on diversity of ownership. We've used both those in-house and those of recognized commercial databases such as e-Investor and Trading Fund Research (TFR) to identify minority-owned investors in underserved economic areas defined by zip code to be targeted for development and growth of this market share.

Gwen closely perused the rest of the document. It clarified that the program's goal was to reach out to this potentially lucrative market and in the process to promote 'vigorously' potentially higher performing investment results presented by the rapidly expanding technology industry. Towards this end, it advised branch offices to promote high-risk and high-return technology stocks to improve the bottom line."

Continuing, the memorandum explained that this PIP program was designed specifically to be applicable "...to trading shares where S/H acts as 'market maker' for developing firm recommended start- up entities, such as small-cap tech stocks that offer oversized upside potential." "This push," it continued, "is particularly appropriate where the company has taken an equity share, having concluded that by doing so S/H would be favorably positioned in a growth business with a promising trajectory. Future production benefits would be expected to flow to the company from such financial support."

The attachment further stated, "While these stocks may present a possible rollercoaster ride to hold, catalysts can swiftly lift positions and the rewards can be rich." It then instructed branch brokers to implement PIP vigorously and to push aggressively the 'BUY' orders in these company recommended 'speculative' technology stocks to these minority small investors. To ensure participation, brokers were further instructed "to define expansively and to delineate and extend where possible valuation of a client's investment assets, risk assessment, and goal objectives." This was to include Growth and Speculation. The broker was then urged "to accommodate the suitability of these trades and revise downward the traditional approach on acceptable risk potential."

Girard's report next explained that the company's research department had concluded that "pushing this program" would increase the company's bottom line through fees, earnings and interest income an estimated 9% a year. Girard had then added that, from the company's management perspective, such a result along with individual client contributions to the program would be expected to have a significant positive impact on year-end employee bonuses and monthly broker sales reward contests. The report ended with the observation that this new policy was likely to represent a win/win for both the smaller, and very small minority client and for the company along with the team's sales representatives. Further it would assist in the company's short-term goal of being viewed favorably as an active participant in new demographic underserved domestic markets, with special appeal to the minority investor community.

Gwen reread the somewhat obscure language a second time, and then a third. She finally concluded that the entire memo on its face stated Stanley, Howe's intent to promote the trading of unreasonably risky stocks in the small asset accounts of its minority clients – like Sammy. This would help expand S/H's client base to include blue-collar persons of color, improve their ROI, albeit temporarily, all while concurrently increasing the company's bottom line. To encourage brokers to engage in this high-risk trading, the company offered various financial rewards and incentives to its sales force.

In short, to Gwen this document evidenced illegal securities conduct and arguably established criminal *scienter*, (the company had the required criminal *intent*). Gwen was certain the firm would not like to see pictures of its executives walking in handcuffs into waiting police vans – like happened years earlier when the government cracked down on anti- trust violators.

Taking a deep breath, Gwen leaned back in her red executive chair while holding a tissue tightly around her raised injured finger. Her face flushed, she began to feel uncomfortably warm as she realized she maybe had found the elusive pot at the end of the discovery rainbow, the legendary 'hot document'. But how to make a copy to take with her? If she put it in the copy pile she'd never see it again. Even with all the documents Anna needed to review, this one now stood out, thanks to her bloody fingerprint.

While sipping from her water bottle, and racking her brain for a solution, Gwen came up with a plan, one that perhaps only a lawyer could devise. Yes, while she'd agreed not to remove papers, really she'd just be temporarily borrowing them, no risk they'd be lost. Besides, Anna, when making her unfair demands, had thereby acted with 'unclean hands', making the terms of the firm's one page form unenforceable. With this reasoning, Gwen silenced her ethical voice, legal concerns, and set out a course for action. Now it was time to be stealthy and strong for Sammy.

Gwen called a meeting of her team. She explained that she needed someone to do an errand for her that might be a little awkward but, in Gwen's view, was within the spirit of NASD discovery. Was anyone willing to take it on? Adam's hand sprang up. She couldn't have been more thrilled, despite a high-pitched voice whispering in her ear, *maybe too quick*? Shush, Gwen's brain responded.

"Great, Adam, let me explain to you what's involved."

Gwen dismissed the rest of her crew and Mary back to their reviewing chores while Adam ambled over to her chair. Gwen, speaking softly, told him what she had found and raised the logistical issue of how to make a copy. Adam offered his hi-tech advice that there was a new mobile phone that had a built-in camera. She asked if he had one with him but alas learned that the nearest such phone was in Japan. And so she decided on a replacement plan, one that didn't involve international travel.

"Adam, I'll call Patty, Anna gave us her extension number, and tell her that you have to leave for an hour on another case to file a Motion at the courthouse before it closes at 4 p.m. Then, Adam, you'll surreptitiously, for there's likely hidden cameras in this room, place the ... um, let's call it 'Judy', then you put Judy in this envelope that I've marked 'Motion to Dismiss, *In re Graves* case'. Once outside the building ask around for a copy place. I know there's one nearby. Then make one copy of Judy. You'll need to buy an envelope and stamp. Mail the copy to my home." Gwen gave him a business card and wrote her home address on the back. Following so far?"

"Yup, very 'sleuthy', exciting."

"Good. Then you put the original in a coat pocket or someplace safe, and retrace your steps back to this room. The guards in the reception area should let you back up if you mention you're with me. Am I going too fast? And more importantly, are you comfortable with this?"

"Actually, Attorney Wilson, sorry, Gwen, it sounds like the most exciting thing I've done since I moved here, even more exciting than finding my neighbor's cat in my trash can. I'm in."

"Now, Adam, the final issue is how do we get the original back in the box?"

"How about this. I'll wait some after I return and just put it back into the same file while putting other documents back in that box. Simple and sweet. Maybe I'll even bring you back a coffee to add some credibility to my story."

"Adam, I can see I've got my man. Oh, one more thing. Don't be alarmed if you see guards with guns. Anna said they're walking around due to some security issues, mostly to scare potential thieves. She said she finds it comforting, but between us, it gives me the creeps."

"Just makes it more like a James Bond thriller," said Adam. "I've no problem with guns. Used to target shoot myself."

Their plan went off without a hitch -- or so it seemed. Gwen had opened the conference room door so that she had a view of the elevator. Her pulse throbbed while she waited. When she saw Adam get off the lift and walk back towards the conference room she began to believe all would be fine. Adam was just ten feet away from safety. But as he walked towards her, fleet-footed Anna and a security guard intercepted him.

"Excuse me, associate. I understand you left the building without notifying me. You should have let me know first." The guard behind Anna, Gwen noticed, placed his hand on his gun. Casually, Adam stopped, then said, "Hey, Anna, so sorry. Is that a problem? Gwen asked me to file a motion in a case while we were downtown. I didn't realize I had to sign out or something. Gwen had let your secretary know about this at lunchtime."

Gwen, hoping to diffuse the tension with some bluster of her own, joined them in the hallway. She jumped in, "Anna, come on. I let Patty know as you requested. Stop with the bully stuff."

Anna appeared ready to capitulate, but then she said, pointing to Adam's jacket pocket, "What's that paper?"

Adam looked down and smiled. "Oh, you mean this?" He removed the offending item and gave it to Anna. "See, Anna, you're making a mountain out of a mole hill. Just the envelope for the motion I filed. You're acting like I stole the queen's jewels."

"Hey, it's empty. Where's the court-stamped copy showing the time and date of filing?"

"Uh oh. Was I supposed to get that also?" Adam pulled his fingers back through his hair and turned towards Gwen. "Sorry,

Gwen, looks like I messed up." Then Adam faced the guard and said, "Hey buddy, why don't you remove your hand off your Glock now? The safety's not on. You shouldn't walk around that way with a loaded pistol. One of the first lessons I learned when shooting my gun. You could have accidentally killed someone."

The guard stood back, his face reddening, and clicked the safety notch on his gun as Adam suggested. Anna's face had turned ghostly white and Gwen wondered if she might faint. In any event, Gwen, who knew nothing about guns, made a mental note to read the hunting magazines in her office, or seek a lesson on gun basics from Adam – who appeared surprisingly knowledgeable for a California techie.

Time to end this scene, Gwen decided. Forcefully, like a New York bulldog, she stepped in between Anna and Adam, smiled, took the coffee cup Adam was holding for her, and said to Anna, "Time we get back to the boxes so we can finish today, Anna, and you can get back to work." Before Anna could respond, Gwen turned and, pushing Adam ahead of her, walked back to her big partner chair.

For a moment, Anna stood twiddling her thumbs, then to Gwen's surprise, she followed Adam into the room, sat down next to Gwen, and removed her heals. She waived the guard off, and rested her now shoeless feet up on an empty chair, and rubbed her eyes.

"Hey Gwen, sorry. Just trying to do my job. Lots of pressure here. And I'm exhausted. You understand, if anything goes wrong it's on my head as the junior lawyer. Lucky you. Not only to have your own gopher, and such a nice version. Must be good to be the partner. I have another two years to see if that will happen for me."

Gwen relaxed. All had gone well, and it wasn't really Anna's fault, that's the price of litigation these days. After all, they were both sisters at the bar. Time to shoot the breeze, thankfully the only shooting to take place. "Yes, I worked at a big city firm so I know the anxiety."

"Yeah, I know that. In the Big Apple. Pretty nervy to give that up for small-town law. Don't know that I'd be able to do that. Hard enough as the 'girl lawyer' to not be asked by male associates, newer hires than me, to go get their coffee. Anyhow..." Anna pointed to the box on the table. "This here your pile of papers to copy?"

"Yes. There aren't too many so far, despite the fact my team has reviewed almost 25 boxes. Can you have Patty send them to me tomorrow?"

"I think we better aim for the next few days. I have deadlines to meet the rest of this week. Friday should work." Gwen smiled. *Sure. You'll make the lawyer 5 p.m. Friday dump so I'll spend all weekend at work. No way, lady. You're right. I'm the partner, and I say this stuff will just wait until next week. That's why I work for my own firm and make the negligible bucks.*

"I'll be busy on another case rest of this week, so that should be fine, Anna."

"Oh, and also, Bradford's approved the Respondents' revised Answer which you should get any day. I don't think there are any surprises but it sets out in the pleadings for the Panel the basis of our defense. No counterclaims as I recall. I expect we'll follow through with our disclosure demands in a few weeks, just a heads up. Enjoy your coffee. Let me know when he's going out again for another. I could use a little fresh air and might join him. I didn't notice a ring. Is he married or taken?"

"Don't think so."

"Great. Oh, one more thing. I don't want to make this a criminal case or anything, but I would have liked it if you had checked in with *me* like I asked before your associate left the building, not my secretary. We have confidential documents here and I need to keep track of what might be leaving the room. Nothing did, right?"

"Anna, first, I let your personal secretary Patty know -- as I thought you requested. I assumed she'd speak with you if that were an issue. Second, this is a small case, no nuclear secrets to steal here I believe." Gwen now resorted to offense. "You know, this could have been done much more expeditiously if you had culled the documents a teeny bit more carefully. At least three quarters of the materials were duplicates or didn't apply at all to this case. Just trying to play games are we Anna?"

"Right. Anyhow, I need to be careful as my butt's on the line if there's a screw-up. Okay, I'll be in my office if you need me. Otherwise, we'll talk next week to make sure you've gotten our response."

Anna rose, gave Adam one more long glance, then walked out. Gwen sifted through another box for a half hour or so, then gave the box to Adam with a pink sticky tag marking the location where the Judy memo had been removed. Adam sat down and took off one of his loafers. He rubbed his foot while quickly removing Judy from the inside of his shoe, then, leaning over, surreptitiously placed Judy back in the file where it belonged. He winked at Gwen and gave her a dimple smile.

Gwen's headache seemed to improve instantly. How had she been even a teensy bit suspicious about Adam? Okay she'd known him only one day but still he'd been smart and savvy.

As to her case, all had gone well and she was sure no one would notice that Judy now had a crease where it had been bent, well mostly sure.

CHAPTER FOURTEEN

To hell with 'tough'. Thanksgiving had come and gone and no word of settlement in Sammy's case. Gwen cracked her knuckles, and then broke down and called Anna. It had already been weeks since Gwen had supplemented her discovery request with a long list of documents not provided in the 40 boxes reviewed, including copies of still missing monthly financial statements Martha and Linda had been asking to see. At the same time Gwen had promptly responded to Anna's discovery request, forwarding copies of the few relevant documents stored in Sammy's, now Olanda's, basement. Since then, only silence from the other side.

And she was increasingly worried about her Complainant. During these weeks she'd spoken with Sammy periodically to update him on the case's progress. He had started to complain that the suit was taking so long, to which Gwen reminded him that she'd told him so, that cases at times crawl rather than sprint. Recently, Sammy mentioned that he'd been thinking about going 'home' to the islands to stay with family. Gwen now worried not only about the case but also whether, despite his promises, her client would hang in there to the finish line.

Her patience with Stearns, Foster wearing thin, and her client flailing, Gwen had decided to blink first. She picked up the telephone and called Anna to see, subtly, whether the investment firm was ready to talk settlement. Into the speakerphone Gwen casually suggested to Anna, "...perhaps it makes sense for both parties to explore agreements on procedural issues and maybe also a long term resolution."

There followed a pregnant silence, during which Gwen's heart momentarily paused its beating. At last, Anna spoke up, stating, "I see, Gwen. I guess I have no problem with that if you like, benefits both our clients maybe. But I'm really busy on this other case, so I suggest we meet at my office again. While I'd enjoy a visit to the mountains, especially now that the slopes are open, I don't see that happening in the near future. And I want a date when Bradford is available."

Gwen agreed to travel and was happy that the senior and a name partner, Bradford Foster, would be attending. After an exchange of phone calls, the date Monday, December 9th, was set.

And so, as planned, on that day Gwen and Mary boarded the 1:15 p.m. express train to Concord, the roads being icy. As the train swayed, Gwen focused on reviewing her notes and outlining her position. She wanted to appear prepared and confident. Thankfully, the city had cleared and sanded the walkways as she and Mary trudged in their boots the ten blocks from the station to the firm's office. To take their minds off falling on black ice, Mary decided to share her extensive repertoire of lawyer jokes.

"Gwen, how many lawyers does it take to screw in a light bulb?"

Smiling and thinking back to the Bar Association meeting, Gwen pronounced "Four."

But Mary just shook her head no. "Sorry, Gwenie. The answer is..., ready, how many can you afford?"

Gwen couldn't help smiling a bit. And Mary's scheme worked, for before Gwen knew it she and Mary had arrived at the building's reception desk without any broken bones. As before, they rode the elevator up to the twenty-third floor and sat in the lounge area to wait for Anna. Gwen straightened her red scarf, added for a "power" image, placed her attaché case at her feet, and then appraised the English fox hunting pictures on the wall. *Are they to remind me of the fate of the fox?* Then she moved on to the employment ads in the *Wall Street Journal*. Gwen noticed that Mary was reading an old issue of *Glamour* which she'd found buried underneath the current issue of *Golf Digest*.

After twenty more minutes a middle-aged, impeccably suited woman approached Gwen.

"Attorney Wilson? I'm Jennie, Attorney Foster's personal

secretary. He's so sorry to have held you up but he's stuck in a meeting that's gone on longer than expected."

Gwen assumed her wait more likely served as the announcement that the negotiation bell had rung.

Jennie continued, "He's reserved the twenty-seventh-floor conference room for today's meeting so please follow me."

Gwen and Mary trailed behind Jennie on the way to the elevator when they almost physically ran into Bradford Foster who was rushing down the corridor. Foster recovered his balance, and then, wearing a slight smile, he heartily shook Gwen's hand. Gwen at least was grateful that she could still maneuver her fingers afterwards. *Maybe when you get to his level, you don't need to show you're macho by crushing your opponent's digitals; you just try to rip off their arm.* She appraised Foster. He was tall, slightly balding, exuded Ivy League with his metal-framed glasses, had the gauntness of a runner, and was dressed in the partner's power uniform – dark blue suit pants, white custom fit dress shirt, red tie, gold cufflinks that matched his Phi Beta Kappa or was it Harvard hanging key. In his mid-50's, Gwen assumed, he exuded the comfortable ease of a man who'd been granted by birthright access to opportunities that had led inexorably up the ladder to his accustomed success.

Foster continued with the preliminaries. "Gwen, I've reserved a room upstairs. Hope you don't mind if we go by the stairs? My way of getting exercise, what with the snow and ice already covering the roads."

Gwen could relate, as she'd tried to squeeze in a similar 'getting fit' stairs climbing routine from the street level into her first-floor office in the two-story building. And, smartly, she'd come prepared this time, wearing her rubber-soled boots with good arch support.

"No problem, Bradford. I enjoyed my step class last time, helped me prepare for my tennis game."

As they ascended Bradford offered small talk to create, Gwen assumed, a 'we're all friends here, let's be civil' atmosphere while at the same time playing the lawyer's name-dropping game to remind her of his *bona fides*. Gwen was determined to not let down her guard. "Used to play a little in college. But Harvard's varsity men's tennis team was tough to break into, lots of ranked players. So I did squash. Now, thanks to my knees, it's pretty much golf."

Finally, sweating and her thighs on fire, Gwen reached the landing. Bradford led her and Mary into a small bow-shaped conference room with a majestic view of the New Hampshire landscape. Gwen tried not to be impressed at how it differed from the view seen from her conference room – a charming old brick wall covered in areas with creative graffiti. Gwen introduced Mary and, with the three of them seated across from each other at the long conference table – Anna had not yet appeared – Foster began the settlement chess game.

"Well, Gwen, I've reviewed again your complaint, that is, Statement of Claims in the Perez matter and discussed this case at length with Bill Wadford – you know him, I believe, Stanley, Howe's in-house counsel. While we appreciate this matter has been difficult for Mr. Perez, and we are aware of his market loss, my client, to speak frankly, insists it has not engaged in any wrongful conduct. In fact, my client is adamant that Mr. Perez's account decline was due to his own actions, or, at best, normal market forces."

Gwen looked at her notes, then at Foster directly. Her turn to reply to this opening chess move. (*Pawn to e4.*)

"Would you be more specific, Bradford, how you concluded this from the evidence so far established? From my...."

Bradford interjected, "I think it...."

Gwen, continuing more loudly, not wanting to allow him to control the conversation, said, "...my case review, the facts – as my experts tell me – establish that your client's broker, Mr. Murphy, with Stanley, Howe's awareness and support, engaged in unsuitable investment activities and churning." Gwen picked up her pen and pointed to a typed sheet she showed Bradford. "On this last claim alone, the numbers, Bradford, speak for themselves. The high churning ratios are there. Even when I use the industry's unreasonably favorable guidelines."

Foster played with his tie. "I can't disagree more. I'm not questioning...."

"Sorry, let me finish my point, please. I'm comfortable that an Arbitration Panel will agree with our analysis. This case risks not only your client's paying Mr. Perez his market losses but even more – what he should have earned." Gwen stopped. *Had she put Foster on the defensive? (Queen's Knight to f3.)*

Unflustered, Bradford answered as if she'd said that the legal pads on the table were out of alignment. "To the contrary, Gwen, the record shows a man in control with significant prior trading experience. He continually pestered his broker, demanding unreasonable trades despite repeated warnings. Mr. Perez was actively involved in the trading and margin account and responsible for his losses." (*Foster's Bishop to c5, where it was ready to attack Gwen's Knight.*)

"Bradford, I just don't see any confirmation of that, except maybe for the self-serving statements of Murphy and his former supervisor, whom as we know is deceased. And, by the way, I have yet to see documents from this Supervisor's file, or his replacement's. These are important to my case. I hope you are not hiding them?" (*Only a one-space pawn move.*)

Gwen tried to remain patient at this feint and jab game.

Foster went in for checkmate. "Gwen, we've produced what we are able to find. We're encountering complications in record maintenance still from 9/11 which as you know hit the securities industry very hard. I'm sure you're not insinuating bad faith on our part. As to Mr. Perez, have you taken into account that Mr. Perez himself continued to withdraw money from the brokerage account as if he were using it as a bank credit card to pay his bills – and the IRS? My client assures me that their algorithms show it was these withdrawals that were primarily responsible for the margin calls. Plus,..." Foster hesitated, leaned forward in his chair, his right hand adorned with its Harvard ring, and, holding one of the firm's Mont Blanc pens to punctuate the air, he said, "... Mr. Perez used some of these funds to start a manufacturing business – that failed, then he secretly opened and transferred money from his initial account into a second account in the name of his cousin, or aunt is it? This was done to cheat his wife during the divorce case, her lawyer told my client. Nice guy."

"The transfer was suggested by Murphy, and to help repay his aunt for her loan/gift to him. This money was not part of the marital estate so it wasn't subject to the family court's division of property. In any event, any withdrawals were minimal, sensible based on the account's rosy picture painted by Mr. Murphy, and the result of my client becoming disabled and so having reduced income." Gwen's chess pieces were moving backwards. (*Time to castle her King and rook?*)

She made a note to have Linda check her numbers again. And the dates Sammy opened the second account. And she wondered how Foster knew about the t-shirt episode? Was there more she didn't know? Foster's confidence, if deserved, threatened placing her King at risk of checkmate. Gwen's heart sank into the lower part of her stomach.

Is my case a lost cause? Am I chasing a shadow? She inhaled deeply and, after cracking under the table a few knuckles on her left hand, continued, "Bradford, I think the Panel will be persuaded by my experts' view of the evidence. And by the testimony of my client who comes across as credible. I suggest your client consider again the aggravation and financial risks of continuing to contest this matter." Gwen wondered if it was time to place this case in a bigger context, or would she be upturning the apple cart by playing the culture card so soon? What the hell, she decided to throw it all out there. Thus she added, "And the statement Stanley, Howe is making to the hard-working people of the Dortman community by fighting its own investor after causing him to lose all his money, what is the benefit? It's harming its own good will. The message it is sending is not good."

The tension in the room had risen as the conversation continued with each advocate repeating their differing positions. Anna arrived, sat down but, like Mary, remained quiet. Gwen expected the meeting was close to ending without indication of settlement interest, but maybe an opening for a nuisance 'get this fly out of my face' offer, when there was an unexpected loud knock on the door. All parties jumped. In walked Jennie with Gwen's lawyer friend John Seduka. John walked over and sat down in the leather chair next to Mary.

Gwen did a double take. *What is John doing here? True, I've consulted briefly with him on the case, but as a law friend, not co-counsel. Yeah, John's helped in rounding up my student associates, but he's had no role in the case preparation or drafting, nor filed an appearance. And how did he know about this meeting?* Then Gwen remembered that she'd mentioned it when she'd complained to John that she was being outnumbered and likely outlawyered. Gwen gave Mary a look of 'what gives', and Mary responded with a shrug and open mouth astonishment.

John, oblivious of the tension already in the room, took off his suit jacket, loosened his tie, and then said, "Hi, sorry to be late. I had another meeting this afternoon at court that went longer than I expected. Bradford, I believe? I don't think we've met." John rose and reached over the table to shake Foster's hand. His elbows resting on the table, John continued. "John Seduka. I'm on some State Bar committees, former chair of the real estate committee, but I don't recall meeting you at any meetings. Boy, lot of traffic out there. Didn't remember that this was such an issue but I guess it's almost commuting time. We even get congestion like this North of the Notch these days. Right Gwen?" John went on like this for a few minutes, talking quite loudly about whatever came into his head. Then he directed himself to the case. "Have I missed anything?"

At this point, Gwen was fuming. *What the hell does John think he's doing? I've been moving this discussion towards settlement. Now John comes in and thinks its happy hour? Is he that desperate for a legal fee that he's barged in on my case? And what's that odor? Surely John didn't come here after getting loaded?*

John said with a slight slur that Gwen had missed initially, "I've reviewed your claims, I mean, um, defenses, Bradford, and, god damn, I just don't buy 'em. This is a case where our demands are reasonable and your client, your really rich client, should get off its frickin' duff and do the right thing and make an offer to help this poor man out, this working class bloke who's overcome so much discrimination and stuff. No more frickin' bullshit that will just drag this case on for more time than it's worth, just for a win thanks to your client's unlimited funds. This is a small matter, so get them to penny up, show some moral spine, and make this fricken' case go away." John began to hit the table with his hand in a tight fist. His face was turning red, even in the room's dimming light. But he was not to be denied.

Gwen thought that John's banging was the end of his monologue, but no. "We have a family man hurt here, forced to live mouth to mouth thanks to your guys. Just 'cause he speaks Spanish, *el hable español*. Well that won't help this matter go your way, you know, the racial thing. By the way, Brad, can you get your secretary to get me a bottle of water? Or better yet, orange juice? Need a little pick-- me-up as goin' all day 'fore this meetin'." John looked around the table and noticed Anna. No lady was too much on the "other side" to chat up. "Hey, you must be Anna, correct?" John gave her his best toothy grin and pushed his blond locks off his forehead.

Anna looked totally nonplussed, which indeed was how Gwen was feeling, along with muscles ready to kill. "I am."

"Nice, Anna, to connect a face with a name. Gwen told me you've been very co-operative on this case." Gwen almost fell over in her chair at this. "Nice to see Bar members respect each other's roles, you know, without exhibiting any, um, without feeling any personal negative shit. No reason to act nasty I always say. Just be courteous and we'll get along fine while helping our clients and justice." John finally ran out of words and sat back in his chair, arms akimbo and chin up, looking satisfied with his effort.

Bradford Foster recovered from the unexpected visitor's assault, and opted to take charge. "Well, John, you surely are direct, but I believe seriously misinformed about the case. I'll see what I can do about a drink." Bradford got up and called his secretary on the private phone. Then he sat back down and doodled on his pad.

During the wait, John removed his loosened tie, opened his shirt collar, and slouched backwards, twiddling with his pen and playing with the paper clips he took from the cup in the middle of the table. He carefully arranged them in a circle shape. Gwen was afraid he would decide to put his feet up on the table.

After the pause, and before John could add his two cents worth again, Gwen decided that, as the meeting might be ending soon – and her chess game hadn't been too successful – maybe now was an opportune time to bring up the Girard memo. She wanted to infer its existence but not affirm that she was in possession of an actual copy. "Bradford, I think you should know that I've learned from third parties about a disturbing new program your client is pursuing that raises issues of, how shall I say this, overreaching in minority communities and taking advantage of persons of color -- like my client. I believe it's called PIP, developed by your client at the executive level, and recently implemented in this region to affect my client's accounts. And a program, if I understand it correctly, that lends great credibility to Mr. Perez's claim of unsuitability. Are you aware of it?"

Silence followed. Bradford, continuing to draw figure eights on his legal pad, finally looked up at Gwen, his face and ears she thought turning slightly ruddy. After drinking from his water glass and adjusting his tie, he said, "That is a strong accusation, Gwen, one I adamantly refute on behalf of my client. And should you pursue this line of attack, absent evidence, I would consider it to be slanderous."

But Gwen noticed that Bradford's doodles had started to become darker and less controlled. *He knows.*

Thankfully, sloshed John remained mostly quiet over the next half hour as the parties spat further, their last negotiating gasps, over who did what and who was in the wrong. John got his glass of orange juice and sipped it slowly until it was gone. Gwen worried he would interrupt the give and take to ask for more. Finally, Bradford rose and offered, "I think we've covered the main issues here. I will talk with my client and explore again their settlement position, but, to be honest, Gwen, I would not hold much hope that they are willing to budge. I, or Anna, will let you know if further talks appear likely to yield a conclusion to this case." Turning to Anna he instructed her to remind him to follow through and then thanked Gwen, Mary and John for coming.

Gwen said as a final retort, "Bradford, I'll await your phone call, and looks like we can start moving this case forward towards a hearing date. I know my client is eager to have his day in court, or I guess I should say arbitration."

Coats on and ready for the winter freeze, Gwen, Mary and John silently descended to the lobby. Once outside the building, they revisited the meeting. Gwen started by saying to John, "I'm really livid at your appalling behavior." Biting her lip while trying to stay calm, she further let him know how angry she was and that he had stepped over the line of acceptable lawyer protocol. "John, do not ever again show up at *my* meeting without consulting with me beforehand. First, if you're looking for a fee in this case, it's on a contingency, I have no client funds to pay you. Second, you are not co-counsel. You cannot act like you represent my client when you do not. That's dangerous territory – for both of us. Third, friend, if you ever come to a meeting with me and opposing counsel again where you are even slightly tipsy, I will file a complaint with Bar

Counsel. Do you get it?"

"Hey Gwen, no need to be so nasty and in a huff. And I'm perfectly fine, just maybe a reaction to some cold medicine. Anyhow, I was in the area and thought I'd give you some support, some male support. Didn't mean to butt in where I wasn't wanted. But, well, you consulted with me on this case, remember? I did review some of the documents, help you set up the discovery and all. And I think my involvement will be good for your client. A male lawyer can give your side credibility with some of the cretins on the other side who don't know what to do with a woman lawyer except to try to f... her. Oh, sorry Mary. Don't want to hurt your young pretty ears. Thought it was good, my acting like the bad guy and all, Gwennie. I wouldn't expect a full share of any recovery, but, you know, I think we can get this settled with my help. Up to you."

"Yes it is. I already have experts on this case, and, to my knowledge, you have no securities law experience. This is not the purchase of a four-bedroom house where your real estate experience would be a plus. Am I being sufficiently clear? I appreciate your help so far with arranging my interns and all, but bottom line – you are not in."

John shrugged, and raised his arms as if offering a blessing to peace. "No problem, Gwennie. Who knows, as I said, if I can be of help I'm here for you. Just trying to serve a close colleague. Take care of yourself and see you at the next Bar meeting." Giving her a winning smile, John put out his hand but Gwen ignored it. Then, patting his hair in place, he walked, mostly straight, down the block towards Gwen knew not where, maybe to another 'bar' meeting.

Once he'd departed, Mary said, "Well, that was an interesting experience. They didn't seem eager to settle. And what was John thinking? I always thought he was a good egg."

"As far as John goes, Mary, I don't know. I love the man in many ways. He's been a good friend to me over the years. I don't think I implied I wanted him on the case. Who knows? Maybe he's having money trouble and this was an opportunity to reach out and make a claim as contingency counsel, get a little piece of the pie, so to speak. Sad, though. Seems like practice pressures are making him seek liquid relief, always a troubling sign for litigators. I've seen it before."

"Do you think their position has something to do with Sammy's being Hispanic?"

"I'm not sure I understand their reluctance to at least make an offer of some kind." Mary suggested that, compared with the industry's quickness to offer money in the Carpenter case, this firm seemed to have dug its heels in on this case. "Maybe these firms only settle with clients who fall within the top 10% echelon, and with whom they want to maintain good will? Now that Sammy has no money, he doesn't present possible future sales. Is the real issue here racism? Is that what we're missing?"

Gwen looked up and shrugged. She wasn't sure herself how she felt on this issue. But she wanted to get feedback on another concern she'd been having. "Mary, one more thing that's been troubling me, not sure if it's my imagination or not. I've been feeling a little like Stanley, Howe's been a step ahead of me, like they have access to my prep notes or drafts of documents, something. Maybe it's just good, experienced lawyering, but ...."

"I know what you mean. It's hard to put a finger on it. Still, sometimes I feel like there's a pestering poltergeist – or hidden spy in our midst."

"Anyways, bottom line is that, at the moment, Sammy doesn't seem to be a good candidate for a quick win."

Early for their train, Gwen and Mary waited in the station's small restaurant. Each ordered coffee. While Mary read a magazine, Gwen thought about the meeting and some of its troublesome reveals. *Damn clients, they never tell you all you need to know, the good, the bad, and the ugly – no matter how much they promise. As a contingency case, this can prove – damn it –*

disastrous for my practice. Did this day put her trust in Sammy in doubt?

No matter, in her bones Gwen believed Sammy had been wrongly served. Maybe he'd contributed to the mess but no client was perfect. We are human and we make mistakes. We are human and we make mistakes. She should know that. Gwen was sure of one thing – Sammy needed legal help. But was it up to her to provide it? Is her chess piece a foolish knight tilting at windmills?

"Train leaving for Middleton," the conductor announced. Fifteen minutes for train to Middleton."

Carrying the remains of their coffees, both women picked up their bags and walked over to the gate for their ride home.

CHAPTER FIFTEEN

As the train neared their stop, Gwen remained in a funk. Her hopes for a quick conclusion of the case were fading. Mary, sitting across from her, had entered nod land soon after the train's wheels began turning. But Gwen, adrenalin flowing still, tossed and turned in her seat.

Outside her window, night descended like a dark shroud over the winter landscape. At last, exhaustion got the better of her and, finally giving in to the car's shaking, Gwen eased into a shallow slumber. Her mind wandered on its own back in time, back before Perez and his cute family, before Brian with his sweet smile, way back to her early childhood, to that fateful summer day when her family's train ran off the tracks.

Screech! Tires desperately grabbing the road. The acrid smell of burning rubber. Pounding sirens. Blue lights shining in the twilight.

A small blond boy lying on the ground. Still.

It was a warm hazy 'nothing special' summer afternoon in Queens, New York. Outside her family's two-story brick attached house, parked cars lined the street, creating a barrier along the curb running to the end of the block. A ten-year old girl with long brown hair tied back in a rubber band, her legs splayed out, sat on the sidewalk happily playing jacks.

Mark was there. Wearing for the first time his New York Yankees white and navy striped pajamas, a present at his recent sixth birthday. In his small hand he held a child- sized baseball in a child-sized leather glove that bore the imprinted signature of Mickey Mantle. A new and already beloved birthday present from his dad. Mark turned sideways and threw the small ball against the cement stoop, then caught the ricochet in his glove. Again and again. He didn't miss any.

Annabelle from down the street came and sat down to play with the little girl, Gwen.

Sylvia, Gwen's mom, was inside resting, very pregnant again –
with the baby who was to be named Arthur after her husband's
grandfather, the young chemist who'd fled White Russia to escape the
clutches of the Czar's army and somehow had arrived at Ellis Island
to make a new life. Gwen watched the small red rubber ball, go up in
the air two feet and then hit the ground only to shoot up again. Before
it hit the cement sidewalk the second time, Gwen scooped up the
eight jacks -- small star shaped metal pieces -- in her left hand and
with her right hand she caught the ball. Gwen was excited for if she
did it two more times and picked up first nine and then ten thrown
jacks, she'd win the game. Gwen was practicing to be the best jacks
player on the block. Annabelle, who was two years older than Gwen,
took out her jacks set, and began to play as well. The girls took turns,
each time the same process: throw jacks, throw ball, pick up jacks,
catch ball.

HONK! HONK! HONK!

The air screeched as the car horn cried and cried out again its
warning. The honk gave way to a loud thud intermingled with tire
screams. Then ominous silence, followed by a woman's shrieks.

Gwen dropped her jacks and looked around.

Where's Mark?

It was her job to watch him while her mother rested. She was a
big girl now and ready to help her mom. Standing up, Gwen looked
for her baby brother – his blond head, his white baseball shirt.

Chaos, neighbors running, police cars with whirling blue lights.

Gwen squeezed through the closely parked cars into the street –
even though she and Mark knew this was a 'no-no.' She looked at the
distraught, bent over, crying woman who was being supported by a
policeman. She looked like her mother but was fancier dressed. Then
she saw on the ground the familiar little body. Red paint had splashed
on his white Yankee pajama top. Gwen thought, 'It can't be Mark,'
for he was always in motion. She stared at the still figure until one of
the neighbors grabbed her gently around her shoulders and walked

her back to her house. The neighbor placed Gwen on the front steps and told her to stay there. She did.

That's when her very pregnant mother appeared, wearing her nightgown. She had opened the front door and she now ran past Gwen in her slippers into the street where there was all the noise. Gwen could see a big white van drive up the street and stop in front of her house. She watched as the little boy, hugged by her mother, was placed in the van and the van, siren's sounding, rushed down the street.

Dusk came and darkness began filling the world until the streetlights went on. Gwen was cold all over. At some point her father arrived and led Gwen, sitting alone and shivering, into the dark empty house.

The image of the red stain stayed with Gwen, despite therapy and her Brian. Many a night she'd woken up and heard the sirens again and smelled the burning tires. Gwen, like any good auto accident lawyer, would from time to time reassess the incident's facts and her conclusions. She had been in charge; it was her responsibility to watch Mark as he played; she, the big sister, had stopped watching him to play her own game. Each time the trial's verdict remained the same: Gwen was responsible for Mark's death. Yeah, there were mitigating factors, just sugar to help the medicine go down. She'd been ten, still a little girl; her brother had ignored the road rules in his excitement; the timing of the passing car was so unfortunate. She, Gwen, understood all this. But the flashbacks revisited, uninvited, unwelcome.

After much therapy over the years, Gwen had begun to understand how the tragedy had impacted on each of her family members. As to her parents, they never talked about 'the accident'. Each one was left shattered and empty, alone in their pain, struggling to move forward, questioning their own guilt, assigning family blame. Each felt the shame of losing a child. Gwen's brother Artie was born, early but healthy. It seemed like the family's bond might be strong enough to bear their new burden. But the long nights took their toll.

Sylvia gradually receded more and more into her bedroom, comforting herself with pills and soap operas. As time passed and Gwen grew up to be a most responsible teen, she passively accepted from her mother the responsibility for much of Artie's care – as if this mothering task were a deserved penance for what she viewed was her selfish mistake. Sylvia, hurting, emotionally disabled, distanced herself from Gwen, as if just seeing her eldest child brought back Mark's ghost and punctuated his absence from her life. And so, over her childhood and young adult years, Gwen accepted both roles as Artie's sibling and caretaker. Gwen's father Martin withdrew as well. He tried to assuage the pain and loss by spending long nights at work. Then one day, when Gwen was sixteen, he sought refuge from his grief in California where, Gwen later learned, he found a second family, one without all the difficult memories. Her parents' divorce soon followed. Gwen hunkered down in school, worked at the supermarket for extra money, sent out applications for college, and demanded nothing.

The train slowed down. 'Middleton, Middleton' the conductor yelled as he walked through the car. It was their stop but Gwen was still lost in her memories. As she groggily woke up, she wondered what had set her off after all these years of putting those family images in a locked box? *Was it the hanging pictures with scenes of those poor foxes facing death? Or the red coated riders bringing it? Or maybe it was seeing the many happy family photos and souvenirs that filled the Perez house?* To ward off despair, Gwen silently repeated her now well-known mantra, taught her by friends dealing with trauma and shame, '*We are human and we make mistakes. We are human and we make mistakes.*'

Mary rubbing her face after her snooze, shook Gwen awake and then grabbed her shoulder and pushed her out the train car before the door closed on them. With their arms intertwined, the friends walked down the platform. Gwen entered her cold Prius and Mary climbed into her waiting van, and both women drove home on the wet snow after a very long day.

On the way home Gwen sang with her car's radio that was playing the music of Sam Cooke:

It's been a long, a long time coming,

but I know a change gonna' come, oh yes it will.

Gwen's alto voice filled the air.

CHAPTER SIXTEEN

Gwen was fit for bear. Holding the cordless phone to her ear, she paced between the comfy leather chair and the window overlooking the forsythia bushes, still sleeping under the layer of January's snow. Poor things, she thought, several more months before they'd start greening here above the Notch. It was a lovely sunny Saturday morning for doing chores -- and she'd wasted it waiting for the arrival of Steve the Contractor. When they failed to show, Gwen, finally reached Steve on the phone. After repeated apologies, Steve assured her that his crew would be there bright and early the next day, yes, Sunday morning, to replace her broken sliding door. Not only that, but true to the above the Notch culture of 'we care', he promised her a ten percent discount for her inconvenience.

Accepting the outcome, Gwen took a deep breath and finished her second cup of coffee while working on her weekend crossword puzzle. *What five letter word means...* The phone rang. Was the contractor having second thoughts?

Gwen answered, expecting it was Steve again. Still feeling some 'bear', maybe at cub level, she said grumpily, "Hello."

"I'm sorry, is this Attorney Gwen Wilson?"

"You bet. Don't tell me there's been a change?"

"Hi, maybe I'm calling too early on a weekend? This is Adam Webber. I helped you with some discovery in the Perez case a month or so ago last term. I hope I'm not bothering you?"

Gwen, having a rapid shift in attitude, replied in a friendly tone, "Hi Adam. No problem. You just got me after dealing with a contractor who didn't show up." She added with enthusiasm, "It's great to hear from you. And thank you again for your 'undercover' work. Adam, how can I help you?"

"I enjoyed my day working on your case. In fact, it was the most fun I've had since I started law school. Starting a new term and I was wondering if maybe you might have some legal work I could do in your office, sort of interning I guess? I'm a quick study and think I could help with research, drafting or whatever."

"Interesting idea. Let me think a minute." Gwen paused, her heart pounding. Yes, she would welcome interacting with Adam again, and, well, also getting some legal help. And who said an intern couldn't be slightly graying at the temples? "You know, Adam, I think that's a wonderful idea. You remember I have a paralegal, Mary Dunkin? You met her that day. Sometimes she can't do the legal work that a law student can do, so I think this might work out fine. You're finishing your first year, right?"

"Yes, can't believe it but at the end of this term I'll be a 2L."

"Did you have a weekday in mind?"

"I don't have classes on Friday, so wondering if that works for you."

"Yes, that should work fine. But, well, I can't pay a lot. You know I just have a small-town solo practice. What money did you have in mind Adam?"

"As I think I mentioned before, I'm fortunate in that money's not a problem for me. I have enough from my prior career. The experience is what I'm after. How about the same amount as you paid us that day, I think it was, um, $15 an hour?"

"I can manage that," Gwen said, exhaling built up carbon dioxide. "Thank you for calling. I think this will work out great. I'll put together some matters for you to review and I look forward to seeing you Friday morning, all right?"

"That's super. See you then. Oh, I guess I need to dress like a lawyer?"

"You can leave the tie at home, Adam. But remember to wear shoes."

There followed silence on the other end.

"Just joking, Adam. About the shoes, that is. See you Friday."

Gwen hung up, aware that she was feeling happy. *What is it about Adam that makes me feel shaky inside?* She barely knew him, but they had survived together the perils of the 'hot doc' scamper. She looked at the framed picture in her bookcase of Brian grinning in his ski jacket. He looked so young, as if he lived in another world. But then again, it had been another world, a time before terrorism and airport security, and *Star Wars*. A time of youthful idealism and conviction. Another world.

Gwen averted her eyes from Brian's picture for even now, years later, her heart hurt when she looked at his face. *We're in a new year, Gwennie, 2003. Maybe it's time I finally get on the life plane and travel to this world?* She'd known for years that Brian would have wanted her to move on with her life. Still, she'd stayed stuck in low gear, unable to climb that commitment hill. But Adam may be just what the doctor ordered – bright, mature, confident, a little dark and mysterious, and, oh yes, sexy like his doppelganger, George Clooney. What would she wear to the office on Friday? She couldn't remember last when that question had caused a smile and a flurry of emotions.

Chinese fortune cookies: Who knew their power?

CHAPTER SEVENTEEN

The office door opened. Gwen glanced up from her computer. There stood Judy, officious and fabulous as ever. "Are you free for lunch? A new client called about some real estate closing and wants to know if he can come in today at noon?"

Gwen stopped revising her draft motion. "Make it late this afternoon, or better yet tomorrow morning. I've a working lunch to review the Perez case with Martha and Linda. It's another gal get--together over Happy Family with chopsticks. Lunch seems like the only time when we all don't have other commitments."

Gwen was early, although she'd been able to smell the Dragon Lady's enticing aroma for at least a mile. Walking between the two red plastic dragons guarding the front door, then past the bug-eyed fish with fangs swimming round the fish tank and guarding the liquor supply, Gwen successfully entered the eating area. She grabbed the only empty booth in the back. As she sipped her tea and reviewed her papers, Linda arrived and sat down. Martha soon followed. Gwen passed around the bowl filled with hard noodles.

"Let's order as I have a 2 o'clock meeting," Martha said.

Gwen checked her watch. "Got it. That should give us enough time."

Gwen waived the waiter over and Martha requested her usual sushi fix and White Cosmo – which came adorned with an edible lotus flower and paper umbrella. Linda and Gwen ordered from the multi-food luncheon specials menu and both requested tea. The women gossiped and laughed until their lunches arrived, ate quickly with their wooden sticks, although a fork for Linda, and then Gwen began the case preparation.

"As I indicated in my recent email, no settlement in sight in Perez so looks like we need to prepare for arbitration, which is the purpose of our meeting. Before I begin the case review, I just want to talk a little about the role of an expert witness in an arbitration hearing as it's a little different than in a court trial. Generally, an expert witness is there to assist the panel of arbitrators on the facts, but in our case the panel members – although we still haven't gotten the list of the three selected – are likely quite familiar with securities law and the workings of the industry. Again, likely the Chair will be a lawyer, the other two, likely not. Despite their familiarity with the field, you're there to be a guru for me and to explain to the Panel our position, how Respondents violated federal and industry rules. And finally you'll help calculate damages. What else can I tell you? In an arbitration case, pre-hearing fact-finding as you know is quite limited. So we may first learn what Murphy claims happened on the fly as he testifies. You can help me cross-examine him. Which in practical terms means I'd like you there likely the second day as well as the first. As to your testimony, I'm usually permitted to ask you leading questions, and if there are objections, the panel will probably just allow the answer in the record – and later determine it's worth.

"One more thought. I understand that the panel may focus more on industry customs, practices, what they think is 'fair' rather than the law. So we want to present Sammy in a positive light." Gwen sipped some tea, checking her list of issues for the meeting.

"And two other big things. As an expert, you can give your opinion, state conclusions – because you are experts. And, big surprise, they'll have their experts at the hearing, so having you there, my friends, helps me from being too outgunned. That's it. Any questions Team about the procedure? I just don't want you to worry too much. It will be a piece of cake."

Not hearing any questions, Gwen moved on. "Linda, have you had a chance to review the financial documents I faxed?"

Her hair pushed back with plastic barrettes and wearing her usual gray skirt and white blouse, Linda nodded yes, adding, "But I'm missing still some monthly Stanley, Howe statements, Murphy's commission reports, and even tax returns and bank statements if they're relevant. I'm not sure I have a good grasp of his assets and expenses during the period he traded and going back a few years.

And any information on Sammy's claimed second account for his aunt. I'll send you a list."

With her eyes looking up to the ceiling as if for Buddha's assistance, Gwen said, "I know there are gaps. I've requested everything relevant. Several times. Even called the NASD to see what my realistic options are, but couldn't find anyone actually assigned to our case. The problems I'm learning of arbitration rules and the agency's slow recovery from the 9/11' disaster. I doubt Sammy's files from his basement are complete either. And I don't think he's holding anything back. I can ask him to contact his uncle who prepared his tax returns to see if he can get missing files, and his bank statements, although maybe they were sent to Olanda."

Gwen then turned to Martha who as usual looked nifty, lots of initials from eyeglasses to shoes. Gwen dutifully puffed up her blue and white checked scarf and hid her walking sneakers under the table as best she could.

"Your thoughts?"

Martha finished making a notation in her pocket calendar and removed her rhinestone-framed eyeglasses that now hung on a crimson string around her neck.

"It's clear to me that the stocks Murphy purchased and sold, and I'm thinking that probably *any* stocks, were far too risky for Sammy. I've highlighted that on this sheet here." Martha placed a two-page spreadsheet between the soy sauce and the hot mustard. "This shows the risk level for each of the disclosed trades on a scale of 1 to 5. Almost all are in the 4 or 5 category, meaning higher and very high risk. In my view, no way was his account handled properly. I can state that they didn't treat him the way I would have done any client of mine based on his age, assets, and goals. But that's why I work on a flat fee and not on commission."

"Good news I guess, guys. So, if there's a hearing, Martha, you can address the industry requirements for suitability and the meaning of these numbers. And Linda, as to excessive trades, churning, you ran some numbers, right?"

"Yes, but again, I didn't have all his financial statements so I needed to extrapolate some." Putting aside her lunch plate, Linda also handed out several typed pages of numbers.

"Gwen, look at that number circled in red in the fifth column? That's my calculation to establish the turnover ratio. I divided the total value of annual purchases by the account's average monthly balance. This is the standard test for churning, as you said, unnecessary sales made by Murphy to benefit him. As you expected, it's high, sometimes over 6, which typically indicates churning. But I don't have actual commission figures so we'll also have to estimate there. And on this page I've also calculated the cost-equity ratio, or breakeven percentage to measure how expensive the account's trading strategy was. As you can see, Murphy's trading required the account to earn 15%, also indicating churning.

Gwen appreciated all the work her experts had put in, and the numbers seemed promising. "Looks like we're scoring good. Can we come up with a damage figure, one maybe a little bit high so there's room to maneuver?"

Pointing to a line on her sheets with her finger, Linda continued, "I show on this chart the loss from sales and margin calls for a randomly selected period, and the higher value of the account if it had been invested during that time in a conservative fashion. Generally it was a good market during this period. I didn't add anything for the non-financial damages like emotional distress that you mentioned. I did, however, estimate interest and fee expenses based on calculations from what data I could find. Assuming a broad approach, I think we can argue with a little audacity and best case scenario that his losses were in the vicinity of $160,000, thanks as I said to the bull market."

Gwen was thrilled with all of their input. Why had she doubted her case? In any event, these numbers clearly exceeded the frivolous threshold, any lawyer's worry, and raised that issue underlying Sammy's case, why no settlement offer.

"This is all good, guys. Gals. Seems like Sammy's case is taking shape. But to make our case we'll also have to show that Murphy had control of Sammy's account. Knowing Sammy and his limited understanding of the market, it seems incredulous to me that this is an issue, but I expect it will be. Murphy's control seems self-evident if you just look at the names of some of the stocks he bought, names I can't even pronounce, let alone remember. Not Sammy's idea of quality stock, like, you know, words we know, Ford, General Electric.

"All this again raises the question of what are we missing? I've had no news of any settlement interest. Bottom line, sorry guys, looks like we're headed for a hearing. As of now, the arbitration date has been set for Wednesday, March 25th, with the hearing to continue for the next two days if needed. Assuming no delays, which based on Respondents' dilatory actions up to now I think an unlikely premise, that gives us more than two months to get our case together." Gwen paused and checked her list again.

"Any issues with the date?"

Gwen was thankful that after Martha and Linda checked their calendars both said they could make the dates work.

"Great. This train is starting to roll. As of now, the hearing's set at a law firm in Concord rather than at a hotel; maybe the case is too small. So, no luck in my getting everyone to travel north. Not ski season, or at least good snow time. There are three arbitrators but I haven't, as I mentioned, gotten their names, bio's. I did review the proposed list, and as expected, lots of concern about conflict and all. I've objected to a few, and I can object I guess again once they are designated, but that's likely to send our case back to the end of the line. Not an option for me. Sammy is already talking about moving back to his island home."

Gwen stopped and drank some warm tea, noting that Martha's

Cosmo was almost down to the lotus stem.

"You said you'd need us two days, is that right Gwen?"

"Martha, good question for all of us. If I can't settle this, and I still have a tiny hope that may happen, you'll both be there maybe half a day to testify, after probably Sammy's testimony that first day and probably half a day the following day, assuming Larry's first one up."

Gwen stopped and played with the sweet and sour sauce bowl, using her chopsticks to make little waves. "I still can't understand why they're willing to spend more money arbitrating then to work out a solution. Ridiculous. What with experts, travel, hiring a fancy litigation firm, they'd save money even if they made a really low-ball offer."

"What don't we know, Gwen? I'd sure love not to have to testify, as you know," Linda added.

Gwen bent her chopstick almost in half. "Either Sammy's not on the up and up, or maybe they don't want us to open some floodgate that would be available to lots of other investors? Who knows? As arbitration decisions are confidential, or supposed to be, not sure of their risk. Also, I think the company has hired other counsel, for the hearing itself, don't know why as I thought Stearns, Foster was doing a good job. A New York firm with more arbitration experience I think. But surely higher price-tag. And their regional counsel in New Jersey may also come to the hearing. Could be they just want to visit their summer homes in New Hampshire on the company's dollar."

"Bet that's it, Gwen," said Martha. "New York's pretty horrible in March, museums crowded, much better to enjoy mud season."

While tapping her fingers on the table, Linda offered, "Maybe they'll just keep getting continuance dates until they can enjoy their summer homes."

Surprised at her humor, Gwen and Martha both laughed.

Linda continued, "Anyhow, what's the procedure Gwen – as

I'm a little nervous even thinking about having to testify?" Gwen noticed that Linda's face had turned pale and her left hand was now playing a silent Mozart concerto. She thought that maybe asking Linda to help had been a reach, but she didn't know anyone else with Linda's skills, or who would not have demanded an exorbitant hourly fee.

Gwen needed to cheer up her team. "No worries, guys. It won't be bad. In fact it might be fun! After all, justice is on our side. Arbitration's low key. We'll be in a conference room, like in your office. No one will be there but us and Respondents' handful of suits. Sammy will go first so you can get your feet wet."

"Whom will you question first?" asked Martha, checking her platinum dress watch and then refilling her tea.

"Sammy will put in the facts. It's important that we have a basis for your opinions. While I guess hypotheticals might work, better to have the issues clear. Then, I'm not sure, but maybe I'll start with you, Martha, to establish the unsuitability of the trades, and then Linda to focus on overtrading and damages. I'll send you an outline of my questions so you can prepare. And don't forget to give me a CV to send to the other parties' lawyers, the number of whom seems to be increasing daily."

Gwen checked her watch and saw she needed to speed up to cover the other items on her checklist. "There are two more things to discuss and I'll be quick. I won't tell you how but I've gotten a copy of a confidential executive memo detailing an investment program that Stanley, Howe designed – which if it actually went into effect I think would substantially help us make our case. What us lawyers call a 'hot document' I guess. It pushes brokers like Murphy to make high-risk trades, especially of high-tech developing companies, for its small investor minority customers like Sammy. The goal is to increase the company's profits. The program is called the 'Pinehills' Investment Program', PIP. But I'm worried if I force this issue now, the company will claim the document was gotten through violation of the discovery rules and thus should not be admitted into evidence. Or they can just deny the program ever went into effect. Martha, would you know of anybody, some friend, who might be willing to do some behind the scenes investigation into this PIP program?"

"Send me the information, better mark it confidential, and I'll see what I can do. That would be a big step up for sure. And encourage settlement if we can find out anything."

"That's the way I see it. The second thing is to keep good track of your time and expenses. We'll submit these in any damage claim, along with my and your fees."

Gwen checked her watch, a non-digital Wal-Mart special. Where did the time go?

"Okay, ladies, to summarize, with emotional distress – which are likely iffy as allowable expenses, attorney's fees, expert fees and other expenses, interest, seems to me I can now demand an initial settlement offer of $230,000 – and not be reduced to laughter."

"Wow." Martha's carefully lined eyebrows shot up. With a little shrug she lifted her empty --but for the umbrella – cocktail glass in a mock toast, "Ladies, why not!"

Raising their small white porcelain cups, Linda and Gwen responded in unison, "Why not!"

CHAPTER EIGHTEEN

The red blinking gasoline tank finally caught her eye. *Damn, I need gas!*

"Adam, sorry but I need to stop for gas."

"I think there's a station up ahead on the right."

"Great, see already I knew you'd be a help tonight. I hope it wasn't too inconvenient – joining me to meet with Sammy on a Friday night?"

"Hey, Gwen. This is exciting. I'm actually going to meet a client, which is cool. So far all Sammy's been is a name."

"Yes, it's nice to leave the books and remind ourselves that all this is about real people. How's it going so far, interning? You've been in the office, what... three weeks I think. Just for some praise, your work has been good, amazing actually considering how long you've been in law school." Gwen was feeling unsure how to handle Adam's legal work; being his boss while separating out her personal attraction to him was a bit weird, and yes, uncomfortable. She kept wanting to ask him, 'is that okay' when she delegated a task to him. Sure, sometimes she'd do the same with Judy and Mary, but they were friends, like family, and long-term employees – not temporary student help. How did all those men do it all these years, carrying on personal relationships with their secretaries – and at the same time acting the boss? *Gwennie, maybe it's the gender thing, after a lifetime of being on top, they just expect that's how it works? Give yourself another fifty years of bossing and likely it will come easy.*

Gwen pulled into the gas station – which advertised in Spanish not only non-branded gas but also coffee, hotdogs, and lottery tickets. After filling up, less than ten gallons thanks to her hybrid, Gwen managed to locate the coffee shop, El Café, operated by another of Sammy's cousins. Since her client was still without a car, she'd agreed to meet at the café so Sammy could walk there.

And as he was now working for another cousin who owned a painting company, Friday night was the time they both were available, even if it meant Gwen driving from her mom's nursing home. As her car approached the intersection, Gwen saw Sammy waiting outside the restaurant, vivid in his red jacket that matched the intersection's traffic light. After all three were settled at one of the Formica and chrome tables, Gwen was pleased that after his trip home to the islands Sammy appeared more relaxed, maybe even, thanks to island cooking, a few pounds heavier. Gwen began with small talk to ease any tension.

"Hi Sammy. You're looking good. I brought a special friend with me tonight, my new intern, Adam Webber. Adam will be helping me on your case."

Sammy nodded.

"Glad you're back and happy. How was your trip home?" With animation, Sammy replied, "It good, Attorney. *Bueño*. Sisters and aunts feed me lots, make me big." Here Sammy blew out his cheeks and patted his stomach. "All happy to see me. Say want me stay. Life, it easier there. But miss boys, so okay at home as I see them."

What with the snow clogging the roads and the cold demanding hats and lined gloves, Gwen could sure sympathize with Sammy's view that balmy ocean breezes and sunny walks along the surf offered distinct attractions. After these preliminaries, Gwen got down to work as she had lots to cover.

"Sammy, the reason we are meeting tonight is that your arbitration hearing is scheduled for a little more than a month from now. It's important that we start preparing for the hearing. So tonight we'll begin reviewing the issues, going over your testimony, practicing your answers, okay? Remember, the hearing will be the end of March."

"Sí, I know, and stomach it hurt when I think 'bout it." Closing his eyes and then rubbing his face with both hands, Sammy added, "Attorney, my case, it take so long, it now new year. Tire me out, all the waiting."

Sighing, Gwen nodded. "Yes, Sammy. But we're in the home stretch. Almost top of the 9th inning, remember, like we discussed? And really, for a legal matter, this case has moved fast, trust me."

A short pudgy middle-aged man wearing a once-upon-a-time white apron approached their table. "*Bienvenido, señora – and señor*," he said with a grin. Facing Sammy he asked in English, "This the good *abodaga* that help you?" Assured this was indeed Sammy's famous attorney, Emilio bowed slightly to Gwen. After he'd brought over espresso coffee for Gwen and Adam, with a plate of biscuits, Gwen opened her folder and started asking Sammy questions about issues raised at her meeting with Bradford. She asked if Sammy took money out of the investment account to pay his bills. "Sí, but Mr. Murphy, he tell me it okay. I gave him all my money in bank account, then when I got hurt at work, I needed to use stock money to pay bills. He say no problem, I making money so I can do that." Sammy then described how also he'd bought his oldest son, Marcus, a computer for school. "Old one no good, too slow, *comme la tortuga.*" Here Sammy grinned and used his hands to show how a land turtle crawls.

Gwen and Adam laughed, which felt good after a tense day, and Gwen was pleased that, when relaxed, Sammy was a little bit of an acting ham. Gwen commented, "Old computer sounds like the speed of my computer. Yes, good answer, Sammy. If their lawyer asks you this question, you should answer just like you did. See, Sammy, you will be a good witness, so no worries." Gwen continued with her review, next asking, "Sammy, did you use the account's money any other time?"

He shrugged, and then played with the zipper on his jacket. "I don't know, so long ago. Maybe some, not more than couple times. Let me think...." Sammy paused and started to count on his fingers. "Before account no good, took money to buy machine for t-shirt business with cousin. We go into business after I leave plant 'cause of my back. Maybe cost, you know, $500 dollars, my share. And I use money to pay tax. I not know I owe, see, when I on disability. And money I save, I need to give Mr. Murphy to pay for margarine."

Sammy rubbed his face, then added, "I pay rent one month, and like... small things like that." Gwen was relieved it seemed so reasonable, but at the same time concerned. Linda hadn't mentioned any statements where she'd noticed these withdrawals. Were there other documents she hadn't seen?

Moving on to another troubling subject that came up at the meeting, Gwen asked, "Did you transfer money from your investment account with Mr. Murphy to another account he opened for you, one you didn't mention to your wife Olanda? Remember, I need you to be honest with me, Sammy. I can only protect you if I know everything, even if it is hard to tell me." Gwen knew that if the Panel thought Sammy was a 'cheater' on his family, as Bradford had implied, his case would be seriously hurt as arbitrators often stressed fairness as much as, if not more than, the letter of the law.

Sammy glared at Gwen, his words rushing out. "No, never put in other account for me. Like I say before to you, I tell Mr. Murphy move money into Mariah account. She my aunt who own store on island and help me pay margerine. It her money." His lips tightly pressed together, Sammy looked at Gwen and then added, "I promise I tell this to Mr. Murphy, he know. He say Mariah account can make good money for Mariah." Sammy again began playing with his jacket's zipper, moving it up and down.

Gwen jotted down a note to herself that Sammy shouldn't wear his zippered jacket on the stand, then asked, "And you did this when?" Gwen tried to be nonchalant, but she fully expected that the Respondents' lawyers would try to picture her client as a rat cheating on his wife during a divorce.

Staring at his fingers, Sammy said in a voice so low Gwen had to lean over, "Don't remember date."

Gwen tried again to firm up the time period. "Sammy, was this after your wife filed for divorce?"

Sammy rubbed his eyes again, which suddenly appeared wet with tears, then nodded. "It hard time for me, painful to think back. I so unhappy, angry, I not feel good in head. Olanda say want divorce. See, it not wife money and not my money. So I no want to list on form as *my* money. Tell this to person helping me at court. I no had lawyer, no can afford."

Sammy's body slid down on the bench and his face, round cheeks and all, looked deflated, as if Gwen had punctured his happy birthday balloon. But she needed to go on to one more subject before calling it a night. "All right. Now, one more question, Sammy. The firm says that you told Larry, ...um, Mr. Murphy, what stocks he should buy for you, that you called him every day and told him what to buy and sell. They say you got stock tips at work, on your computer, or from television shows. Then you'd call and tell Mr. Murphy what to do. Is this true?"

Gwen held her breath while she waited for Sammy's answer, as this was legally an important point – showing the extent to which Sammy had control over the accounts.

"No. Not happen like that. I not know how to use computer, you know, no Google name of stock on Internet to pick good one. Just know email, son he show me how to do that. And, like I say to you before, I no good at remember name. I hear at work, other guys, they say name of good stock so fast, I no, how you say... know name, not say like General Electric, Ford."

"Think back some more, Sammy. Did you mention to Mr. Murphy any special stock?"

Sammy sat, head down. He started moving the saltshaker back and forth. "Maybe. I think when I still work, Pete wrote down on paper name of stock he said was good, and I say letters to Mr. Murphy. Not sure of name now."

Gwen's heart dropped to her feet. Was this a one-time thing, or a pattern? And did it matter? After all, Sammy had given Murphy discretionary control over his account so Murphy had authority to trade on his own.

"Attorney, like I say to him all the time, I say only buy quality stock. I say IBM, Ford. You know. I name good companies. He I say one to pick stock. Why I pay him fees. I am telling you truth."

Giving the sign of the cross, Sammy added, "I swear on my Bible."

Gwen decided to push him more. "Come on Sammy. You say you only suggested one stock to buy? You did talk with him often, right? It would have been reasonable to pass on tips from your friends, or what you heard on television."

Sammy fidgeted in his seat, and looking at the table said, "I remember I say to Mr. Murphy, buy stock in this company, Claritan – no that for my allergy. Clazit..., don't know name now. Friends at work say my company, it go to buy it. Secret. They say stock price go up when people know. Sure thing, they tell me. So I tell Mr. Murphy. And friends – they right. Stock price go up. Mr. Murphy say he buy for him also and stock make him good money. He thank me, say good tip, I good player on his team."

Instantly Gwen's mind rang the bell 'illegal insider trading'? But as far as she remembered that claim could present a double-edged sword, maybe applying to Sammy as well as if he were still an employee. She tucked that possibly useful settlement issue aside for the moment. She had enough on her plate. What Sammy was saying rang true for her. She'd doubted all along that Sammy would have been able to pronounce, let alone remember, the names let alone abbreviated trading names of some of the tech company stock Murphy had bought for his account. Still, unless there was something there, why would the firm be fighting so hard? Did they have evidence to show that Sammy was a gambler, that he spent lots of time checking out the market, maybe on TV, looking for deals? After all, he had access to a computer and knew about Google for stock checking, and, yeah, he did risk all his family's assets to play the market. He must have understood there was some risk….

Gwen turned to Adam who had remained silent so far. "Adam, anything I missed?"

"I think you touched the major issues."

"I go home now?" Sammy stood up. Gwen rose as well. "Good job." She shook Sammy's hand, reminded him of the hearing date, adding that he needed to be there. "This is your chance to tell your story. No show, no win. You understand what I am saying?"

"Yes, I be there. For sure. I give you my word." Sammy crossed himself again.

Gwen thanked Emelio who had come out to give her a container filled to the brim with his restaurant's special pudding. Pressing her hand he muttered, *"Gracias abodaga."* Gwen was speechless at this gesture, so she gave Emelio a smile and hand squeeze in return.

The Prius's engine purred as Gwen pressed the power button. After dropping Sammy off at his cousin's down the street, and after leaving Adam at the place where he'd left his bike – as he'd declined a ride to his apartment, she thought about the meeting. Did she trust Sammy? Did she like him? Did that matter? He sure had enviable community support. She knew at this point in the case she was in for the long haul, or at least through the hearing. Thankfully she did feel more confident in his case, even if Adam had commented as he left, "Not so sure I think this guy is on the up and up. Reminds me of some con artists, gamblers I ran into at Vegas, looking for the quick buck. But probably I'm wrong, Gwen. Too cynical in my old age.

Is the glass half empty or half full? Whatever. As Chris used to tell her when surprised by a client's conduct, "It is what it is."

CHAPTER NINETEEN

Gwen, her arms loaded down with New Hampshire statutes, walked into her office's library/conference /intern room to return the heavy books to their designated place. She was super busy these days trying to jockey her case load to allow time to prepare for Sammy's hearing set to start in two weeks. Surreptitiously she stopped and watched Adam as he typed on his laptop, fully engaged in whatever he was doing. When he paused, Gwen quickly interjected, "Adam, you can go anytime you want. Don't want to hold you up from weekend plans. TGIF and all."

"Hey Gwen. Just finishing this memo on the legal doctrine of 'unclean hands'. I assume it's in connection with the document, or as us undercover spies say, 'Judy', that I helped you copy. Didn't learn about this yet in school. Have a minute?"

Gwen nodded yes.

"Here's the definition." With eagerness, Adam relayed, " 'A legal doctrine, a defense to a complaint, which states that a party who is asking for a judgment cannot have the help of the court if he/she has done anything unethical in relation to the subject of the lawsuit.' Gives the court the right to dismiss the suit or not grant judgment, so can be pretty powerful it seems."

Gwen thought about the impact of this equitable principle. It covered not just violations of court rules but 'unethical' conduct. What if the other party was the first to act unethically, did that wipe out the second party's bad conduct? What if one was a minor miscue, the other a big 'no no'? Her brain began exploring the various hypotheticals. Before she could respond, Judy walked in, coat on body and arms loaded with mail. "Bye guys. Have a great weekend."

Gwen checked her watch as her stomach was gurgling. "How did I get so hungry? Seems like I just finished lunch."

"You know," Adam said, "I'm starving too. All this brain

exercise."

Exercise. Gwen had forgotten to do her chair warm-ups, let alone leave time for a run.

Adam started putting the law books back. Turning towards Gwen, he said, "Hope I'm not being too forward, but..." Hesitating, his ears turning a slight shade of pink, he went on, "What I'm trying to say, Gwen, is that I don't have dinner plans." Pushing his fingers through his hair, he continued, "God, I feel like a teenager again. Would you like to go out for dinner? Um, ... I'm messing this up. I mean would you like to go for a bite – with me that is? I'd really like company. You pick the place." Looking at his feet he added, "Better some spot not too fancy as I'm wearing sneakers."

"Sounds like a good plan. But, Adam, no one's waiting at home for you? We've never talked about, you know, our personal lives. No significant other, kids, dogs, turtles?"

"Nope. Just me these days."

"So it's a yes. But I first have to make a brief stop at my mother's nursing home. How about we meet after that?"

"Hey, I don't mind waiting in the car as I took the bus this morning instead of my bike, thanks to the rain. I can do some homework while I wait."

Gwen thought it odd, just a little, that Adam lacked his own car. *Maybe he's an avid green energy person?* "Okay, if you don't mind waiting, Adam. But it's my treat."

"Super. Just need a minute."

An hour later Gwen left the nursing home, her mom tucked in for the night. After putting on her seat belt, she sat quietly behind the wheel, needing time to recover from her usual overwhelming sadness as she confronted her mom's disappearance slowly but inexorably into dementia's grasp. Adam sat silently, giving her space. She appreciated his sensitivity.

Driving up Route 49 to the rotary, she took the exit to the bright neon lights of the Circle Diner. "Hope you don't mind just plain food, Adam, with a selection large enough to please a statewide political convention. No pretentions, sort of fits with the expectations here above the Notch – fine as it is, and doesn't claim to be more. The owner is a former client of mine who became a friend. And the price is right, at least for my budget."

Adam smiled, a wide grin that showed off his dimples – and excellent orthodontia. "Great with me Gwen. I've fond memories of diners." He added, "And if I leave my baseball hat on, I think I'll be properly dressed."

Gwen smiled, appreciating his sense of humor that reminded her of Brian's, a hint of sarcasm to make the humor less sappy. They entered through shiny silver doors. The restaurant's chrome-covered walls reflected the lights hanging from the ceiling and transformed the diner into a mock-up of a television game-show set. Gwen thought nothing romantic here, but the casual atmosphere made her instantly relax.

"Hey Gwen, this place is amazing. Should be on the National Registry of Historic Places. I haven't seen one of these chrome babies since I was a kid in knickers. All that's missing is the full-size figure of Elvis strumming his guitar."

Lila from Down East, one of Gwen's favorite waitresses, came over to their table, order pad and pencil ready. "Evenin' Gwen, good to see ya'. Been too long."

"I know, Lila, too busy at work these days."

"You both look hungry as a moose in dead of winta'. What can I get ya' tonight? Specials are turkey meatloaf and vegetable lasagna, comes with homemade corn bread."

They ordered drinks, Gwen a glass of Chardonnay and Adam orange juice, and both requested the meatloaf special. Gwen leaned back and spread her arms out on the booth's padded red, somewhat cracked leather seat. Sipping her wine she asked, "Adam, tell me a little about yourself? As I recall I think you said you were from the West Coast. And you worked with computers before law school?"

"Right you are. Good memory." Adam went on to talk about

growing up in a wealthy suburban section of Northern California, studying physics in college, working in his dad's shed on weekends on a new kind of computer chip device. Gwen didn't exactly understand this part. After his second year he dropped out and, with a childhood friend, worked on this idea for an improved ... something that made the computer work faster.

Gwen chimed in, "That would be great for my computer, speed it up that is. Sorry, please go on."

"Well, soon we were making these chips for a fair price and the business took off. Making money was nice, you know. Still, after a few years it lost its allure."

"I'm ready to try that out. See if I get bored."

"Trust me, Gwen, you're too smart and curious to settle for boring. Anyhow, fortuitously, a big conglomerate made a buy offer. My friend and I accepted. And that pretty much set us up for life, financially. Shortly after, I began my party tour.

Lila came over and placed their platters on the table. Gwen wondered when the rest of the baseball team would show up for their portion. Adam smiled at Gwen, ate some meatloaf and started on the fresh corn bread.

"Hope I'm not boring you, Gwen?"

"Hey, really, I'm enjoying learning about your life, Adam. Mine is so dull by comparison. Go on."

Adam continued his tale of post-work life. "The rest gets a little sad. Maybe I should stop there."

"I know sad too, Adam. No problem, why don't you continue."

"All right." Moving the brown gravy around with his fork, Adam went on, "While I was traveling 'round the world I stopped in Amsterdam. Figured maybe a little weed, tulips. That's where I met Kila. You know, sometimes in life there's just magical karma." He snapped his middle finger and thumb. "Well that happened to us. We were biking in the countryside, each checking out the tulip farms. I literally ran into her." Raising his arms and bringing he hands together he said, "Bam! We both fell down, entangled with each other, and after that we just clicked so that our lives became entangled as well.. We lived on a houseboat on one of the canals for a while so she could finish school. Then we traveled. And we floated with the current. One month we were volunteering in Somalia. We built clean water systems for poor villages, far better than giving aid. Next thing we knew we ran climate tests on a boat in the Arctic. We even brought in nets on a Norwegian fishing boat. The years passed. Rich, good years."

"Sounds idyllic." Gwen was ready to sign up, to be a camper again.

"It was. Best years of my life." Adam now used his fork to play with the green peas, rolling them around on his plate. Gwen watched as a few became engulfed in the gravy.

After a moment of silence, Gwen said softly, "Don't mean to pry, Adam. But what happened? I gather Kila is not here with you?"

Slowly, Adam nodded. He drank more orange juice, mussed his hair, tapped on the table with his fingers. In a barely raised voice, he said, "One of life's blows. Life's whims. You've got the world on a golden platter – then before you blink, the earth shifts. Like enjoying the beach on a summer day. Blue sky. No clouds in sight. Surf's calm. All's great." Adam unfolded his paper napkin and crunched it into a ball. "Without warning, the tsunami hits. Don't know how to explain it otherwise. Sucks big time, that's all."

Impulsively, Gwen reached out and took his hand. "Yeah, I know what you mean. It's as if blackness descends like fog and you can't imagine seeing blue sky ever again."

Adam looked at her, his eyes misty and his lips tight. Then he said, "I see we've traveled down the same road."

As they sat silently, Lila came by, picked up their plates, balanced them miraculously on her forearms, and then asked, "You want me to wrap that up for ya'? Shame t'waste it."

Gwen, her eyes misting, just asked for the check. "It's a special club we both would prefer not to belong to, I'm sure, but there we are. Adam, what happened after that?"

"The tsunami was cancer." After blowing his nose, Adam went on, "One day she found a lump on her breast. Not enough months later, the C monster won."

"I am so sorry."

"Hey, you know, it's gotten easier. Time heals, between the hurt."

"How long ago was this?"

"Three years, four months, maybe going on three weeks since I lost her."

"Losing a loved one – you don't really get over it. Not like a cold. But you learn to move on." Sitting up straight, Gwen added, "At least I think that's what they say happens."

Lila returned with the check and to see if they wanted more drinks, on the house. Adam ordered his third orange juice, Gwen now wondered if he were Vitamin C deficient. They sat for a while, neither speaking. Adam looked around the large restaurant and smiled at the two young children at the next table who were busily coloring their paper placemats with crayons from the box provided. He didn't seam eager to leave, nor was Gwen. Soon, they were chatting about the legal system, the Red Sox, and the need for alternative energy. Before Gwen knew it, another waitress came bringing a plate of homemade warm rice pudding with two spoons, a gift she said from the owner to thank Gwen once again for her legal help.

While they scooped up the gooey pudding, Adam nonchalantly quizzed Gwen about the Perez case, her strategy, the evidence, the weaknesses she saw in her arguments, her settlement goal. Gwen hesitated, a little wary of revealing these secrets. Then she remembered that he worked for her and just wanted to be prepared. *Hey Gwennie, don't be foolish. No paranoia required. Besides, it will be good for you to get feedback. Just as if the suggestions were from a 'real' associate.* And so, with her arms crossed, feeling still a little defensive, she hushed her doubts and clued Adam in to her case plans. And when he asked about where the copy of the hot document was, having remembered it he said thanks to his research on unclean hands, she told him.

Lila returned and cleaned up the dishes, subtly reminding them that there was a long wait for the table. They took the hint. Gwen dropped Adam off at his bus stop and then drove home to her empty house. Before retiring for the night, she stopped to look at the framed picture of Brian standing on the top shelf of her living room bookcase, almost out of sight for 'shorties' like her. For the first time in a long while, she smiled at him, climbed on a chair and retrieved the picture which she move to a lower shelf, next to the one of Artie.

Sitting down on her comfy chair, Gwenn realized that, wow, she'd enjoyed dinner with Adam – was surprised they'd found so many connections, had common experiences, and that in many nice ways Adam reminded her of Brian.

She vowed to see if Adam might be free for dinner next Friday night, but this time at her house. She wrote a note to remind her to ask Judy if she knew of places where Gwen could get take-out dinner that looked and tasted like homemade.

CHAPTER TWENTY

Do I still have a client?

She couldn't blame Sammy if he were feeling angry and exasperated, for that's how she felt when she received last week a letter from the NASD informing her that the Perez v. Stanley, Howe matter had been continued until June 17, 2003, 'due to one of the Panelists' unexpected conflict with other on-going litigation'. No apology or further explanation was offered for the delay.

While Gwen was glad she finally had a panel, this was not good news – for her, for Sammy, for her experts, or she thought for Justice. Then she remembered Mary's comment that maybe the Respondents' lawyers were gearing for a hearing schedule that coincided with their summer vacation plans, ergo likely making tax deductible some of their expenses when enjoying sailing on Lake Winnipesauke. Could that apply as well to the panel members? She'd pooh-poohed Mary's suggestion, but now Gwen wasn't so sure; Mary may have been on to something.

Finding her Lawyer's Diary, Gwen confirmed that Sammy's appointment was indeed for today, Friday May 16th at 3 o'clock. As it was a Friday, she'd re-arranged her visit time with her mom. She could feel her anger rising; it was now at thigh height thanks to her short legs – but going up fast.

Gwen was already feeling sad as it had been almost two weeks to the day since 'The Old Man in the Mountain', the state's 40' high granite hunk, had died a tragic death. On May 3rd, he had lost his 10,000-year-old battle with gravity, slipping from his spot on top of Franconia Notch. All that remained on Cannon Mountain was part of the forehead; the distinctive nose and jutting chin were now mere boulders below. Gwen was missing him. She routinely checked for his presence when driving through the Notch. When looking from just the right spot you could see jutting out of the mountain, like the sudden appearance of an apparition, the profile of an old man. His strong rugged face stared out over the surrounding peaks, protecting the Notch from danger.

The whole state had gone into mourning after this loss of New Hampshire's iconic symbol, one seen on all state license plates and many tourists' t-shirts. And, indeed, she felt as if she'd lost a friend, a distant if imposing family member. But in a way, the loss resulted from human error – failure by the rock's caretakers to install the needed screws to keep the old man's craggily face in place. Gwen wanted to remind her fellow 'New Hampshire clan of her mantra, '*We are human and we make mistakes*'. Still it was a lesson that the laws of the Universe, that is, gravity, would have its way.

As the minutes passed and no Sammy, tension crept up her body. This was the problem with contingency cases – where the client had no financial investment. She knew the wait had been hard on Sammy. And *Bali Hi* was calling him to the Dominican sun where his sisters would pamper him, the Island's ladies flirt with him. Hell, she'd probably listen to the song '*Come to Me, Come to Me*' and hop on the next plane were she faced with his options.

But Gwen couldn't afford to let this case drop, not after the many billable hours she'd invested in it. Getting ready to give up and leave – better to spend her time sipping Chardonnay and watching the moon rise than waiting for a no-show client – she jumped when the doorbell buzzed. When she opened the front door there stood Sammy in his red ski jacket, and this time with a new friend, more likely, Gwen surmised, cousin.

Gwen greeted him with a forced smile, adding, "I was worried, Sammy, you'd forgotten our meeting."

"Hi Attorney. Sorry, had to wait for Juan, my friend here, to finish work so he drive me."

"Sammy, you have no car still?"

"Give mine to son, Marcus. No money for insurance."

Gwen had Sammy follow her into the library/conference room while Juan took a seat in the waiting room. Gwen explained to Sammy that their meeting was again to prepare him for the hearing. As she began to review various exhibits with Sammy, he suddenly stood up. "Attorney, I no feel smart today. I no sleep well, worry all time. Wife she not talk to me, not let me see boys on school nights." Tears formed in Sammy's eyes and Gwen appreciated the emotional toll the case was taking on him. She wondered whether she would hold up any better if she were in his shoes.

"Attorney, my case it take so long. Like say before, no good for me."

Gwen paused, exhaled deeply, and then said, "Sammy, unfortunately we need to finish the case after all our hard work. You have been brave and strong taking on the big investment firm and the bully broker. I'm sure your sons are proud of you. As am I. Just hang in there a little longer."

"But I not remember well no more, it been so long. I no be good, no answer questions smart."

"That's why we're preparing today." Gwen got up and stood beside Sammy. "And you are wrong. I've worked with you for over a year. Trust me. Many clients feel this way as their court date approaches, and they do fine. I'm confident you'll be fine too."

Sammy sat down and lawyer and client continued their case prep work. But Gwen noticed that Sammy became more and more confused and flustered. Some of his answers now differed from what he'd said previously at his meetings with her. Gwen began to worry that maybe it was all too much for him.

"Almost done, Sammy, just a few more issues to review. You'll be surprised how easy it will be once the real thing happens." She repeated again, "I have confidence in you, Sammy."

But by now Sammy was grabbing his stomach and taking in deep breaths. Would he collapse on her again, as he'd done at their first meeting? Instead, Sammy pushed himself to his feet and announced to the world, "I no can do more. I done answering questions for day."

Gwen realized she felt the same way. She was done for the day too. In fact, she felt exhausted and after this meeting more worried about the hearing becoming a fiasco. What was she thinking taking on this case alone? Facing a baseball team of litigators with her female crew of above the Notch friends? What were her options? She considered her choices. None looked good. *Damn them for not settling*! Staying positive seemed the most sensible course going forward.

Showing Sammy support, she nodded her head, gathered her energy, and responded, "No problem Sammy, no more questions. I think overall you did fine." She then gave Sammy a pasted smile, aware that she was learning acting skills not taught in law school. "Now remember the hearing is in a month. I gave you written directions before. Let me know if you can't find them. Do you have transportation to the city?"

Sammy put his hands over his ears, and then placed them in his pockets. In a low voice she had trouble hearing, he spoke to the carpet, "Attorney, I need tell you thing important for hearing."

Gwen's stomach curdled on cue, anticipating dire news.

Rocking back and forth on his heels, Sammy finally said, "I not happy in head, I miss boys, miss house. I see Doctor and he say no good for health. I make plan to leave end of week, go home to islands, live with sisters, family, work in store, and help cousin in business."

Gwen's legs turned numb and pain began pressing above her eyes. Was he riding off into the sunset?

"Attorney, I no quit. I promise. I make plan to be here. I fly home for hearing. Juan promise he take me from airport. Or Carlos. Don't worry," Sammy waved his hands in the air, "I be there. For sure. I swear on my Bible, I be there. I show my boys I no give up."

Collapsing into her office chair, Gwen said softly, "Sammy, if you do not show up you will surely lose." To herself Gwen added, *and you better be there, buster – or I will hire my own version of the All Mighty!* "Be brave, tell your story. Sammy, they say real courage is when you do something you think is right, even when you are afraid. We can do this together."

Just then the doorbell to her office rang. Gwen heard Judy open the door and a whole lot of noise entered. That's when she learned that Juan's painting crew had arrived for a 'Sammy surprise', planned with Judy's secret help. Soon her bookcases were moved to the middle of her office and covered in protective cloth, ladders were propped up against the walls of her office, each one holding a man in painting overalls, with paint roller. Soon her drab office was miraculously being transforming from dull green to a soft, warm taupe, all to the steady beat of Latin music.

Juan came over to Gwen and said, "You know, Attorney, our family and friends, we want to thank you for helping my cousin. You now big celebrity in Dortman, attorney who help for free Hispanic man get shot at what fair. That's a big thing to us."

Gwen thanked Juan, and then added, a real smile now on her face, "It already looks great, as Judy said, better color, calming." Then she yelled to the painting gang, including Sammy who was now busy painting the trim white, "Thank you all! *Mucho gracias.*"

Gwen stood for a while transfixed as they changed the room from blah to nice. Clients for sure hadn't done this at her big New York City firm. They more likely would have sued her – as a way to negotiate the lowering of their bill. She gave a silent cheer. *Another plus chalked up – or smeared on – for the small town practice life.* After watching the magical moving rollers, Gwen left the Picassos to their work and closed herself in her conference room where she joined Adam and Mary doing work.

Soon though she rose and announced to all, "The hell with this." She went in to her waiting room, moved a bunch of chairs against the wall, opened the door to her office, invited Mary and

Adam to join her and Judy. For the next hour the four of them moved their best to jive and dive and jump and jerk to the beat of the sound emanating from her office. Gwen moved like a chicken on steroids, and the rest, with arms up, danced their personal versions of 'one two *cha cha cha*', 'one two *cha cha cha*'. Soon laughter competed with the beat of the brass.

Every twenty minutes or so Gwen would stop and stare at the change in her office for, like a hanging dull chrysalis, it was being reborn as a beautiful butterfly.

CHAPTER TWENTY-ONE

Today was to be a Sunday in the park with Adam. As Gwen and Adam approached the green space, her eyes were dazzled by the bright lemon-yellow bordering the perimeter thanks to the late burst of the forsythia blossoms. Clad in sweats and Red Sox baseball caps – pink for Gwen, blue for Adam – the couple walked their rented bikes between and around the stopped cars, thankful that Sunday morning's traffic was light. When they reached the crosswalk Adam gallantly stuck his hand out to stop traffic while Gwen rolled her bike across the street. As she waited at the entrance for Adam, Gwen noticed that her thighs were slightly shaking. *Is there such a thing as bicycle flu?* The prospect of actually getting on the two–wheeled contraption engulfed her in fear. She would be, voluntarily, encountering more physical danger than she'd experienced since, well, going down the birth canal.

When Adam had asked her if she had time for a bike ride on Sunday, Gwen's initial reaction was to choke on her sandwich –– that she was eating as usual at her desk while catching up on completing her time sheets. Once she recovered, she mentioned that she hadn't ridden in quite some time.

His response – "It's like, well..., riding a bike Gwen. You don't forget how. Once done your muscles remember for life. No big deal."

So, spur of the moment, she'd agreed. But looking at the high seat that moved in unison with the rest of the bike, she was reassessing the wisdom of her decision. Placing her Sox cap in the bike's wooden basket, she put on the rented helmet with fins that resembled the ones those crazy racecar drivers wore. She already was struggling walking the bicycle and worried what it would be like when she actually tried riding it. Adam took off without issue, as if biking were just different legs to walk on. Not so much she. Gwen pushed down on the pedals until the right one was at the top of its cycle. Hands now grasping both handles, she straddled the gizmo, thankfully a girl's bike, so one foot was on each side, resting on the ground. So far so good. Then, shifting her weight, she pushed down with her right foot on its designated pedal, glided briefly, rested her butt on the hard seat, then quickly lifted her straggling left leg and placed it on the left pedal once it came to the top of its cycle. This time she pushed down with her left foot, and moved forward again until her right pedal was once more high at its arc, then repeated pushing down with that foot, all this happening while the wheels were spinning round – and thankfully still vertical. Oops, as the bike began wobbling, her left hand pressed together the break device on the handlebars, causing her to briefly touch down on the ground with her right foot while the wheels slowed, only to use it to kick off the ground again. She then pushed down hard with her left foot, butt back on the saddle, and there she was, moving, still upright, all good.... legs now pumping like car pistons. Air blowing against her face, scenery passing by in a blur. Feeling taller. Yes. Left foot down. Glide. Right foot down. Glide. Left foot again. Pedals moving faster. Hands tighter on handlebar. Glide. Then it happened. She was doing it! Up, down, up, down, her knees chugging along. Okay, her hands were now numb except for her palms which hurt, and were perhaps permanently indented from the pressure of holding onto the handlebars as if her life depended on it. Which she suspected it did. But, no matter. The ground was disappearing underneath her moving bicycle and the wind blew against her face.

With joyous relief and a tingling in her heart, Gwen yelled, "Hey Adam, this is a little bit fun!" Soon she was experimenting with kicking her legs out wide and then removing her hands, one at a time – and only for a second – from the rubber covers on the handlebars. She even worked up the gumption to click back and forth on the attached bell as it sang out 'kechung, kechung'. Yeah, she'd already learned bike lingo for 'here I come', *kechung, kechung*.

"Hey, Gwen," Adam shouted to her, "You're a sight to behold."

From her new perch high in the sky, at least for her, and in front of Adam, Gwen watched the world pass her by. Yes, the trees dressed in their new leaves were resplendent in June's green. Azaleas showed off their purple and pink not quite fully blooming flowers. The pruned beds sprouted baby plant life with gusto.

And then her moment of flying came to an abrupt end. Thank goodness Adam yelled ahead, "Don't hit the old man!" Just in time Gwen squeezed hard on her handbrakes, caught the ground barely with her right foot, and steered her front wheel sharply to the right. She almost fell, but regained control just in time.

"Guess I shouldn't be too ambitious," she offered. Still shaken and unsteady on her feet, she walked her bike around the next curve. "Adam, how about if we stop at that bench, just to catch our breath?"

And so they spent the morning biking with periodic stops to munch on apples, Judy's homemade chocolate chip oatmeal cookies, and generally to enjoy springtime in New England. Gwen found it easy to talk with Adam. They stopped and gossiped about the park's visitors: couples holding hands; fifty-somethings trying nifty basketball moves that no longer came easily; young men ogling the partially clad parading teens of the opposite sex. It was like the dirty white piñata of winter had suddenly been burst and all the hidden candy of June had been displayed before them, lit by the sunshine. A time when those living about the Notch, humans and black bears, celebrated at last the Earth's revival after its long, cold winter's sleep.

At one rest stop Gwen noticed two men in the distance across the pond. Were they staring at her and Adam through their binoculars? "Hey, Adam, look at those two men, see them behind the pond with the water fountain? Weird looking, you know. Maybe it's their funny clothes, large basketball pants and white undershirts. One guy actually has on black socks with leather shoes. And get those shades and brim hats. They don't look like 'Notchers' at all."

Adam stared at them and then quickly stepped back into the shade of a nearby tree.

"Ha, they look like some movie *mafioso* trying to pass as birders." Gwen said, laughing, as she waved at them.

"Hey Gwen, cut it out. Lets move on. I think this way's a shortcut to the entrance. We need to return the bikes soon or there'll be a penalty payment." With that, Adam quickly turned his bike in the opposite direction of where they'd been going, and started pumping his pedals.

Gwen followed, but was a little unsure what had seemed to change his mood. Over the next hill, well, incline, Adam turned and with a smile back asked, "How did it get so late?"

"Minute by minute, buster," Gwen said, using one of Brian's favorite sayings.

"Very funny, biker lady. I guess it's my turn. Time flies – although today I guess it rolls -- when you're having fun. And Gwen I'm having fun."

Gwen smiled for she was too. Who would have thought she'd so easily become a 'biker'. Maybe next spring she'd join the big bikers rally – and wear a leather jacket and pants.

They took turns walking and riding the five miles back to the rental store and retrieved Gwen's car. Surprised, Gwen noticed that after all that exercise she wasn't even tired. *Are my chair workouts finally paying off?*

And so it happened, on a warm and perfectly lovely New Hampshire spring day, Gwen and Adam began their courtship. After the bike escapade, they started doing 'couple' activities together. When time allowed, and the days were longer at this time of year, they went to wine tastings, flea markets for lost treasures, mostly fun junk, and visited the annual Lupine Festival held in a quiet hamlet tucked away at the foothills of the White Mountains. Amidst the crowd of tourists and locals, Gwen took pictures of the majestic blue and purple flowers that bloomed only for a month, briefly engorging the valley with dazzling color.

When their energies lagged, they spent down time at Gwen's house reading the Sunday newspapers, eating New York bagels, and doing the crossword together in ink.

Some days they enjoyed espressos on Gwen's patio while watching her birdfeeder's cardinals and jays and nuthatches battle for seed. Other times when Gwen did client work at her kitchen table she'd glance Adam's way as he napped on her recliner, blanketed by case books and class notes.

Then one night it seemed too dark and drizzling for Adam to go back to his apartment on his bike. So, he didn't.

CHAPTER TWENTY-TWO

Settlement. The word rested in Gwen's mouth like a delectable chocolate: sweet, sensual, sinful, satisfying. But, unfortunately, she'd heard nothing from opposing counsel in the Perez case that even intimated an interest in settlement – and the hearing was now a month away, July 16th instead of June 17th, thanks to the most recent continuance. Another NASD letter had arrived, another 'we're sorry but...', and yet another date for her and Sammy and Martha and Linda, and now Adam to shift their calendars around. This time the excuse was an unexpected medical procedure required by Mandel, Murphy's lawyer, due to some injury involving a golf cart. As Mary was not loath to tell her, the lake water was still cold in June. Gwen doubted, however, that even the NASD would hesitate to continue the case until ski season.

Now that there was another time gap before 'batter up', Gwen decided it was an opportune time – once again – to take the bull by the horns, or at least the rose by the thorns, and explore an amicable resolution. Who knew, maybe the new date imposed unpleasant difficulties for the Respondents' side as well.

"Hi Judy," she called out her open door. "Would you please see if you can find the phone number for Stanley's in-house attorney? I recall his name's Wadford?"

While Gwen was putting together last week's time sheets, Judy walked in and placed a small tab on her telephone. Gwen picked up Judy's note and dialed the number.

A woman's warm welcoming voice answered the phone with the rote "Legal Department of Stanley, Howe. Jennifer speaking. May I help you?"

"Yes, I'm trying to reach Attorney Wadford. Please tell him Attorney Wilson is on the phone to discuss the case, Perez v. Stanley, Howe."

"Certainly. I'll put you through to his secretary."

While waiting, Gwen doodled a fierce six-legged dog with a bird sitting – or was it shitting – on the pooch's head. She couldn't decide which animal her subconscious thought she was, otherwise known in legal parlance as the 'shitor' or the 'shitee'.

"Hello, Attorney Wilson?"

"Yes."

"This is Marilyn, Attorney Wadford's secretary. Please hold the line, he's just finishing a conference call and will be with you directly."

Gwen doodled some more, this time trying her hand at a two-headed giraffe that had stripes like a zebra and wore high heels. Clearly, thanks to its height and shoe preference, even at a sub-conscious level, this creature wasn't meant to be her.

At last, Gwen heard a deep voice on the line. "Bill Wadford here. Hi Gwen."

Tucking in her chin, trying to imply tough but nice, Gwen said, "Yes, hello Bill. Hope I'm not contacting you at a bad time. Sounds like you're having a busy day."

"No problem, Gwen. With summer coming up seems like all lawyers in the state want to get their cases resolved so they can go on vacation without worry."

"Ah, you got me there. Do you have time to discuss the Perez case? As you know, there's been another continuance so we're not set for the arbitration hearing to start until Wednesday, July 16th. With this time reprieve, it seemed a good time to touch base with you and see where we're at in terms of an agreement."

"Yes, Gwen, I'm aware of the changed arbitration date. I hate these summer changes as it impacts on my family's vacation time at the Vineyard."

"Not so much for me or my client who's been eager to tell his story for months now. But before we all get into litigation crunch mode, I thought I'd explore again whether there's interest in maybe resolving this matter. We all know how much energy and uncertainty is involved in trials." There, she'd spit it out, and hopefully without having resorted to pitiable pleading.

"I hear you. But, Gwen, between us, I did discuss this case with the General Counsel and our head of Litigation last week. I don't think settlement's a go at this time. Based on our experts' reviews, and the opinion of outside counsel, I'm told we're not prepared to make any offer, that we're comfortable our case is strong and the Panel will decide in our favor."

Gwen furrowed her brow, still trying to figure out what she was missing in this case. "I see. That sounds pretty definitive. Let me make sure I'm clear on your position, Bill, before I – and you – spend lots more hours preparing. Your firm has no interest in compromise, despite the positives of avoiding the cost and expense of a hearing, is that correct? And this position applies to both the firm and its employee Larry Murphy?"

"Yes, on both counts. That's what I've been told, Gwen."

Gwen decided to press more on the chance she might get some clue of their thinking. "As you know, Bill, arbitration's a little bit like throwing the dice in Vegas. A sympathetic investor can influence the Panel's position. And, knowing Sammy's story, I believe my client's most sympathetic."

"I understand, but we take the view that NASD arbitration is a fair forum for our claims; the Panel are all persons familiar with the securities industry and its standards, and we believe that supports our side. Gwen, I did try even to see if I we might make a token offer without any admission of responsibility on our part, but, well, even that's not looking likely."

Gwen sat back and played with her paper clips. "I see. Bill, I appreciate your being up front with me. I am disappointed as this will be an expensive exercise for all, one that I'm pretty confident could have been avoided. Let me know in the next few days if anything changes." Gwen quickly added before Bill could hang up, "In the meantime, just a reminder, you owe me documents pursuant to my last discovery request. I'd like confirmation that you'll be producing them by the end of the week. I'd prefer we avoid fighting over another Motion to Compel and sanctions with the NASD, but if necessary I will do that."

"Sure, Gwen. Should be no problem, but just to make sure, I'll follow up today with my paralegal. I understand your position. As to settlement, I'll do what I can as I wouldn't mind having the time to focus on my other work. Thanks for calling."

With that Bill hung up and Gwen sat there, phone in hand. *Not good.* She began to pull on her knuckles and speculate again as to the firm's possible motivating factors for holding firm. *There's something I'm missing here, some unknown negative in this case that's raising the bar even on settlement talks. Is there information Sammy's not told me? Some facts my experts haven't seen? Am I wrong on the law? Or is there another influencing factor, maybe Sammy's Dortman address? Or skin color?* Gwen sat and stewed.

Then she thought of her hot document, copies safely ensconced in her house and office, and pondered whether to mention it in another talk with Wadford, one before the hearing. Then Gwen remembered she'd not heard back from Martha as to whether her friend had found any information affirming Stanley's implementation of PIP. She tickled a note in her Diary to check that out tomorrow.

Without that, is my position too weak? Do I need to push to force them to put in more effort so at least there's an annoyance factor? Or a legal mistake that show's my ignorance of this legal area of the law? Is there an ethical issue I need to worry about if I use the 'Judy' document? Am I willing to risk my reputation to win this case? And why should I worry about my conduct when it's Stanley, Howe and Murphy who have nefariously and immorally cheated my client? Who, after all, is in the wrong here?

She began to doodle a big bad wolf dressed in a summer bikini with little sneakered feet running towards her house of hay... Then she drew 'SuperIntern' riding in on a white horse with the name 'Adam' written on its saddle.

CHAPTER TWENTY-THREE

Gwen turned off her desk lamp, the office's overhead lights, and locked the front door behind her. Her car was the only one still in the parking lot. After throwing her 'homework' on the back seat, she belted herself in, put on her 'hi' lights, and drove toward home. On the way she stopped at a client's house to have papers signed and at the local market for their complete turkey cooked dinner. She'd be eating for one as Adam was spending the night at his place finishing an article for one of his school's journals.

At the top of the hill with her ranch house in sight, and the prospect of a glass of wine, some mindless television, and a warm bed, Gwen felt the day's tension oozing out of her body. It had been half a dozen years since her move to Middleton and her search for housing that didn't have elevators and doormen. She'd fallen in love with her house at first sight, with its backyard of open meadows extending to woods and what seemed to her at the time high mountains. The house featured a large white front porch where she could sit on a rocking chair and watch the sunsets, a cozy wood fireplace, and wide oak planks on the floors that offered character.

At the time it seemed almost too large with three bedrooms, two baths but it came with visions of country life, a summer garden, fallen leaves to rake, and friendly neighbors who'd gladly offer a cup of flour if needed for that pie. Thankfully she had enough funds for the purchase from the quick sale of her 23rd floor Upper East Side studio. And, except for a needed water heater, roof leak repair, the occasional skunk family taking refuge under the porch, and the need to hire someone to shovel the snow and mow the lawn, it had been a quite happy 'human-house' relationship.

Walking up her front path, arms loaded with books and dinner, Gwen reached for her house key, unlocked the front door, and turned on the entry light. After putting her bags down on the nearest kitchen chair, she entered the living room to put her coat in the closet and almost tripped. Damn!. Gwen looked down and saw a fallen lamp in her path.

Then she saw the bigger wreckage strewn across her living room.

What the hell's happened? Did a tornado make a wrong turn in Pennsylvania and veer seriously off-course towards Middleton?

Holding on to the kitchen table, legs slightly wobbly from the shock, Gwen looked around and realized that her home had been ransacked. Papers were strewn everywhere, furniture overturned, pictures dumped on the ground.

Ignoring her heart palpitations, Gwen called out, her voice tremulous, "Anybody here?" After a few more calls and no answer, gathering her courage with the help of her Swiss Army Knife stored in the kitchen drawer, a camping gift from Brian, Gwen picked up the house phone and dialed 911. After the recording stated 'this number is for emergencies only,' a woman's voice asked the reason for her call. Gwen dutifully provided her name, address, and that her house had been robbed. She then opened her front door and waited for help, not venturing further into the house alone.

In under ten minutes Officer Lambert, or Charlie as she knew him thanks to a prior school matter she'd handled for his family, drove up in Middleton's orange and black police vehicle. He got out of his cruiser and walked over to her, one hand on his gun belt. Gwen wondered if he were too young to shave.

"You all right, Attorney Wilson?"

"Yes, Charlie. Gwen, please, we have history together. Pretty shaken up I guess, but the strange thing is, from what I can tell from a quick look around, it seems like there's a big mess but nothing's been taken. Televisions, computer, stereos, all there."

Charlie led Gwen through the house for a closer inspection. Other than her much-used address book and her pick-it-up home safe stuffed in her bedroom closet behind her boots – nothing appeared to have been taken. *Why the mess then? What had they been looking for? Or was the mess to make this look like a run-of-the-mill robbery?*

"Looks, Gwen, like whoever did this may have come in through your glass slider out to your patio. I noticed that door wasn't locked."

"Lock doesn't work again so I use the stick when I'm inside to lock it.

I guess I presumed if anyone wanted in that badly they'd only need to break the glass. You know, Charlie, I'm not sure what this is about. I have nothing valuable, and our neighborhood's so safe I often don't even lock my doors. Anyhow, all appears okay now. Charlie, can I get you some coffee or water? I could probably use some bourbon if you don't mind, still shaking a little."

Charlie nodded. "Water thanks. And I don't mind if you help yourself to something stronger. That is, unless you're under twenty-one. I won't card you – this time. It's scary to deal with an intrusion into your home."

"I sure appreciate your support." As Gwen was getting the water, her kitchen phone rang. She picked it up, preparing to let into some marketer who had the nerve to call so soon after she'd been robbed.

"Is this Attorney Wilson?"

"Yes."

Gwen didn't recognize the voice.

"Good evening. This is Brad calling from OnGuard Security. I just got a call from one of our security guards that your office has been broken into. Notes say sometime early evening. My man searched inside but found no one there. The premises are now secure. Do you want me to call the police?"

Gwen inhaled deeply. Could tonight get worse? "How did they break in? And was anything stolen as far as you can tell?"

"Ma'am, no signs of break-in the report says. But that doesn't always mean much these days with all the hi-tech tools. Office equipment was still there based on our list. Looking at the report it says there were papers thrown around. Did you have anything valuable in your files, like money or whatever?"

"No. Just regular lawyer documents. Brad, were any of the pictures moved?"

"Not that it says. Hidden safe?"

"Yup. Thanks Brad. No need to contact the police as I'm in touch with them already." Gwen turned to Charlie and let him know about her second break-in.

"I don't like coincidences," he commented, the concern evident on his face.

Charlie again checked out the house, told her all was clear, and instructed her to make sure she locked her doors and left the outside lights on overnight. He assured her he'd drive by the house on his rounds 'to be on the safe side'. He also asked that she report the break-ins at the police station in the next day or so. He added that would help with any insurance claims and update the department's records.

Gwen, now on her third bourbon and feeling mellow, agreed to all, gave him a hug – after all, he was a former client – and thanked him for his diligence. She also shuddered at the thought of doing Charlie's job, walking through a strange dark house knowing it was possible a burglar might be ready to pounce from behind a Lazy- Boy recliner. She was glad she was a part of the legal system that worked only with paper, not guns. Her lone likely assailant was an ornery yelling judge.

After Charlie had left, Gwen pondered the double break-ins. Maybe she did have an idea what they were looking for. Was it too far-fetched? She'd kept her two copies of the "hot" document in the Perez case in her safes, the one in her bedroom closet and the one behind the apple picture hanging in her office above the coffee-maker table. She knew the first one in her home was no longer there. She hoped the thief enjoyed her copy of her vehicle registration as well as original birth certificate and other personal papers. First thing tomorrow she'd check her office safe, which hopefully had been better hidden. While drinking her coffee, decaf, and ignoring the television show's commercial, she considered who might know about her safes. Her office staff, of course, but they didn't know about her home safe. Although maybe she had mentioned it to Judy in case she died or disappeared. The only other person she could think of who maybe knew of her home safe was Adam. As to her office safe, she and Judy knew the combination but that was all except… Gwen remembered she had told Adam about the 'Judy' locations during their meal at the diner. But did Adam know the combination for her office safe? He had seen Judy open it but still… And anyhow, he was busy at school, or so he'd said and the law of physics she thought from her college days said you could only be in one place at a time. *Gwennie, there must be a simple explanation. I just have to think of it.*

Gwen made sure again all her doors were locked, took some Tylenol for a growing headache, and went to bed. Finally, on the verge of sleep, the telephone next to her bed rang. She jumped, her mind suddenly alert and alarmed. Good news usually didn't arrive at that hour of the night. Picking up the receiver she heard a faint 'Hello'. The voice was so quiet she wasn't sure anyone was there.

"Hello?"

After more silence she heard whispered, "This Sammy. Speak to Attorney?"

Then she remembered she'd given Sammy her home number in case he needed to reach her urgently. "Oh, Sammy." Gwen could feel her blood pressure spike. "You surprised me. Yes, this is Gwen. You got me at home. It's very late. What's the problem?"

"I hurt. I walking home tonight after watch Marcus play basketball game at school. No one there on street. Then big man, he come at me. Hit me hard with fist in my face, say I should not make trouble. Say in English, then he say in Spanish. Hit me again in my stomach, not so hard. I scared, never to me happen before."

Gwen sat up in bed and rubbed her eyes, furiously trying to focus after all that bourbon. "Sammy, are you hurt? Do you need to go to the hospital? I can pick you up and take you there." Gwen didn't add that she'd need four cups of strong coffee first.

"No, not need you drive me, Attorney. Nose, face hurt but I be all right. Went to cousin where I stay and cousin's wife, almost nurse. She help me. But I worry. I afraid he or other guy may do again."

Frantic, Gwen asked, "Do you think they were looking for money? Someone wanting drugs?"

"No ask for money. Just hit, tell me stop, then he go. Leave me on ground."

"I think you should call the police."

"No police. I okay. Sorry, I call you as I worry it about my case, but I leave soon for Island."

"Sammy, I'd be surprised if there's a connection. No lawyer I know would risk disbarment. Still, I don't like this. I don't like this at all. I will check with the other lawyers. Stay safe, Sammy."

What's going on?

Gwen tossed and turned under her covers. Sure, Dortman isn't the safest place. Still, it's pretty obvious from Sammy's clothes he likely has nothing valuable to steal. Can there be a possible link to his case? Surely a fancy firm like Stanley, Howe wouldn't risk possible licensing trouble over Sammy's likely losing complaint, not when they could have settled for diddlysquat. To set the goon squad on her client makes no sense. Unless it has to do with the 'Judy' document somehow, maybe frighten us to drop his case. Not likely, but still, as Charlie said, and the great Hercule Poirot, I don't like coincidences.

Gwen decided she'd draft a motion explaining the assault on her client and robbery of her office and demand that the NASD assign a security guard to the hearing – without cost to Sammy. That might get the Respondents' attention in any event. Gwen punched her pillow, threw off her covers, peeked at the bedroom clock. At last she padded over to her kitchen drawer, removed her twelve-inch cook's knife, and carefully placed it under her pillow. Yet, even with this protection, all night she listened to Charlie's patrol car drive by. She was glad she'd set out on her driveway a thermos of hot coffee and a bag of cookies --slightly stale, but still they were chocolate chip.

Early the next morning after arriving at her office, her face drawn with anxiety, Gwen moved the coffee pot and reached behind the apple painting in her office. Holding her breath, she turned the knob on the built-in safe, using her birth date numbers. Success. A click. Gwen, her breathing abated, opened the safe. She didn't need her glasses to know that the safe was empty.

**** **** ****

After the robbery Gwen was relieved to have not only her long kitchen knife to sleep with for protection, but also Adam whose snoring presence made her feel safer. At the same time, a squeaky voice asked in her ear whether the robbery raised trust issues not resolved with orange juice and eggs. What did she really know about this stranger who sat in her living room offering witty sexual innuendos? Yes, he was smart, confident, funny, and sensitive to her needs. And fun to be with, made her feel special. And all in such an amazingly short time.

When she quizzed Adam on his whereabouts the night of the robberies, he told her he'd been at the library late doing legal research for a professor, and showed her his notes. Likely true as he'd stayed in his apartment that night, yet she was aware she only had his word on this. *Does trust fill in the rest?*

After Gwen described the thefts, Adam asked, "Anything important taken?"

"Not really. You check the local paper and the biggest crime in Middleton might be someone stealing a bicycle off a porch. But I had two burglaries in one night. Yet they didn't take anything of real value, even cash. How do you figure that?"

Adam shrugged.

"I should mention, though, that strangely they did manage to take both my copies of the Judy memo."

"Yes, the document I heinously smuggled."

"Well, let's say it was the one we briefly borrowed. But I thought you knew that it was hidden in my safes? Didn't I or Judy mention that?"

"You must be mixing me up with another boyfriend or intern."

"Ha-ha," said Gwen.

"Hon, maybe they found your key hidden in your underwear drawer and then it was easy to figure you had a safety box in your bedroom?"

Gwen stopped eating, her fork in mid-air. "Yes, they did. How'd you know that, about the key I mean?"

Adam's cheeks turned slightly red, understanding his *faux pas*. "Good question. Don't know, just my experience I guess; I remember that's where Kila kept her diary. And splurge money."

Gwen stared at him, her mouth open.

CHAPTER TWENTY-FOUR

After leaving a phone message for Judy that she would be in late, and with Adam in tow as he was getting a free lift to school, Gwen drove to the Middleton police station to report her recent robberies.

Over the sound of the morning news on the car's radio, she casually asked Adam a question that had been nagging at her. "I was wondering, do you have a problem with your eyes? I notice you don't drive a car."

Staring out the window for what seemed to Gwen miles, Adam finally turned to her. "No eye problem, something more. Gwen, it's not a story I'm proud of but you've a right to know the bad as well as good about me."

"I'm listening," Gwen said, turning off the radio.

"Goes back to my Kila days. After she got sick, and then became really sick, and we were going from treatment option to treatment option in the States, I was under lots of stress and pretty angry at the unfairness of it all. Started drinking. Progressed before I knew it from beer to the hard stuff. It became a problem. I was a good driver, used to drive sports cars, but within two months I had two auto accidents, both my fault. I almost hit a child. I pleaded to two DUI's and my license was suspended. That forced me to accept my problem real quick and get help. Did AA, stayed away from booze. Still do both."

"I've noticed, the orange juice that is."

"Found I didn't mind biking places so haven't felt the need to drive a car. Not that I don't trust myself. To be honest, I guess I'm not sure of my limits, and don't want to test it, both the alcohol and the penchant for racing. So, I avoid the encounter with both. I do have a California license that ... um....I may need to renew. If I really need a car these days my neighbor lets me use her truck."

Gwen's fists tightened on the steering wheel. "Thanks for sharing. I remember my dad having alcohol issues, trying to forget but thankfully he also found out that booze didn't help. Instead he preferred one day to skip town. No more said."

They both entered the glass and chrome police building and Gwen filled out her report about the incidents. As they were leaving, a woman approached from down the hall shouting, "Stop! Attorney Wilson, hang on a minute!"

The middle-aged, slightly plump woman almost tackled Gwen in her zeal. Stepping back to avoid becoming an assault victim, Gwen recognized that the woman was Sarah, the local newspaper's crime reporter.

Breathing heavily after her short sprint, Sarah said, "Attorney Wilson, I'm desperate for a story. Can you help me? You're my last hope! Don't need anything fancy, just something hinting at criminal will do. Even a lost puppy case, I'm so hungry. Please, I'm on deadline and have an editor who will not be happy unless I give him some copy."

Gwen noticed that during this confrontation Adam had continued walking towards her car, his back to Sarah. To prevent Gwen from similarly departing, Sarah grabbed Gwen's arm, and then stuck a small tape recorder in her face. Not wanting to offend the reporter by threatening to sue her for criminal battery, thereby giving Sarah her much needed story, Gwen pasted on a smile and offered to help. Sarah had referred some cases to her in the past, and Gwen didn't want to burn any bridges unnecessarily. Besides, she liked Sarah and appreciated that it was a tough job for a woman to do – reporting on crime.

"Sorry Sarah, nothing more than a local robbery at my house to report. No injury and nothing of any value taken. Maybe some kids wanting a fun night out."

"Hm. Anything else? That's a pretty short article. Door broken? Police think part of a serial thing? A little more, maybe list of what was taken, and I can make it fill the space."

"I'm in a rush, Sarah, so not sure I can help you much more. Maybe you can catch Officer Lambert and he can help you."

Gwen rushed to catch up with Adam, Sarah trailing behind.

Sarah, spurting ahead with a speed that beckoned the Olympic trials, she effectively blocked the exit door with her body, like a linebacker. This time she held the tape recorder in front of Adam's face. Smiling at him, and Gwen could have sworn also sticking out her boobs and seductively raising a hip, Sarah said to Adam, "Hey handsome, do you have anything to add about the robbery, or better yet, a story? I could take you out for coffee on the paper if you want to share some information."

Adam, his face twisted in anger, barked loudly, "Get lost lady!," then he pushed past her out the front door and got into Gwen's Prius.

Startled, frozen in place, Gwen watched this scene unfold. *Where's that venom coming from?* She said to Sarah in a sweeter voice then she felt, and with an apologetic smile, "Sorry, he's a student interning in my office, and, fortunately for him, getting a ride as he's late for class. He'll be in big trouble with his professor if we don't hurry so got to go."

With that Gwen jogged behind Adam – aware she finally was getting in a run. Undeterred, Sarah again miraculously raced in front of her. With a small camera that appeared from nowhere, she took a quick picture of Gwen and then of Adam through his side window. The flash lit up his face. Turning towards Gwen, Adam glared, and then scrunched his shoulders down in the seat. Nothing if not persistent, Sarah ran in front of Gwen as she was getting in the driver's seat, and snapped another picture, this time with Adam's face in the background.

"Hey, I didn't agree to that," Gwen complained, the light from the flash still blinding her.

"Don't worry, almost positive it won't run. Not much of a story, even for a slow news day. But I need some visual. And no lawyer I know would object to free publicity!" Sarah then reached inside Gwen's car before she could close the door and yelled to Adam, "Sarah Denarra at your service," and handed him two of her business cards. She left another card on Gwen's dashboard. "Just in case something comes up I can help with." Then she was gone pursuing her deadline story.

Once back on the road, Adam, his voice now calm, said, "Didn't realize the time. Can you put the pedal to the medal? I'll be late for class unless we hurry. Not a good thing when it's my turn to be called on."

"Roger, Captain," Gwen said and put her car into gear. But she felt a slight frisson of what felt like fear emanating from Adam's side of the car.

On her way to work, Gwen began to think again about Adam's actions with Sarah, the robbery, and what did she really know about this tall dark stranger she was sharing breakfast with most mornings. She did know that since the robbery she'd been relieved to have Adam as her houseguest, even though he was busy finishing up his classes thanks to the school's quarterly class schedule, and his law books and notes had spread out like her lawn's crabgrass and now covered much of her living room floor. Not only did she feel safer for his presence, but she felt happy, enjoying the cutesy banter of intimacy they'd been sharing. Nice.

At the same time, a squeaky voice asked her frontal brain whether she was being smart. Hadn't the robbery raised trust issues, a fire she couldn't quite put out with breakfast orange juice? What did she really know about this stranger in her living room offering witty comments and crossword puzzle answers? Yes, he was smart, confident, funny, and sensitive to her needs. And they connected emotionally over their grief. And he was fun to be with, made her feel special, competent, cared for.

And all in such a short time. *Am I rushing too much because I'm lonely? Feeling the years creeping up? Afraid of closing my life choices?*

CHAPTER TWENTY-FIVE

"We have a problem, Houston."

Martha, who was studying her handheld calendar, raised her eyes over her half glasses and asked, "What gives Gwen? Have you joined NASA?"

"My wish. Always thought it would be great to circle the Earth and see several sunrises in one day. Let alone touch Mars. But I wasn't tall enough for that to be an option. Best I could do is watch the July 4th rockets red glare this past weekend. Martha, let's wait for Linda and then we can talk about the latest Perez news."

Linda magically appeared on cue, weaving her way through the tables in the café filled with customers drinking lattes. She sat down on the comfy leather banquette that faced the raging fireplace, even though it was July.

Gwen said, "Hi team, thanks for coming on short notice, but I thought I needed to share the Perez news with you as soon as possible."

Martha and Linda stared at her, their welcoming smiles fading fast.

"The news is a little good, and maybe a little more not so good. Yesterday I got one of those one-page letters from the NASD. They have changed our hearing date so it is set to start on Tuesday, August 19th, thankfully still this year. Seems that one of the Panel members will be out of the country on the latest July dates. I hope the now *fourth* I think revised hearing date is workable for both of you. At least this letter stated that there would be no more continuances. Ha. Respondents have promised no more delays. I intend to hold them to that. Also, the case will be heard now at a law firm's office in Manchester instead of at a hotel in Concord. Means a longer drive, but not too much. Also, Stanley, Howe has hired additional counsel who'll be taking the lead, an Attorney Josiah Day. He's a big name with a New York firm and, interestingly is a person of color. Is this date change okay with you both? I expect we're really still talking about the first two days when I put on Sammy's case and when Larry testifies."

Martha checked her calendar and frowned. "Not great. If I move a client I can give you that first day. But I'm flying to Spain early Friday morning on combined business and family time, and have some urgent matters to handle the day before. Sorry Gwen, I won't likely be able to be there if something comes up during their presentation and you need me."

Linda said she needed to check with her office but it appeared the nineteenth would work, sufficiently post-tax season extension time she added. Linda continued, "Just to vent Gwen. This has been some pain-in-the-ass experience. All these last-minute delays, I don't know how you maintain your sanity. At least April 15th stays the same every year. Remind me never to agree to do this again!"

"Not fun?"

With a puckered face as if she'd sucked a lemon, Linda added, "No, not fun. Maybe good for my career as you suggested; we shall see. Sammy does appear to have gotten screwed so I'm still in. But deadlines should be deadlines."

Gwen remained quiet. She played with her knuckles – a nervous tick not unnoticed by her friends - - and turned the drinking straw in her latté in circles. "Despite their admonition, I could request another date change, but I'm worried there would be a significant delay if I do that. And every delay makes me more anxious Sammy will get cold feet. It seems like we have no choice but to hang in there and go with the new date. So August 19th it is. Now for the second not-so-great reason for our meeting.

Martha interjected, "You mean the continuance is the good one? Uh oh. What's happened?"

"I was able to do more research now that the Panel members are set and the NASD gave me access to more agency files. Turns out that the initial disclosures I got from the agency providing panel members' backgrounds were outdated and incomplete. Maybe the timing with the chaos after 9/11 explains it, don't know. The chair of the Panel, the lawyer who worked for a firm representing both investors and companies, remember? Well, two years ago he changed jobs. Now he specializes in defending hedge funds and the big guys, I don't know, like J.P. Morgan. Not exactly Sammy friendly, you think? And the other two guys look even more like industry shills thanks to their recent work. Unlike other NASD cases, we weren't offered a neutral panelist, a so-called public person, as an option. And then there's the fact that I was right. I did object to one of the appointed industry member way back in the beginning. But he has somehow re- appeared. I assume my paperwork got misplaced – or the agency couldn't find anyone else interested in our client's small allegations of fraud."

"Doesn't this give you a chance to have the panel excused?" asked Martha.

"Like I was saying, maybe I could demand a new crew but that would just result in more delays, meaning again the hearing wouldn't likely happen until next year. See, all three panelists need to be available, along with all the many lawyers, plus Murphy. Think how hard it's been for the three of us to get together, other than at lunchtime? Delay as you know favors their side so there's no reason for them to be accommodating. Just presents a greater likelihood Sammy will have moved on."

Martha commented, "You're right, Gwen, not great options. Do we have any real choice? I say we just bite the bullet. As we've known Gwen from the beginning, Sammy's case was always a long shot, a small guy taking on the big boys, and in their own house so to speak, and with their own rules and unmatched resources."

Gwen nodded, "Yes, the fox protecting the chicken coop. Unlike those hunting pictures in the law firm's waiting room, in our case it appears more and more likely that the fox has the upper hand. But wait, you haven't heard the best in terms of lousy news."

"God, Gwen. That sounds ominous," Linda said. "This meeting is becoming a real downer."

"You think? As I was saying, when doing further research I found arbitration history for this lawyer who's heading the Panel. The story ain't pretty, ladies. I came upon a decision he wrote a few years back in an investor fraud case. Scaringly, it raised similar claims to Sammy's. This claimant also was ready to retire and lost all his money thanks to his broker's risky trades and fees. *Our* Chair wrote the decision holding for the company and broker on all the investor's claims. Specifically it ruled that: the investor controlled his account; the broker was more credible; and no industry standards were broken. What's the difference between this case and Sammy's? The Claimant in that case was an upper middle- class, educated, white guy, mid-level executive, whereas our client is, well, to be blunt, a low- income disabled Hispanic with a GED. But who knows if that harms or helps Sammy's case?"

"I wouldn't put money on it helping," Martha said. "Can I use the 'f' word?"

"Help yourself. That pretty much sums it up appropriately," Gwen added. "Warning guys, better check all those contracts you sign that now mandate arbitration if there's a dispute. Allows the deciders to be industry pals, to be inherently biased you might say. So, for example, should a panelist issue a large award favoring an investor, you can bet that guy's less likely to sit on a future panel – and I assume make some easy money. The securities industry, at least through its arbitration procedure, has found a way to set the rules, restrict the deciders, and, thanks to no appeal, put closure to the disputes. All done confidentially behind closed doors. Now, true, many investors are happy with arbitration, it is quick and can be much cheaper, no promises given it will work for our client."

All three women sat around the table glumly and stared at their coffees.

Gwen finally broke the silence. "As I said, I think our best chance is to put on our case, try to embarrass them into doing the right thing, maybe raise the image of an Hispanic David who's fighting to protect his family with his little slingshot against the powerful gigantic Goliath. Of course this all assumes that Sammy shows up and is believable. And that I can get a better handle on the case as they've swamped me with an overload of paper, yet still have failed to produce many of the basic documents you both have been asking for. Mark my words, these will suddenly arrive right before the hearing. And, to be honest, without depositions I'm having trouble even understanding the meaning of what I've been given. I never thought I'd fall in love with the Rules of Civil Procedure, but I sure appreciate them now. Between us, my friends, I am feeling more and more in over my head." Gwen sipped her latte, then put on a smile and said, "But we shall persevere! Justice awaits those who are noble. Or is it, those who are ninety?"

Her joke received no smiles. Gwen knew that her friends were not happy with today's tidings, and likely were pretty fed up with the whole process.

Martha, sitting with arms crossed and twisting her large diamond ring, said, "Gwen, I presume you meant that 'noble' stuff sarcastically."

"Well… I admit that I'm revising my ethical lines here. Which leads me to ask what's happening, Martha, with that memorandum we had talked about?

"Funny you should ask. I just heard back from my friend who advised that there are rumors in the back offices of trading firms that Stanley, Howe has implemented some kind of trial balloon involving an aggressive marketing program directed at communities of color with hopes of increasing the company's market share, otherwise known as diversity expansion. But all has been hush, hush, so that's just talk as of now. He did say that there were concerns about the program's potential legal traps, thought company execs wants to keep the program confidential for now--

until they see if it is successful and safe. Gwen nodded. She couldn't do much with rumors. And, without copies of the Judy memo, she had less leverage to raise this issue in a push for settlement.

All three women sat silently, aware that the road ahead had become harder. Finally, Linda stood up and gave her usual direct appraisal. "As to the date, not much else we can do. As to the case, I agree with Martha. We're right and the hell with the one-sided law. I've got to go."

So it was settled, on August 19th – arbitration is a go.

Gwen moodily walked down the blocks to her office. How had this case that had seemed so promising become so risky? As she passed Polly, the tall bronze statue of a twirling young lady with long wide skirt and happy face, Gwen reached out and rubbed the lady's fancy dancing shoe. Built to honor the main character of the town's most famous children's author, Gwen hoped there might indeed be some truth to the legend that those who touched her foot would encounter some sunshine in an endeavor that at the moment had seemed bleak.[1]

• [1] See, e.g., <u>Shearson/American Express v. McMahon</u>, 482 U.S. 220 (1987), a case decided several years AFTER Sammy's case where in a suit against a brokerage firm alleging, like Sammy did, violations of Section 10(b) of the federal Securities Exchange Act of 1934, the anti-fraud provisions, the Supreme Court held that the brokerage firm could compel the customer agreement's mandated arbitration provision as it is federal policy under the Federal Arbitration Act to favor arbitration. As such, the Majority Opinion held that courts are required to rigorously enforce such agreements.

CHAPTER TWENTY-SIX

Gwen tottered into the kitchen under the weight of her groceries. She'd stopped on her way home as the only option in her refrigerator for dinner was – eating out, and she was too tired for that. Putting her bags down on the counter, she noticed Adam was fast asleep on the recliner, his Contracts casebook resting on his chest. *Who is this person who's become a focus of my life these last few months? And why have I allowed a virtual stranger to grab hold of my heart?* She wasn't someone who fell hard for great looks. While Brian was adorable with his hazel eyes that changed from gray to green with the light. He also had a nose that imposed. More importantly, he was gentle, solicitous, funny quirky, and nerd smart. They'd fit with such ease as a couple, like two puzzle pieces. Or like PB&J.

Was that true of her and Adam? Okay, by most standards Adam would be considered a super catch – were she to be man fishing. Good looking, smart, assured, and rich even, maybe. But at nearing forty his jowls were thickening just a little and fine creases extended from his eyes. Then there was the start of a little paunch. But most women, including Anna, would mostly say a ten on the "wish for" scale. So what was this guy doing asleep with a law book in her armchair? She, after all, was just a small-town lawyer making a somewhat living in a non- glamorous part of ski country. With modest grades in the glamour department—short when in sneakers, hips that held up her pants, unimpressive cheek bones, light brown eyes that benefited from glasses, and "scintillating" auburn locks that didn't look at all blond.

Then there was his changing bio. *Am I gullible believing this charmer's story? Is what he's told me even credible, outside a daytime television show?* Gwen thought she'd noticed red flags in his biography – small contradictions, far-fetched coincidences. And what was his nastiness with that nosy reporter Sarah about?

More concerns filled her head and whirled around, blanks in the Adam picture. *Yes, he is bright, very bright. So why is he enrolled at a third tier law school? Where's his apartment, and why haven't I met any of his friends? And isn't it fortuitous that he arrived at my doorstep like an unexpected birthday gift during the Perez case?* While preparing the 'salmon with lemon dill sauce' meals, that is, putting them in the microwave, Gwen asked herself whether their jigsaw pieces fit.

She looked up as Adam made movements in his chair.

"Hi there, chef. Didn't realize how tired I was." Adam pushed down on the recliner and sat up.

"You're excused for as I recall, reading legal opinions is a soporific experience. And, big guy, you've been burning your candles at both ends lately, what with your helping me, finals, and working for that professor."

Adam got up and walked over to the kitchen, enclosed her in his lovely hairy arms, and gave her a knee-melting kiss.

"Hey you," she said. "You're going to spoil me. But it sure is nice. How hungry are you?"

"Not that hungry. For salmon at least."

And so they enjoyed pre-dinner appetizers, and began another night of a newly formed couple discussing their day over salmon.

After dinner, Gwen hesitantly asked Adam, "I was thinking that maybe it's time we talked about us. I know very little about you, really. Yet here you are essentially living with me. In fact, worming your way into my anatomy." She picked up her wine, poured a glass of orange juice, and walked over to the couch, libations in hand.

After sipping his juice, Adam smiled at her. "Have I come on too strong, Gwen, pressured you? It seemed to me we both have seen life and know what we want, and that we seem good together."

"Don't get me wrong, Adam, I'm happy that you're here. I just want to know a little more about whom I've been welcoming into my life. And I guess you also don't know much about me. I come with lots of baggage, I can tell you."

"Carrying luggage is something I do well," he said, grinning now. "Being a porter was a back-up career option."

Gwen could have sworn his eyes were twinkling, like that star hanging low in the sky at night. Okay, that was probably Venus, but it was bright. She grinned back, wondering if happiness were catching like the chicken pox.

"Very funny. You are such a cut up." She went over and gave him a peck on his cheek. Sitting down next to him, trying to appear nonchalant while her stomach was churning up a rip tide, she continued, "So, humor aside, tell me again, but this time more than an outline, all the dope I'd expect to read in a Hollywood tell-all magazine."

Resting his contracts book on the floor, Adam stared out the picture window, his face furrowed in thought. "Yes, Gwennie. You are right. You deserve to know whatever you want about me. Relationships demand trust. And honesty."

Bingo, she thought. "I agree," she said.

"Not always easy to go back." Adam rose from the couch and sat back on the recliner, facing Gwen. Taking a deep breath, his arms resting on his knees as if he were about to give directions in a huddle, he began, "I think I told you the basics. How I grew up outside San Francisco. My dad taught Physics at the state college. I went to a day school, sort of like a non-boarding prep school. It was connected to the University's education department. Got a tennis scholarship and went to Stanford. Didn't make the team after all that. Met and broke up with lots of co-eds. A friend was starting a tech company. He asked me to join in as I was good at computers. More fun than studying physics, so I left college. Working in his dad's shed we developed hardware to make faster running motherboards. You know, what operates all computers. The money started rolling in."

Gwen's antenna had shot up. Weren't there slight variations

from his prior life resume, where, as she recalled, he'd been the one who recruited the friend? And the shed was his dad's garage? Are there other slips? Or am I over-reading his story's shifts, responding from my fear of joining an intimate relationship? *Can I --should I – open myself again and risk the pain of a broken heart?* Gwen wasn't certain she had the courage to find the answer.

Adam rested one foot on the coffee table, and then continued, "The money was nice, for a while. Hard to believe maybe, but, you know, it's not such a big thing. I did enjoy the toys it bought. And the control. I spent a few years luxuriating in the material goods, dating starlet types. I got bored so did risky challenges. Crazy stuff. Not much seemed out-of-bounds."

Gwen was curious as to how the other half lived, those not physically and emotionally risk adverse. "Like what? For me a risky challenge is trying to do the *Times* crossword puzzle on a Friday when they're way out of my league."

Nodding his head and grinning, he said, "Yeah, that can get your adrenaline flowing." Then Adam's face turned slightly red. Sitting up and looking directly at her he went on, "Not sure you want to know. Some of it was stupid, scary, not covered by my life insurance. Did skydiving, swam with sharks, kayaked around glaciers. With a grin he added, then there was the less healthy stuff."

Gwen placed her hands over her eyes as if in mock terror. "Maybe we can skip those. I'm just a middle-class kid from Queens."

"Probably good idea. Then, as I told you, I met Kila. Life got more serious. We were now two, and when she got pregnant, soon to be three. Time to grow up. As you know, after travel we settled in Amsterdam. She went back to her job as a curator at a small Dutch museum. I worked on a travel book." Adam sipped more juice and stared out the window. Rubbing his hands together, he continued, "And then there happened that horrendous day. See, I usually met her and we'd bike home together, but I was napping, actually sleeping off too much beer that afternoon. So it was the rare time she was biking home alone. A truck driver, I later learned high on weed, failed to stay in his lane. On the turn a the corner he ... The EMTs couldn't help her, or the baby."

Adam sat back and hugged a throw pillow so hard his fists turned white. To Gwen, something in his story didn't sit right. Then she remembered.

"Adam, I thought you'd said Kila died from cancer?"

Adam coughed and then took another sip of juice. He turned his face away and this time rubbed the back of his neck. The silence extended. Tightening his shoulders he finally went on, "Hon, you caught me. That's not exactly what happened. The cancer story, just not mine. I borrowed it from a friend's life story. See, if she died that way I wouldn't feel guilty, responsible for her death. Easier for me to swallow and for you to accept. Just a slight shift in the facts, but a big difference in my feeling of guilt. If I'd been there that afternoon, biking with her, not home thanks to too many beers, well..., she'd have been more visible, maybe we'd not be at that spot, ...so many ifs. Getting sick and fighting together against the disease, I'm so much less at fault. I can focus on the love side of us easier. You know what I mean? But she died on me. And I lost my baby. And the thing is I'll always feel fucking guilty."

"I can't imagine your grief," Gwen countered, but of course she did. She still woke in the wee hours thinking of Mark and the "what ifs": what if the blue car had come a few minutes earlier, what if Mark had caught the ball, or... How would her life have changed if earth's molecules had been arranged just a little bit differently that day? And maybe she too might want to stretch the truth somewhat, and avoid the pain – and shame – of feeling so culpable.

Adam walked to the sink with his empty juice glass and poured himself a glass of water. He gulped it down, returned to his chair, and then continued. "After that, you know, her being gone, and the baby, my not saying goodbye, I floundered." With a slight smile he added, "Maybe I shouldn't say that since we ate the poor salmon. Anyhow, I was a mess."

"What sane person wouldn't be?"

Adam nodded. He then reiterated his troubles when returning to the States, his sad trail of drugs, drinking, gambling. Gwen marveled that he could seem so matter-of-fact describing his woes. Continuing in this cool manner, he added, "Nothing mattered, just oblivion. I was languishing, lucky to get through the days without trouble, no more than that. Finally got into legal trouble – but I told you about that. I understood I needed to accept that Kila wasn't coming back." Pausing, Adam stood up, turned on the lamp next to the chair and moved the throw pillows to the couch. "Helps, hon, if I have more light. Anyhow, where was I?'

Gwen said, "Pretty down and out."

"Yup. Boy, reliving this, hon, it ain't easy. So be it, I promised you my story. At the bottom of this destructive time, like I said I knew deep down that I had no choice but to clean up my act. So I came up with the idea of hiking the mountains, sort of my own Appalachian trail. Did I mention this to you already, can't remember? As an athlete, I'd found challenging physical demands in school had helped me overcome depression, angst. And it worked, hiking the hills, that is. Like others before me, I was saved by exercise and nature's glory. And I discovered more. It was this connection to the wild and nature's amazing world that helped me regain my belief in myself. And that I had a role that could be meaningful. And there it is. I got clean, found an important cause to steer my ship towards, and came to accept that life is a series of losses, some inexplicable – and we need to focus on today. You know the rest."

Gwen was moved by Adam's struggles, how could she not be. But she found that her stomach, her usual barometer for candor, was churning. *Is Adam's tale a little ajar, like a container lid that doesn't quite fit? Didn't he say before that the environment issue was Kila's?* Maybe she'd misheard. His story sure sounded sweet, like redemption in a romance novel. Was she being too hard? After a pause, Gwen gently asked Adam to finish and tell her about his life in Middleton.

"No problem, Gwennie, much easier tale. A year or so ago, after my park experience, and I'd decided Kila would want me to live life with gusto, I applied to law school. I got into the local one here. For a nice fee they didn't care I hadn't taken the LSATs – or even graduated college. Got credit for 'life experience'. Or, you know, they checked out my bank account. But the school's accredited and, to my surprise, it works really well for me, allows me to be a star and connect with my Profs. Don't need a big firm job afterwards. So, here I am. Making Kila proud. Making me whole. Giving my life focus, meaning. And, thanks to you, happy."

"Sounds like law school's worth the tuition. And your apartment, life in Middleton?"

"Not much to say. I live – when not here with you – in a small apartment in an older couple's house, the people who lend me their truck when I need it. Maybe not fancy, but it has a great view of the mountains, is an easy bike ride to school, and meets my student needs. As I said, I actually enjoy law school, the Socratic method – which isn't so different from the logic of computer programming. I haven't made friends I can talk to. They just seem like kids, you know. You are my best friend." Adam reached out his hand towards hers. "I do know one thing, Gwennie. I'm falling head over heels in love with you. And it's great and, you know, scary. I didn't know I could feel this way again. Sometimes when I wake up next to you, I can't believe my luck. There it is."

Gwen's heart thumped like the cartoon rabbit's lucky foot.

Adam stood up and stretched. He walked around the room, straightening up his law stuff. Opening the front door he inhaled the cold air. She joined him and pointed out the star low in the sky that she surmised was actually the planet Venus. "The Roman goddess of love, and victory. Maybe a good omen?" Gwen decided she preferred this twinkling ancient fortuneteller to her paper Chinese cookie fortunes, although, admittedly, the last one about the dark stranger had been pretty nice. Holding her loosely in his arms, Adam said, "Of course, with Venus on our side, victory will be ours."

After walking around the living room and checking out some of Gwen's souvenirs of life, Adam said, "Sweetie, it's your turn. As you said, I also don't know much about you."

Gwen could feel sweat already forming on her forehead. Was she ready to reveal all? "Should we have desert first? Or watch the news? There's also a documentary on TV about some Central American spider's mating dance…"

"Ha-ha. No way, funny lady. How about we stick to you."

Gwen sighed and then, feeling surprisingly tipsy, sat down. The full weight of what he was asking had struck her like a Mack truck. The room had become uncomfortably warm, in fact, roasting. Walking into the kitchen, she poured herself a glass of cold water. *Hey girl, time to trust the moment, to let go my goblins and phantom visitors, to face my past.* Cracking her knuckles behind her back while trying to appear blasé, she said, "If you want, Adam, it will be my turn."

From across the room he responded, "Yes, I do want. I want you which means knowing about your life, your story." His brown eyes focusing like darts on her, he continued, "Talk to me about you. Not the professional attorney, nor your practice. I've seen your CV. I want to know more about the fabulous woman I'm falling in love with. The one I've met who's sexy, kind, yeah complex, smart, funny, and maybe a little distant and aloof." Adam, after placing another log on the fire, sat down on the couch, legs crossed, and intently looked in Gwen's direction.

Gwen gathered her strength and thought back on her past. *Adam's done it, shared his secrets. Now, if I care about him and what we might have together, it's my turn. As do we all, I have a story. Haven't I learned anything from my family's experience?*

Not talking makes feelings fester like an infection. Silence can destroy even a loving relationship. I can do this.

"I think you know the basics – oops I think you said that." Gwen then repeated her biography: childhood in Queens, dysfunctional family after the Mark event, fancy law school, the Big Firm stress, Brian's death, the move to Middleton, joining Chris's firm to get away to a healthier practice, a healthier life.

"I don't regret my decision to throw in the big lawyer towel one iota. But, Chris got sick – a heart attack. He left for sunny Florida. I still miss him. I make enough money to get by, at least I did. I believe I'm helping my clients, fighting to make things right, that's important to me. Until recently, you can say I've generally enjoyed the small-town practice. Now, I don't think so much." Gwen stopped and played with her hair, trying to look inward yet knowing introspection was not her forte. "These past months I feel more the stress from my responsibility to my clients, of being in charge. I'm more troubled by the law's dysfunction, and find I'm exhausted from the long days." Massaging her tensed shoulders, she added, "I feel this weight pressing down on me, like it's attacking my spine and my spirit, my soul, my young lawyer idealism."

Softly Adam said, "Doesn't sound like the life of a happy esquire."

"Not so much these days, work wise anyhow. So, get your diploma soon for if I'm to continue I may need an associate, one who will accept low pay in exchange for other benefits."

Adam laughed. "Hang on for another year or so and we shall see. There you go, distracting me with your comic touch." With his arms folded tightly on his chest, he said, "So far feels like facile surface stuff, speaking about romance novels. Which I admit I don't read. But it won't do, Gwen. Yeah, I know – and generally knew-- what you call the basics. All nice and admirable. Part of why I'm falling for you. But, hey there, you weren't fully fuckin' honest, were you, with your neat little tale? You didn't even attempt to tell me about the 'behind the scenes' that helps explain the basics. I'm still left with the question, why's a smart, attractive woman like you not tied down with a good man? I think you like men." After a pause he added, "Unless maybe you like both?" Adam's eyebrows had risen in suspense.

"No, just men. Although I love puppies of any gender."

Adam rose and paced around the coffee table, his mouth grim. Suddenly, he stopped. With his arm raised towards her, he loudly exclaimed, "Damn it, Gwen. Yeah, cute --but more deflection."

Gwen sighed, knowing he was right. Silly, spurious attempts at humor would not hit the mark, or shield her from the self-awareness he was asking for. *Am I ready for it also?* She shrugged and came up with, "Okay, I'll try better." But, without thinking, she found herself in lecture mode. "You know, Adam, amazing ladies can function without being sewed to a man. A woman's fulfillment isn't tied to having a man in her life. Unmarried women survive all right without collapsing into a puddle of melting Jell-O. They don't lack self-worth, satisfaction, or value in society."

Adam gave a low chuckle. "Thanks for the feminist lecture. Yes, women are complete people in their own right. Now can you move on and help me understand better who you are, what you feel, what you dream of. That's the way forward for us. Gwennie Wilson, you're a smart, sassy, accomplished person who has a picture of a handsome man on her bookcase that she's never mentioned except briefly in passing. No discussion of relationship, commitment, a future family, children. And you've avoided all talk of *your* family, whom I know nothing about except that I see you are a good daughter to your ailing mother. I will like you, maybe love you, no matter what you tell me. Remember, I like baggage."

The hours passed -- although her watch said it was only minutes later. Could she trust Adam with her darkness? Was it her *Id* or is it *ego* voice that boomed in her ear, *'Yes, fool, yes. Way past time for you to face it and fess up. Grab this life saving rope already.'* Gwen folded and unfolded her fingers on her lap. When she couldn't fidget or fiddle any more, she bit the bullet and began.

"Of course, Adam, I want a life partner, preferably a sensitive, caring being having two legs, not four. I do want hordes of children – well two. But, for whatever reason, and throw in bad luck, timing, it hasn't happened."

Frowning, Adam said, "Weak beginning. Fate isn't the answer alone. I noticed this picture of two guys in ski clothes behind the fake plant. God, Gwennie, not even a real plant, one that you have to nurture and that may one day die. Riskless."

"Very observant Adam."

"So, will you tell me about them? I might be able to help. You know, I have gone through my own loss and stages of grief."

Gwen walked up to her bookcase, reached up and removed the framed photo of Brian and Artie. She moved her fingers softly over the picture, and then rested it on her lap. "It starts further back, Adam, in my childhood. You said I was a good daughter, but that's not always been the case."

"Gwennie, I can't imagine you hurting anyone intentionally, let alone those you love. What could have been so bad? Were you a drug gang member? A serial killer? Or more likely, did you disappoint your folks by not selling the most Girl Scout cookies?"

"Very funny."

"Sorry, and I mean it. Didn't intend to be flippant, just feeling anxious about all this honesty, as I'm sure are you."

Gwen sighed deeply. Pushing her mind back to a place she'd spent so much energy avoiding over the years, in halting painful sentences she revealed to Adam the family story of her brother Mark's death and its consequences. After a long pause, she added, "My parents never verbally blamed me. In fact, after their and my lives were coming apart, and I recall a stab at outside help, they sat me down when I was older and told me that my brother's accident -- they couldn't actually say 'Mark's death' – was tragic but no one's fault. They tried to comfort me with all the excuses I knew myself: I was too little for that responsibility, bad timing, he knew not to run into the road. Bottom line, they said, was that we can't control life. But I never in my heart of hearts believed they meant it. My mom surely also felt her own guilt that she placed Mark's care for just a little while in a child's hands – mine. In some ways, I think the guilt became all she had to keep her going."

Adam rose. "What, have *you* really forgiven *them* so easily? Where's *your* anger in all this? You remember 'anger'? It's one of the seven steps of grief. Anger. Where's your anger at this parent who made you, yourself only a child, be the responsible adult? Your mother had other choices – and she made the wrong one. Where's your anger at your brother who even at six years old knew better?"

"No, he was a kid."

"And we haven't even come to your father whom I gather gave in to his grief and couldn't find the strength to help his exhausted wife more, and then to hold your family together. What did he do, the man of the house? He gave up and left."

"He tried. How can I blame him for it being too much."

"He was a parent; he didn't do his job. Where's your anger at him?"

Rising from her chair, her cheeks red with emotion, Gwen hollered, "Shut up! No, Adam, you have it wrong." Hitting herself with her fists, Gwen shouted, "Me, Adam, it was *me*. I was the one in charge. I was the one who was selfish, thinking only of me. I knew better."

Shaking his head vehemently, Adam retorted, "No, Gwen, you were a child, a little girl playing with a friend. It was not your job to be a parent. You have the right to be angry at your parents, and your brother." He approached her, arms out as if to hold her."

But with her own arms pushing back fast and furious, with tears welling in her eyes, Gwen shouted, "Stop it! Stop forgiving me." Without thinking, she picked up a pillow and hurled it at him, but he ducked in time and moved out of harms way.

They both sat down to catch their breath and control their

emotions. After a few moments, Gwen said, her voice noticeably cracking, "Stop blaming my family. Please. They don't deserve it. They suffered so much thanks to my mistake."

Quickly Adam answered, "As did you, Gwen, and in part due to *their* actions. You have the right to be angry at them about that. Isn't it time to own it and move on?"

Gwen didn't move. But she thought about what Adam had said. Picking up the tossed pillow and placing it gently back on the couch, with a slight smile cracking her face, she mumbled, "I guess I know now why they call them 'throw pillows'."

Adam, a smile slowly spreading across his face, retorted, "Who knew you had such a good arm. Watch out Boston Red Sox."

The temperature in the room now having cooled, Gwen said softly, "Yes, Adam, you're right. It is time for me to deal with the anger issue. And maybe it is true that we all shared in Mark's death, and the harm we caused each other afterwards." After pausing again, she added, "But, do you know the irony that keeps bugging me? I spent my youth babysitting plenty for all the neighborhood kids – and not one of them got so much as a scratch on my watch. Still, I didn't protect my own baby brother. How do you figure?"

Adam shrugged. "Such is life's unfairness."

"Ha. As you've told me tonight. Is that why I'm so hung up on fairness? And maybe also it explains my need for control? Which the law establishes conveniently through lots of rules."

"How's that been going, controlling life's demands, stresses, with law?"

"Yeah, not so great at the moment."

"Do you think your decision to take the Sammy case is related to all this? You were taking a real risk; you didn't know this man, owe him anything, yet you took the case on contingency. After all, wasn't he the one responsible for ruining his life, gambling with his family's savings? Even risking his family's house and business, all to make a quick buck, drive a fancier car? Maybe you wanted to bring some control to what you saw as imbalance, to use the law to shift the scale so Sammy was made whole despite his mistakes and misplaced trust?"

"Maybe I listened a little to my empathy gene, I'll admit. And belief in the fair application of the rules."

Grabbing Gwen's hands for a moment, Adam continued, "Because, honey, no matter how we constrict our life to fit within the lines, we can't control everything." Pacing back and forth in front of the coffee table, Adam added, "You told me that Brian died in a ski accident. Did you know that in our country *each year* some 40 skiers die from ski accidents, many by hitting trees? And as to Mark, 12,000 children annually are killed, the leading cause being parents who back up and run over them. I know this because I looked it up. Yes, we can opt to live in a bubble, like that boy with a weak immune system. Or we can live in the real world. Then we face the risk of making mistakes, for we are only human, and hoping that luck and fate protect us from the messiness brought about by our lives."

Gwen murmured, 'We are human, we make mistakes.' She sat down on the couch, too exhausted to even move the throw pillows out of her way. "So, counselor, how do we learn to forgive ourselves?"

"Accept you meant well and life can be cruel no matter how good a person we are. Say to yourself, as you just did, but mean it this time, 'I am human – so I make mistakes." Then add, 'But I am a good person – so I will forgive me.'"

Gwen twisted in her seat and thought about what Adam had said. Sure, she'd probably read the same message in those books on grief. Somehow, however, tonight, accepting forgiveness sounded right, advice she could take to heart.

"Thanks, Adam, this has I think been helpful."

"Ha. Hey, Gwen, dearest, sorry but we're not done. You haven't yet old me about Brian. He's the guy in both pictures, right? I know he died in an accident and his death broke your heart.

Is there more you can share? As I did about Kila."

Gwen got up, put Brian and Artie's picture back on the bookcase, but this time in front of the fake plant, and walked around the room, picking up the cups left in the living room and depositing them in the kitchen sink. When she had no more obvious distractions available, she sat down in the rocking chair, rocking back and forth a few times. Staring at Brian's picture she replied to Adam, "You're right, time to disclose all."

To her surprise she found herself back in New York City, a young career woman with a fantastic future awaiting her, before tragedy struck. "I was working too many hours at the firm and had no social life. So my brother Artie invited me up to his friend's weekend house in Hudson, about an hour and a half North of the City. I took the early Saturday express train from Penn Station to Hudson. I expected to be communing with nature from Adirondack chairs so I was casually dressed, my hair up in a ponytail, sneakers – you know the look – and I carried an old backpack from college days. Sitting across from me in the car was this nerdy but not bad looking guy doing the *Times* crossword. He was writing, then erasing his answers. So I offered to help. We spent the trip trying to finish the puzzle. I actually wasn't much help – he clearly was smart and sharp. I remember we laughed a lot. When the train pulled into Hudson we politely exchanged phone numbers. I never expected to hear from him again."

Gwen got up and poured, then sipped, some of the remaining wine. "To make it short, Brian and I met up in the City, we discovered lots of common interests, we went to out-of-the way museums, ran in the park, checked out and rated the neighborhood bagel stores, well, just had a great time. And I fell in love. Head over heals as they say. For the first time in too many years I felt wanted, prized, complete. He moved in with me and after a few months we were engaged. He bought me a Woolworth's ring, went down on his knees before the ape house at the zoo, and we celebrated our togetherness, and laughed. We were both working,

Brian was a guru at a non-profit, so we did dinners out on week-days and on week- ends museums, cocktails with friends, even marches for good causes."

Adam nodded. "Sounds good. Sounds healthy. What happened?"

"You know about the ski trip and Brian's accident. What you don't know is that I was the one pushing the trip, making arrangements for us and Artie, even though my brother said skiing was risky that late in the season, could be icy. I didn't listen as I wanted badly to get away from work, and, ever practical, the rate was cheap. At the last minute, my luck, I got an assignment from a senior partner, so I ended up having to work. We'd paid for the tickets so I decided it made sense for Brian and Artie to go without me. Brian wanted to pass, said he should be there to make me a nice dinner after my working all day, but, pushy person that I am, when I'd made up my mind, I insisted. He should have fun and spend time with Artie, I told myself, feeling generous of spirit. I recall yelling at him that if he didn't go he wasn't being nice to my brother who'd scraped together the plane money. And didn't he want to try out the new skis I'd saved up for and given him for the holidays? Talk about a guilt trip.... I guess literally. Lovingly, Brian went."

"Go on," Adam said. "You had a special relationship, one maybe I'm a little jealous of, if I'm truthful."

Gwen pushed her shoulders back, blew her nose, wiped her teary eyes, then with a second wave of determination, she continued. "Brian was a good skier. Despite maybe looking nerdy, he actually was quite a graceful man. According to Artie on their last skiing day Brian went down the Black Diamond trail, my brother behind, for the last run of the day. The afternoon sun had melted the snow and then the wind and cold air had made it granular and icy, and they were contending with late-afternoon shadows across the trail. Artie thinks also the new skis were maybe still a little stiff. Whatever, not great decision, Artie admits. Brian skied ahead. Around a sharp turn he lost control, his skis skidding on the ice. Artie saw him veer right, be unable to stay on the trail, skid over the plastic barrier, and stop only when his chest hit head on a big fir tree.”

Gwen stopped, the image flashing in her head. She put her hands over her eyes but the devastating picture of Brian dead in the snow wouldn't leave.

Adam silently gave her time to recover and finish her tale.

In a quiet flat voice, almost whispering, Gwen ended her story.

“I flew out to be with them. Brian was in the hospital for thirty-four days and six hours before they turned off the machine. He never regained consciousness. And Artie, who'd been there and saw it all and spent helpless hours at the hospital with me, never forgave me. And maybe himself for not saying ‘no’ to Brian's eagerness to do one more run. And, like you and Kila, I didn't have a chance to say goodbye.”

Adam handed Gwen a Kleenex and she wiped her eyes. “To complete my sad story, after I lost Brian I stopped functioning. All went downhill, my own Black Diamond, and I had my self-punishing crash, some of which I've mentioned. Well, I took time off from work on not great terms, holed up in my closet of an apartment, watched soap operas in bed and became dysfunctional – just like my mother had done. I became her.”

“Unlike Sylvia, you have a strong force for life, Gwen.”

“You think? Maybe you're right. I held on. When spring arrived, I put my head out my window, felt the sun's warmth on my skin, and decided to see the blue sky again. That's how I ended up here: a thirty-something single, momentarily facing impoverishment, emotionally damaged, but generally I think, you know, surviving, working with some success I hope on finding a place for myself that is comfortable and fulfilling. That's enough I think.”

“Once again, how have you dealt with the anger issue?”

“Mostly, until tonight, not admitting it's there, except for my anger at myself. But in the middle of many nights I've asked myself, why did Brian not protect himself better? He knew the dangers. Hell, even I know most ski accidents happen on the last run of the day, and as you've told me skiing into the woods and hitting a tree is a major cause of such injuries. Why didn't Brian, you see, place more importance on his responsibility to me, why didn't I have priority over the thrills of one final run? And Artie.... I put Brian in his care. And he didn't step in and say no. He didn't do his job. Sound familiar? But Artie wasn't almost eleven like I was. And yes, damn it, they were both human and humans make mistakes."

"All good," said Adam.

"And so I've learned tonight that you and me, we had similar paths dealing with our grief. I, like you, 'floundered' and did really stupid self-destructive things. I dated the wrong kind of guys, trying to prove I was unworthy of real meaningful love I guess. When not watching old televisions reruns, I'd wander the City's sketchy bars at night, willing to be picked up by strange scruffy guys. I remember one time I met this handsome super friendly waiter while vacationing in the Caribbean. He was attentive and charming and a gambler who talked that lovely lilting Island talk. Told me how amazing I was. I was filled with self-loathing and gobbled it up. I actually invited him to live with me in New York and paid his expenses. After two weeks where he mostly spent his time emptying my bank account, I sent him packing, along with lots of travel money. Crazy. But I couldn't help myself, like an addiction to shame."

"Then what?"

Gwen paused and rubbed her neck muscles. "At the rational level I try to forgive myself, acknowledge we all do stupid things and that's the nature of life, at least on this planet. And I have made progress."

"All good," said Adam.

Gwen said into the living room space, "As you said, hon, life's a series of losses. You said losing Kila was like having a dark shadow that blots out the sun. Well that's also how I felt. And at times, unexpectedly, I still do. The pain from losing him, my better half, lingers. It's inside me yet, ready to erupt when I'm least prepared." With her eyes closed, she said softly, "I think you understand." She heard Adam speak into her ear as his arm reached out, "Shit, yes, I do. But you know I've found it gets less heavy."

Staring through the picture window at the dark shadows thrown down by the distant mountains and the moon, Gwen muttered, "And there it is." Her face twisted to him now, with shoulders slouched, she added, "See, Adam, in my own way I've hurt all the men I cared about in my life. I helped cause my dad to flee, harmed Artie, killed Mark, and then virtually killed Brian, even from almost 2,000 miles away. And so... how can I trust myself? All the males in my life, the people I've given my heart to, have left me. I worry in the back of my mind that I am dangerous, like the Black Widow."

Adam rose suddenly with such force he almost knocked her wine glass off the side table. "*Excuse me?* That, my dear, is total crap. Surely you know that? As we've both said for the past hour and years, mistakes happen – by all of us. But that's not cause for a life sentence of penance. Loss, it's the nature of the universe. Runs from birth to death. Everything becomes eventually mass to be recycled as stardust. You and I, we need to find the courage and fortitude to live in the now. *Carpe Diem* my darling Gwen. At least that's what I've learned. And that we are still good people, even if some of our choices may have had sad consequences."

Gwen got up and smiled, surprised to feel as if a great weight had been pushed off her shoulders and the darkness around the edge of her distant vision seemed less bleak. She blew her nose and felt even better. "Or so the books say, for as you can imagine I've read them all. Gone through my seven stages of grief. Am working on the 'forgiving' part. Do you realize that the word implies to give, like a gift to oneself? I'm learning how to accept that gift, to accept the painful feelings, to try to learn from them, and to cherish that, well, I'm not a lowly amoeba."

Adam approached Gwen and wrapped her in his arms. "Hey, babe, I understand even amoebas, at least in their own primitive way, embrace."

"One more concern, Adam, before we call it a night. We've both had special loves. Can we love again, do you think?"

"You bet. Of this I'm certain. As we go through life, I think that as adults we have many loves. The first fresh love of the teenager, the love when starting a family and raising children, the love seniors have for each other as their abilities diminish and they face a 'nearing' the end date. If we're lucky we can experience these with one person. But, with our divorce rate being what it is, it would surely be a downer if all were over before we moved through our stages of life."

"That's comforting, I guess," said Gwen as she rose and stretched out, finding thankfully that she could still touch her toes. "Here's to my Uncle Howard. His wife died after they were married and inseparable for some 50 years, then he met widowed Marcia and they had a second love. Thankfully, as he lived to be 102."

"Gosh, I hope I don't have to wait some 50 years for our love to blossom," said Adam as he reached for her hand.

CHAPTER TWENTY-SEVEN

Notch. N-O-T-C-H. Gwen wasn't sure she'd known the word before moving to Middleton. Now Gwen was peeking up at the towering granite rising above the two-lane road in Notch State Park. Slowing down, she scanned the top rocks out of habit for a view of the craggy Old Man in the Mountain standing as sentry to the park. But for the past year all that remained of the strong granite features were the jagged rocks of a jutting chin, thanks to the force of gravity, and a few missing screws. With Adam by her side, she drove slowly past all that remained of his splendor, a painted sign along the road bearing the famous profile. Life is about moving on after loss, she mused, and forgiving ourselves for mistakes that can't be taken back, like a famous profile.

"Adam, look out your window and up. That's where the Old Man used to be."

Adam stretched his neck. "I see it. Shit, that's some cliff. Will his fall hurt the tourist business?"

"Well, there's still the Flume, another natural wonder. And other attractions in the area. We just passed the exit to the Robert Frost Museum, the poet's home for many summers. Now a working museum, can you believe, for poets. Nice views. Hikers come to walk the Appalachian Trail, an experience I guess like your walk in the wild. In summer there's Profile Lake and a sandy beach. In winter there's good skiing. And you can always pan for gold in caves at one of the tourist places."

"Nature, poetry, nah, but gold. Now you're talking. Okay, Gwen, time for me to know. What is a notch?"

"Not learned in geology are you? Yeah, me neither. As you can see, we're going through a narrow pass between mountains, created by Mother Nature, not dynamite. But I think, you know, in New Hampshire it's more than geological splendor. There are three such rock features I think in the state, but Franconia Notch is the one I call the notch. It acts in a way like a border, separating the prosperous growing southern part of the state from the scenic, mostly wooded, certainly less affluent, and rural area to the north, that itself stretches up to Canada."

Gwen looked up again at the granite cliffs. "I'd say, to over generalize maybe, folks up North, like the Old Man, can be more craggy, self-reliant, individualists. You know the kind, people who want to do things their way without all those government regulations. Like their license plates state, they're prepared to 'live free or die'. I'd also say they are likely to be more generous, open-minded, to practice old-fashioned neighborliness. Also, they want directness, no pretentions. And, well, they live close to the land – farmers trying to eek out a living in rocky soil, and, yes, hunters but mostly respectful of nature."

"You know," Adam smiled while looking at the towering granite, "this really is impressive. Maybe not the Rockies, but it will do for majestic."

Gwen nodded, without saying more.

Once out of the park and back at 60 mph speed, Gwen drove the half hour to Plymouth, home of one of the state university's campuses, to meet with Anna Patman, finalize the Perez document exchange, and agree on uncontested hearing exhibits. It seemed that while Stanley, Howe had hired a New York attorney, Day, to run the hearing, they'd also kept on board Stearns, Foster – and its associate Anna – to carry on the mundane work. She'd brought Adam along ostensibly to make sure the documents were properly marked. And, oh yeah, so they could have time together out of the office.

Getting off the highway, Gwen turned left off the exit and drove to the Common Skier, a popular upscale Inn and restaurant. Inside the Inn they waited for Anna in an area that offered a roaring fire – despite the fact that it was mid-summer and the snow had long since melted, as well as wood puzzles and board games made by local crafters. Gwen and Adam competitively explored their 'play' options while waiting.

As Gwen was about to knock down Adam's wood brick tower, Anna bounced in, out of breath. "Hi Gwen, sorry I'm late." Gwen noticed she was decked out in golf clothes. "Hope you don't mind my informal attire but I'm playing golf with a partner after our meeting and won't have time to change. There's a nice mountain course nearby. Pausing, she noticed Adam had come along for the ride. Standing up straighter, maybe with chest out just a little, or so Gwen thought, Anna smiled at him as she added, sweetly, "How nice Adam could join us." Adam smiled back, but Gwen noticed that his dimples were hardly visible.

Over their lunch of burgers topped with Vermont cheddar and the fixings, Gwen and Anna argued over missing documents, the terms of a confidentiality agreement, and procedural issues like the timing of final production and where paralegals would sit. Adam watched silently as the two women bickered, then bit into their hamburgers, then bickered some more. Finally, Gwen signed some papers, Anna rose, then handed Gwen an armful of documents that Gwen loaded with Adam's help into her backpack.

"Glad we could get this done quickly," said Anna. "I'll put together in binders the exhibits we've agreed to be admitted into the record and have copies made for the Panel members and lawyers, and will send you a copy of course. That should expedite the hearing. Am I missing anything, Gwen?"

"Well Anna, you still owe me many of the documents on the list I gave you today, including the remaining monthly client statements. To summarize what you've promised today: one, you'd get these to me by early next week, and that they'll be included in the hearing notebooks, unless I say otherwise; two, no additional documents will be included in the binders without my prior approval; and three, any disputed records will be included in a separate binder with similar copies for all. I have your word on that, right?"

Nodding, Anna said, "I see no problem, but as I've explained too many times to mention, the final word is with my boss, Bradford, and I guess now Josiah as well."

"Yes, I was wondering about that. Why the change?"

"No clue at my level. I do know, between us, that Bradford's pretty pissed. Not only because of the impression of no confidence it may give, but it represents lost income." She then thrust the bag with the duplicate files over her shoulder and got up to leave.

As Gwen and Adam had planned on the drive down, Adam momentarily stood up to block Anna's exit, while Gwen casually asked, "Before you go, Anna, it's maybe our last chance to discuss resolving this case and avoiding the hearing costs. So what gives? My client's clearly made a colorable legal case."

"Sorry, Gwen, but I was told Stanley, Howe's not interested, something about they won't 'roll over for this guy'. For some reason they really don't like Mr. Perez."

"So it seems. You know, he's a picture of the American dream, before, that is, he met Murphy. Immigrant made good, night school, nice family, worked hard. Well, you know that from my pleadings."

"I gather there's more 'there'. Looking at Adam, Anna added, "By the way, Adam, if you need any job references, career advice, whatever, here's my card." Anna held it out for him. "Just give me a call. Maybe I can connect you with some of my friends at other large firms. I think you'd be attractive to their hiring committees." Giving Adam a lingering grin, Anna pushed against him as she left for her golf game.

Buckled up and backing out of the parking lot, Gwen asked Adam, "What are you thinking about the case?"

Pursing his lips, Adam ventured, "I think we're up against the wall. Something's up their tight ass that they're not saying." Squirming in his seat, Adam gazed out the window, and then said, "You know, Gwen, I had some misgivings about your client, I think I mentioned that, and maybe I still do. But if you look at the big picture, as you said, he's presented a facially sound claim and you have experts to support them. I don't know much about settling cases, but I do know about cost-benefit decisions in business, and this just doesn't seem to be a case you litigate."

Gwen laughed. "Maybe, Mary is right, the company's goal is less sinister, like extending the hearing until the corporate honchos can justify a trip up North during the beautiful summer season. And I'm dumbfounded that they're bringing in a top litigator at this stage of the case. A teeny bit worrisome, you think?" Gwen could feel the bile start rising up her esophagus tube or whatever part of her anatomy was meant for such conditions. If she thought she was in over her head before, seems like now she was, like the Old Man before his great fall, on precarious turf. *Am I also missing some screws?* But, on the positive side, discovery was moving forward, finally, and the hearing was only a few weeks away.

CHAPTER TWENTY-EIGHT

One day to lift off, but she had no client – again!

Damn it! It was late afternoon on Monday, August 18th, the day before the arbitration hearing was to begin, and she had been unable to reach Sammy! He was supposed to have contacted her as soon as he got off the plane this morning from the Dominican Republic, but so far, no word. *What should I do, he's going to be my first witness?*

Gwen paced up and down the fake Persian rug in her office, her head beginning to throb, worried beyond measure. This was what she'd feared at her darkest moments – a contingency case with – poof – a disappearing client. She was surprised as all these weeks Sammy had dutifully kept in contact with her from the Island. Gwen understood Sammy was scared. And the long trip made it that much harder to face the hearing. Sure, she became a little concerned when he'd notified her he couldn't get back to the States earlier to prepare for the hearing than on Sunday, August 17th, due to unspecified 'family reasons.' Then Sammy had changed his arrival time to this morning, although Gwen had told him that was cutting it too close. But he'd given her his word that he'd be there on the "soul of the Blessed Angel of Mercy and all the Saints in heaven," so Gwen hadn't pressed. *Was that a mistake? Should I have had him swear over his rosary beads as well?*

She went over in her mind her scenario for the hearing and her options now. Could she put on a case without a fact witness? Did she have anyone else to step in and testify about the events? While Martha and Linda would be able to address the legal issues, they couldn't effectively testify in a factual vacuum. She was certain Olanda would be a definite no to helping as a filler. Plus there was the problem that Gwen had no idea what she'd say on the stand.

UGH!

As Gwen was ready to send Adam out to visit Sammy's cousin

in Dortman to scout the scene for her missing client, at 5:20 p.m. her phone rang. Scowling, Gwen picked it up at her desk. She heard a faint voice.

"Attorney, this Sammy."

Gwen let out a long slow sigh. She didn't know if she were more angry or grateful to hear his voice. But she did know she was definitely not a happy camper.

"Sammy, where the hell are you?"

"In Syracuse."

"What? Say that again. Where?" Her voice rose in octave and volume.

"What the hell, Sammy, is going on?"

"Plane to Boston, it land in Syracuse."

Gwen paced the floor, the phone in her hand.

"Why in the world are you in Syracuse, Sammy? Was there a problem with the plane?"

"My plane make special landing. No accident, it 'cause of me it land in Syracuse."

"Sammy, I don't understand. You told me your flight was direct to Boston. And your plane was to land this morning."

"It was."

Gwen paused, rubbing her temples to assuage the sudden pounding in her head. "I don't understand, if no plane trouble, what? Is there bad weather on the Island – or in Syracuse, so it was delayed? Sammy, you remember I told you to return earlier, just to avoid such problems. You can't rely on the airlines these days to follow their schedules. And why didn't you take a direct flight?"

"Yes. I took direct. But, see...."

A long silence followed. Gwen feared Sammy had hung up. "Sammy, you there?"

"Yes, Attorney," he said so softly she had to press the earpiece against her ear. Sammy continued, still sounding as if he were on the other side of the globe. "See, it my fault. I so nervous I got sick on plane."

"What? Do you have the flu or something?"

"No, I get sick, sick from worry. I no can breathe. Chest hurt. Don't be angry. All on plane, they angry at me."

Gwen inhaled slowly and tried to speak without an edge. "Sammy, did you call the flight attendants?"

"Yes."

"Then?"

Gwen listened intently as Sammy told a story she would not have

believed if she heard it on the nightly news. It appears that, despite the aid of a doctor who happened to be traveling on Sammy's flight, okay, an obstetrician, the captain determined it was necessary to make an emergency landing so Sammy could get medical help for his chest pain and breathing difficulty. The nearest airport available turned out to be Syracuse and that's where Sammy and all the passengers and crew set down unexpectedly. And where after a brief stop all but Sammy went on to their Boston destination.

At the Syracuse airport Sammy was taken to the health center where a doctor administered one of those little white pills and within an hour Sammy was feeling better. The airline put Sammy up for the night at a nearby motel, as the last flight to Boston had already left. They then insisted he stay to tomorrow to make sure he'd be all right to fly – or, speculated Gwen, wouldn't impact another flight and cost the airline thousands of dollars. Thus, Sammy's call from his motel room.

"Attorney, Doctor here he say I good to fly tomorrow to Boston. Company it tell me no can fly their plane again, never. Sorry. I so upset. It hard for me to talk. Company it make plan. Now I fly to Boston tomorrow afternoon, not in morning. So no arrive Dortman until late evening. I be there no let you down."

"Yes, I understand." Gwen knew she had been forewarned from her first introduction to Sammy when he had a panic attack in her office from stress. How would he possibly perform when giving testimony at the hearing, a situation where his stress might be even greater? Should she arrange to have a doctor on call at the hearing? Should she bring some little white pills for Sammy – and for herself? Gwen swiveled back and forth in her chair, trying to get her bearings. What to do? Warm and clammy, her body tense and tight as if encircled by a very large knee brace, Gwen stood up and paced

in front of the cooling breeze from her window air conditioner, well, actually more like a minor gust.

"Listen to me, Sammy. Do you hear me?"

"Yes, I here."

"Sammy, you need to get on that plane tomorrow. Can you do that? Should I arrange, I don't know, for some limo to drive you from Syracuse?"

"No. I take pill as Doctor say tomorrow and I be good to fly. They assign person to help me get to plane. You see, I be there."

Gwen noticed that her voice finally sounded firmer. "All right Sammy. Let me think." She doodled with her red 'edit' pen, drawing wolves with concentric red eyes and large canines. Her plan was for Sammy to tell the facts of his case, hopefully get some sympathy from the Panel, and then Martha and Linda were to swoop in and, with the facts in the record, they'd give their expert opinions to establish his legal claims. Speaking into the phone, Gwen advised Sammy of the newly revised plan.

"All's not lost, Sammy. We'll still go ahead with the hearing. I'll call our experts tomorrow instead of you to testify. We'll just work a little backwards. But you get here tomorrow, you hear?"

Before hanging up, Gwen made arrangements to meet Sammy the following evening in Dortman so they could review the day's happening and prepare his testimony. And maybe she could calm him down. She then telephoned Martha and Linda about the change of plans – which she was certain they would not be happy about. That chore done, sweating despite the air conditioner blowing on high, she collected her file for tomorrow and called Adam. She warned him to make sure there was cold beer in the refrigerator, and maybe an Adam shoulder massage as well. Then again, her entire body-- not just her shoulders — felt like it had gone nine rounds with the great Ali.

Have I averted a crisis? She shook her head, hoping that the alteration in presenting her case would work out after all. It was manageable, maybe. Unless the Panel took the position that her experts couldn't testify as there'd been no record made of the facts on which they were basing their opinions – the usual procedure in trials, and then, well it would likely be over. Linda and Martha had made it clear they were not available the following day.

Gwen shivered, acknowledging that this was definitely not an auspicious start to the long-awaited arbitration hearing. Way off her radar, in fact maybe more so than when Sammy's plane found itself way off its own radar destination thanks to its unexpected and unscheduled stop at the Syracuse airport.

CHAPTER TWENTY-NINE

Opening night on Broadway. The Sammy show was about to begin.

Wednesday, August 19, 2003, had arrived at last. The Perez v. Stanley, Howe *et al.* arbitration hearing was set to start. After well over a year of preliminary work, and the ups and downs of litigation where she'd prepare for the hearing – only to have it repeatedly delayed, the Perez case was in the batter's box. Would she get through this first day? Gwen wasn't sure. Despite leaving her house at 7:30 a.m., thanks to traffic she hadn't arrived at the hearing room in Manchester until almost 9:40 for the scheduled 10 a.m. start time, her stomach already churning up anxiety. Martha and Linda were to arrive later at 11:00 a.m., Gwen having anticipated that the Panel would be busy with administrative matters until then. Was she cutting it too close? Her experts were so frustrated by the NASD's process, she was trying to impose on their overfilled lives as little as necessary. As it is, thanks to their busy schedule they were only able to commit to being present today. Adam, who had offered to skip his classes to help out, wasn't to assist until Sammy's arrival the following day, and Mary had a long-arranged family wedding obligation that was priority. So she was starting this ride solo, not even a co-pilot. Just like her hero, Amelia Earhart on her first brave and pioneer flight, not, Gwen hoped, like the one where her plane became lost, disappearing over the Pacific Ocean.

Off the empty elevator and down the hall into the conference room at yet another law firm, Gwen pulled her overstuffed briefcase on wheels up to a chair at the end of the large oval table and sat down, sweating already from the exertion of lugging all those papers around. She already missed her bagman, Adam. To her surprise she was the only person present. Yawning, she already felt tired, thanks to Sammy's unexpected non-appearance she'd worked late into the night reviewing her direct exam notes and exhibits for Martha and Linda. Inserting a piece of caffeine loaded Buzz gum into her mouth, she waited for that artificial kick of energy. Great gum, a two for one – helps keep her eyes open and also fosters salivation when nervous. Despite chewing mightily, her world was beginning to sway. *Had the cleaning crew removed the room's oxygen?* Gwen inhaled deeply, feeling as if she were waiting at the dentist's for a root canal. *Lighten up, Gwennie. Do your best and stick it to these creeps who let greed ruin a man's life. Even if you don't win, at least you've stood up for fairness and right – which counts for something.*

Still, she felt as nervous as when she'd taken her bar exam after law school graduation. She expected being jittery – for this was her first NASD arbitration and she wasn't sure exactly what the rules were in reality. There was also the fact she'd be outlawyered by experienced Esquires who were super litigators. At her Big City firm she'd been 'the Anna', the senior associate that handled pre-trial matters; the firm saved actual court time for its 'high hourly rate' partners. Since being in private practice, sure she'd had her share of small trial cases, but almost always they settled before the hearing, albeit sometimes on the courthouse steps. Sadly, Gwen thought, there were no steps at this building to offer such a reprieve. So Gwen gave herself a team talk. *Gwennie, once the hearing starts, you'll be okay. Hell, even the great Lawrence Olivier threw up before each performance, and yet he managed to act pretty well. Courage, remember Amelia.*

Fifteen more minutes passed. Gwen remained the only person in the room. Had she gotten the time wrong? Was she in the middle of a lawyer's nightmare, arriving at court only to find out that the trial had happened yesterday – or been delayed again. She busied herself by laying out her papers in neat piles on the table. She placed her yellow legal pad and purloined Mont Blank pen in the ready position. And waited. Her watch's hands moved, yet no one entered. Gwen, with no more tasks to do, looked around to check out the conference room.

It was palatial. Green leather chairs lined the lengthy mahogany table. Next to the erected dais for the three Panel members at the front of the table was a small table for the stenographer who would record the hearing and mark the Exhibits. Both were covered in gold colored linen. Gwen suspected they were also used as tablecloths at corporate luncheons. *There I go again, making jokes, using humor to lessen my anxiety. Gwennie, this is serious, we're dealing with truth and justice.* But she knew she'd resort to humor again to help deal with the tension.

What else about the room? It was ornate, fancy moldings, plush green carpet, matching brocade curtains that framed the ten-foot-tall windows. Kept out the sunny blue-sky world outside. Dangling above the conference table were four large crystal chandeliers. Sets of old law books, impressive in their dark leather bindings, filled the bookcases lining three walls. Gwen loved the stuffy smell of the written law, almost like cherry tobacco – imposing, powerful, and steeped in tradition and history. Hanging were paintings of, surprise, English hunting scenes, the hounds and riders eagerly chasing over hill and dale the desperately fleeing vixen. She wondered what it was with these big law firms and their affinity for fox hunts. All in all, the room had the air of a private men's club soaked in heritage, power, 'old' money. A place where the masters of industry and Partners Committee read their newspapers or balance sheets after lunch before nodding off – and women were not permitted. Tough, she whispered to these ghosts of Christmas past. A new day has dawned – fox hunting is supposedly banned in England, and women can now participate in this lawyering game.

The grandfather clock struck 10 a.m. The chimes of Pachelbel's Canon rang out in the room, empty but for Gwen. Gwen reviewed again her client's written Statement of Claim and her outline for today's testimony. At last she heard a squeak as the door to the hallway opened.

A short, handsome man holding a well-used leather briefcase, dressed with flair in a light beige linen suit with bright blue handkerchief and matching silk tie, walked in and approached her chair. Gwen noticed he wore his Harvard Law class ring. *Should I have worn my Phi Beta Kappa pendant –or maybe my SDD sorority pin?* A black lawyer, Gwen assumed this must be Day, as to her knowledge there were maybe only a handful of members of the N.H. Bar who were 'persons of color'. Like much of New England, her state had remained overwhelmingly racially white. The message she took away was that this was a man who managed to rise through the WASP ranks of the big law firm thanks to his top-notch talent and hard work. Was Stanley, Howe's selection of Day, nevertheless, intended to neutralize any insinuation of racial bias by the company?

Hand extended, the man said, "Good morning, you must be Attorney Wilson?" His voice, Gwen noticed, was pleasantly deep and musical.

"Yes," Gwen nodded. She shook his hand, and almost lost the use of her favorite middle fingers – fortunately absent jewelry – to his crushing grip.

Smiling, the man said in a friendly manner, "Seems like we'll be getting a late start today. Pardon me, forgot to introduce myself. I'm Josiah, Josiah Day. Stanley, Howe has asked my firm to handle this arbitration hearing on their behalf. I'm assisting their inside counsel whom I believe you've worked with, Bill Wadford."

Day handed Gwen his business card and then seated himself across the wide table from her. Gwen decided not to offer him one of her business cards in exchange, as displayed on its back was a pretty picture of the Notch and cascading waterfalls. She thought that, perhaps, it didn't convey the hard-nosed shark lawyer image appropriate for Complainant's Counsel. She wrote a note to herself to order more boring cards.

Gwen sat some more on her side of the table and waited. Quietly chewing her gum she doodled on her legal pad, looking suitably at work. She almost started pulling on her knuckles to calm herself, but they hurt too much from Day's handshake. Gwen again reviewed her opening remarks, a culmination of many hours of work during the past week. Over the next twenty minutes the room slowly filled up, each new entry walking over and politely— okay, some not so politely – introducing himself to her. It felt like being on a receiving line at a Bar Association dinner without the pre-dinner happy hour. Before long, sitting on the other side of the table – according to her notes – were: Day — a senior partner at a New York City firm that she knew had branch offices around the world including China; Day's associate Donald Moss; the brokerage firm's inside senior counsel, George Donovan and his help-mate, Bill Wadford; David Gordon, Wadford's junior associate; and bringing up the rear was Martin Mandel who represented Sammy's broker, Lawrence Murphy.

Murphy himself was present. Gwen studied him carefully as this was her first time she'd seen him in person. *What did this force of evil look like? Can one see evil?* Murphy she decided looked like some of the more senior finance guys at the car dealership where she'd bought her Prius. He had a large frame and chiseled features that had slouched over the years into puffiness. He wore a bulky college ring on chubby fingers, open plaid shirt, and tried a comb-over to cover up his receding blond hairline. Gwen surmised he'd once been a 'big man on campus,' maybe football player or frat President, but whose glory days were well behind him. He was leaning back in his chair and laughing over something with his lawyer Mandel. *Not too worried, huh? Just wait until we put in our case, Larry.*

More people arrived. Gwen added to her count another lawyer who represented Murphy's Supervisor along with his client. Three additional people sat down on Respondents' side, later identified as expert witnesses. Finally, sitting in fold-up chairs behind this row of the 'big league' players was the 'minor league' team comprising two young lawyers in suits, whom Gwen assumed were first or second year associates, and three paralegals armed with numerous brown file folders. Missing, Gwen noticed, were Anna and her boss Bradford Foster whose law firm, as Anna had said, hadn't been hired to attend the actual litigation of the case. In all, Gwen counted seventeen male 'suits' in opposition. At least Sammy was doing his fair share to support the legal profession.

Except, that is, for her.

It hit Gwen then like an unseen foul ball at Fenway landing in the row where she was sitting -- she was the only woman in the room. Not only was she taking on an all-male baseball team, she was doing it as the lone female. Admittedly, she had been a sort of star on her high school softball team -- she could throw the ball to first base without it bouncing. But she doubted that there'd be any softball pitching at this star-studded hearing. While she'd often been the first member of her gender at legal events, she still wished that science had found some way to bottle testosterone, just to make the playing field a little more level should she need some extra aggressive confidence.

It was almost 11 a.m. and no sign of the Panel -- which would make the male count total twenty. Doodling some more along the edge of her legal pad, Gwen closed her eyes and focused on remaining calm, and on salivating so she could talk when called upon. As she'd already chewed and disposed of her pieces of Buzz, she poured herself a large glass of water from the pitcher on the table near her seat and drank. Then she gave herself another pep talk, like she'd done she now recalled when it was her turn to bat in high school.

Gwennie, you've been the only woman before in many situations. No big deal. You go girl and make them work for their money. After all, you're as smart as them or in the same ballpark, you probably lead with three state bar admissions, you have a chest they can only envy, along with archery and canoeing camp awards, and you grew up in Queens, home of the chutzpah. And, as the Old Testament might say, Hear ye Hear ye, all you so-called winners, here sits Gwen, kin to David, who with her legal brilliance and wit will shoot the stone that brings down the greedy Goliaths — so that virtue and justice shall reign throughout the land.

The clock ticked by, minute by minute, for another twenty spaces. The suits were conversing avidly amongst themselves and on the room's four telephones. It appeared that those new-fangled mobile phones were unable to work thanks to lack of adequate reception. Gwen wondered if she should go check on Martha and Linda, but worried she might then be late should the hearing start. Gwen heard a squeak. The conference room door opened. The noise ceased. All eyes watched as three men entered, walked down the aisle, and sat at the Panel's table. A frisson of cold air appeared to sweep across the room, or at least on Gwen's side.

Crossing her arms in front of her, Gwen sat back and studied the new entrants. She presumed that the tall thin-haired man, looking like an academic in his metal glasses, except for the fact that he was wearing a custom-tailored suit, was the Panel's lawyer and Chair, Jay Sawyer. Sitting to his left was a much older man sporting a gray goatee. He was dressed in a madras short-sleeve sport shirt worn under a bulky yellow sweater, despite the fact that it was August. The sweater was adorned with an insignia that appeared to be a golfer swinging a club in front of a palm tree. Gwen assumed that the wearer had a tee time later that afternoon. The third Panel member sported a thin mustache below a noticeable nose, balding head, and wrinkled dark suit with bowtie. He appeared to be what he was – a numbers driven accountant. Trailing behind the men was a short, stodgy, older woman. Her red reading glasses, hanging on a cord around her neck, jumped up and down on her bosom as she entered. In her hands she carried a cardboard box as if it's slightest tilt could upset the apple cart. Walking over to the side table she set up the stored tape-recording machine. The woman then put on her headphones, removed a tape from her box and inserted it into the machine.

Time to begin. Gwen picked up her pen and faced toward the

Panel, making sure her shaking hands were underneath the table. The Panel members conversed. Finally, as the grandfather clock clanged once on the half hour, the Chair spoke.

"Good morning counsel and parties. I'm Jay Sawyer, the Chair of the Panel. I apologize for our delay this morning. It couldn't be helped. Before we go on record, I want to address one administrative item. I have been informed this morning that the NASD, that is the National Association of Securities Dealers, the entity running this arbitration, has ruled in favor of Claimant's Motion for a security guard. This guard should be arriving after noon and will attend for the remainder of the hearing. Is that all right?" Sawyer looked down at his papers. "Let me see, Attorney Wool ... Wilson, correct?"

Gwen stood up. "Yes," glad she didn't have a more difficult-to- pronounce last name, as Sawyer seemed to stutter with Wilson. Still standing, she added, "Also, I'd like to bring to the attention of the Panel and Respondents a recent change. Due to unforeseen health circumstances my client, Samuel Perez, will not be attending today's hearing. But he shall be available and will be testifying tomorrow. As such, I am fine with the guard not being here today."

Turning to the woman at the small table, Sawyer said, "Loretta, we're going on the record now. Please turn on the tape machine." Overseeing the room, Sawyer added, "First, we'll identify ourselves." All watched as Loretta pressed the button and the tape in the machine began to move in clockwise circles. Sawyer continued, "This is the matter, NASD Case Number 58365, Perez v. Stanley, Howe, LLC and Lawrence Murphy. That is the broker correct?" he said, turning to Respondents' table.

"Yes. Attorney Martin Mandel for Mr. Murphy," came a distant seated voice from the other side of the table.

Sawyer nodded, and then said, "As the record of this hearing is being taped, I'd appreciate it if all participants remember to speak into the microphones set out on the conference table. I want to make sure we get a good, clear record." Shifting his gaze towards Loretta he cautioned, "Please let me know if you have any difficulties with the taping."

Gwen pulled the distant mike closer to her. She was feeling like she was part of a Congressional hearing, or a T.V. quiz show, or seventh grade debate for Class President, except she didn't have a grant of immunity or a chance at stardom or power.

Looking at his notes, Sawyer went on, "Now we'll identify the arbitrators. I'm Jay Sawyer, Chair of the Arbitration Panel."

The man sitting in the yellow sweater on Sawyer's left then spoke. "I'm James Grimes, the industry representative's Panel member." Gwen thought he sounded gruff.

The third Panelist, the accountant, stated his name was Elias Pollippi. He sounded like a lower octave version of Linda. Both Grimes and Pollippi looked at Sawyer, clearly deferring to his running the hearing.

Sawyer began by getting up and handing out to all counsel updated conflict disclosure forms for the panel members. Gwen quickly reviewed them and, heart clinching, was stunned by the changes between the disclosures provided her by the NASD and the revised disclosures. All panel members stated recent connections with either Respondents or industry members that were not previously made known. Most troubling were Sawyer's revisions. His indicated he'd changed law firms and that his present firm represented large financial institutions, including Stanley, Howe. Sawyer denied up front any conflict issues since, he said, he hadn't worked yet on any matter concerning the Respondent. Gwen thought that was a little like saying his family robbed banks but he hadn't yet been involved in a robbery at this bank.

Sawyer, looking up at the assembly present, then said, "Now, for the parties. Counsel please identify yourselves and give me a brief idea of which witnesses you are intending to call, and whether they are fact witnesses, expert witnesses, or, of course, parties to this action."

All counsel complied, Gwen naming Sammy and Martha and Linda as her party and expert witnesses.

With all the parties identified, Sawyer read from his notes, "Will the parties confirm that they have accepted the composition of the Panel?"

Gwen hesitated. She could not imagine a group of so-called neutral deciders with clearer ties to the industry. But, as she'd explained to Martha and Linda, her options were not good. In fact, they were lousy. Were she to object and the case then be returned to the NASD for appointment of a new panel, and with the questionnaires and other time-consuming work involved with that, there would surely be an extensive delay in the hearing date, maybe into 2004. This was an unacceptable option. Sammy was having trouble attending today's hearing. A few more months in his Dominican paradise – she didn't like her odds that he'd show up again. Gwen, twisting the pen she was holding so hard her fingers hurt, reluctantly responded, "Yes for Complainant Perez."

The opposing counsel quickly echoed their affirmations and the Panel members were officially accepted.

Sawyer continued on the record. Reading from a prepared statement, he quickly stated in a monotone, "This hearing is now formally opened and submitted to this Panel in accordance with the NASD Code of Arbitration Procedures. All awards will be final and are not subject to appeal. Counsel wishing to assert objections will hold their objections until the close of testimony. Arbitrators may ask questions during the matter. If at the conclusion of this hearing the Panel determines that there appear to be violations of the Securities and Exchange laws and regulations, this Panel shall submit this matter for possible further investigation and disciplinary action."

Gwen sighed, both with exhaustion, apprehension, and relief. At last it was happening. She stood up and, her face flushed with adrenalin, explained to Sawyer that her expert witnesses were available and in the hallway. Then she advised Sawyer again that

Sammy had become ill while traveling, and on doctor's orders he would not be available to attend the hearing until the next day.

Sawyer paused, looked at his fellow arbitrators, and then asked if Sammy were under medical care. Gwen replied that he was. Sawyer nodded to Gwen's relief and he asked all counsel to have their witnesses present in the room. Gwen rose and strode out the room to find Martha and Linda. They were sitting in the nearby waiting room reading magazines. Gwen filled them in on the proceedings so far and they followed her into the conference room and sat at her side. Gwen smiled, pleased that her team was expanding. Now she had a catcher and shortstop. When all witnesses were present, except for Sammy, Loretta rose and swore them all in. Sawyer then excused the fact witnesses from the room, but allowed Martha and Linda and the other expert witnesses to remain. Murphy, as a party, stayed seated. Gwen noted that this brought down the number of suits opposing her by two, so the count was now fifteen men verses a grand total of four women – if Loretta were included. 'The times they are a changing', she sang to herself.

Sawyer continued with the numerous administrative tasks. He had Loretta mark the panel's collection of the agreed-upon exhibits and pleadings. It was Day's turn to rise. Holding up three thick black binders, a feat that impressed Gwen, he began, "The parties have agreed that the documents included in these binders may be used for reference during the hearing at counsel's discretion to assist the Panel. And the documents stamped with Exhibit numbers, basically the first two volumes, have been agreed to by counsel for inclusion as evidence in the official record." Gwen presumed these were the materials she'd reviewed at her luncheon meeting with Anna. Day then had one of his associates hand out a copy of these binders to the Panel members and to Gwen. Gwen, with no time to review the contents, assumed on faith they included the appropriate papers she'd seen. Gwen knew that unless a fact was admitted into the record, it couldn't be considered by the

Panel when they were deliberating.

But Gwen hadn't remembered there being so many documents. Should she take action or accept Day's representation? Hesitantly she stood up. Talking into the set-up mike she stated, "As you can see, I have just received a copy of the so-called Master File. I join Attorney Day in hoping that its availability to the Panel assists in expediting this hearing –- and rely on his representation that it is complete. I note, however, there have been a number of documents FedExed to me in the past few days that were to have been produced many months ago. I do not waive my right to object to and to strike should any of these be introduced. Further, while I respect Mr. Day's claims that these binders contain only documents accepted as relevant, I wish to retain the right to review these documents to assure their accuracy." There, she'd spoken and survived. *And, what the hell, it isn't so bad.*

Day again rose. "I agree that going forward we can deal with these newer materials separately should the need arise." He remained standing.

Sawyer listened to the preliminary finagling with a blank face, then said, "Thank you counsel. I conclude that the record of documentary exhibits marked into evidence in these binders has been agreed upon, except for the documents mentioned and supplemental materials and documents not included on a list to be provided by counsel. That should assist us moving forward. So let's proceed that way. I'd now like to move on to opening statements."

After this initial skirmish, Gwen could feel her competitive juices rise up in her veins like energy from a power bar. She was ready to take on the bad guys and fight for Sammy.

CHAPTER THIRTY

The opening statement, a time when lawyers present an overview of their case, what they'll prove, how they'll do it, and a finish exuding the reasons why they should win. It was, Gwen thought, like opening a bottle of fine champagne, it should offer anticipation hype, a crisp, powerful, well-balanced body swirling in the bottle, bounteous bubbly promises, and the prophesy of a special warm relationship.

"Will you begin on behalf of the Claimant, Attorney Wilson?"

It was time, now or never as they say. Grimacing with apprehension, Gwen picked up her handful of index cards and arranged them on the table, placed her shaking hands again below the table. She stood and faced the Panel with what she hoped was now a confident smile. Sadly, she was again the lone ranger on her side, as Martha and Linda were in their own space getting ready for their time at the plate and Sammy, well hopefully he was on his way from Syracuse.

Gwen began. "This case is about broken promises and broken trust. You will hear how my client, a Hispanic man who immigrated to this country as a young man to grab the American dream. He worked hard at blue-collar jobs, went to night school to better his prospects, and was able to achieve a version of that American dream: a middle-class life for him and his family, and to give a good start to his three boys so they would do even better." Gwen stopped and checked her notes. She wished she'd prepared a glass of water. With parched mouth she continued, "But this dream was destroyed by Respondents."

Gwen continued Sammy's story, how he relied on Murphy's promises, trusted the Respondents, and how they cheated him for their own benefit, putting their interests above their promises to him.

Mandel stood up, yelled "objection," and then denied that his client was self-serving. Gwen responded that she was allowed great latitude during her opening, and, anyways, her claims *ipso facto* showed she had a basis for this charge.

Sawyer stared at Mandel. then said, "I think we can move on counsel. This is not a jury trial. We understand the claims and are prepared to allow room for a degree of embellishment during opening statement. Please sit down."

Gwen was relieved that Sawyer was applying the standards applicable to a court hearing. She secretly carved a "notch" on her 'hearing belt'.

Gwen, continuing from where she'd left off, said, "Claimant, Mr. Perez, that is, Sammy, also placed his trust in Stanley, Howe, an established nationally recognized *full-service* brokerage firm. But both persons...."

This time it was Day's turn to rise and interrupt. "I object at characterizing Stanley, Howe as a 'person'. It is a corporation that did not as such earn commissions from trades."

Gwen moved around her chair and closer to Sawyer. "Mr. Chair, I appreciate that Respondents' counsel wish to disrupt my opening, but their objections are frivolous and delay this hearing."

"Go on, Attorney Wilson. Please start where you are comfortable." Sawyer smiled her way.

"Thank you." Gwen walked back to her seat. Despite her pounding heart, to show that they hadn't flustered her, she managed to calmly pour herself a glass of water, sip and then move on. "Mr. Chair and Panel members, we shall show that both Respondents, the firm and the person, took improper advantage of Sammy – the broker in order to make commissions and achieve rewards from his employer, the company through greed to make more money and to promote their investments."

Gwen moved her index cards around to the one with her next point. "My client, Sammy Perez, is not a trading whiz like Mr. Murphy. No, he's the opposite, a trading novice. He is a 57 year old blue-collar worker who until injured worked in the same manufacturing job most of his adult life." Gwen was starting to feel some rhythm as she relayed Sammy's experiences as set out in his Statement of Claims. The words started flowing out like the tide as she got her sea legs.

After skimming through her cards to ensure she'd covered all her items, Gwen went on to her finale, reiterating briefly Sammy's claims. "To summarize, we will show that Mr. Murphy's trading was excessive by industry standards; that...."

"Bullshit!" Larry Murphy bellowed as he stood up, his face turning red. Slamming his fist down on the table, he again shouted, "Bullshit. This is total bullshit. A total fucking circus act. I'm not going to sit here another minute and listen to this crap." Gwen was relieved that the likely hundred-year-old table was hard mahogany wood, and that she wasn't within striking distance of the clearly disturbed Respondent.

After a brief shocked silence, Sawyer leaned into his microphone and with a fixed stare towards the broker admonished in a loud and judge-like firm tone, "Sit down, Mr. Murphy. We will not allow such emotional outbursts at this hearing. I understand that this is difficult but you must leave it up to your attorney to speak on your behalf. You will have your turn to tell your view of what happened. I trust, Mr. Mandel, that you will control your client going forward." Mandel nodded and spoke quietly into Larry's ear. Sawyer, having restored decorum, looked towards Gwen, then he nodded, and she continued.

"Claimant will further show through the evidence I've described that Mr. Murphy controlled Mr. Perez's account; engaged in unsuitable trades; and exacerbated this risk through the use of margin." Gwen heard a commotion at the far end of the table and, turning, saw Murphy, red in the face again, this time in angry discussion with his lawyer. Regaining her focus, she concluded in a symphonic Fourth Movement flourish, "We will show this Panel that Sammy lost all his life savings along with his family's money, thanks to Respondents' wrongful conduct. We will establish that if properly handled Sammy's investment would have been worth today $175,000 or more."

Gwen stopped and put down her notes. Looking directly at the Panel members for emphasis, she hammered in the nail. "It is Mr. Perez's contention that through greed, negligence and willful violation of this country's laws governing security transactions, and their own industry's standards, Respondents Stanley, Howe and Larry Murphy forever changed for the worse Sammy Perez's life and that of his family." Maintaining eye contact with the Panel, Gwen placed her notes on the table and sat down. Secretly she hoped that no one else was aware of her left thigh shaking.

Gwennie, the worst is over, the beginning. Good job overall. Too bad Sammy wasn't here for his longed-for moment – finally telling his story to the people that hurt him.

Chatter and murmurings filled the room. Sawyer turned to his right and advised the suits that it was now their turn for opening statements. Day rose and quietly walked over towards the Panel's table. Speaking without notes in a mellifluous, mesmerizing voice, Gwen knew she was seeing a star litigator in action. She'd just been the warm-up act.

"Mr. Sawyer and Panel members, this is a case of sour grapes by a gambling man who was seeking a quick win at the roulette wheel so, like his work buddies, he could buy a new car. Contrary to Attorney Wilson's selective and at times misleading and fallacious statement of the case, Respondents will establish without doubt that my opposing counsel's client, Mr. Perez, was a sophisticated investor, one who had traded in risky stocks before and..." Here Gwen admired that Day slowed down and put special emphasis on his words, words that established *scienter*, intent. "... he knew well the risks of the market and margin trading. He understood speculation, sought a quick win, and gambled his family's future away. In short, he was a committed gambler. Additionally, Mr. Perez's constant *daily* demands and directions to his broker show beyond doubt that he, Sammy as his attorney refers to him, was the one who controlled his account, not Mr. Murphy. It was Mr. Perez who was driving this bus. We will establish that his claims are without merit."

Day went on smoothly contradicting each of the points that Gwen had made. As to the margin calls, Day claimed they were caused by Sammy's own actions in using his account funds to pay his personal debts. Finally, Day, in a soft voice that brought silence to the room, stated that Sammy, indicative of his gambling mentality, seriously overstated his assets to Murphy to satisfy the asset guidelines the firm required to support underlying risky trades. Concluding, punctuating each point with his right hand and its bone-crunching fingers, Day stated, "Members of the Panel, Mr. Perez is a knowledgeable, calculating investor. Respondents just did their job by following Mr. Perez's directives. You will, we are confident, determine – as have Respondents – that it was Mr. Perez who drove this bus. And if it went off the road, that was solely due to his driving. Thank you for your time." Day gave the Panel a brief nod and sat down.

The Panel members nodded back in turn. Sawyer wrote down some notes to himself. Gwen wanted to applaud Day's performance, but instead poured herself a second glass of water and had a long drink. She wished it were something more substantial, like Pepto-Bismol. Day had been good, earning his big bucks and confirming his reputation as a master of his trade.

Attorney Mandel rose. "On behalf of Mr. Murphy I waive his opening remarks as I believe Attorney Day has been fully persuasive addressing the same issues. However, I would like to take this moment to request that the Panel advise us of their proposed hearing schedule. It would be helpful to me if I can have an understanding of how long we will go on particular days. I regret but I have to fly to Miami Thursday evening for another hearing. I apologize that due to the late notice of this hearing from the NASD, I was unable to extend that hearing date. I believe there are other attorneys present who similarly are trying to jockey several demands on their time."

Sawyer consulted with his fellow members, and then said, "In general, we were planning on going until 4 p.m. each day until we finish up. As also some of you may have to do, the Panel members are also jockeying several matters at this time. So, let's take a lunch break now and see you all back here at 2 p.m. sharp with the goal of going later today due to our late start."

Loretta turned off the recording machine and all male persons got up and quickly left the room.

Gwen sat for a moment to vegetate, then, cool as a cucumber, she went into the hallway looking for Martha and Linda. She found them in an empty office.

"How did the remainder of the morning go?" asked Martha as she put down her pen.

Tightly pursing her lips Gwen shrugged, then elaborated, "A little contentious, some warning shots of the battle to come, and I wished Sammy were there. All the Panel needs to do is look at him in his red ski jacket, or golf jacket, and then compare the claims that he's sophisticated with what they see. First impressions count for something. But, moving on. We start again at 2 pm with Sammy's case. Linda I'll call you first. I decided it makes more sense to introduce the data first and then Martha can put it into the trading context. And Linda, no sweat, I'll just be going over the outline I emailed you, so no surprises from me."

"Do we have time for lunch?" Linda asked.

"Almost forgot!" Gwen smiled. "Hey, don't worry amigos. I planned ahead." Her stomach gurgling, Gwen handed out to her team sandwiches she'd made the night before. "No sushi I'm afraid, Martha. Nor, unfortunately, did I bring fortune cookies predicting 'big victory coming'."

All three women sat in the empty office munching on turkey and Swiss cheese sandwiches – and wishing the day were over.

CHAPTER THIRTY-ONE

Gwen expected the fireworks were about to begin. As she and her team walked into the room, suffragettes ready to take on the male bastion in their suits, her dozen or so opponents were surprisingly already seated, and looking loaded for bear. While entering, Gwen noticed a man in blue leaning against the back wall, an object dangling from his belt. Gwen assumed this was the NASD security guard wearing a weapon – gun or long flashlight.

As soon as she and her experts appeared settled in, Sawyer announced, "Please call your first witness, Attorney Wilson."

Linda rose but before she could move to the witness seat, Day yelled out, "Objection." Clearing his throat, and with his right hand pointing at Linda, he began the afternoon with an aggressive thrust of his legal dagger.

"I move that this Panel not permit Claimant's *expert* witness, Ms. DeNardi I believe, to testify at this time. Claimant has presented no *factual* evidence on which his expert can base any opinion relevant to these proceedings. As such, her testimony would be without a proper foundation."

Gwen appreciated that Day wanted to appear to be earning his $500 plus an hour fee in front of in-house counsel, and she had expected his motion. Gwen knew that Sammy's failure to testify had set up this claim. Sawyer furrowed his brow. A ruling against her would likely terminate the proceeding then and there – as her only other witness was Martha, and, like Linda, Sawyer would view her testimony as fatally flawed absent a factual basis in the record.

Gwen stood and offered what she hoped was a persuasive argument in Sammy's favor. She reiterated that Sammy's absence was on doctor's orders, and that her client would be testifying tomorrow. She then appealed to the discretion of the Panel to permit her to change the order of her witnesses rather than to delay the hearing. She asserted that the Respondents would not be harmed by this change. "Ms. DeNardi has been on my witness list for many month, she'll be testifying about Respondents' own documents, prepared by them and included in the Binders without objection by them. Mr. Day may then cross-examine regarding any expert opinions Ms. DeNardi may offer."

She'd done her best. Would that be enough to save Sammy's case?

After a brief consultation with the two so far silent Panel members – whom Gwen was calling in her mind 'Tweedledum' and 'Tweedledee', the Chair issued the Panel's ruling. With her heart pounding, she heard Sawyer state, "The Panel denies Attorney Day's Motion." Gwen was so relieved she barely heard Sawyer continue that if she failed to provide a factual basis tomorrow with Sammy for Linda's assertions, then the Panel would allow Day to renew his Motion. And, well, without any expert testimony in the record, Sammy would not prevail.

Quickly standing up before one of the other suits could raise a related objection, Gwen said, "I call Ms. Linda DeNardi."

Linda, her face as pale as her white blouse, walked stiffly to the designated chair. 'Scared woman walking', Gwen thought. She placed several small index cards on her lap. Dressed in a basic gray suit, her reading glasses hanging on a string around her neck like a plastic amulet, Linda looked the part of a nondescript CPA. But then again, Gwen wasn't complaining as she herself was wearing a five-year-old off the rack navy suit, fake gold necklace, and flats, comprising the dress attire for court of an above the Notch female lawyer, generally a/k/a, her. Alas, her custom-tailored attorney attire from her Big Apple law firm days no longer quite fit around the hips.

Reviewing her notes, Gwen started with a series of preliminary leading questions regarding Linda's background to establish she qualified as an 'expert'. In these, Gwen did most of the testifying and all Linda was required to do was to say "yes."

Gwen's questions covered Linda's employment, professional licenses, academic degrees, stock trading experience. Both Gwen and Linda began to relax some thanks to this litany, their statements less marked with 'ah's' and "um's," their voices firmer and more confident. Gwen moved on to specific questions about Sammy's case, trying to set out the facts that Day had demanded where possible. And she continued asking leading questions beyond the preliminaries, hoping the Panel would adopt a relaxed evidentiary approach befitting arbitrations.

"Ms. DeNardi, did you have an opportunity to review Mr. Perez's account statements provided by the Respondents?"

Before Linda could get a word out, Day jumped up, arm raised. Gwen, admiring his quickness, suspected he was good at playing 'Whack-a-Mole'. Day stated, "Mr. Sawyer, if the witness is going to use notes I have the right to see them and to obtain a copy."

Gwen groaned – silently. Would Sawyer stick to his trial standards after all? That would allow ongoing bickering over whether the question was properly framed. Sawyer came out somewhere in between, a position Gwen expected would be the case going forward on most issues. He said, "If the witness would put her notes away until she needs them, please. If she can't testify without them, she may use them to refresh her recollection. At that point I'll have copies made for Respondents' counsel and the Panel. Loretta, we have access to a copy machine, correct?"

Loretta nodded yes.

Continuing, Gwen took Linda through Respondents' financial statements. They reviewed the initial profits and then ongoing losses in Sammy's trading accounts and what the market was doing during this period so as to assess how his account would have done better if his funds had been invested appropriately. Initially Gwen had to repeat several questions as Linda, her face tight with anxiety, was having difficulty focusing. However, once the questions involved number crunching Linda became adept in answering.

On the issue of Sammy's damages, Linda stated, "I calculated the value of the securities and margin accounts, divided the total by the number of months the accounts were open, the product giving me the 'average' investment amount, which I named the "AIA." I next took the costs of the purchases from the statements, divided these by the AIA for each of the months I was looking at. But I note..." and here Linda, appearing now sufficiently relaxed that her mouth formed a pout, looked up at the Panel and stated, "I was not provided with all the statements for each of the years involved. So I was forced to extrapolate from the year-to-date information in the statements I did have. But my numbers should be on the whole reliable."

Gwen hoped the Panel had understood that, as it was a little Greek to her. Still, it sounded expertise-like, which could only be good. Gwen moved on to get to the bottom line. "What was your calculation as to how much money Mr. Perez lost?"

"The statements were a little confusing as in a different format than I've previously seen, but I calculated he lost in the vicinity of $135,000.00 which includes out-of-pocket losses from the numerous margin calls plus interest, fees, and other expenses." Not exactly an impressive number for the Panel of bigwheelers, but surely not negligible either, at least for an investor above the Notch.

"Do you have an opinion as to what Mr. Perez's account would have been worth had it been invested in low-risk security funds over the several years that he maintained an account with Stanley, Howe?"

Linda, her eyes raised so they were looking over her glasses, confidently stated "approximately $148,000. It was a bull market generally." Gwen stopped to let the number sink in for the Panel members. She smiled at Linda, took a sip of water from her glass, and played with the paper clips she'd set aside in case she needed them. Turning, she looked at Murphy down the table, then at the Panel, and then turned back to face Linda again. For the first time in her life she was glad that her mother had forced her to take ballet classes as a child, from which she had acquired the graceful arm movements she was now displaying.

Moving on to establish more 'facts' for Day, Gwen handed Linda a piece of paper, then said, "I'm showing you, Ms. DeNardi, Claimants Exhibit No. 3, a document entitled 'New Account Statement'." Gwen stopped, rose and gave out copies to the Panel, Linda and, via "Please pass it down," to all the main line participants, one of the many times she wished she'd had Adam in her corner acting as an associate to help her. With document in hand, Gwen informed the Panel, "This document for your reference is Bates stamped Number 417 and appears I believe at p. 132 in the second black binder."

Turning back to Linda, Gwen asked, "Ms. DeNardi, do you see the box in the upper righthand corner that asks the applicant to check off one of the five stated trading options?"

"Yes, I do."

"Looking at this box, what are the investment objectives checked off?"

Putting on her reading glasses, Linda read, "Growth, and ...um...also speculation."

"Are you familiar with Mr. Perez's federal income tax returns for the past three years?"

"Yes, I've reviewed them in connection with this case. They're pretty basic, especially the last year when he filed as an individual rather than as married. I didn't prepare them so I can't personally vouch for their accuracy, but they were prepared by a certified accountant."

"Thank you. Based on your review of these returns, what is your opinion as to Mr. Perez's approximate average annual income during this period?"

"He earned about $43,000 a year, give or take some change, less of course when he went on disability."

Sawyer suddenly spoke up, "Disability. Um... excuse me, did

you say disability? He was on disability?"

"Yes, I'm not sure of the date."

Gwen thought she'd been clear in informing the Panel of this significant fact, but it appeared not to be the case. She went on with her questioning. "Ms. DeNardi, for a family of five, would you consider that to be below the state's average income?" "Based on my firm's in-house reporting that reviewed state income data, this is at the lower end of the medium range for family personal income."

"Objection," bellowed Day. "Speculative. Where is this data?" Sawyer commented that the Panel were generally familiar with this public earnings data, and he then nodded to Gwen to continue, adding, "Move on, Counselor."

"Ms. DeNardi, just a few more questions. Did you come to an opinion about the level of trading by Mr. Murphy based on your review of the account statements?"

"Objection," yelled Mandel, who followed Day's lead in jumping up before speaking.

"Mandel here, Counsel for Mr. Murphy. Panel members, there's absolutely no foundation for any valid opinion, let alone confirmation that this witness is qualified as an expert on this subject."

Sawyer leaned forward. "I think we've dealt with that, Attorney Mandel. But, Ms. Wilson, you may want to revisit this factual issue when your client testifies. We'll allow the witness to answer, subject, as before, to our assessment of its value." Looking at his watch Sawyer added, "Can we see if we can get to the final points of your witness's testimony, Ms. Wilson?"

Linda sat quietly. Finally, Sawyer leaned over towards her chair and told her she could answer the question if she were able. After adjusting her legs and pulling down her skirt, Linda answered, "Yes, I did see a trend. As money came into the account, soon afterwards there were frequent equivalent or greater purchases out."

Gwen followed up with questions designed to affirm Linda's professional expertise to satisfy Mandel's complaint. "Ms. DeNardi, are you familiar with the rules and standards regarding excessive trading activity?"

"I believe so. From seminars as part of my annual CPA required courses, and client work over the years. From, well, usually a tax perspective."

"Do you have an opinion based on your training and experience whether the trading you observed appears to be excessive in terms of industry norms?"

Day jumped up this time. "Objection, again as my colleague stated, no foundation. Surely the Panel has been more than lenient in allowing in unfounded testimony, but there is a line where such approach goes beyond the boundaries of fairness, Mr. Sawyer. The evidentiary rules exist for a purpose, and flaunting them as Ms. Wilson has consistently done is unprofessional and harmful to my clients' case."

"Again, I think we'll allow it for now," said Sawyer tersely, "subject to the same assessment standards the Panel has previously expressed. But my patience is wearing thin, Mr. Day. We are facing a late start, a change of witness scheduling, and a minimal time period reserved for this hearing room, especially when considering *your* co-counsel's time limitations. I will not allow a pattern of interjections for the purpose of interfering with the progress of this case. Now sit down, sir."

This statement was followed by silence in the large room. Day responded by focusing on documents in the binders and writing notes. Gwen, trying hard not to smile with satisfaction, looked down at her legal pad and shuffled her note cards, as if she were preparing to deal a bridge hand.

Linda paused, and then looking directly at the Panel said, "Yes, I do." Without waiting for Gwen to ask her to explain, and not hearing an objection, she continued. "It appears to me, the trading that is, was excessive. My review of the current literature on churning of accounts further confirms my observation. The applicable standard 2-4-6 Rule, generally applied in the industry, is that for a conservative investor, such as Mr. Perez, an annualized turnover ratio of 4 is presumptive of churning. A ratio of six is pretty indicative of excessive trading." Linda now spoke quickly as she was in her world of numbers. "Reviewing Mr. Perez's account, I calculated the turnover ratios to be well over these standards. Mostly they were in the neighborhood of 5.5. In one year it was much higher, as I recall 6.44."

"Did these ratios in your opinion exceed the industry norm?" Gwen asked.

"Yes, they did, for a client like Mr. Perez." Linda stopped. But when Gwen didn't ask a follow-up question, Linda again took the bull by the horn and expanded on her answer, saying, "My opinion is that Mr. Perez's account exceeded the turnover norm generally accepted in the securities industry."

"Was there any other information that influenced your conclusion of, using the common term, churning, in his account?"

Day stood up. This time he said in a speaking tone, "Mr. Sawyer, I apologize for interrupting, but may I request a brief recess?"

Sorry his ass! Gwen had been ready to go in for the kill. Trying not to look annoyed, she informed Sawyer that she was almost done. Nevertheless, after consultation with his colleagues, Sawyer announced a ten-minute break. The suits jumped up in unison as if a men's choral group ready for their oratorio section. Soon they were either busy using the limited number of telephones or had disappeared from the room to find cell phone reception. The Panel members likewise left. By contrast, Loretta retrieved a sandwich from her bag and began to eat her snack.

Gwen used the break to rub, with Martha's help, the throbbing knot between her shoulder blades. After this first-aide, and telling Linda she was doing super, to reduce the tension on her team Gwen spent the remainder of the break gabbing with Martha and

Linda about their weekend plans. She had assured her friends this experience would be fun, after all. Laughter soon was heard on her side of the conference table. Before Gwen could describe Sunday's garden standoff with the red squirrel, the Panel returned, Loretta's recording machine swirled, and Gwen went on with her questioning.

Picking up a thick book on the table, Gwen opened it to a page with a blue tag sticker, and asked Linda, "Just to clarify my terms, Ms. DeNardi, I'm using "churning" to describe the process where a broker excessively buys and sells securities...."

Day jumped up without missing a beat, not to be cowered for long by Sawyer it seemed. "Objection. Leading."

Sawyer ignored him. "Please continue," he said to Gwen. She finished her definition, "That is, buying and selling for the

purpose of generating more commissions. Is that your general understanding of the term?"

"Yes," stated Linda.

"Did you see frequent in-and-out purchases and sales?"

"Objection, already testified on this, Mr. Chair," offered Day.

With no ruling by the Panel, in the silence Linda continued, "I did."

Gwen jumped in, "Are you aware that churning can violate federal SEC Rules, including 15(C) Sections 1-7, a copy of which Rule I note for the Panel is included in Binder 1 at p. 15, and other securities laws?"

"Objection!" shouted one of the other lawyers sitting at the end of the table. "Not within expertise," another finished the thought.

Sawyer stared down the table. "Gentlemen, please identify yourselves for the record when you speak. I'll allow you to participate should you wish after Attorney Day's cross-examination, provided that you do not create confusion on the record, and...," Sawyer looked around the room, then added, "well, you are not overbearing in light of your numbers. Are we clear?" Sawyer waited for a response. Hearing none he turned to Linda and continued, "Ms. DeNardi, you may answer, and the Panel will give it the weight we deem appropriate."

"Yes. That's what I understand is the law from my accounting work for my clients with substantial securities accounts."

Gwen looked through her note cards on churning. Satisfied she could check off each item on her list, she moved on to her next subject. "As regards the issue of margin accounts and their suitability for Mr. Perez, Ms. DeNardi, did you take a look at the margin account in Mr. Perez's file?"

"Yes, I did. I was surprised to see the use of margin...."

"Objection," said Day. "No foundation," added the voice of Murphy's attorney, Mandel. After he'd identified himself, Mandel added, "The question relates to information beyond the scope of the witness's expertise. As such, she is not permitted to offer an opinion."

Sawyer almost stood up, before saying, "Gentlemen, you are trying my patience. Please. Only one lawyer objecting per question at a time. As before, we'll allow the answer and we will assess the weight it should be given later. Continue Attorney Wilson."

"I believe there's a question outstanding regarding the use of margin accounts?" Gwen said to Loretta.

"Please, Loretta, read back the last question," Sawyer directed into the microphone.

Loretta found the place on the tape and repeated Gwen's question.

Linda finished her answer that margin trading is far riskier. Gwen then went over with Linda – as she had on the issue of churning – what a margin account is and why it would be inappropriate for use in Sammy's account. Thanks to their having practiced this Q & A before, Linda was prepared to give her input. She explained the increased investor risk as, "If the value for the assets supporting the margin loan goes down, then the investor may have to come up with more money, an amount that will satisfy the firm's set minimum collateral value required to maintain the account."

"That's a handful, at least for investment novices like me. Can you offer an example?"

Linda paused, and when there was no interruption, continued. "Sure. So, if you have a no-fee checking account at a bank, and it is free if you have $500 in your savings, but you spend this savings making the amount in the account below $500, then you have to add more money to meet the bank's requirements or you start paying fees on your account. In a securities account, if your pledged assets decline in value, and this leaves your account below the firm's set minimum, that's when you could get a margin call. The investor either comes up with more assets or the broker has the authority to sell the investor's stock in any account with the firm to make up the difference, *even* if at a loss. And there usually are fees imposed for this."

"Did that happen in Mr. Perez's account?"

"Yes, many times."

Gwen passed out copies of her next document. Then handing a copy to Linda she asked, "Ms. DeNardi, I'm showing you Claimant's Exhibit Number 5, a letter from Stanley, Howe's Office Practice Supervisor, a Mr. Clifford, to Mr. Perez. Have you seen this document before?"

"I have."

"Did this letter influence your opinion as to whether Mr. Murphy engaged in excessive trading?"

Linda said, "Yes it did. The letter addressed to Mr. Perez states...."

Day stood up. Gwen wondered if he were getting tired. She knew she was exhausted just from watching him rise and fall. Day said to the Panel, "Mr. Sawyer, the letter speaks for itself. Reading it will only further extend this already long day and, as you have noted, our tight time-schedule. Additionally, it is in effect hearsay as it is being presented as the testimony of a third party."

Sawyer paused, jotted down some notes, perused his copy of the letter, and then asked, "Mr. Day, the letter came from your client, correct?

"Yes."

"And it is included in full in the binders? And where would that be?"

"Yes," answered Day. "It is at p. 118 in Binder 2."

"And Mr. Clifford is dead, am I correct in that?"

Day answered, "Yes."

Sawyer turned to Gwen, "Ms. Wilson, do you intend to have your witness read the entire letter?"

"No. It will only take a few moments at most to read into the record the relevant part, which I've highlighted for the Panel members and counsel. As I will have follow-up questions, this will not effectively lengthen my examination."

"Okay, thank you." Having made up his mind, putting down his copy he turned to Linda and said, "Ms. DeNardi, why don't you continue please. And counsel, in future it would be helpful to the Panel if you note in the record where we may locate an exhibit."

Squinting through her glasses, Linda read, "I want to call your attention to the substantial volume of trading in your account. This high level of trading has resulted in significant transaction costs." Looking up at Gwen who nodded her head to go on, Linda continued, "That's the highlighted part. In sum, from my perspective, this letter supports my conclusion that there was excessive trading going on in Mr. Perez's account."

"Thank you." Gwen raised her pointer finger, opened her mouth as if to ask another question but, instead, stood silently as she reviewed her checklist, confirming that she'd gotten what she needed to into the record. Fixing her eyes on Day, she said, "I have no more questions of this witness."

Gwen sat, drained of energy. How had she done? Martha affirmed her performance with a hidden fist bump.

Smiling to herself with relief that one witness almost done, Gwennie expected it would be a gravy train from here on out. She just had to sit and jump up at the appropriate times, like Day did and say objection. *Hey, after all that anxiety, like the law boards, it wasn't so bad! In fact, it was almost fun, okay maybe a little like being on the edge of a cliff and looking down at a gorge filled with thundering water, but I didn't fall in. And maybe I gave Day a reason to think settlement?*

Sawyer looked at this watch, then said, "I think we'll continue straight on due to the time crunch and begin cross-examination, if any." He got affirmation from Tweedledum and Tweedledee that this was fine with them, then turned to Linda. "Ms. DeNardi, would you like a brief recess?"

With no choice other than to finish, Linda said, "No, I'm ready to continue."

Gwen worried how Linda would hold up to Day's bluster. True,

Linda had grown more confident during direct, indeed Gwen thought she'd metamorphosed from a timid CPA into a CPA lioness. But would she end her role in this case with a roar?

CHAPTER THIRTY-TWO

It was time for Day's cross, the event Linda had been dreading all these many months. Would she be able to withstand Day's blistering attack?

Sawyer started the hearing by asking Respondents' side of the table, "Counsel, who will be handling cross-examination of this witness?"

Standing up, Day responded, "Members of the Panel, Josiah Day as co-Counsel for Respondent Stanley, Howe. I shall be doing the cross of Ms. DeNardi on behalf of both Respondents."

Day walked towards the Panel and stopped across from Linda's chair. In his beige suit and audacious bright blue tie, Day exuded charisma that commanded the attention of all eyes in the room. Gwen watched in awe, hoping to learn from a master. Clasping his hands together in front of him, Day started to speak without any notes. He began by renewing his prior unsuccessful motions that Linda not be allowed to testify, then he added an objection that she was not qualified as an expert as a matter of law, as lacking "the requisite knowledge and expertise on securities trading."

Sawyer after briefly whispering with the other Panel members reiterated his previous rulings and instructed Day to move on.

An auspicious beginning for Sammy's case? Maybe, but Gwen worried this might also turn out to be the high point of Linda's cross. Walking back to his seat, Day picked up a black binder in each hand. Facing Linda he said, "Good afternoon, Ms. DeNardi. As we converse this afternoon, I will be referring to documents contained in these binders, documents previously admitted into evidence by counsel for all parties. Let's begin by looking at Exhibit S397, titled 'Profit & Loss Statement'." He paused while his associate – *cute, Gwen assessed, but not nearly as cute as Adam* – gave copies to Linda, all counsel and the Panel. "Please, Ms. DeNardi, focus your attention on the first page of the Exhibit marked 'Summary'. Do you see that, Ms. DeNardi?"

Linda put on her glasses and looked through the multi-page document, then at page one.

"Yes, I think."

"I'm sure you recognize it – for it is a standard format for showing cash flow, correct?"

"Yes, I recognize the format but I don't recall seeing this document." Linda twisted in her chair towards Day.

Gwen was desperately trying to figure out whether this exhibit had been one of the documents she'd reviewed and approved with Anna, or something that had been added more recently to the binder. *Ugh, why didn't I keep better records! And prepare a chart of the thousand or so documents by Bates and Exhibit number so I can tell when I got what.* She did know that, as she'd expected, late last Friday afternoon half a dozen boxes of additional materials, supposedly responsive to her discovery requests of months ago, had been delivered to her office. They currently remained in piles on her maroon carpet. Sure, she could have complained about Respondents' *faux pas* one more time, but she knew that ship had already sailed, unless of course she demanded a continuance until... what would in effect be hell freezes over. Still she decided to put her grievance in the record if possible.

Day continued, "Now, does it show next to the line headed 'cash out' the amount of $11,000 on that page?"

Raising the document so it was closer to her face, Linda said, "Yes it does."

Day continued, "Now, showing...."

Gwen jumped up. "Excuse me, Mr. Sawyer, but I would appreciate it if Mr. Day goes just a little bit more slowly so that I can follow his line of questioning. I appear to be less swift than Ms. DeNardi, so I apologize, but I also note from looking at my document summary that I do not have a record of receiving this document before, at least that is before the last weekend when I received a truckload of long-overdue discovery material from Respondents."

Day gave her a cutting look with his cold almost black eyes. She smiled and stared hard back at him, as if she had the power of Medusa, but alas he didn't turn to stone.

Addressing Linda again, he said, "Please let me know if I'm moving too quickly, Ms. DeNardi, all right? I do not want to rush you."

"Yes, thank you."

"Now, do you see on the second page of this same form, the mid- section? I've marked it with a blue tag. I'll wait while the Panel members – and Attorney Wilson – find the marked section. Are we set?"

The Panel members nodded, so Day went on, "Isn't it true that this line is a debit reflecting cash taken out of the account?"

Linda looked carefully at the document. "Yes, that appears to be the case."

"And, Ms. DeNardi, do you see the notation just to the right of this amount? It states doesn't it that this money was used to pay the IRS for overdue taxes in the amount of approximately $40,000?"

Linda cautiously answered, "Yes, I guess so."

Day continued without pausing, "Therefore, these were funds removed by the Claimant Mr. Perez from his securities account with Stanley, Howe, weren't they?"

"Um..., yes, it seems so." Linda was beginning to sink down into her chair.

Day, almost leaping forward, bore in to attack Linda's effort to equivocate. "Excuse me. 'It seems so,' you say? You told this tribunal that you are an experienced accountant; you are familiar with this form you said, but you can only guess what this means?"

Her face blushing a pink to match her lipstick, Linda answered, "Well, yes, I gave you my view based on what appears on the form." Fidgeting in her chair, Linda continued, "I don't know when or who wrote those words, or even who removed the funds."

Yeah, Linda, give him a fight for his money, Gwen silently urged.

Walking closer to Linda, Day continued on the attack. Rocking forward on his toes, his voice rising with sarcasm, Day said, "Excuse me, are you claiming some stranger came in and just decided to insert these numbers out of the blue? Sorry. Withdrawn." Back to using his mellifluous voice, he continued, "Ms. DeNardi, I am correct, am I not, that this figure represents funds debited from Mr. Perez's securities account – by him or at his direction?"

Gwen rose, "Objection, he is badgering the witness. She has already answered this question."

"I think we can move on Counsel, and the Panel directs all attorneys to remain courteous in these proceedings." Sawyer tapped his pen loudly on the dais as he spoke, then looked at his watch and frowned.

Day responded, "I'd like an answer to my question."

Sawyer said to Linda, "Do you need the stenographer to repeat the question?"

Gwen chimed in that she'd objected as already asked and answered.

Linda shook her head no, hesitated, and then said, "As I said, they are listed as a debit on the account."

Sawyer was already moving his fingers through his hair and grimacing. The other Panel members seemed unperturbed.

Day continued, "You agree, then, that this withdrawal constitutes a reduction in equity, a basic concept in accounting. These funds for unpaid taxes were withdrawn from the account, correct?"

Gwen thought of rising again, offering her asked and answered line a third time to show her support for her witness, but decided that would only emphasize the issue. Linda was on her own. Gwen felt like a mother waving goodbye as her child got on the school bus on the first day of school, and *this* bus driver looked grumpy and mean.

"Yes." Now understanding what appeared to be a basic error

when calculating damages, Linda, head down and feet pulled in, was transforming once again, but this time from a CPA lioness back into a slightly timorous mouse.

Day, pointing at the documents held in his left hand, persisted, "Assuming this is properly stated, wouldn't this reduce your calculations of losses in the account?"

"Yes, if that is correct."

"Do you have any reason to believe it is not?"

"I don't know."

"Come on, Ms. DeNardi, that is a simple yes or no question?"

"Well, no I don't – at this time."

Gwen rose to offer Linda more help. "I object to further questions on these documents. It hasn't been established who prepared them or that they were timely provided to Claimant. It is my ...."

Day cut in, speaking directly to and over Gwen, "Counsel, you agreed to what's in these binders as admissible documents. I presume you reviewed them before such admission." Turning towards the Panel he added, "I further note for the record that we did provide Attorney Wilson with an earlier version of this statement. The one presented today is merely a slightly updated form."

Before Gwen could respond, Sawyer interjected, "Counsel. I will not have this become an unsightly war of words. This is an arbitration hearing; there is no jury here to be impressed by your verbal retorts. I assure you, theatrical dramatics do not influence our decision. And I believe the Panel members are fully capable of understanding these forms. In light of our time constraints, there is no need to elaborate on each of the lines, Attorney Day." He then directed Day to move on.

Gwen's stomach sank to the floor, bumpily. Her case was starting to slide downhill, and Day's cross had barely begun. Who knew what Black Diamond moguls lay ahead? Yes, Anna had promised the binder's approved Exhibits would only include documents Gwen had approved, and it would not be updated without her knowledge. Yet here Day already had admitted that was not the case. What were her options? These documents 'spoke' for themselves, so she could hardly claim foul too loud. At the same time Sawyer clearly was not interested in this tit for tat epee contest. She decided her best option was to address any damage on her re-direct – if she had time for one.

Day continued, "Ms. DeNardi, isn't it true that you have to consider the turnover ratio in the context of the client's objectives, risk profile, what he told the broker? That is the cornerstone set forth in the cases, correct? You have read the legal cases underlying your opinion?"

Linda sat frozen in place, her hands tightly grasping the chair's side arms. She looked at Gwen for direction then gave a stab at an answer. "Not sure what you are asking. But, um, I... um...believe that's so."

Gwen rose to help. "Mr. Chair, Attorney Day is fully aware that Ms. DeNardi is not an attorney. Her opinions as she's stated are based on CPA professional material. Thus, I move to strike his last question."

Sawyer responded by nodding to Day to move on.

Day continued with his wrecking ball, and Gwen thought, based on the smirk on his face, he was enjoying this destruction.

He next said, "Ms. DeNardi, I show you S00657. Mr. Sawyer and Ms. Wilson, it is in the smaller binder, at p. 37. The Bates stamp number is in the lower right-hand corner of the paper." Day waited, and then went on, "Have you had sufficient time to review this paper, Ms. DeNardi?"

Linda nodded her head yes.

"Ms. DeNardi, I'm sorry but you need to speak up for the record." Sawyer gave her a faint smile.

Linda dutifully said, "Yes."

Day pursued his point. "Doesn't this page show a copy of a check in the amount of $11,000 made out by Mr. Perez to himself that was written against assets in his security account?" Without waiting for an answer, Day said, "And doesn't S00755...," here Day and his assistant passed to Linda and all present copies of this second document.

"This Exhibit at the same time shows, doesn't it, a credit of this same amount, $11,000, into Mr. Perez's *personal* bank account? Do you see where I am?" Holding up the paper, he pointed at the line on the page with his pen.

Gwen jumped up this time, objecting on the basis that these exhibits hadn't been timely provided so her witness could examine them when doing her analysis. Sawyer was not impressed, and moved the questioning on.

Linda looked at the papers in her hand. Gwen noticed that her right knee had begun to shake up and down. "Yes, I see. But I don't believe these were provided to me before today."

"Really? You might ... "

Gwen interjected, "Objection, I wish to state for the record that...."

"Chairman Sawyer, I object to opposing counsel's...."

Sawyer hollered, "Stop both of you. I will have decorum." Sawyer then blamed both of them and told them he wouldn't countenance such conduct. And if it happened again there'd be consequences from the NASD down the road. Gwen assumed this meant money fines, something she definitely wanted to avoid. Finally, Sawyer told Day to continue and Gwen to stay seated. And that's how it went through the afternoon that remained.

Day repeatedly showed Linda moneys paid by Sammy from his account for various personal expenses, most all in small amounts for living costs. Day then moved on to claiming that his client was in full compliance with the NY Stock Exchange maintenance requirements when it came to margin trading and that Stanley, Howe's set equity value in a margin lending account satisfied this standard. Linda repeatedly exclaimed that she had no knowledge of this, except that the margin maintenance value she read about far exceeded what the firm used for Mr. Perez's account, thus increasing the latitude of the firm's profitable margin trading for Sammy. Gwen understood this to mean that if the bank required you maintain $300 of assets for free checking instead of $500, then more customers could participate in the program. If the program were to be profitable, it meant more money for the bank. Or something to that effect. When Day asked for specifics as to the source of her belief, Linda was unable to provide any other than refer to general common accounting educational materials.

"Now, one more question Ms. DeNardi."

Gwen's stomach immediately tightened. She hated these pregnant promises, as they often were followed by disasters. She'd had enough tsunamis already for one afternoon. Gwen held her breath, waiting for the sky to fall.

"You said you noted the investment goals of Mr. Perez checked on his New Account Application. You understand, don't you, that the suitability of these goals is based on information the investor provides the broker, correct?"

"I believe so. Although that's not my field."

"You don't know what information Mr. Perez provided to Mr. Murphy do you?"

"Well, no. I wasn't there. But as I said before, I have reviewed the New Account Application and Mr. Perez's tax returns."

"Yes," Day raised his voice for emphasis, "but as you said, you don't know what Mr. Perez told Mr. Murphy verbally because you weren't there. You don't know whether the broker was told by Mr. Perez that he owned considerable property in the Caribbean, had a manufacturing business on the islands, and other claimed assets, isn't that correct?" Having made his point Day concluded, almost as an aside,

"You need not answer that. I have no more questions of this witness."

Day sat down. Mandel followed with, "I have no questions for this witness at this time."

Reluctantly, Gwen rose as time was becoming even more of an issue. "I just have one or two questions on redirect, Mr. Sawyer."

When Sawyer affirmed it was her turn, Gwen asked, "Ms. DeNardi, based on your review of the statements in Mr. Perez's' Stanley, Howe securities accounts, initially his accounts did well, didn't they?"

"Yes, that appears, um...that is, it was my impression that was the case."

"At times, the account statements showed a total value of about $140,000, occasionally even higher, correct?" Gwen noticed out of the corner of her eye that Day had started to stand up but then as quickly sat down.

"Yes."

"With that in mind, that his account had substantial funds, and accepting Mr. Day's representation that there were several minor withdrawals by Mr. Perez from his account, isn't it true that the totality of the amounts allegedly withdrawn, when compared with the total, using just simple division would show such withdrawals were minimal, and they did not substantially lessen Mr. Perez's financial loss?" Gwen realized her question was long enough to be confusing, so she tried again. "In other words, any such difference in numbers representing trading losses between yours and Mr. Day's are minimal when viewed in the context of the total value of the account?"

"I would say yes."

"And, moreover, it may well be- indeed we shall show- that in light of the bull market and the initial growth in these accounts, Mr. Murphy encouraged such withdrawals, correct?"

"Yes."

"No more redirect," Gwen said and sat down. She tried to look confident but knew her pulse rate was probably a nice high number. When no re-cross was requested, Sawyer dismissed Linda. She got up and quickly exited the room. Gwen and Martha, both holding their pens so tightly that their knuckles were white, gave her supportive smiles as she walked by.

"Okay. Let's take a short five-minute break and then I'm determined that we make a substantial effort to finish with Claimant's next witness tonight. I'm correct, Attorney Wilson, that you've told me your next witness is not available after today?"

"Yes, she has travel commitments that were made before the last hearing extension."

Looking around the room, Sawyer advised, "Therefore, gentlemen, please make arrangements to stay later today." Gwen looked at her watch, 5:15 p.m., already past the initial four o'clock closing time. She rose and walked out with Martha. They found Linda drinking a bottle of water in a quiet corner down the hall and joined her.

Gwen gave her a hug, then said to her friends, "Hey guys, it wasn't too bad. I think we still have a good shot at a W. They didn't really attack the churning claim, and while maybe Perez did divert some of the funds, and we don't know whether Murphy encouraged this, Sammy still lost a bundle. And we can address the 30% maintenance guideline Day admitted Stanley, Howe sometimes used, which Linda believes is lower than any accepted trading standard. So we're still in the game. In fact, I think we're ahead. And when Sammy arrives, maybe he can clarify some of those withdrawals. Could be they were connected with margin calls. As I recall, he did take some money out to start up that t-shirt business, but only after he'd lost lots, including his job."

Gwen shook Linda's hand, said thanks, and asked her if she wanted to leave or stay.

"I've got to stay – as Martha and I drove in together. But I think I'll meet you at the donut shop across the street. I've had enough for, well, for forever."

Gwen sat quietly with Martha during the wait. She thought about calling Adam and decompressing, but better to wait until she could do so with a glass of wine in her hand – while he micro-waved dinner. She would just sip the Chardonnay, close her eyes, put her feet up and maybe rest her head on Adam's chest. Then she remembered she had to meet Sammy that evening and groaned out loud.

"Everything okay?" asked Martha.

"Just remembered how long my day will be. Oh well..." Gwen looked around the room watching the busy suits at work, probably updating their time sheets and making plans for a fancy business paid dinner. With her gut feeling unhappy, Gwen understood that her DNA was not designed for confrontational warfare, even if at times it proved a power trip for her ego. She'd long ago accepted that going to law school involved making a bargain with the devil – agree to a sometime testosterone-bolstered life in exchange for fighting for justice. Her internal nature was geared – like most women she knew – to mediation, compromise, let's not forget empathy. These were not exactly highly valued traits for litigators. Sammy's case fit in to this bargain, as she was helping the little guy get a fair shake. Okay, and there was also the part about saving her practice.

But was that enough anymore? When she was young and full of optimism about the law, 'standing up to wrong' was enough of a goal. Today, she wasn't sure she still maintained the will, stamina, or belief in legal institutions to continue the day-to-day small practice grind, especially as often the reward was ephemeral. Not only was she disposed to pass the baton in the race to those younger and eager souls, she was, she realized, maybe even disposed to just drop it on the ground and walk off the track.

CHAPTER THIRTY-THREE

Gwen's star witness, Martha Stoneham, pulled down her skirt, arranged her blouse and made herself comfortable in the witness chair that had now been placed next to Loretta. Dressed in a white linen outfit set off by gold around neck, wrists, and fingers, Martha presented a contrast to Linda's 'backroom accountant' look. Gwen knew that she had to use her time wisely as the evening had already started to darken and she absolutely had to have Martha finish her testimony today. That meant leaving enough time for Respondents to finish so they wouldn't dare claim they hadn't had enough time.

Gwen began her questions by establishing that Martha satisfied the 'expert witness' credentials. She quickly reviewed Martha's qualifications: twenty plus years of managing a multi-million-dollar portfolio of clients' accounts, bank portfolio manager, CFA – 'chartered financial analyst' certified, experience with suitability and churning rules, continuing ed. classes on these issues, and Chief Investment Officer to a national banking firm prior to joining her present firm as a partner. She then asked Martha, as she had with Linda, to summarize the documents she'd reviewed in this case, Martha added that many she thought were missing. Martha also affirmed that she'd held two conversations with Sammy.

Gwen asked Martha to summarize her findings. "I learned that at the time he became a client of Stanley, Howe, Mr. Perez had liquid assets of almost $60,000. I put his total net assets in the low six figures if you included his retirement and benefit plans, wife's business, and house equity share. I also became aware from our conversations that he is currently disabled and earning perhaps half of his prior income and is now divorced, all making his assets lower." Turning towards the Panel, Martha added, "Based on this information, I concluded that his financial situation at the time he opened an account with Stanley, Howe appeared minimally sufficient to carry him through his senior years and to provide for his family and the education of his children. As regards his objectives, according to the account application form, which he told me he didn't complete..."

A cry of "Objection!" came from Marty Mandel and others at Respondents' side of the table. Mandel explained, "Ms. Stoneham is relaying hearsay so I move to strike her last response."

Sawyer stared at Marty, shook his head, then responded, "Gentlemen and Ms. Wilson, let's move on. Do I need to repeat myself? As with Ms. DeNardi, the Panel will give Ms. Stoneham's testimony the weight it deems appropriate. It is getting late and unless you want to stay for the weekend – and if necessary I will hold a session at my offices on Saturday, Attorney Mandel – we need to speed up. Does everyone understand that? It has been a long day, some of us still have to go to our offices tonight, so, I implore all, let's get moving."

Silence filled the room. Then Martha continued her answer. "As I was saying,

Mr. Perez's investment goals on his new account form – which I consider essential to determining suitability – were listed as growth, meaning to me a fairly aggressive approach to trading, and speculation, which I believe was totally inappropriate. However, as I noted, my opinion just offered is based on the limited materials I had access to." Facing the Panel, Martha continued, "I found a surprisingly large number of missing documents I would have expected to have been produced, at least documents that I insist on having for my clients, for example, the completed account agreement – items I consider basic."

"The new account form was incomplete?" asked Sawyer, surprise lighting his face.

"I saw two forms. The one signed by Mr. Perez had several blanks, and the second one, a copy it appeared, had notations on the back that I couldn't decipher."

Gwen followed up. "What else do you believe was not

provided?" Gwen was glad Martha was running with her answers and didn't require her to pull teeth. Besides, after her recent cleaning by Drea the dreaded hygienist, she wanted nothing to do with teeth for a while, like maybe decades.

Martha ticked off missing items on her fingers: "Telephone notes, memoranda about conversations, summary notes about assets, proof of retirement benefits, prior trading experience. I also would have liked to have had research notes about stocks purchased, especially as so many were small hi-tech startups where Stanley, Howe was market maker, and, let me think, also the basis for in-out trades, and importantly a long- term plan for the account. As I said, I consider all this basic client investment information pursuant to the due diligence obligation to KYC – Know Your Client." Martha paused and sipped some water from the glass on her right. Her diamond ring's faucets flashed off the chandelier lights. "Also, I'd like to have known why a margin account was opened. Just filling in the details would have been helpful."

Gwen paused, letting all sink in. She thought about going over the list and asking more questions to emphasize the incompleteness of Murphy's file, at least as provided to her. Needing to move forward, she pressed on. After all, these Panel members – all experienced in securities sales – knew all this as well as Martha did. And, after Sawyer's recent pique, she didn't want to upset the applecart.

"Ms. Stoneham, based on these documents and conversations with Mr. Perez, do you have an opinion whether the registered representative, Mr. Murphy, and his full-service firm, Stanley, Howe breached their legal obligation to Mr. Perez to invest in suitable products?"

Day rose again, like the 'Old Faithful' hot spring repeatedly shooting upwards at Yellowstone Park. "Objection, no foundation for an opinion, especially one on law. Unless Ms. Stoneham also has a 'JD' attached to her credentials which she forgot to mention."

Sawyer responded, "It would be helpful, Attorney Wilson, if

you set more of a foundation before your witness gives an expert opinion, despite our time pressure."

Taking this advice while marking in her mind that Sawyer called her 'Attorney' when he appeared to be advising her on what she should be doing, Gwen worked on going more slowly. She reviewed with Martha the standards applicable to determining if a course of trading is 'suitable' for an investor, and followed up with clarifying Martha's experience in applying these standards.

Gwen was impressed with how comfortable and commanding Martha was. No wonder she used her as her own financial advisor, to the extent she had any savings to protect. Day must be regretting his objection, she hoped. She continued on her roll.

"Ms. Stoneham, can you explain what you understand 'suitability' means?"

"I consider suitability to be at the heart of providing sound investment advice. It goes to whether the client's accounts are being invested sensibly and prudently for that client's financial position. This is required, as the members of the Panel are aware, as I said before, by the industries' Know Your Customer rule. It obligates both the broker and the investment firm to use due diligence to ensure that their securities recommendations – be it purchase, sale, or exchange – appropriately take into consideration the suitability and reasonableness of the proposed action."

Day rose as if to object, but then sat down. Mandel got up and briefly walked over and conversed with Day, and then returned to his seat. Gwen was sure all of this was to push Martha off her track as she was doing so well.

Martha, ignoring the sideshow, continued her testimony. "As I was saying, the KYC rule includes assessment, as we've discussed, of the client's financial situation, investment knowledge, investment objectives, and, of course, risk tolerance. The process begins with the New Account Application, which is why that form is so important as it provides relevant client details and the client's motivation for investment choices."

You go girl.

Martha then added, "As I said, based on this industry standard, the financial advisor should have a reasonable basis that the purchase conforms to the client's financial needs and objectives.

That is why I would have liked to have seen more supportive documentation regarding the trading history in Mr. Perez's account."

Gwen was now getting to the meat of the case. Filet Mignon here we come. "Were there specific concerns you had when reviewing Mr. Perez's accounts?"

"Yes. As I mentioned, I was concerned that someone close to retirement age seemed to have so much of his portfolio invested in two primary business areas, technology and telecommunications. Both are traditionally volatile sectors of the economy." Martha paused, playing with the many gold bracelets hanging from her wrist, then, looking directly at the Panel, she stated, "Vehicles in general stocks as I'm sure you are aware, which in this case were most of the account, carry high risk, particularly when primarily made up as here of telecommunications issues with limited or no earnings.

But my opinion on suitability is not related to profitability. There were some profitable investments and some not profitable. The other issue that stood out to me was that the account was a margin account. Mr. Perez had limited assets, and so such a risky vehicle is definitely not appropriate. The risk is compounded when the stock selection itself is quite volatile, as I noted was the case here. And it appears that the unsuitability of margin turned out to be case. Mr. Perez was approaching retirement at that time. Even if his assets were substantially greater, the general standard for a client of that age is to invest only up to 25% of his assets in equities."

"Did Mr. Perez's portfolio exceed that amount?" "Yes, it was all invested in equities."

"100%?"

"Yes."

Gwen continued, "If an investor has little sophistication with the stock market, does this affect suitability?"

"Clients should understand the risks associated with various stock purchases but, even if an investor is more sophisticated than Mr. Perez is – and he is *not* informed based on my discussions with him, the investments should still be suitable."

There followed Martha's understanding of Sammy's lack of financial sophistication marked by repeated objections of counsel up and down the table, claiming 'hearsay', and 'without foundation', all of which Sawyer responded to with his usual admonition that she could answer for now and the Panel would determine later what weight to give her response.

Gwen now focused on closing the circle, asking the expert opinion question, "Do you have an opinion as to whether growth and speculation were suitable investment goals for Mr. Perez?"

"Absolutely not. In my opinion, his account maybe should have been invested in safe products, such as government bonds, maybe a limited number of low-risk vehicles."

"What is your opinion as to whether the investments made by Mr. Murphy were suitable for Mr. Perez?"

Again, after a series of denied objections, Martha stated, "In my opinion *none* of the investments in his account were appropriate/"

"None?"

"No, none."

Gotcha, Gwen shouted silently, ready to give Martha a congratulatory hand fist. Gwen let the opinion echo through the room. She punctuated Martha's statement by visibly making a check mark on her legal pad. Taking a sip of water from the glass on the table, organizing her note cards, she looked up at Martha and went on with her questions regarding Sammy's churning claims. While Linda had dealt with this issue, Martha was so impressive, Gwen thought it a good idea to go over this charge again.

"Did you notice whether there was frequent account activity?"

Martha then discussed the extensive trading in Sammy's account, "It appeared to me the intent was to purchase stock, make a quick profit, and sell it quickly."

Day, rising, stated in a slightly higher tone than before, "Objection."

"What's the nature of your objection?" Gwen asked him.

Before Sawyer could act, Day said, "Sorry, my fault. Go ahead. No harm, no foul."

Gwen was annoyed, sure that the intervention was just to slow down her good rhythm. She looked for her hammer to whack him one, but she must have left it in the toy store. So she moved on, like a matador going in for the kill, except of course she was almost a vegetarian and preferred to pick up spiders and carry them out the front door if possible. Still, damages needed to be addressed, so she persevered, sword in hand.

"Do you have an opinion on what would have been a reasonable return on these accounts if invested suitably?"

"Industry standard is Treasury Bills rate of return." "Have industry standards been satisfied here?"

"I have an opinion – which I just gave. No."

Day's final assault, "Move to strike, asked and answered."

Gwen decided it was time to stop, even if not with a big bang. "Thank you, no more questions."

Now, all that remained to make Sammy's case was for her client to show up and testify.

CHAPTER THIRTY-FOUR

Today was Day's day. Gwen was prepared to take notes from the maestro litigator on how to do a top-notch cross-examination of an opponent's witness. While she had respected Bradford Foster's smart chess moves, Day was a member of the New York 'best-rated litigation lawyer' club, and he was a dangerous shark ready to bite. She had no doubt that he would go for the jugular when questioning her experts if he thought it would help his client's case. Gwen tried to hide her concerns by busily organizing her area of the conference table. Water glass to the left, highlighters laid out on her right, and aspirin in her briefcase. No one needed to see the state of her knuckles, which for the moment she held under the table.

Sawyer reached for the microphone on the dais and gave it a quick tap with his pen. Satisfied that it was on, he glanced at his watch and then asked Day, "Shall you be cross-examining Ms. Stoneham?"

"Yes, thank you, Mr. Sawyer."

Sawyer signaled to Josiah to begin.

Walking around his end of the oval table, he moved closer to Martha. Then, in a friendly, respectful tone, as if he they were socializing over drinks, he began his questions. "Ms. Stoneham, I must say you have an impressive background. Admirable accomplishments. It is nice to see that there are members of our finer sex who find securities trading as fascinating as I do."

Martha politely smiled back. Gwen sent a mind message to her not to be disarmed by his pleasant manner, to remember that was how the Big Bad Wolf had gotten to eat Little Red Riding Hood. But she knew the reception in the room couldn't handle cell phone service, and so doubted it transmitted her brain thoughts. She assured herself that Martha was one smart cookie, a savvy woman who'd spent her life dealing with men who thought they were sharper than her. So, Gwen watched warily as Day worked his skills, switching on a dime from ingratiating colleague to hard-nosed litigator.

"Wouldn't you agree, Ms. Stoneham, that the definition of suitability in regards to an investment account is not a fixed concept?"

"I'm not sure I follow."

"Let me see if I can explain, then. What is an appropriate risk for one investor may not be appropriate for another investor, right?" Before Martha could respond, Day continued, "Let me put it more simply if you like."

Trying to make her presence felt early on, in hopes of cautioning Day not to overreach on her watch, Gwen called out, "Objection." She then said, "Ms. Stoneham is a highly trained professional and does not need simple questions, just clear ones."

Sawyer looked up at the ceiling as if for divine guidance, then said, "Attorney Day, please continue without the characterization. You know better." This was followed by another watch glance and admonition to all to move along.

Day dutifully nodded and back to his mellifluous tone and manner, said "I'm sorry, Ms. Stoneham, if I was unclear. Please let me know if you don't understand the question. As I was saying...."

Squirming, Gwen realized her objection had allowed Day to repeat his question. *Don't grab at the bait, Gwennie. Martha's a big girl, well able to handle herself.* Gwen made a point of sitting on her hands.

Martha, continuing her answer, said, "...when you are considering the appropriateness of an investment strategy, what is reasonable for a thirty year old is likely different from what is reasonable for a sixty year old like Mr. Perez nearing retirement, correct?"

"Yes, as I thought I'd said, I agree with that."

"And what is reasonable for someone who just lost a job may not be reasonable for someone who was awarded a large promotion, or someone who has outside income versus another investor who depends on his job for income, correct?"

"Yes, of course."

Gwen waited for the ball to drop. At least Martha was following her advice of not responding more than necessary.

"So, you'd agree with me, wouldn't you, that a broker should consider the broad financial position of an investor, in other words, all the assets in his portfolio when assessing what is acceptable risk?"

"Again, yes. Again, I believe I've already stated that."

Picking up on this comment, Day added, "And you also stated, correct, that a broker should be guided by the financial sophistication of his client, his prior trading experience, his knowledge of risk, his ability to withstand losses?"

"I agree. Once more, I believe I discussed all that when I stated that I thought the broker in this case failed to follow these rules."

"Yes, you set out for the Panel what *you* think the standards are in the industry. Now, let's be a little more specific. You said you reviewed Mr. Perez's account documents." Getting no answer Day continued. "I show you Exhibit 8. Mr. Sawyer, it is included at p. 58 of the first binder. For ease of reference let my assistant hand a copy to the Panel and to Attorney Wilson."

Gwen watched as the cute associate did his job of handing out these papers, for which he had prepared by spending three years at an expensive law school, passing a difficult exam, and working 100 hours a week since then.

"I believe Attorney Wilson reviewed an earlier prepared version of this document before with the Panel. But the substance of both is the same. Now, ..."

"Objection," yelled Gwen. What was Day doing here, subbing documents? "I object to any change in documents that I haven't reviewed, nor had an opportunity to review with my witness. This is outrageous, Mr. Sawyer. After much effort, Counsel for the parties had an agreement, and it is a clear breach for Attorney Day to unilaterally exchange what is a key exhibit in this case."

Sawyer turned and consulted with both 'Tweedles.' then stated, "Attorney Day, are the documents essentially the same? Why the need to switch?"

"I assure the Panel this change was inadvertent, my associate included the final version contained in the file, which I had understood until just recently had been the one reviewed by Ms. Wilson. Other than perhaps for minor contract terms, there is I believe no substantive difference that would impact on this matter. I will be pleased to provide Panel and Ms. Wilson tomorrow a sheet showing the exact differences if the Panel wishes."

Sawyer looked stymied. After a long pause he finally said, "Mr. Day, based on your assurances, that won't be necessary. However, it would be helpful if you submit such a comparison during the next several weeks to the Panel and Ms. Wilson, at which time Ms. Wilson may file a Motion to Strike from the record with the NASD should she so wish."

Day gave the Panel his assurances, and Gwen secretly added a second notch to her litigation belt. Day then continued his cross.

"Ms. Stoneham, can you see Exhibit 8, the document is titled 'New Account Agreement'?

"Yes."

"Do you note the boxes checked off at the top of the agreement?"

"Yes."

"Please tell the Panel what they say?"

"The boxes say that Mr. Perez's investment goals are growth and speculation."

"And you have previously pointed that out to the Panel. Now please look at the bottom of the form. Whose signature is that?"

"I don't know who actually signed it but it says as best as I can decipher 'Sammy Perez.'"

"Do you have *any* factual basis to question the veracity of this document? That is a yes or no question. As you noted, it is complete and signed by Mr. Perez."

Gwen noticed that Day's tone was beginning to up the *ante* on nasty confrontational. She'd wondered how long it would take him to get there.

Martha said, "I don't know..."

"Yes or no?"

Martha ignored this direction and continued, "... who had checked those boxes. Based on the profile on the application, in my opinion they are not appropriate goals; they allow way too much risk."

"By your non-answer I believe the Panel should take that as a no. So, if we agree that Mr. Perez did fill out that form, doesn't that affect your opinions to this Panel? Doesn't it make any trading goals acceptable if carried out at the customer's direction?"

"No."

"No?" Day displayed astonishment, his eyebrows flaring upward. "Is it your testimony that a broker should be able to just ignore a customer's direction?"

Martha looked at Day but did not respond.

Day moved closer to her, leaning forward over the conference table as if he were a linebacker about to pounce.

"Excuse me," Gwen said into the microphone, "I'd ask Mr. Day to give the witness more space."

Taking a step back but still leaning in, Day continued, "So, Ms. Stoneham, let me see if I have this right. It is your opinion that in a standard discretionary account, the investor's agreed upon trading objectives and directives can be ignored by the broker?"

Martha calmly answered as if Day were one of her students. "First, there are varying degrees of broker control in accounts. And it is my opinion that, based on Mr. Perez's lack of financial sophistication, his reliance and trust in the firm and Mr. Murphy, the fees he paid for their services, his repeated verbal directions to only trade in quality stock — which it appears were ignored, and that Mr. Murphy completed highly risky trades without consultation with Mr. Perez, present here was the 'essence' of broker control irrespective of language in any form agreement." Martha twisted in her chair and faced the Panel. "These factors warrant in my opinion greater 'suitability' scrutiny."

Martha then explained further. "But I would also say yes to your question. In my view it is appropriate for a broker, especially at a full-service firm such as Stanley, Howe, to independently use his -- or her – training and skill to make a determination as to the suitability of the risk presented. In sum, it is my view based on my training and decades of management that any registered representative with a full-service firm like the one here should not engage in trading that is inappropriately risky based on the totality of information available to that broker. Certainly not without explicit clarification and warning to a client regarding any client proposed trades, none of which safeguards were present here." Martha paused and, looking squarely at Murphy, she said, "It was Larry Murphy who effectively drove this bus. It is clear to me, and I suggest should be as well to this Panel, that Mr. Perez didn't even know how to handle a stick shift. At best he was a passenger on this bus, and sadly for him Murphy drove it into a ditch."

Martha's answer was met with silence. Gwen noticed that the Panel looked at her with apparent alarm. Grimes sat there with his mouth open, like he'd swallowed a fly. Gwen surmised that in their world, ethical considerations did not top their profit-making concerns. They accepted that Murphy was acting as a salesperson for the investment firm and that, unlike lawyers and financial advisors, he'd undertaken no 'fiduciary duty' with Sammy, that is, the duty first to act in Sammy's best interest, not his own.

Nice try guys, but you're wrong. As to suitability and churning of customer accounts, the law is clear. Based on federal statutes, regulations, industry rules, judicial decisions, as she'd set out in a Memorandum attached to her Statement of Claims, the law protects the foolish or ignorant investor from a broker's overreaching.

Now, Gwen just had to convince these industry lifers that Larry's conduct had exceeded even their permissible bounds of overreaching.

Day, believing he'd scored one for his team moved on. To Gwen's surprise he started by addressing again Martha's professional training, an issue Day had commended her on. Gwen was at a loss as to how this would help him. Still, she felt the hairs on her arms rise. Were his prior kind words just a set-up for an attack? What nefarious trick was he trying to pull?

"Now, Ms. Stoneham, I see here on your CV, about two-thirds of the way down, that you obtained an advanced 'Banking' certificate from the School of Banking at Webster University, isn't that correct?"

Martha nodded yes, then spoke into the microphone, "Excuse me. Yes I did. Some years ago now."

"Let me see if I have this straight. You claim to have gotten this advanced degree... um... certificate as part of a *degree* program offered at the banking school, am I correct?"

Martha didn't flinch. "Yes."

Without pausing Day went on, "I don't want to belabor the point, Ms. Stoneham, but Webster is my *alma mater*, and I appreciate firsthand that it is a fine school; indeed I consider it to be an excellent school. And as a member of the school's Board of Trustees I know a little bit about its programs. Frankly, Ms. Stoneham, I have never heard of an independent School of Banking at Webster."

Now Gwen got it. The old legal maxim is that if you can't win on the law you try to win on the facts, and if you can't win on that, well then you attack the witness. And that's what Day was trying to do, raise into question Martha's integrity, her credibility.

"I'm sorry, is there a question there?" asked Martha, trying to turn the tables.

Day stopped and without blinking glared into her eyes. Raising his voice he rejoined, "You bet there is!" Walking back and forth in the aisle behind his chair, without taking his eyes off Martha, he stated, "So if I called the Registrar for Webster right now, and I have his phone number here, ..." Day held up his yellow legal pad, "... and I know him personally. So, if I asked him about this School of Banking and this degree, er... certificate that you say you earned, you are testifying under oath I remind you, he would know what you're talking about?"

"Yes, he should."

"Well, I did contact Jim Collins yesterday and he told me, Ms. Stoneham, that there is no, and never was a School of Banking at Webster? Knowing that credibility is an essential requirement for any witness, aren't you telling this Panel that they can't have confidence in your testimony? For lying..."

"Objection, objection. This is outrageous that..."

Day continued, speaking more loudly to drown Gwen out. "...about such a minor matter may well establish concerns about what else may not be the case, wouldn't you agree?"

Martha smiled slightly but her eyes were like ice. Gwen had heard the expression 'if looks could kill'..., and she thought she was seeing it now. Martha pulled her skirt down and pushed her hair back, then calmly stated, "I don't know whether this program is still operating, as it has been a number of years since I enrolled in that course, as my CV reflects. But I can assure you...." Martha looked up at the Panel, "I did attend such a program and I did earn such a certificate."

Sawyer asked her to tell them more or would she like to change her testimony. Gwen held her breath.

Martha sighed, flashed her large diamond ring while straightening her suit jacket, and then turned directly to Day. In a flat clipped response she stated, "No, Mr. Sawyer, I will not change my testimony one iota. While I am surprised at his, that is your friend Jim's lack of historical knowledge about his own school, I did enroll – as stated on my CV – in a two- year program offered at that time in what Webster described as its School of

Banking. Neither of us are recently out of school, are we Mr. Day, so we are going back some time. Perhaps Mr. Collins is sufficiently younger he has no institutional memory. No matter. The program I was in involved part-time study over the summer on campus and the remainder of the program was off campus – which was its great appeal to me as I was working and raising my two children at the time. I earned and received the certificate I listed and, if you like, I will try to find a copy of it – which I presume is probably somewhere in a box in my basement.

As you know from your own experience, Mr. Day, Webster is an excellent university and it was a rigorous program. I still look back fondly not only at the collegiality of my fellow students, some of whom have risen through the professional ranks with me – and I'd be happy to give the Panel their names, and the support of the faculty for those of us trying to acquire additional skills while already dealing with a heavy load. Along with the many hot summer nights when on campus studying, I also was lucky to be enthralled by the Worthington Center's numerous cultural programs that left me with a love of classical music. I presume you also knew that place well, Josiah, during your student days."

In the silence that followed, all eyes in the room turned to Day. He quickly walked to his chair, his back to Martha and to Gwen – and to the Panel. Speaking towards the lawyers down the table, he murmured, "I don't think that will be necessary."

After reviewing papers on his desk, Day faced Martha again to continue his cross. "Ms. Stoneham, to summarize, you've testified that Respondents engaged in, let me see, inappropriate investment strategy, high volume trading and inappropriate investment vehicles, correct?"

"Yes, all of the above. Primarily because of what I understand to have been his income, limited assets, age and lack of investment knowledge."

"Kindly respond to my questions, please. That required only a yes or no response."

Gwen decided it was time for her to speak up and exert her presence in order to protect her client. "Objection. Would the Panel please advise Counsel not to continue to harass the witness? It is more than enough that he has cast unfounded aspersions on her character. Now Mr. Day wants to have his cake and eat it too, testifying about her prior testimony, and then objecting when she clarifies his own unfounded testimony included in his question. If Mr. Day wishes only yes or no answers, perhaps he should leave the testimony to the witness."

Turning rapidly toward Gwen, Day started to respond before Sawyer's gavel yielded silence in the room. Sawyer followed this with, "Move on, Attorney Day."

Combing his hair back and straightening his tie, Day drank some water and then renewed his attack. "Now if a client represents to his broker that he has substantial assets outside of what was disclosed on the application form, would that affect your opinion? That is, as regards suitability."

"It could, depending on the capital amount. But I'd want to know why it wasn't disclosed on the form. The broker should make inquiry. There are no documents, notes, anything I saw that showed this was done. But, yes, I'd want to know what assets and net worth were not disclosed."

"Are you aware of the performance of Mr. Perez's employer LCD's company stock?"

"It performed well, providing stockholders with substantial paper earnings. Until a significant later decline I believe."

Day pressed, "In sum, Ms. Stoneham, if a client makes financial disclosures regarding assets, such as a claim that he has a retirement plan valued at hundreds of thousands of dollars, or valuable real estate located out of the country, and these asset claims are unsupported by documentation provided by the client, isn't that all the brokerage house need rely on? Isn't it the obligation of the client, not the broker, to be honest? Surely, clients can be slick and unreliable, right? I presume you have experienced that."

"There are times when I believe reasonable investigation by the broker is called for."

"I see. So the firm must hire its own private investigators to ensure their clients are being up and up, on the level, with them?" With his right arm moving up and down repeatedly as if he were chopping wood, and his voice rising, Day continued, "Wouldn't that yield chaos and innumerable conflicts that would negatively impact on the smooth efficiency of the market? And thereby result in excessive fees and costs to honest investors? And market strangulation? Strike that." Day took a sip of water and then removed his jacket. "I hope the Panel doesn't mind, but it is quite warm in here."

"No problem," Sawyer said. "I will check on the air conditioning situation for tomorrow. Please continue, Attorney Day. But be aware of the times constraints as it is getting quite late."

"Thank you, Mr. Sawyer, I am almost finished." Day took a moment to review his notes and several documents. Then he was ready for his next attack. "Now, Ms. Stoneham, are you aware of the fact that Mr. Perez went through a divorce during the relevant time period?"

"I became aware of this."

"Are you aware that Mr. Perez transferred money from one Stanley, Howe trading account to another account opened at his request by Mr. Murphy shortly after Mrs. Perez had filed for the divorce? And that this second account was undisclosed to his wife, thereby *hiding* these moved assets, and, Ms. Stoneham, that the family court when it became aware of this attempt to cheat, the judge froze this second account?"

Gwen felt like someone had wacked her in the chest. Had the court ruled that Sammy had cheated? She'd briefly reviewed the Separation Agreement reached in Sammy's divorce, but it appeared to provide for the standard division of marital property. Was there more 'there'? Rising, she stated, "Objection. This question states facts not in evidence, addresses a matter irrelevant to these proceedings, is hearsay and without foundation." But Gwen knew that it was very damaging if true as often panel members relied on their feelings about the investor Claimant – and who likes a man who cheats on his wife and children?

Sawyer jumped into the fray, clearly alert. As now did Tweedledum and Tweedledee. "I think it goes to who owned this account and the credibility of the Claimant, so I'll let the question stand. You will have the opportunity, Ms. Wilson, for redirect if you like." Looking at Martha, Sawyer added, "You may answer."

"No."

Day, recognizing his advantage, played out this line of inquiry as if he were a violinist playing a long high note before an audience. "Mr. Perez didn't tell you this, did he, in your two communications? Nor did he tell you why his wife is not participating in this hearing, did he?"

Gwen objected again, further mentioning that under the divorce decree, this was Sammy's account and so, with his wife's consent, his case.

Martha was silent, not showing that this news *if* true made Sammy out to be a slimy, reprehensible, deceitful spouse in her mind. However, Gwen doubted that the Panel would be as open-minded.

Day said, "Were you aware that Mr. Perez had prior investment experience, and that this involved his controlling his account activity?"

"When I looked at records provided by Attorney Wilson, there was one reference to a small transfer into Respondent's firm from a non-operating account at Freedom International. Freedom, I understand ..."

Day broke in. "Excuse me, please just answer the question asked. That was a yes or no question."

Martha ignored this interruption one more time and completed her testimony, adding, "...is a discount brokerage firm and I am not sure whether it is still in existence. Anyhow, despite some research, I was not able to review copies of any statements from this account."

Day repeated, "Please answer the question whether you were or were not aware."

"Although you asked two questions, my answer to both is yes, subject to my prior comment."

"Ms. Stoneham, does the existence of this prior account with Freedom International, and the fact that there was some trading on margin in that account, and I refer you to..." Day thumbed through his yellow pad, then gave the reference location, Exhibit 157 in the third black binder at pp. 450 to 455. "Did this prior trading influence your opinions given today?"

Gwen rose. "Objection. I note for the record that I requested copies of any such third-party trading documents from Respondents and did not receive any response prior to this hearing. Thus I did not see these documents nor agree to their inclusion in the binders and I object to their admission."

Sawyer asked Day, "Is that correct?"

"It appears, Mr. Sawyer, we just received copies of these documents ourselves and included them in the binder as being highly relevant. Copies were recently provided Attorney Wilson I believe..." Day consulted with one of his assistants, then added, "Yes, yesterday. Additionally, it was our assumption that these documents were in the Claimant's possession – as he was the investor and acted as a trader."

After consulting with his *compadres* on the dais, Sawyer advised that the Panel would allow this testimony and admit the documents, and that Gwen would be provided sufficient time to review the material and conduct, as was her right, a redirect of Martha, or to renew her objection. He then instructed Day to move on, noting that Ms. Stoneham could not have relied on this prior trading since she testified she was unaware of it.

Gwen kicked the legs of the table with her foot until her toes hurt – a little. Once again, the relevant power of the parties counted

– to her detriment. She had attempted to obtain these records from Freedom International, the firm where his wife's cousin had briefly traded for the family before he had become ill and moved back to the islands. But Mary had been unable to even locate the firm. Yet, somehow Day had been able to get copies from the apparently defunct business.

Gwen knew from Sammy about this trading, thought it irrelevant as so long ago and family related, but she should have discussed this better with Martha. She'd been waiting for the documents to arrive –which they never did until it seems yesterday. *My fault, I'll have to clean this up when Sammy testifies.*

Day went in for the kill. "Ms. Stoneham, let me get this straight. Would Mr. Perez's trading on margin and in speculative stocks previously, suggesting a prior pattern of gambling, alter or affect your testimony today?"

"No. The strategy followed here was not suitable."

Pacing back and forth, his arms crossed, Day finally stopped and stated, "Come on, Ms. Stoneham, isn't it a question of *who is driving the bus?* Mr. Perez was driving the bus at his prior account and he continued to drive the bus and pursue the same speculative strategy in the Stanley, Howe accounts in question. Isn't that correct?"

"Objection." Gwen stood up one more time, struggling to come up with something to say. "Mr. Day is testifying again. He can't establish his own facts. There is nothing in the record to support his assertions."

Day smiled, then looked at the Panel. "Members of the Panel, first Ms. Wilson accuses me of creating facts. But as she full well knows, of course I have to impute facts based on the documents available – because it is HER witness who has failed to testify – so that there are no facts in the record. Talk about having your cake and eating it too..."

Gwen's attempt for a save didn't matter, however, as Martha responded on this important point. "I don't know what role Mr. Perez played regarding the Freedom account, but even if he might have been driving at the prior brokerage house, that was different. It was a discount brokerage where there are no assigned commission-based advisors. And it was I gather years ago. Here, Mr. Perez paid high fees to get the recommendations of a professional, Larry Murphy, and his firm and both failed to provide those skills."

At this point Sawyer said, "It is getting quite late. Attorney Day, how much longer do you expect to be? Perhaps we should continue this tomorrow, maybe start at 7 a.m. if Ms. Stoneham might be available?"

Gwen noticed that this comment appeared to eat up the oxygen in the room. Like the suits, the thought of getting up at 5 a.m. left her sitting with her mouth open.

Day paused, looked at his notes, consulted with co-counsel, and then said, "That's all I have."

"Would any other Attorney wish to ask questions of this witness? No? Then any redirect?" Sawyer asked Gwen.

Gwen knew Day had been effective. Even she was beginning to doubt Sammy's story. She made a lame attempt at redirect and hoped to have Sammy clarify some of the factual assertions Day made, some of which were new to her. *Damn it again! Why don't clients listen to their lawyers when told to give them all the information, the good, the bad, and the ugly?*

Martha prepared to stand up and leave when Sawyer turned to her and started to ask his own questions. Gwen had begun to relax and think of maybe a nice cup of hot cocoa before bed – it would be too late for Chardonnay – but sat forward, instantly alert.

"Ms. Stoneham, it's my perception that you are testifying that in your opinion this customer should not have been trading in stocks at all?"

"That is correct. He should have been in minimal risks."

"So in terms of suitability, you are saying that, based on industry standards for brokers, this customer was involved in unsuitable trades and thus the Respondents violated the law?"

"Yes."

Sawyer nodded but wasn't done. Looking at his legal pad he asked, "If there were some conversations between Mr. Perez and Mr. Murphy about assets not reflected in the documents, such as the availability of pension assets for example-- do you have an opinion whether industry standards would have prohibited the alleged unsuitable trades?"

"I would need more information, so, I guess, I do not have an opinion without more. But I would be highly doubtful that this would substantially change what was in Mr. Perez's best interest. And, as I've testified, I saw no evidence in the record verifying any verbal representations of additional assets, and these should have been there if that was the basis for trades."

As Martha was starting to stand, Sawyer again went on with his questions. "Do you have an opinion whether industry standards would have prohibited the alleged unsuitable trades – even if they were based on requests initiated by the customer?"

Martha stopped and sat down again. Swirling her bracelets, she paused before answering, then said, "You mean if the customer wanted unreasonable trades? Well, yes. As I've stated, I believe carrying out such requests is improper and wrong under, for example, the 'know your customer' rule."

Sawyer leaned back in his chair. After whispering with both Panel members he said, "I want to thank counsel and witnesses. We'll adjourn for today, continue tomorrow at 10:30 and go at least to 4 p.m. I apologize but I have some matter that came up at my office so I cannot be here earlier. Mr. Perez will testify, so we should finish with Claimant's case tomorrow. Thank you all for staying late."

Martha stood up, gathered her notes at the table, and walked out of the room with Gwen, who marveled that her expert witness appeared so confident, trying to keep up stride for stride behind her, despite her short legs.

Gwen wasn't so sure the day had gone well. Sawyer's

questions especially troubled her for they implied that he was taking an overly narrow view of a broker's duties to his client. Maybe he was just being thorough. But Gwen expected that the battle for Sammy's financial recovery, already an uphill fight thanks to the NASD forum, the Panel's industry leaning proclivity, and the fact that she was facing a powerful baseball team comprised of legal stars, well, it had now become even more of a steep climb.

No problem, Gwennie. I've been running some with Adam. With my recently enhanced quads, in my stylish pink running sneakers, I'm ready to climb that mountain. After all, I live in the Granite State, home of majestic mountain ranges, and the Appalachian Trail. As the song says, 'Ain't no mountain high enough'.... Gwen, free at last from the confines of the conference room, and with no team member to see, began to do a little shimmy á la The Supremes while singing about mountains on the way to her car, pulling her luggage behind her.

Tomorrow, assuming her client showed up, she'd finish putting in her case, and thankfully have her personal porter there to help her. Tonight she'd meet with Sammy and grill him for *all* the truth.

****** **** ******

The road through Dortman was dark. Following Sammy's directions, she drove to the coffee shop next to the Chinese restaurant near Sammy's family house. Bone tired, her feet dragging, she entered the small empty eatery. She took in the dozen tables covered in red and white checkered linoleum tablecloths, each one presenting a plastic flower in a tiny clear vase and rows of condiments, most of which she couldn't identify. Okay, she recognized the red ketchup bottle.

At the table near the entryway sat Sammy, but not the sad Sammy she knew. This Sammy wore a colorful Hawaiian shirt, talked animatedly with the waiter, gesticulating his points with his moving hands. He even smiled, his grin lighting up his face.

Sammy walked over to her and gave her a strong handshake.

"Hi, Attorney, like I promise you, I'm here. I all ready to be smart tomorrow."

Gwen smiled back, and she meant it. Seeing her client so happy was a pleasure. But she knew it was time to get down to work or she'd fall asleep on the drive home. "Sammy, glad you got here all right. What an unexpected adventure – for both of us. How are you feeling?"

"I feel good. White pills of doctor work. Not so anxious." Sammy stopped and rubbed his eyes. Gwen saw tears forming. "And saw my boys today, so I very happy. They get big!" Sammy raised his arms up and made a big circle. "Miss them so it hurt in me. They call me at night many times. Hard, but they gonna' come to visit all family when school on vacation, if it okay with Olanda, and I save money to help pay cost. And I give Olanda present from islands, nice jewelry made by my aunt. She say she like and she allow me to sleep at house tonight so easy to meet with you."

"Is she upset about this court case still?"

"I think not so much; she say boys proud and I strong to take on big company." Sammy again smiled but this time his chest stuck out a little, exuding pride in himself.

"Sammy, we better start as I'm really tired and we have a long day tomorrow. Are you okay with that?"

"Yes."

A tall young woman wearing jeans, a t-shirt that read 'You Can Do It!', and dangling earrings approached. She said hello warmly and asked Gwen if she would like a dish of homemade rice pudding saved for her. Gwen nodded eagerly, aware that her empty stomach was grumbling, and began to organize her notes to review with Sammy. The waitress soon returned bearing a bowl of warm, thick rice pudding with raisins, melting cream and fresh cinnamon. Then the young woman looked at Gwen and solemnly added, "We are all so proud of Sammy. See, he's not rich, not a powerful Latino. Still he's sued this big American company that cheated him. And you've helped him do that. All our community wants to say *gracias* to you. We're all rooting for you and Sammy to win."

After she left, Sammy explained, "She my niece. She go to college next year."

Gwen sampled the dessert and smiled with delight. With the warm welcome and thoughtful treat, she was beginning to rethink Sammy's offer to be his family's guest on the islands. The tangling cinnamon taste still on her tongue, Gwen started going through her list of questions. They worked for an hour, Gwen squeezing in a bite of the spectacular desert when she could. Finally she said, "Enough. We need to stop so we are not too tired tomorrow." With furrowed brow, she added, "Sammy, just making sure you have a way to get to the hearing."

"My cousin Benny, he drive me. Leave early."

"I think you have enough relatives in Dortman to fill Fenway

Park and you are lucky that they care about you so much." Gwen momentarily thought of Artie and promised to herself she would reach out to him again once this damn case was over. Maybe even arrange a vacation visit to the Coast.

After confirming one more time with Sammy that he'd be at the hearing by 9:30 in the morning, Gwen remembered to suggest, "Maybe, Sammy, take one of your little white pills before you leave." She thought about asking him to bring one for her, but figured that with her sensitivity, the little pill might put her to sleep for the remainder of the hearing. Wishful thinking, but probably that would be malpractice not covered by her insurance.

CHAPTER THIRTY-FIVE

Welcome to 'The Sammy Hearing'. Day Two. Sammy's day to tell his story.

But will my client show up?

Thanks to Adam rolling her litigation bag, Gwen pranced into the conference room at 10:05 a.m. arms free to sashay. But to her dismay no one else was there to appreciate her stylish arrival. Except for Adam sitting to her left, she faced a room of empty chairs. She already missed on her side of the table the gender and, of course, professional support of Martha and Linda, but they'd given her what time they had – after the fourth hearing date change. As to the empty chair to her right, it would soon be filled by her client, any time now.

The cherry grandfather clock in the corner, a beautiful antique she'd love to take home and place in her living room, now read 10:10. Gwen began to worry more seriously where Sammy was. Today she'd dressed in her other 'court' suit, the gray one, and a turquoise short-sleeved silk-like blouse. She accessorized with her gold, filigreed pendant – a 'sweet sixteen' present from her father, maybe not as prestigious as her Phi Beta Kappa pin but more noticeable. Adam was handsome of course in his navy suit, with subtle pinstripe, set off by a dark and light blue striped tie. And then there were his boat shoes, great for pulling in the anchor on a cabin cruiser. Other than his footwear, he looked like a well-paid lawyer.

While waiting for the show to begin, Gwen took in a deep "calming" breath and pretended she was listening to waterfalls in a yoga class. Adam placed his legal pad on the table, and then piled high a dozen or so books containing case law and federal statutes – a portable law library – that he'd lugged into the room. Just in case reference to 'the law' would be needed. *Damn, no sign of Sammy yet.* She felt tense, anticipating that this long-awaited day would be long and demanding, that is, if Sammy actually showed up.

Another deep breath.

At 10:15 a.m. Day walked in – attired in a light gray linen suit with Cerulean blue shirt and 'contemporary' green tie, apparently designed by Sesame Street kids practicing their numbers 6, 7, and 8 with orange and yellow crayons. With matching handkerchief and Harvard Law tie clip – Gwen wondered if he'd bought out the school's jewelry offerings – Day successfully looked the dandy courtroom litigator featured on television shows. He nodded to Gwen from across the table. She smiled back as if greeting an old friend. And in a strange way *she* was feeling a sisterly connection to Josiah. Maybe there was something genetic connected with having the JD degree. Or they'd both had to struggle with professional survival despite being non-members of the 'old boy's club'. Day's compatriots walked in, and last – except for the missing Complainant, the 'Tweedles' arrived followed by Loretta and her tapes, all taking their seats at the makeshift dais.

Sawyer started off the day promptly at 10:30. "Good morning lady and gentlemen. Again, I apologize for my need for a late start this morning. Shall we begin?" Looking directly at Adam, Sawyer added, "Is your client present, Attorney Wilson?"

Gwen rose and felt all eyes drilling in on her. "My client is expected momentarily, Mr. Sawyer. I met with him last evening and I expect he's been delayed in traffic." Gwen coughed, her throat already tight from anxiety. Sipping from her cup of hot tea from the café in the building, Gwen presented the only other person on her team who was actually present. "However, I would like to introduce to the Panel and counsel my associate/intern, Adam Webber, who will be assisting me today."

Sawyer stared at Adam over his reading glasses. "Welcome Mr. Webber. Are you a member of the New Hampshire bar?"

Gwen assumed Sawyer asked this question because he was struggling to fit Adam into the proper law firm intern slot, thanks to his slightly graying hair. Without hesitation Adam stood up and said. "Not yet, Mr. Sawyer, but I hope to be soon. I am a law student interning in Attorney Wilson's office." Adam was careful not to state that he'd just begun his second year.

"I see. No problem with your joining us today, Mr. Webber." With that matter done, Sawyer continued to more pertinent issues. "I'd like us to start promptly as I suggest it may be a long day and I have an appointment at my office late this afternoon. Any matters I should be aware of before we begin?" In a louder tone, staring at Gwen, he added, "Except of course the continued absence of your client, Ms. Wilson." Sawyer looked up and down the conference table but no one raised a hand. "On the record, Loretta, please. I do see that our security guard is with us again."

"I have one matter," Day said as he raised his arm.

Sawyer nodded. "Yes? Now is the time while we are once again waiting for the claimant, Attorney Day."

"Members of the Panel, we have here this morning a fact witness, Mr. Cavanaugh. We request that he be allowed to stay in the room during the hearing so that he can assess Mr. Perez's facility — assuming he arrives – with English."

"Any objection, Attorney Wilson?"

Already Gwen felt unprepared. Had she known of this? "I was unaware of this witness prior to now."

"The question is, do you object?" Sawyer asked, his eyes narrowing from impatience.

"No, except I request that, as with fact witnesses, Mr. Cavanaugh be directed to leave the room after I complete a half hour of my direct of Mr. Perez. That should allow him sufficient time to observe without breaching confidentiality."

"I think that's reasonable. The ruling of the Panel is that Mr. Cavanaugh can remain during the preliminary questions to observe Mr. Perez's command of English, but once we get to more specific questions about the facts of this case, he will leave. Attorney Day I trust that you will handle that."

Taking off his glasses and then raking his hair back with his fingers, Sawyer surveyed the room with a stern glare. "Before we begin I want to point out to Counsel again that we are on a tight schedule. Let me punctuate. Neither I nor the other Panel members will condone efforts to delay this matter – or to act in a manner that is more appropriate for courtroom conduct. Am I making myself clear?" Sawyer glanced around the room but no one spoke. "Fine. I will hold you to this standard. Please call your next witness Attorney Wilson."

Gwen by now was feeling flushed. *Damn, where's my client?* "Mr. Perez assured me he would be leaving Dortman by 7 a.m., so I apologize once more to the Panel for this unexpected delay." *Could he be dead? Lost? On a flight back to the islands?*

"I'm sure he'll be here momentarily." Gwen sat down, poured water into her glass, and was ready to wring Sammy's neck. To relieve the growing stress, she squeezed rather than cracked her knuckles under the conference table, not wanting to make any popping sounds that might irritate Sawyer, or alarm the security guard.

During the lull Sawyer shuffled his papers, spoke with the Panel members, then took off his jacket and folded up his shirtsleeves. After more minutes of delay, he spoke into the microphone, "I'm not happy, Attorney Wilson." Looking left, he added, "Loretta, we're off the record. To save time while we wait, would you please swear in Mr. Cavanaugh?"

After Loretta accomplished this, all in the room sat silent, waiting for Sammy's entrance.

The minutes ticked off, slowly, one by one. Gwen admired again the grandfather clock. When Sammy still hadn't arrived five minutes later, Day rose, waived his arms to get the Panel's attention, and then said, "Please be advised, the Respondents are ready to present their defense, including a Motion to Dismiss based on Claimant's no show."

Sawyer sighed, then said, "Ms. Wilson, if Mr. Perez fails to show by 10: 55, I will ask Respondents to call their first witness or have the Panel address their motions...." Fixing his eyes on Gwen he continued, "As such, we'll see how – *or if* – we proceed from there. I remind you that your prior witnesses' testimony was subject to your laying a factual foundation."

Gwen sat, listening to the clock's clicking noise as its minute arm moved towards the eleven spot. She tried to not do anything that might draw attention to Sammy's empty chair. To relieve her tension, and neither a little white pill nor a Pink Cosmo being available, she whispered to Adam, "So, what do you think of the hearing so far?" She added a 'ha, ha' – but was not smiling.

Adam whispered back, "It will be fine, babe. I have confidence in Sammy. Maybe he had parking issues. Anyhow, my first impression is that there is a definite gender gap in the room. Oh yeah, and a diversity issue."

"You noticed? Both? I always knew you were keenly observant. More seriously, might as well give you a legal lesson, 'Interning 101'. We're facing a top-notch securities law machine. I'm out of their league in knowing how to play the system."

"What do you mean?"

"Take discovery, to the limited extent it's allowed. There was the initial fiasco with all those boxes of unimportant and irrelevant documents, as you know only too well. I, of course, complied with the NASD deadlines. Then, despite my importuning the NASD for months about their non-compliance, right? In the last few days they've produced dozens of significant ones, leaving me no time to review them with Sammy or my experts."

"Don't you have recourse for that?"

"That's just the way this industry governed arbitration game is played, I gather. The NASD is still trying to find their way after 9/11. The whole industry suffered great personal loss. If I file motions for more time, or relief, well that's a disaster for our side.

Can you see Sammy coming back months from now? I'm just praying he shows up today."

"I get that. So, accepting that the glass is half full, onward we go."

"That's the spirit. Here's hoping the rest of my cast arrives and we actually get off to see the Wizard."

At 10:53 on the dot the door opened and into the room stepped Sammy. Gwen almost laughed when she saw that in August he was wearing his large red ski parka that almost swallowed him whole. She'd suggested he wear a sports coat, and that's apparently what he thought she meant, and well it made sense if looked at from his viewpoint. Underneath she noticed the colorful flora of his Hawaiian shirt. It was as if a bouquet of tropical flowers had just been delivered in a red vase – making a fashion statement different than the others in the room.

Gwen jumped up, walked past the guard, and led Sammy to the chair next to hers. She spoke softly into his ear, "Hi Sammy. Am I relieved to see you, mister! I was worried about you." Sammy stammered an explanation for his delay and assured her he was ready to testify, adding that he'd taken his medicine like she'd said.

Gwen got to her feet and said into the microphone, "My apologies to the Panel and Respondents for my client's delay. He assures me he and his driver left his residence at 7 a.m. this morning to get here, but they encountered an accident that held up traffic above the Notch for well over an hour. An unusual event, for sure. Something about a loose moose. He is here now and ready to testify."

Sawyer sat back and exhaled a long breath that was picked up by the sound system. After removing his reading glasses and rubbing his eyes, he nodded to Gwen, put down the pen he'd been repeatedly clicking, then said, "Good morning Mr. Perez and I'm sorry to learn about your unpleasant trip this morning. In fact, it appears you have had difficult travels this week. My name is Attorney Jay Sawyer and I am chair of the arbitration panel. As I'm sure your lawyer has advised you, we are the three members of the NASD's appointed Panel who will listen to the testimony, then consider the evidence presented in the record. It is our task to make a recommendation to the NASD, the agency governing this arbitration, whether you have provided sufficient evidence of a violation of the law by the Respondents. Do you understand that, Mr. Perez?"

Sammy said in a voice so low even Gwen had difficulty hearing him and she sat next to him, "Yes, sir."

"Good. Now, Mr. Perez, we are using a microphone today so that we can record what is said. But I still ask that you speak up when you testify. Do you understand?" Sammy nodded.

"And, one more thing, Mr. Perez, we need to speak into the microphones set out on the table in order that the machine records on tape what we say. Do you understand that?"

"Yes, sir. I try speak loud."

"Good. Oh, yes, I also want to tell you, Mr. Perez, that if you do not understand anything asked, because it is confusing or is difficult English, you should let me know. Will you do that? I think we should be all right as your Counsel has not requested a translator."

Again Sammy nodded yes, and then when Sawyer pointed to the microphone, Sammy dutifully stated, "Yes sir. I okay with English so far," into the device.

"Thank you, Mr. Perez. I'll now ask the stenographer to swear you in as a witness. Loretta, please turn on the tape player."

Sawyer paused and all looked at Loretta. The tape began to roll and Day 2 of the hearing finally began. Gwen suspected that the tape had recorded her loud sigh of relief that they were finally off and running. Sawyer immediately announced, "Okay. We're on the record. This is the second day of the arbitration hearing in the matter, Perez v. Stanley, Howe *et al.,* Case No. 8745."

Gwen helped Sammy move the 'witness' chair closer to the Panel's table. She was concerned he would speak too low for the machine to record his voice. Talking into his ear, her back to the Panel, Gwen gave her client a quick final bit of advice -- something she'd anticipated doing an hour earlier.

"Sammy, just do the five things – like your fingers – that we discussed last night and you'll be great." Here Gwen held out her left hand and raised a finger for each point. "One, speak slowly." Gwen stretched out the word slowly to help him focus as he was understandably nervous. "Two, speak up and into the microphone." Gwen moved the microphone closer to him. "Three, listen, listen, listen to the question and make sure you understand it before answering. Four, Sammy, most importantly, focus on answering *only* what is asked. Don't volunteer. I will make sure you say what you need to. Trust me. And number five, tell the truth – as you know it. Now, a big cleansing breath and you'll be fine." Sammy did as he was told and, using his lungpower, with fists clenched, he exhaled his tension.

Sitting back down, Gwen noticed Cavanaugh, the language expert, was leaning forward in his chair, eagerly and intently listening.

She started her direct examination of Sammy with easy questions to give him time to relax. "Please state your name."

"Samuel Emanuel Perez, they call me Sammy." Sammy's voice was as she remembered, high pitched and it rose upwards towards the end of a sentence. Musically nice, at least to her untrained ear. Gwen, nevertheless, instructed him again to speak up as even she had difficulty hearing him – and she was only three feet away.

"Thank you. Mr. Perez, I'll use 'Sammy' then as we proceed." She believed it important she make her client appear a likeable 'average' person, not an investor tycoon, and using 'Sammy' would make that easier. Of course she couldn't change the other overwhelming differences between her client and the Panel members, but it was a start. "Where do you reside Sammy, sorry, that is, where do you live?"

"I don't know."

Gwen, ready to move-on, stepped back. "I'm sorry, um...where are you living now?"

Sammy sat silently. Then, after a deep breath, he said, "With brother-in-law's cousin, at 3692 Lawrence St., Dortman, New Hampshire, don't remember other number. But at my sister when on Island, Benelux 5, Las Terrenas 35503. That, you know, the Dominican Republic."

Sawyer, who had been leaning in towards Sammy, interrupted. "Attorney Wilson, I'm having a little difficulty hearing. I think it might be helpful if we move Mr. Perez's chair further away from the tape recorder. My experience is that if the seat is too close there's a tendency not to speak up."

With Gwen gesturing, Sammy got up and moved his chair to the spot Sawyer was pointing at, and Gwen continued. "Mr. Perez, that is, Sammy, are you the Claimant in this case, the person bringing this suit?"

"Yes, I sue."

Gwen asked Sammy about his age, education, occupation, immigration status just to confirm that he was a citizen for the Panel members who might not be conversant with Latino migration to the States, and employment record. When Sammy responded that he no longer worked because he was disabled, Sawyer lurched in his chair. Gwen was alarmed, for Martha had already stated this fact, but it seemed it didn't register with the Chair.

Sawyer asked, "You say disabled?"

Sammy explained that he had hurt his back at work over a year ago and had depression after losing his money, and was now on disability. Gwen then had Sammy recite his efforts to achieve the American dream starting with his work as a cleaner, that he'd tried to improve his skills taking classes and then gotten a better job as a systems tester of electronic circuit boards, and his decision when offered to take early retirement.

"What income are you receiving now?"

"From pension about $600 a month I think, plus disability and some from small savings."

To ensure that the factual basis for Martha and Linda's

testimony was in the record, Gwen then had Sammy explain that with his wife's income their combined annual earnings had been about $55,000, and now less since he'd stopped working.

Gwen looked up at the Panel. "Mr. Sawyer, at this point I request that Mr. Cavanaugh leave."

After confirming that Day had no objection, Sawyer said, "Mr. Cavanaugh, you are excused. Thank you."

Gwen watched Cavanaugh walk out, wondering what damaging things he would say, although, ironically it might hurt Sammy's case more if his grasp of English was excellent rather than wanting. She then turned her attention to those important points that likely were of most concern to the Panel members, starting with Sammy's sophistication as an investor.

"Mr. Perez, was there a time when you opened an account with Freedom Independent, do you remember?"

"I don't remember." Gwen was nonplussed. She'd specifically gone over this material with Sammy the night before. But he was now in this stressful environment, and she'd learned over the years, that changed things.

Sawyer tried to help. "Do you remember the year?"

Sammy played with his lips, then ventured, "I think 1990, maybe..., not sure. But I have account with wife's nephew. Sorry, I nervous, do my best."

Smiling to convey confidence, Gwen continued, "So, Sammy, at the time you opened this account were you married?"

"Yes, reason open account. Wife's nephew work there, said would help us make money. Wife thought good idea."

Sawyer broke in again. "Does your wife work?"

"Yes, she work as ...," Sammy struggled trying to come up with the proper English word. "What you say, she make hair nice, like woman barber? She have own store in Dortman. She also mom to our three boys."

With Sawyer silent, Gwen questioned Sammy about his trading experience at Freedom. Sammy explained that his nephew handled the account 'good', but then he got *mucho* sick and left job. It was up to Sammy to handle the account as the company had no brokers to help, like at Stanley, Howe. Sammy explained he didn't know what to do. He listened to what men at work told him to do, but not always good idea. One friend, he said, told him the name of a stock 'sure to go up and make lots of money', and if he bought on 'margerine' he would make even more. This friend told Sammy how to do this. But stock went down, and after that all kinds of bad things happened in account, and he had no one to help him. He soon lost most all the money in the account, but still had to pay fees for long time. His wife, Olanda, was not happy with her nephew for leaving her and Sammy with 'the mess'.

"Sammy, why did you listen and trade with your nephew?"

"He smart, study at school, say to wife he know about how make money, he take care of us. Only had short time, then nephew, one that help me, as I say, he stop."

Gwen quizzed Sammy on his knowledge of securities trading to establish for the record that he was an 'unsophisticated' investor. Sammy described that he didn't read about stocks, follow the market, or, as Gwen showed, know the meaning of stock terms, such as the difference between stocks and bonds. Gwen tried to give examples so the Panel would appreciate Sammy's lack of knowledge.

"What do you understand a 'market' is in terms of securities?"

"You have cash, you buy shares. Like market I shop at in Dortman for food, you buy, get something, but if it stock, you can also, you know, sell and get money."

"Do you know what 'margin' is?"

"No, don't remember from time I use margarine." Playing with his lips, Sammy finally said, "I think it like auto loan, if you no make payment, the auto place take back your car. With Mr. Murphy, I lose money not car if don't pay."

"Did there come a time, after Freedom, when you opened another securities account?"

"Yes, Attorney, much later. I soon be age can retire. I want use savings good, like my friends at work. I take bus, go to big company in Middleton, 'cause friend say good. This time I want someone who know how to do, want to only buy good stock. Woman at desk say to me Mr. Murphy my broker, I tell him buy only *quality stock*, no want to lose money like before."

"Objection." Attorney Mandel, Murphy's counsel, rose and yelled towards the Panel. "Please instruct the witness to only answer the question asked, not to ramble beyond that. I am having difficulty understanding him otherwise."

Sawyer turned and addressed Sammy, saying slowly, "Mr. Perez, please respond only to your counsel's question, don't add information unless asked."

"Yes, sir." Sammy nodded his head vigorously up and down.

Gwen wasn't complaining, however. She continued to have Sammy elaborate on his opening of his account with Stanley, Howe and his meeting with Larry. Gwen went over the application form with Sammy. He said he didn't remember the form, but he did sign the agreement and also signed his wife's name as Larry directed.

Step by step Gwen put in her case, filling in the facts referred to by her experts, addressing the new account form and other missing information, and establishing that it was Larry who was driving this bus.

Affirming, for example, Sammy's lack of trading sophistication, she asked, "Do you know what 'Growth' means? That box is checked on your application form as an investment goal."

"Don't know, maybe...stock grow up to sky, you know, like plant?"

"Do you know what the term 'Speculation' means for an account?"

"Not sure."

"What do you think it means?"

Sammy squirmed in his chair. "Don't know."

"No idea?"

"No, maybe something do with...." Sammy pulled on his ear, and then crunched his fingers. "Sorry, I not know."

"Sammy, did you fill in the boxes where it asks for your investment goals?"

"No. No do that."

"Did Mr. Murphy ask you at any time what your 'investment objective' was?"

"I tell him many time I want only good stock, like IBM, Ford. Safe. No want to lose money like years before."

Gwen could tell Sammy was getting tired. He was fidgeting in the chair, playing with his jacket zipper, and rubbing his eyes repeatedly. She had only a few more areas to cover. She hoped he'd hang in there to the end.

"You said you went to Stanley, Howe because it was a full service firm rather than a discount firm like Freedom, that it offered benefits. Do you know what they are?"

"Objection, leading." Day didn't even deign to rise, and Sawyer didn't respond.

Sammy nodded his head, saying, "I know from friend. They in charge of your account, like my manager who in charge of my team. Broker know business good, call you and he tell you how stock doing, give you good advice, you know, what to do. It cost money to use, but I don't want to lose like before so I say to me, 'Sammy, do it right."

Gwen went over the margin account and that Larry hadn't explained to him how it worked.

"Sammy, I'm showing you Exhibit 22, Bates stamped # 334875, in the second binder I believe," and here Gwen waited as Adam passed out copies to the Panel. "Sammy, this exhibit is a maintenance form requesting additional funds be added to your account, a margin call. Do you remember receiving this, and what did you do if so?"

Day rose. "Objection."

"He can answer," Sawyer said.

"I no see. Never 'til you show me. It turn out it sent to old post office address, not to address where I live."

Mandel rose and called out, "Objection, hearsay."

Sawyer turned and said to Sammy, "Mr. Perez, how do you know this?"

Sammy, facing the Panel, explained that Gwen had shown him the envelope with the closed Post Office address and statement that it couldn't be forwarded. At that point Gwen pointed the Panel members to the page where the copy of this document was included in the binders. Gwen then went over Sammy's expenditures in his account, his use of it to pay his Visa bills, his loan to his aunt and need to keep that money separate. She then dealt with the numerous margin calls for more money, and the impact on Sammy's account of his spending down the account's assets.

"Did you understand treating your account like a bank checking account might affect your margin account?"

"No, for sure." Sammy played with his jacket zipper again and checked out his various pockets. Twisting his legs and shifting in his chair he finally said, "No understand that when use it, Stanley credit card, could lose all. Just thought give me so can take money out, you know, then that money not make more money."

Gwen paused and looked at her list of topics on her legal pad. She consulted with Adam briefly, just to check on his list.

Before she could finish, Gwen needed to address several damaging issues. First was that Day had claimed that Sammy was a gambler. Problem was she hadn't had a chance to go over these questions with Sammy beforehand. But she didn't believe he gambled.

"Sammy, to put it bluntly, are you a gambler?"

"No. Never. No want hurt family. I put my trust in Jesus my Lord. No play at cards, no go see horses like friends."

"Did you go to casinos?" "No, never."

As to Day's assertion that Sammy attempted to hide money from his wife, an issue that clearly troubled Sawyer, Gwen confronted it directly. "Sammy, why did you move money into a second account?"

"I borrow money from my Aunt Mariah on island for t-shirt business, I gave my word to pay it back. I told this to Mr. Murphy, he say put in account for her, make her money and he move money. This Mariah money, not mine. And not wife money."

"Why did you not tell your wife about this different account?

"It not my money. In divorce wife had lawyer, did good. She got the house, beauty business, bank savings. I get bad Stanley account and retire fund. I pay back Mariah what can."

"Sammy, did there come a time when you were contacted by the investment firm, someone other than Mr. Murphy about concerns with your account?"

"No, never."

When Sawyer looked again at his watch, Gwen knew it was time to finish. She focused on the heart of her case, that Murphy controlled Sammy's account and he cheated Sammy to fill his own coffers.

"Sammy, who was in charge of your account, who made the decisions about what to do?

"It broker, Mr. Murphy, he in charge. Why I pay fee. When I say I worry all time about black line for my account, it go down, Mr. Murphy say to me what he always say, don't worry, Sammy. It be fine."

Gwen said, "In fact it wasn't fine, was it? Who made money with your account?"

"It him, Mr. Murphy. I pay lots fees. I one who lose all life savings, and my family's money when they try help me."

"Sammy, who was 'driving the bus' in your securities account: between you, Mr. Murphy and Stanley, Howe?"

Sammy sat silent, looking down at his hands. He pressed on his chest and Gwen worried he might be sick again. Then, after exhaling air, he raised his arm and pointed to Murphy, blurting out so all could hear, "He, Mr. Murphy. He drive, then he make big crash of bus." Sammy raised his arms and clapped his hands together loudly, likely waking up any suit who might have been snoozing. Sammy then added, "He one that ruin my life. Now no wife, no boys no home. I work hard all life." Turning to the Panel, Sammy said, "Sir. It Mr. Murphy, he one drive bus."

Gwen let Sammy's outcry fill the room's silence. She noticed that Murphy was writing on a notepad and smiling. After one last review of her checklist, she said to the Panel, "Thank you, Sammy, I have no more questions on direct."

Gwen sat and stared blankly. She knew she was spent.

The suits, other than Adam, broke into murmurs and whispers. Sawyer broke the chatter, stating, "We'll resume after one o'clock, the arbitrators will have the room until then." To everyone's surprise Sawyer didn't get up but instead looked at Sammy and asked a question directly.

"One more question if I may before we break. Mr. Perez, showing you Exhibit 24, Ms. Wilson it's at p. 54 of Binder 2, if you would share it with your client." Sawyer and everyone waited while the logistics were completed. "Have you seen this document before?"

Sammy held the piece of paper up to his face. "Yes, sir. It is about money I use for machine I bought."

"Can you tell me about the T-shirt business?"

Sammy looked up at Sawyer. "As I say, after retire, cousin want open, you know, t-shirt business. Sell t-shirts on street. You pick out picture or letters and tell us size of shirt and we make on machine. He had done this before on island so he say to me he know business. Tell me good way I can make money, see I not working then. I give cousin money to buy machine. I buy also parts for business, and maybe it all cost $750. Mr. Murphy say can take out of account with him. We try, work hard, but everything go wrong. We not start good time of year, you know, it too cold outside to sell t-shirt. And machine we buy, it not work good, break many time. We did maybe for three, four months. No good. We not make money so we close. Only thing I have left is machine."

Sawyer continued, "Did there come a time when you re-financed your house?"

"Yes, um, ..." Here Sammy rubbed his head, as if to help him remember. "Yes. I went to take money from bank. I use money to give to Mr. Murphy to invest, I don't remember how much, maybe $15,000. All wife allow me borrow. Mr. Murphy, he promise it safe in his hands. Say money pay itself off. Pay for Marcus, my son, so he go to college."

Sawyer jotted down notes on what Sammy said. Then, after checking the time, Sawyer asked one final question, "Can you tell us, Mr. Perez, what has been the consequence of your trading experience?"

Sammy's face fell instantly, like a house of cards. "Like I say, it ruin my life very much, hurt family so no *hijos*, now no can live in my house with wife and sons, wife and family angry so no talk to me. All pressure, no good for my health, need see doctor for medicine for my anxious..." Sammy stopped, tears welling in his eyes. After a few moments he blew his nose, then continued, "Sorry. I have illness, depressed now, and hard for me to think good. Like I say, I work hard all life, go to school to make a future, save good, do what people say is right, go to church, thank America I live here. Now I alone, have no future, only worry, and ..." Sammy stopped.

Sawyer wrote himself a note, looked over his legal pad, whispered with the Panel members, and then, rising in his chair, said, "The Panel has no more questions of this witness. We will break for a brief lunch and I expect everyone back in his, or her, seats at 1:00 p.m. Again, as I mentioned, the Panel will be using this room over the lunch break."

Sammy walked over to Gwen. She gave him a hug, maybe not very professional, but the man was a wreck. Then the trio, Gwen, Adam, and the client walked out of the room. As they raced to the fast-food place across from the building, Gwen held on to Sammy's red ski parka – to show her support, and to make sure he showed up for the afternoon session on time.

CHAPTER THIRTY-SIX

The room was eerily empty. Gwen and team – which included thankfully Sammy – had hurried to be back on time, only to learn they were the only ones who'd returned from the lunch break. Slowly, the remaining participants and the Panel's members dawdled into the conference room, chatting away. *When will I learn the unspoken rules of the game, like when a start time means 'the start time'?*

Sawyer began the afternoon hearing session at 1:20 p.m.

"I believe we all are back. Mr. Perez would you please again take your 'chair' and, Attorney Day, who will doing the cross-examination for your side?"

At this point, to Gwen's great surprise, a suit midway down the conference table and Josiah Day rose and switched places. She tried to figure out why the passing of the baton to the relief team, especially when their ace was pitching so well? All she could guess was that there might be billing benefits for sharing.

Addressing the Panel, the new questioner started his cross with, "Good morning. I'm sorry, good afternoon Mr. Sawyer, ... and members of the Panel. Excuse me, and Ms. Wilson."

Gwen thought, "Two balls thrown already." The man continued, "My name is Donald Moss and I am in-house Counsel for Stanley, Howe. By agreement I will be examining Mr. Perez on behalf of my company and Mr. Murphy." Moss then had his associate hand out copies of several exhibits that he would use during his cross.

During the lull, Gwen checked Moss out. Impeccably dressed and groomed, he appeared the stereotypical corporate lawyer, probably head of the firm's litigation department and maybe next in line to be General Counsel for the regional office? Would he be more aggressive than Day? Gwen suspected she'd find out soon enough.

"Good afternoon Mr. Perez. I'd like to start by reviewing with you copies of Exhibits 12 through 18, which were just distributed.

Panel members, for the record, um... excuse me, and Ms. Wilson, these documents appear as well in the second binder at pages 86 through 105. Mr. Perez, I've handed you statements showing transactions that happened in your securities account at Stanley, Howe. I draw your attention to the first, third and fifth lines in Exhibit 12. See where it is highlighted in yellow? These are notations for debits representing checks you've written in this account. Do you see that, Mr. Perez?"

Sammy stared at the exhibits. Moss had spoken so quickly that even Gwen was having trouble identifying the lines. Moss suggested, "Perhaps your Counsel can point out the lines I'm speaking of?"

Perhaps not, Gwen thought. Dutifully she rose and walked the few steps towards Sammy. With the help of her one long fingernail, and the bright yellow markings, she pointed to the lines she thought were those mentioned by Moss.

"Yes, I think so."

"Good. Now, sir, the first of these pages shows a debit in the amount of $11,000. Isn't that right?"

"Debit, you mean...?" Sammy rubbed his eyes, leaned over the paper, and then looked at Gwen.

"Debit. Meaning money you took out of the account in this amount, said Moss."

"I already say 'bout this, I pay back loan to Mariah. She give me money to help me, I family. Then business slow and she almost lost store..."

Moss interrupted Sammy's answer, saying, "Yes, you've testified before on that. But Mr. Perez, I'm asking you to carefully listen to my questions and to respond only to what is asked. Can you do that?"

Gwen stood and objected that Moss wasn't letting her client finish his answer and Sawyer agreed, directing Moss to do that going forward. In the meantime, Sammy answered that he was explaining to all what had happened.

Gwen noticed already that Moss didn't pretend to be cordial; he was ready to attack the jugular. "Now, I direct you to page three of that exhibit. This page also shows further transfers out of your securities account with Stanley, Howe, or debits as we've just discussed, correct?"

"What you say? I don't see where." Sammy held the pages in front of his face as if closeness would produce more clarity.

Gwen rose again. "Objection. Mr. Moss is speaking so quickly that he is pressuring the witness. As the Panel may recall, English is Mr. Perez's second language. I'd appreciate if the Panel would instruct Counsel to go more slowly so my client – and I – can be able to follow and respond."

Sawyer did as Gwen directed.

Moss said at a more deliberate pace, "Yes, of course. Excuse me. Let me know, Mr. Perez, if you do not understand my questions. Do you wish me to repeat the question, or perhaps Attorney Wilson can assist again."

Gwen walked over to Sammy, pointed out the line, and then sat down.

"What you ask again?" said Sammy. After Loretta read back the question and Sammy said "yes," Moss moved on.

"Now, sir, please look at the upper right-hand corner of Exhibit 14 that I have given you. Do you see it? The paper has number 14 on top?" Sammy held up a page and showed it to Moss. Sawyer leaned over and affirmed it was the right one and told Sammy that was it.

Moss then continued, "Now, Mr. Perez, if you look at the upper right- hand corner as I said, there's a notation that a check was written on this account and the account debited in the amount of $1800? And other checks also are listed, correct? This is a yes or no question."

Sammy put the paper even closer to his eyes and moved it around. Then he nodded. "Okay, now see."

"Is your answer 'yes' Mr. Perez?"

Sammy nodded. Sawyer again leaned over and asked him to speak into the microphone.

"Yes, sir. That for son Marcus's computer. He need for school."

"These checks listed on this one statement, if you total them up, amount to almost $15,000, that is, $15,000 out of your trading account in only one month, correct?"

Sammy this time brought his head down towards his lap where he held the forms. While his head was still down he said, "Don't know. Too many numbers. Print so small. If you say."

"Mr. Perez, it is true not because I said it, but because when you add up the numbers, as I presume your expert witness, Ms. DeNardi did before her ..."

"Objection." Gwen said. "Mr. Moss is...."

Sawyer broke in. "Yes. Mr. Moss, please just ask your question and don't characterize prior testimony."

Moss stopped and shuffled the papers on the table before him. He appeared determined but the increased reddening of his ears that Gwen noticed might indicate increasing performance anxiety. She surely wouldn't want to follow Day in examining a witness.

Moss said, "Yes, of course, Mr. Sawyer." Turning towards Sammy he continued, "As I was asking you, Mr. Perez, this document shows that you wrote checks that debited your primary securities account with Mr. Murphy in an amount totaling approximately $15,000 in this one month, December, right? Let me know if you don't understand the question again."

"I don't know what is answer. I guess it what you say. As I say to my lawyer before, I...."

Moss broke in. "I'll take that as an affirmative. And we do not want to raise issues of attorney-client privilege, do we? Now moving on to Exhibit 15, Mr. Perez. That's the paper in your left hand. This document is the January statement from your personal bank account showing deposits equal in amount to several of those debits we've discussed, does it not?"

Gwen listened as Moss went through a litany of expenses paid for from Sammy's securities account, the apparent gist of Moss's claim being that these personal expenses were not losses resulting from Murphy's mismanagement of his account, and that they also confirmed that Sammy was actively making account decisions. And, no matter how awkward were Moss's questions, the methodical approach was successfully making Sammy seem confused and maybe less than forthright and honest.

Gwen was convinced Sammy had been truthful with her, but she'd seen it before. Under the pressures of a hearing, many witnesses, scared, anxious, overwhelmed with the event, would fumble their answers, even if they'd been perfect when preparing with her. She suspected she might react the same way had she waited all these years to tell her tale of woe, and to a school of sharks. But she doubted that the Panel would be so empathetic.

Moss moved on to facts he asserted showed that Sammy was in control, that he was a sophisticated investor who was willing to gamble his money to make a quick buck.

"Isn't it true, Mr. Perez, that you repeatedly made unsolicited requests during your many daily conversations with Mr. Murphy, asking him to purchase stocks based on recommendations you received from your co-workers, your supervisor, and even from your watching CNBC business shows on television?"

"When he there, and most time not, I talk about how account do. No understand company statement, what it say, and unhappy as total money number, black line it go down. I worry lose so much money." Sammy looked up and now pointed to Larry who was busily reading some paper. In the silence Larry looked up as Sammy stood up and with anger finally coming out in his voice, shouted, "He say my money, it safe, be patient. It go make money as good market. He say to me he take care of me, I on his team. I not to worry. Not true. He, Mr. Murphy, he big liar."

Undeterred by this demonstration, Moss went on, "Mr. Sawyer, I ask that the non-responsive part of Mr. Perez's answer, the last sentence, be stricken and that you please instruct the witness to only answer the question I ask."

Sawyer sat up and made a note on his paper. "Mr. Moss, I think we can just move on. We'll consider your objection when we review the record. Need I remind Counsel again – and the witness – that this is not a trial before a jury. The Panel is perfectly competent to appraise the responsiveness of the answer. And, Mr. Perez, please do listen carefully to Attorney Moss's questions, and respond only to what is actually asked. Now continue, Attorney Moss."

Moss again dealt with the issue of who ran the account, trying his best to present the picture that it was Murphy who was on Sammy's leash. "Mr. Perez, weren't you all the time looking out for stocks that would make you rich?"

"No. Most of time I not know about company Mr. Murphy buy for me. He tell me he one who knows, it he who broker. But money, it go down."

Gwen was perking up. It seemed that Sammy was getting a little feisty, fighting back. Maybe the battle was not so one-sided as she thought. The home team was not done!

Moss appeared to take a moment to review his notes. Then, he continued, "Now, let's look more at your use of your Visa card with this account."

Moss then spent far too long reviewing Sammy's use of his Stanley, Howe issued Visa credit card, starting with the charge of $29.95 for the family's Fios internet account. Gwen looked at her watch. Surely Moss wasn't going to inquire about every deduction? What did they say about hammering a nail to its death?

"Mr. Perez, for the past almost decade you've been familiar with the Internet, correct?"

Gwen was almost laughing at the absurdity of trying to claim that Sammy, with his GED and clear lack of business let alone computer sophistication, was somehow an early expert on the Internet.

Before Sawyer could respond Sammy said, "I only use Internet for manage my mail. That only thing I do." Sammy was firm, his lips pressed together and his posture straighter. Then he added, "Only thing I do every day, most important, is read my Bible and pray. No take time use Internet."

Moss realized he had no more Internet claims so he moved on to an IRS letter sent to Sammy about employment.

"That letter is a written request that the IRS sends to prospective employees. The letter explains that you had turned down a position with the IRS."

Sammy replied with animation, his hands gesturing back and forth as if calling Moss out at the plate, "You wrong, lawyer. I not work IRS. When I look for work after old company lay me off, I told instead of stay home and get money, can go to school. I learn type, courses like that. School at IRS office, where I do training. No work at IRS. Don't know why send letter."

Moss was not deterred. "Now look at Bates document #1759, where it says Smith & Browser Academy on top? This page lists a school record, do you see? Look at the last entry in there. Doesn't it show you took in 1975 some business courses at the Academy?"

Gwen finally got it and almost guffawed out loud. *These idiots are trying to show that because Sammy took some training classes twenty-five years ago while unemployed, he is a sophisticated, educated businessman. Good luck.* But she was impressed with their enterprise in investigating Sammy's life, even going back a quarter of a century.

Sammy explained with more patience than Gwen thought she would have been able to muster, "This is same course as at IRS, that name is place I took class. I no go to school there.

Moss continued to chug along with earnestness as to Sammy's business skills, seemingly unperturbed that his cross was making no hits. He handed out copies of several more documents to the Panel and to Gwen. She thought she saw the members of the Panel roll their eyes.

"Backing up a few pages, I give you a copy of Bates document # 1733, and also to the Panel members and Attorney Wilson. Isn't it true that this document is a listing of various business courses you took while employed at your company, LCD?"

"No. You wrong. Those not courses on business; those for safety. You have to go, safety classes. Deal with chemical, fire, how to get out building."

"Okay. All right, the one that has sixteen hours...?"

"I don't see it."

Sawyer, after glancing for the umpteenth time at his wristwatch, leaned over and showed Sammy the line on the form. "Okay, let me explain 'bout this. Union head comes to work, tell us everybody have to go to those classes. I went sixteen hours, 'cause union say have to go."

Moss next tried to "get him" on tax fraud but Sammy again explained that he didn't know he had to pay taxes on money received when disabled, and accountant, his cousin, help him file taxes and correct his $1800 mistake.

Gwen couldn't believe they were trying to claim that Sammy had engaged in major tax fraud. Surely the Panel if they were still listening would appreciate the silliness of this and hopefully be upset at the waste of their time. But then again, Sawyer was looking keenly at the tax documents, seeming to be fully tuned in to the questions. Why, he probably spent more in a year on restaurant meals claimed as business expenses than Sammy earned in a year.

As Moss went on some more about Sammy's tax payments, Sawyer finally had enough. "He's just not sure what the tax laws are. If you have an IRS letter for us to take judicial notice, we'll consider it."

Gwen was getting it – Respondents were not pushing on the weaknesses of Sammy's legal claims, but instead were focusing on her client's character. *Am I in a different universe? Is this what this case is really about? Who is more likeable? Is that the unwritten rule my opponents know will tilt this windmill? And is that why no settlement? They just don't think Sammy's on the up and up!*

Sawyer checked his watch again, consulted with Grimes, and then said, "Attorney Moss, we are running quite late. Can you please see if you can move on."

Moss stopped and unbuttoned his suit jacket. Then, pointing his right index finger at Sammy he made one last jab, "Mr. Perez, isn't it true that you are admitting only that which you cannot deny? You are denying everything that can't be proved, isn't that correct?"

Gwen stood up. "I object." She wanted to say she objected to the whole process of investigating her client and treating him like he was a criminal when it was their company and their employees who had worked hard to make money off of him, and that this process had helped ruin his life. But she didn't. *A foolish slave to decorum?*

Sawyer responded, "You don't have to answer that."

After a brief consultation with Day, Moss announced that he had no more questions for Sammy. Sawyer then asked if any of the other counsel at Day's table intended to cross-examine the witness. Following a pause where no one rose, Mandel, after a brief tête-à-tête with Moss, stood up and said he wished to cross-examine the witness. Gwen immediately felt her body tense. *What are they cooking up as a final attack? Something saved until the end?*

Walking up to approach her client, Mandel asked, "Mr. Perez, you tell this Panel that you are receiving disability payments from the government because you injured your back at work a year or so ago, is that correct?"

"Yes, and as I say, because Doctor say I depressed."

"Mr. Perez, have you painted before, you know, painted houses and such, not art painting?"

"Yes, I do paint when I have my house. Want to keep nice. Olanda help me."

"So you know that painting requires lots of twists and turns and can be hard on one's back, right?"

Sammy looked at Gwen, eyes wide. Gwen assumed he, like

her, was wondering what trap was being set by Mandel. Sammy said, "Yes," but, not done, he added with a nervous smile, "Paint, it easier when I a young man." There was a brief round of laughter from the room as all it seemed could appreciate that older backs don't work as well. However, no one on Gwen's side of the table was even chuckling. Indeed, Adam seemed agitated, Gwen thought, shifting in his chair and moving his legal pad around. Mandel tried to tag along with Sammy's joke. With a smile to the

Panel, he said, "Yes, that's what I tell my wife." More collegial laughter, then Mandel, his tone now aggressive, continued, "Yet isn't it the case that while you claim to be disabled you are working for one of your relatives who owns a paint company?"

Sammy stared at Mandel, shook his head back and forth, and then loudly said, "No. I no work, just help few times when cousin, José, need one more worker. I no get paid. We family."

"Isn't it true, Mr. Perez, that you *did* get paid when you painted your attorney's office, you got paid by not having to pay legal fees in your case? Isn't this another example of your being a cheater, Mr. Perez, of trying to cheat the system as you have tried to cheat my client with this unfounded lawsuit?"

"Objection." Standing up, Gwen continued, "First of all, this whole line of questioning is immaterial to the substance of this case. And Mr. Mandel knows full well that any fee arrangement between my client and myself is totally privileged. I ask that Mr. Mandel's cross be stricken from the record and he be sanctioned for his egregious conduct."

But before Sawyer could respond, Sammy, leaning towards Mandel, piped in, his voice rising in volume, "No, you wrong. That a gift, a present from me and my family to say to Attorney thank you as she agree to sue for me. She good lawyer, help people who live in Dortman take on big powerful company for nothing. No pay. And, yes, back still hurt, but okay as I only do trim, so not so bad. And we only paint the one room. It way my family give back to her."

The room remained silent after this outburst. Sammy had laid it on the line, Gwen thought, the community who helps each other verses the rich who take advantage when they can for more money in their coffers. She knew she couldn't have said it better or more effectively. *So take that Mandel, or as Shakespeare would say, you were hoisted by your own petard.*

Sawyer finally spoke up. "Please move on, Mr. Mandel, if you have other questions. As Counsel for Mr. Perez has pointed out, these questions do not relate to this case. If you want to file a complaint with the state's Disability office, that is a separate matter from this arbitration hearing."

Mandel was about to respond, but instead conferred with his client Larry. He then stated, "No more questions, thank you."

Sawyer nodded, then asked Gwen if she had any further questions on re-direct, to which Gwen gladly responded 'no', and Sawyer excused Sammy. His day on the witness stand was done. Timidly, Sammy walked to his chair beside Gwen, a small man, seemingly lost in a high-powered room of 'important' people. Yet, Gwen thought, a man who radiated a determination to stand up and seek justice.

"Attorney Wilson?"

Gwen stood and looked at Sawyer.

"Do you have any more witnesses to present?"

"No, Mr. Sawyer. The Claimant, Mr. Perez, rests his case."

Gwen thought this sounded sufficiently legalese that it might be a direct quote from an old *Law and Order* show she'd seen.

Gwen's shoulders instantly relaxed with these words. All that remained now was the testimony of Respondents' witnesses. Where she'd be in the position of the shark. She could hear in her head the musical theme from the movie *Jaws*.

It sounded thrilling.

CHAPTER THIRTY-SEVEN

All gravy from here. Sammy and she had survived, the worst part was over, his case was still alive. Exhausted after only a day and a half of the hearing, Gwen newly admired trial lawyers who managed to survive sane and intact when litigating long cases. Thankfully, now that claimant's presentation was done, Sawyer ordered a 20-minute break before Respondents began putting on their case. Gwen, Adam and Sammy quickly paraded out the door, took the elevator to the lobby, quickly grabbed coffee at the deli across the street, and shared their initial assessments.

Sammy was silent, shoulders slumped, head down. Gwen felt badly for him. She had hoped after all the tension and heartache, he'd be elated now that he'd at last 'had his day in court'. Adam also was silent. *Time to liven up this melancholy crew with some praise.*

"Sammy, you did fine today, really held your own with the best." "Yeah. Not so terrible," Sammy said, his face finally showing some animation. But I not like his questions, make me confused, try make me lie."

"That's to be expected, this is what Mr. Moss does for a living. Remember, he's

a seasoned lawyer, done this process thousands of times likely. But it was just the first time for you. Even though a 'rookie', you didn't let him bully you. You answered his questions smartly. All told, I'm pleased with how the day's gone so far and I think, Sammy, bottom line is you advanced your case."

Turning to Adam, Gwen asked, "Adam, your thoughts?"

Adam put down his coffee cup and smiled at Sammy. "I think Sammy did a super job. You told your story and you didn't let them get you angry when they attacked. Not easy. Showed courage." Adam leaned over and gave Sammy a fist bump. Then, he added to Gwen, "And boss, you were – swell as well. A side of you I haven't seen, tough as nails."

After this affirmation, all three cheered up. Gwen decided maybe she'd call Judy later and suggest she check out the office catalogue for a new secretary desk. And she might check the vacation ads over breakfast tomorrow.

Back in the hearing room Gwen looked around, squinting in the light streaming through the window curtains. She noticed that Sawyer had removed his suit jacket and Grimes his golf sweater. Sure enough, across the table the suits had followed the Panel's lead, that is, except for Day who looked cool, calm, and collected. Gwen gladly followed the suits' lead and removed her jacket, exposing her surprising arm muscles. She did notice that Adam remained fully dressed while Sammy's ski parka had been placed in a pile behind his chair so that his shirt's resplendent garden brought a festive island mood to the room.

After checking his notes, Sawyer asked Day and Murphy how Respondents were going to proceed in presenting their case, and whether they intended to begin with Mr. Cavanaugh to address Sammy's facility with English.

Gwen, listening with less then rapt attention to the procedural discussion, thought she heard someone entering at the back of the room. *Who'd be this late for the afternoon session?* Turning to look back, she noticed a pizza deliveryman had entered holding a large boxed pizza pie. Gwen could smell the pizza and salivated at the thought of a nice, dripping, oily slice. Who could have been so thoughtful as to arrange for a late-afternoon snack for the hearing's attendees? Waiting for someone to announce the pizza break, she heard Sawyer direct Day to have his witnesses sit on the chair across from Loretta, not next to her, and began doodling on a new page in her legal pad.

Bang! The noise blasted through the room.

Whoosh. Almost immediately a rush of air whizzed by Gwen's head! She jumped up and found herself standing at the table, her heart racing and brain whirling. Before she could cover her head with her muscled arms, there was another *Bang! What the hell's happening?*

Looking around, Gwen was vaguely aware that time was moving in slow motion only to come to a dead stop, as if someone had pressed the pause button on the room's remote device. Gwen stood frozen in place, unable to move even her new muscles. She instructed her body to duck, but it just wouldn't listen. Failing this, Gwen decided to close her eyes and then to wake up from this terrible dream. But a Mack truck ran her over and she stopped feeling anything.

On the ground she heard a third crack explode. She thought the bang again came from the back of the room, near the pizza guy, but no whoosh this time.

Moments of quiet passed. Gwen opened her eyes. She was lying flat on the ground, her left cheek pressing hard into the thick carpet. She could barely inhale thanks to the big moose sitting on her chest. *I know New Hampshire is famous for its moose but how did one wander into this hearing room? Damnation, what the hell's going on?* Sweat broke out on her forehead and trickled down her face. A wave of nausea suddenly hit like a tsunami. She worried about throwing up her long-ago eaten breakfast on the room's fancy rug. *But I don't feel pain. Will the pain come later, like in the movies?* Biting her lip, for she couldn't get to her knuckles as her arms were pinned to her side, Gwen worked at focusing better. She pushed through the fear freezing her movement and forced her lungs to fill so she could yell for help. At least, thinking like a good lawyer, she thankfully remembered that her will and health care proxy were in place.

Then she heard a faint whimper muffled by the carpet. Suddenly, the pressure on her chest lifted. Able to raise her face, she gasped for air. With effort she rose onto her elbows, then sat up. Adam lay still on the ground beside her. She gathered from his position that as soon as the noise of the gunshots were heard, he'd risked his life to jump on top of her and protect her from harm.

What a gallant knight in shining armor! Gwen reached out to Adam and gently touched his cheek with her now warm and pliant fingers. She was startled when she started to shake uncontrollably. She held on to Adam's hand even tighter.

Then, finally able to move her legs, she leaned down and gave him a kiss on the cheek she could reach. "Hey Adam, you okay? My hero. Can you believe this?"

"Yup," he said. "Think so, just winded. And a little cold."

Gwen thought his voice was shaky. She looked down again at his face but he seemed fine, maybe just a little pale.

"Hey, honey, maybe you should just chill for a minute. Boy, what a team we make. I'm hot as can be, as if I were in Miami sunbathing in the summer, and you're chilled to the bone as if you were sledding in Alaska. I sure look forward to our vacations." Gwen wasn't sure why she couldn't stop talking, must be the adrenalin from almost getting killed.

Turning to her right to check on Sammy, she saw he was nonchalantly playing with the zipper on his red jacket, his face relaxed as if he were on a lunch break. *Is his calm demeanor because of the magical white pill, or living in Dortman where gunshots are not an exactly unknown sound?*

If Sammy seemed calm, elsewhere pandemonium ruled. Lawyers huddled together under the conference table, apparently waiting for an 'all clear' signal as if at a hotel's fire drill. The Panel members were crunched behind their small table. Sawyer, finally getting his mojo back, stood up and scanned the room. Then he walked on what appeared to be wobbly legs over to help Loretta who, with her eyes closed, sat folded on the carpet, her arms wrapped protectively around her recording machine.

Taking a few cleansing breaths, Gwen stood up and looked around the room to find out more what had happened. She could make out a man in the back standing near where the pizza guy had been but the deliveryman was no longer standing there. *Where's he gone? Maybe realized he had the wrong room?* Then she could see on the carpet behind the end of the long table a pizza box lying on the floor, pie pieces spread around, the steam still visible. And next to the box was a prone man in a white delivery uniform. He lay sprawled out on the carpet. He wasn't moving. His face rested nose first in the steaming sauce. Red gravy from the pie had collected on his chest, covering the pizza company's printed logo. Gwen realized suddenly that this red pool was likely not 'pizza gravy" but blood. Then reality fully hit. She was looking at a dead man. Her world began to swim before her eyes. She'd never seen an actual real life dead person before.

At last, men in blue uniform with guns ran into the room. Then came men in white uniforms carrying kits. They amassed in the back where the security guard was standing. Gwen began at last to understand what had happened. The security guard had shot the pizza man who had, for some reason unknown to her, fired two shots directed at Gwen or her team. *Thank God for the guard. Never did I think he'd be needed for actual security when I filed my motion months ago.* Soon the officers cordoned off the crime scene with yellow tape, just like in those cop shows Gwen loved. Her head spinning, she managed to return to her seat and checked again on Adam and Sammy.

Smiling at Adam who still lay quietly, she rubbed the red mark on her face from the carpet. "Hey Adam, told you to expect fireworks today. Of course I wasn't thinking at the time that my premonition should be taken literally. Who knew that securities cases could be so life and death serious? At least you have a story to tell in class that is even more far-fetched than that tort case with the hunters and deer that you were telling me about." There she was again, mouthing off and not being able to stop. Then she heard again the soft moaning sound. Adam's face turned from pale to paler. Her heart shook as if it lost its moorings. Something was wrong. Kneeling by Adam's side she opened his suit jacket.

"No!" she screamed. "Oh my God, he's been shot!"

A streak of red was traveling slowly across Adam's white dress shirt like hot lava creeping over rocks. She felt the shadow of the security guard – everyone's hero of the day – and a policeman standing over her.

Helpless, she called out to them, "He needs help! I think he's been shot. Please. Get help now."

The security guard, resting his hand on her shoulder, told her that the EMT techs were on their way while the cop opened Adam's shirt and put pressure on his chest to slow down the bleeding. He offered by way of comfort, "Don't worry, Ma'am, doesn't look too bad. He should make it." Looking back at their seats, he added, "I think the shot may have hit those thick books on the table first. Likely saved his life."

Gwen looked up at the casebooks and statute volumes Adam had piled on the conference table early that morning –– which seemed at the moment to her like another lifetime. *So the law saved his life?*

"Adam, I knew the law was powerful, but still, to stop a bullet..." She thought she saw Adam's lips curl into a slight smile.

That's my man, always ready to appreciate a bit of irony.

CHAPTER THIRTY-EIGHT

Gwen remained on the floor of the conference room squeezing Adam's hand and watched Adam's shirt bleed blood. Her mind was blank. All she felt were cold shivers that caused her body to shake uncontrollably. The security guard continued to be her hero, keeping all gawkers away – even the Panel members, so as not to contaminate the crime scene. Finally, after what seemed to Gwen enough time for a glacier to thaw – but probably was five minutes – medical help arrived. The EMTs carefully placed Adam on a gurney, buckled him in, and started a drip line. They wheeled him into the building's elevator and an ambulance, lights blazing, was waiting outside. Gwen assured Sammy, who'd remained calm in his chair through all the tumult, that all would be okay and asked him to go home with Benny who was waiting outside the room. She promised to call him when she had news about the hearing tomorrow.

Taking a deep breath to allay her dizziness, Gwen stood up and followed the EMTs out of the building. Fibbing that she was Adam's fiancée – she didn't think saying she was his boss would yield sufficient empathy, she climbed into the ambulance and sat across from her wounded warrior. During the short ride to the hospital she had some moments to think over what had happened. *Who the hell's the target of the assault? Is it Sammy? Is he really a secret gambler in trouble with the Latino mob – if there is such a thing? Surely not myself. That leaves Adam, the actual victim?* Then she remembered his reaction to those two men at the park and his admitting he'd had a gambling problem in the past. *No, Gwennie, he wouldn't put you at risk no matter his prior problems. Didn't he risk his life trying to save you?*

Whatever the story, she knew that she'd never been so frightened in her life. But all parts of her, that is the physical kind, were whole and her team had come through okay, at least in the long term. *So come on, Gwen, you're an ex-New Yorker. You've lived with crime around the corner for years. They say Adam will be fine and the shooter's dead so he's no longer threatening. Get a grip on yourself and deal with this.* Had she lost her 'New York tough' cynicism and replaced it with North of the Notch empathy?

Adam's lips moved. Gwen leaned over, careful not to touch any area near the dried red blood or the hanging tubes. "Hey, babe, don't worry," he said, his voice hoarse and fading. He gave her a lame half smile, one that didn't show off his usual dimples. "I'll be back on my bike soon." He paused, breathing in slowly as he cringed from a sharp pain. "Can you call the school and let them know I won't be in class for a few days probably?"

"Sweetie, you don't worry. The EMT tech said it's probably a flesh wound. Actually, to be more precise, she said the bullet apparently tore a bit of your trapezius muscle which is above the collarbone, and that was the source of the blood. In surgery they'll probably stitched it up. For now you're on Oxycontin for pain and they've started antibiotics. She added that after surgery you'll likely hurt if you try to lift your arm for three weeks or so but you should be fine after that. She said you were very lucky.

"So, seems, sweetie, that you won't have an excuse to miss your exams this term. Next time you want a break from school you need to plan something more effective. I don't know, maybe like a fall off Mt. Kilimanjaro into an ice crevice." He tried to laugh, but the pain wouldn't let him. Gwen continued, "The EMT guys said I could ride with you to the hospital. By the way, I sort of fudged it and told them you were my fiancé. Now that should get your heart pumping for real, probably scarier than a bullet!"

Her nervous humor got a slight chuckle. And so she sat across from Adam's gurney, careful not to crowd his movement, while the ambulance sped to St. John's Hospital. During the trip she closed her eyes, and found herself imagining one day down the road of life when they were old and gray and she was telling their cherubic grandchildren their tale about Grandpa Adam's scar and how he was injured attending a securities arbitration hearing –- and that he was saved from death by the Code of New Hampshire Statutes.

Gwen waited fitfully in Adam's room – or more accurately cubby area. The whole scene brought back memories she'd fervently hoped to the bottom of her being never to revisit. She had similarly sat with Brian after his tragic ski accident, feeling so lonely and afraid and helpless, nothing to do but listen to the room's large clock tick the hours away. She'd prayed then for his recovery, even though unreligious all her life. But there was no divine intervention and Brian died. Now here she was watching Adam in a hospital, as ghost white as the bed sheets, machines all around monitoring his state. But this time the prognosis was good, in fact, very positive for a complete and rapid recovery after he returned from surgery.

Exhausted, her head resting on her hands, almost asleep, a nurse gently touched Gwen's arm, and then told her she had a phone call at the nursing station. Gwen couldn't imagine who knew she was at the hospital or would be calling her at that hour. Had her staff somehow found out? She walked unsteadily to the phone.

"Attorney Wilson, ...um, Gwen? This is Jay Sawyer here. Sorry to call so late but I've been worried sick about how your associate is doing. And, well, also I need to make some decisions about tomorrow's scheduled hearing. Sorry again to pressure you, but are you able to address this now?"

Gwen paused, having trouble switching gears from worrying about Adam living to worrying about Sammy's fraud case. Silently holding the phone up to her ear, trying hard to concentrate on the demands of the hearing, she at last said to this man she didn't really know but who was showing unexpected kindness, "Thank you for your concern, Mr. Sawyer. Jay. It was very thoughtful of you to call. Adam, thankfully, went through surgery and is doing fine, patched up with some stitches, and they say likely to be discharged in a day or so. Fortunately, the bullet magically missed all parts important. Of course, we're all worrying what this was about as none of my team has a clue."

"That's good to hear, about your associate I mean." Gwen could hear Sawyer let out a huge sigh. "The other members of the Panel also wish him a speedy recovery. After a long pause, Sawyer continued, "Gwen, nothing like this has ever happened on my watch. I mean, this isn't criminal court or anything where you might expect violence to break out. I'm still shaking from the event. At least it is a relief to know that no one was seriously injured. A big relief."

"Yes, Jay, it certainly is. I'm grateful. Also, Sammy seems fine, has taken this in stride – indeed better than the rest of us it seems."

"Not wanting to pry into personal matters but it's important to the hearing in terms of security. Do you have any information about what the incident was about? I'm not sure the police know even who the intended target was? Was it involving Mr. Perez? I just re-read your motion for the security guard."

This was the question Gwen kept asking herself. She wished she could crack her knuckles to help relieve her anxiety – but appreciated that wasn't possible while holding the phone. After deeply exhaling as if meditating she said, "At this point, I have no idea. I'm hoping the police will be able to work that one out. I don't have any serious enemies; at least I think I don't. Sure, maybe my car mechanic was a little upset I didn't pick up my car until after hours last week – got stuck at work. Still, I suspect that faux pas doesn't warrant attempted murder."

Gwen could hear Sawyer momentarily chuckle. "I'm pleased to see you are able to maintain your sense of humor, Gwen. I appreciate how appalling this has been for everyone."

Gwen observed once again, "Jay, I don't mean to be flippant but I've learned humor is how my brain sometimes deals with difficult times and painful emotions, sort of like a protective shield.

And this is surely one of those life events. Be assured, I'm still pretty traumatized by all this as well, but am trying to move forward. Which brings me to how did things go with the hearing after I left?" *Why am I being so open with this guy who's likely to rule against us? Gwennie, maybe there is some truism up here in moose country that fellow lawyers are members of the bar's family, sort of like joining the area's Royal Order of Moose lodge.*

On a more firm footing, Sawyer explained to Gwen the facts of the post-shooting. "The police were here for several hours. They of course removed the, um, the shooter. They, let me see, well, ... um, ... sorry if I'm stumbling a little, anyways, they took statements from all Counsel, and um ... all those in the room. Did fingerprints, a new experience for me I can assure you. They seemed pretty thorough. As you can imagine, we're still shaken up. And, between us, I'm not sure I'll recover for some time. Never been so alarmed, and, I guess physically frightened. As you can tell, I'm not a hunter like some of the others in the room who are used to dealing with firearms. But other than for your intern, thank God, no one else was hurt. Not including, of course, the assailant. Also, just to note I made sure that your client went home with his friend – or was he a relative. He seemed all right."

"Thanks for the summary and for addressing Mr. Perez's situation. Yes, I made sure he had a ride home, but appreciate your follow-up." Gwen to her surprise did feel much better after this news. While there were times she might have wished vengeance on Respondents, especially Larry Murphy, shooting them did seem a little over the top.

Sawyer continued, "Yes. The police tell me it looks like it was a professional hit. I hear they found another man waiting downstairs parked on the street – in a stolen pizza van no less. They believe he was the getaway driver. I don't understand this at all. I mean, there's no mob involvement here. Like I said, it's not a drug case. This whole thing is quite disturbing. Maybe the accomplice can provide some clarity."

"Yes, Jay, I am as perplexed as you. But, fortunately, we had our experienced security person to foil the plot. Otherwise, their plan – whatever it was – might well have succeeded, and they'd have gotten away. And with a whole truckload of pies."

"Yes. The pizzas. Which brings me to the other reason that I mentioned for my call. The cops gave the okay to continue the hearing – should we elect to do so. We'll just move into another room on the floor. Not surprisingly, I couldn't find any relevant directions in the NASD's rules. As such, I guess it is up to me as Chair of the Panel to decide how we proceed. But I'd like first to get your input. I've consulted with the other Panel members and Respondents' Counsel and all prefer to return tomorrow to finish the hearing. Many said they've made travel plans and delay would require conflicts with other cases. And, as you know, rescheduling raises the issue of when all would be available to convene together again. This of course can be done. I understand fully that you and your client have been through a traumatic event. So what do you think? Are you up for starting again tomorrow at 10 a.m., or should I advise the NASD that we need a continuance?"

Gwen was torn. She'd like to be there with Adam to ensure that he was getting the best treatment. But at the same time she had an obligation to her client to do her best for him. Delay would likely mean no resolution for Sammy whereas continuing the hearing tomorrow would bring finality and hopefully a good resolution, especially if all those angels and cherubs flying around on the ceiling in the conference room managed to fly over to the new room. Sammy seemed fine and rescheduling presented once more the major issue of his returning from his happy life on the islands. Truth be told, Adam was doing well according to his doctors who said he would escape his brush with death with likely only a token scar. All told, the decision seemed clear.

"Jay, I believe my client would like to continue, and that would be Adam's wish as well. We are almost done. Perhaps we can start a bit later so I can briefly first stop at the hospital?"

"Fine, Gwen. I'll let the Panel and Counsel know tonight we shall convene again at eleven in the morning, and we'll go straight through without breaking for lunch. And I'll make sure security is tight. Again, on behalf of the Panel please extend to your intern Mr. Webber our wishes for a full recovery."

Sawyer hung up. Gwen held the phone in her hand for another minute, wondering if she had heard some momentary, unexpected, but deeply appreciated human outreach. Maybe, after all, this special brotherhood/sisterhood lawyer connection thing was real.

Before she returned to Adam, Gwen called her office. When Judy answered, Gwen updated her on what had occurred. Interestingly, Judy mentioned during their conversation that the other day some man, speaking she thought with a Brooklyn accent, had called the office and asked to meet with Adam today about some new case. Judy told him that Adam would be out of the office at Sammy's hearing.

"Don't know if it meant anything, Gwen, but it seemed a strange phone call." Both Judy and Gwen breathed in deeply at the same time after Judy relayed this news.

Returning to her hospital chair to watch Adam sleep, Gwen's mind raced back over the shooting event. *Will someone try again? Is there still a threat of violence?* Damn it. At least she'd learned one thing during the past day – she wasn't made for a life of crime, despite her New York pedigree.

CHAPTER THIRTY-NINE

Welcome again to Sammy's Hearing, Day 3. The Respondent's turn at the plate. Thank God it's almost over.

Gwen's mood was gloomy, not helped by the hanging slate clouds that muted the morning's light. She'd not slept well, the trauma of the shooting played in her mind like a stuck vinyl record that kept repeating the 'Bang' part of yesterday. And she continued to return to the conundrum: who was the target of the attack and did danger still exist? Other than walking New York City's streets at night and riding in city cabs during rush hour, she'd not confronted real danger before. Well, excepting hunting season – which she survived by not walking near woods without her bright orange vest.

Today promised to be long and difficult. First stop – Adam. After maneuvering through the hospital lobby, intake desk, and nursing station, Gwen finally found his alcove, charitably designated the 'Annex'. Blue curtains separated its five beds. Outside Adam's curtained space sat a uniformed cop, a conspicuous bulge protruding from his belt. Gwen approached, trying to resemble a devoted fiancée.

"Sorry, Ma'am, we can't allow anyone in to see Mr. Weber at the moment."

Gwen heard Adam call in a strong voice from behind the curtain, "Hey Joe, she's my lady – and lawyer. Please let her in or she might sue me."

As instructed, Gwen was permitted to enter Adam's protected curtained space. He was sitting up in bed, looking remarkably human again, and without attached tubes or devices. Even his dimples now showed off when he smiled. Gwen marveled that the body, at least his, was able to recover so fast from a major assault.

"Nice digs," Gwen said. "You must have what we in the North Country call 'Cadillac' health insurance to warrant this room."

"Only the best for the privileged patients admitted through the ER when the hospital has no beds available."

Gwen gave Adam a brief kiss on the cheek, not wanting to risk inflicting any further damage, and sat down on the metal chair next to his bed.

A matronly nurse entered through the curtain with paperwork and equipment in tow. As she began taking Adam's temperature, Gwen asked, "How's my guy doing?"

"Seems to be making an amazing recovery. In fact, I heard the doctor talking about discharging him if all goes well by tomorrow." She added while wagging her finger at Adam, "That's if he behaves himself. He's a fortunate young man."

Gwen wondered what mischief Adam was already causing. Adam smiled and replied, "That's the best news I've had since I learned Mary Leonard had a crush on me."

"Who?" Gwen asked, her eyebrows rising – to her surprise.

"Hey, babe, she was my 4th grade girlfriend."

"You certainly started young."

"Yeah, aren't I lucky I was precocious."

This bit of repartee left the nurse chuckling as she departed. Gwen sat down and checked out Adam's nice cute blue socks that matched the attractive green and blue striped hospital gown that she appreciated didn't quite cover his muscled hairy chest. And then there was the large white bandage covering his wound.

"How are you feeling, honey?"

"Fine. No, really. All sewed up good. I felt worse when I got tackled in high school football –- without the ball. This is not so bad. Hurts still if I move my shoulder wrong way, but I'll heal. Maybe won't even have a scar to tell tales about to my grandchildren."

"My, you are thinking ahead. Are you on meds for pain?"

"Nothing strong anymore. Don't want to miss the daytime soaps on TV."

Her hand covering a smile, Gwen said, "I guess you can't be in too much distress, as I see you've maintained your distinctive droll humor. All good I guess. As for me, I'm still suffering from trauma overdrive."

Adam, his voice serious now, said, "Gwen, I'm so sorry about that." With tears welling in his eyes, well at least the right one, Adam added, "I really don't know why this happened, but I would never knowingly put you in harms way. I hope you know that."

Gwen fidgeted in her chair, played with her hair, stretched out her legs. *Yeah. I do need to know – and he's opened the door.* Arms folded tightly, her fingernails digging into her palms, she asked, "Adam, what is this all about? I can't believe some professional killer came in and began to shoot at me. Or Sammy. So that leaves you. And why the cavalry outside since they've killed the bad guy? Let me know if, well, you don't feel well enough to deal with this now. But we need to, soon."

Adam restlessly moved around in his bed. He momentarily moaned as his gown pulled on his shoulder. Gwen waited. He avoided her eyes.

"Gwen, you know how much I care about you. My time with you.... it's opened possibilities for personal connections, deep affection, I thought I'd lost."

Gwen waited but Adam didn't offer more. Her ears had perked up with Adam's use of the phrase 'you know' – which she'd learned in Psych 101 may imply less than full honesty.

"Okay, bud. Nice words, especially for someone spacey on pain pills. But a deflection, not an answer. Adam, I'm serious." Gwen flinched, aware she almost said 'dead serious.' It was time for her to be brave and put it all on the line. She'd survive either way. *Damn, there I go again with this life and death theme.* "I can't continue how we are without knowing more. I almost got killed. As did my client. So it is tell me now or, well, I don't see our future together."

Adam closed his eyes. Then, focusing on the ceiling, he began again. "Pain pills maybe, but I'm feeling quite lucid. Maybe more

than I want to be.... It appears being 'almost killed' can do that."
Adam grimaced, but this time not from any external movement.
"Gotcha. You're 100% right. It's time for me to explain. I get it.
You deserve the full story."

Gwen sat back and frowned. "Adam, I don't want another
story, I want the truth. Our future together relies on trust. I need to
be able to trust you. Remember the old cliché 'honesty is the best
policy'? Well it is. No more Pinocchio fairy tales. Be on the level
with me or you're out the door, at least my door."

"Okay. Here goes." Adam pushed the electric button on the
hospital bed, raising his upper torso so he could lock eyes with her.
"What I've told you, that I started a computer company and all,
that's what happened. But I may have made myself out to be a
little more 'cool' than the nerd I was. And I did love and lose Kila,
did lose my hold on life after her death. That was real. But I
underplayed my destructive path after she passed. I didn't just
drink. I gambled, pursued reckless encounters, did party drugs. I
wanted oblivion, to block the unfairness of it all. Nothing was too
risky."

Gwen sat silent, her face immobile. "Yes we've both talked
about our destructive actions after Kila and Brian. "How we
wanted not only to block the bad memories, our feeling of guilt,
but to deal with the unfairness of it all. Tell me more."

"Got it. I became friends with a rich guy, Ovid, when partying
in L.A. He was no doubt a charmer, ever gracious, the life of the
party scene. He exuded confidence, was contemptuous of the rules.
Anyhow, Ovid was generous to me, let me stay on his boat, made
arrangements so I could enter the private casino games in Vegas.
And I did, with gusto. Ended up owing the wrong guys lots of
money. Boy was I in over my head! And too full of myself to
notice. Soon learned that being part of this scene was not such a
good thing.

"Go on," said Gwen, anxiously twirling her hair.

"Sounding like a bad Grade B action thriller yet?"

"Adam, I want to hear it all, but yeah, it's out of my league for destructive life experience. Well, maybe not by so much. I hope there's a happy ending. One with ever after."

"My friend offered to grease the wheels with his casino buddies if I helped him out by doing a 'small favor'. So I took an extra bag on the plane home from Cancun. Ovid told me he'd bought some watches as family gifts and he already was at his declaration limit. He'd done this before, not a big deal. I shouldn't worry for customs didn't check Americans carefully, especially those who looked rich. I was a little nervous, but I took him at his word. Didn't want to seem what I was, a twenty- something computer nerd trying to play with the filthy wealthy jetsetters. I stupidly felt I owed him somehow, for all he'd helped me. Jackass, right?"

Adam stopped speaking as his breath became labored. Gwen was about to go and find a nurse when Adam took a deep, slow breath, coughed once, and then continued.

"Easily most stupid thing I ever did! I don't know how to explain it. Thank goodness I didn't have the machismo to be a savvy smuggler. I couldn't pull it off. My first shot and I was stopped at the border. There I was, saying just bringing in some Rolexes for family, when under the trays of watches were hidden bags containing powder. Don't know what kind of drugs, but I knew I was in trouble. The CIA intervened and under torture..., no just kidding. All it took was one meeting in a windowless room with the FBI and I 'spilled the beans', as they say. Some criminal mastermind! In the end I made a deal. In exchange for helping the agency I'd get off without a criminal record.

Anyhow, my friend found out I'd co-operated with the feds, nothing actually happened to him, not sure why, and that was that. But, as you may imagine, he wasn't happy with me. I thought I was too 'small fries' to matter, still think that. I haven't heard from Ovid for years and I don't know if there's any connection between this hit to my past, but it is possible. For all I know that stupid picture of me in the local paper maybe was picked up somehow by Ovid's local friends or family."

Gwen got up and looked through the curtains at the trash containers outside. She studied the traffic on the road leading to the hospital. Some cars were pulling up to the valet parking stop. Women got into wheelchairs and then were rolled through the main entrance. Turning back to Adam she said, "You're right. This sounds like a dime store crime novel. We're North of the Notch people here, quiet rural New Hampshire where chopping down a neighbor's tree may make the front-page crime headline in the local paper."

"Would you like me to continue, Gwennie?"

"I'm waiting with bated breath. But I see you're tired. Should you continue? And I have to get to the hearing soon."

"Now or never as they say. I might not have the courage later, when I'm not taking all that numbing pain medicine. The rest is short. I ended up, as I told you, with some help from my new friends in the Bureau who helped me to find a job and place to live hidden in the Mid-West. I basically tried to wait it out to ensure they'd have forgotten me, but I was slowly going bonkers. It was the winter blizzards that finished me. Violated my California roots. Again with help from a Fed buddy and my savings I was able at the last minute to get into this local law school, as of course I had no school records, hadn't taken the LSAT, or anything. Got in based on my 'life experiences' –– not the one's we've been talking about. My plan remains to use this time to get the training to become an environmental lawyer and help protect the wilderness. In the meantime, I've stayed low."

Gwen was quiet. Was this yet another Adam tale, and a long one at that? "Adam, you're right, sounds like a story from one of those supermarket tabloids. I need some time to take it in. But I also need to get going, as Sammy's case is to start soon."

"Sure, babe. I understand. This all seems insane. It does to me too. And I'm living it. Really, I'm just a middle-class guy who got lost for a while in a different biosphere. Gwen, that happened, you know, years ago. I'm grown up now. I have my feet on the ground. Please, Gwennie, remember it has been really good between us. I mean it, at least for me. You are the best person I know. I'm not sure what's next for now, what's safe, but don't give up on me, please. I do promise you, Gwen, that I will do what is necessary to make sure you and your team are safe. No more danger. My word."

He reached out with the arm closest to her, grabbed her hand, put it up to his mouth, and gently kissed it. Then he added, "One more *important* thing before you leave. My being shot, well, that's all my doing. Nothing brought about by you, you hear me? In fact it was your law books that likely saved me. No crap about "black widow" and all that stuff. Those other times when you've dealt with loss, well, they were accidents. Nothing more. Just the fickle finger of fate acting out. You listening to me?"

"I hear you, my Lancelot. We are human and we make mistakes. Now forgive and move on." Gwen rose, looked long and hard at his face, focusing on what she was feeling, what was her sixth 'truth' sense saying? But all was quiet.

"Got to run, we're trying to finish the hearing today." She stood up and leaned over Adam's bed. "We both know how it's likely to end sad; the case I mean, not you and me. Still, there's always that thing with feathers, at least according to Emily Dickinson."

"Gwen, one thing more that I've been thinking about. The odds of a W aren't good, I give it an 8 to 1 on my radar in favor of the bad guys, if not worse. What's kept you going with this case?"

"Ha! Good question," Gwen said as she gathered up her stuff and was walking towards the exit. She stopped and turned, then addressed Adam. "Quick answer, I took it on because, well ignoring the financial interest in making money to keep my practice afloat, I felt a commitment to Sammy and to his case, to this immigrant having the American Dream who still believes after everything he's gone through that the law will mend wrongs. At least that was my thinking then." Pursing her lips together, she stopped, and then added, "Maybe foolishness I'm thinking more and more these days, but that's a subject for another day. Take care, Adam. And listen to your nurse!"

****** **** ******

At 10:30 a.m. Gwen rushed into the hi-rise where the hearing was being held, and rode the waiting elevator car up to the 21st floor where Josiah Day's law firm coincidently had its satellite New Hampshire office. Emerging into the hallway Gwen was surprised to see Josiah rush towards her and then suddenly stop just before they collided. His distant smirk suddenly changed to a brief smile as he finally recognized who she was.

Gwen took the moment to dive in with the purpose of her visit. "Hi Josiah. I see you're in a hurry. I was hoping we could talk briefly before the hearing starts on a matter that's concerning me. Do you have a moment?"

"Hello Gwen. Sure, but give me a sec while I visit the little boy's room."

Gwen waited, leaning against the wall. She closed her eyes and was almost nodding off when she heard Day's baritone voice yelling at someone to do something. He approached her like a rooster in heat, head cocked and chest out, showing off his red kerchief and tie. She thought she understood and appreciated his showmanship style. He was a black partner – probably the only such minority senior attorney – in an old, venerated New York based law firm. In addition to being a really smart litigator, he likely needed to exude self-confidence and moxie to be accepted by the firm's wealthy clients and bar brothers in order to overcome the historical racial barriers in this staid profession. She could relate, being a woman lawyer dealing with gender barriers in an almost exclusively man's world.

"Sorry Gwen, too much coffee this morning. Hope it's not my

prostate. So what would you like to talk about? And how's your associate? In all my years of practice, that was a first for me. Something to bring up at our next partner's meeting – life insurance."

Gwen's exhaustion seemed magnified by Day's high energy. Speaking fast under the pressure of the hearing start, she began, "Know you're busy getting ready, Josiah; just wanted to cover a few things and not sure when else we could talk. First, thanks for asking, Adam's doing fine, turned out to be just muscle damage and he should be sent packing tomorrow."

"Good news. What else?" Josiah was already checking his Rolex.

Gwen rushed on. "Also, on a related matter, but important. You may remember in my security motion filed months ago I mentioned that my client was assaulted and given an ominous verbal warning to end what he was doing. I understood this to refer to this case thanks to the timing of the event. I recall mentioning this to you but I never heard back."

Day nodded and said, "Yeah, any connection seems speculative to me, although I'll admit the shooter's aim was clearly at your side of the table. And I did send out feelers to the other lawyers and my client. Responses I got were that no one knew anything about some such assault, so I didn't have anything to pass on to you. But not sure heard back from everyone. Anything else? The hearing's going to start soon and I want to get my ducks set up."

"I'm not so certain I can dismiss the connection to this case so readily. While it may not be connected to yesterday's fiasco, it did happen the same day my office and home were burgled. Can you assure me that your client's hired P.I.'s didn't act inappropriately to frighten my client off."

"What?" Josiah rose to his full height, instantly transforming into his bully lawyer mode before her eyes, sort of the opposite of a chrysalis into a butterfly. "Are you accusing my team of wrongdoing?" Leaning toward Gwen, as if to press her into the wall until she cried 'uncle', he added, "That's damn absurd. And coming from a smart lawyer like you. I and my colleagues don't play that way."

Gwen pushed him back with her pocketbook, the female's weapon of last resort. "No. Just following the dots. After yesterday, I'm sure you can understand that I need to make sure my client is safe. I'd appreciate your looking into it more fully to assure me that I'm wrong and that my client is not in danger."

Josiah, pushing his hands out so he could pull his fingers backward, he continued in a softer voice, "Sorry, Gwen. Yes, it was disturbing. I'd be upset too if that ever happened to one of my clients, but fortunately they usually are insulated from exposure to physical injury thanks to their company's security staff." Looking into Gwen's eyes he said firmly, "Fine. To be more certain as you say, I will check further to confirm that no third party from our side breached their instructions. Gwen, if so, I'll deal with that as necessary. You have my word."

Gwen nodded, thanked him and gave Josiah her most charming smile. As she walked towards the elevator she called back, "See you at the hearing Josiah, I think it will be our day." Thankfully the elevator door opened just at that moment and she was gone before he could respond.

But as she was riding down to the 5th floor she fretted. If not this case, why did someone attack Sammy? Did he have dangerous enemies she wasn't aware of, maybe connected with gambling or other debts? She'd been pretty confident the assault was to scare him off, but what if she were wrong? And what might this say about Sammy's honesty? Should she require that future contingency clients take a lie detector test?

CHAPTER FORTY

Where's my client?

Once again, Gwen had to ask where Sammy was as it was 10:30 a.m., and the 'Final Day' of the hearing was about to start — with all present except the man who started it all.

Rather than stewing over Sammy's absence, Gwen decided to survey the replacement meeting room. It was the first one's twin with rich wood paneling, English landscape paintings, glittering chandeliers, and the smell of money. Except this version came with a navy and forest green color scheme – and a ceiling without flying angels. Across from her sat Josiah Day, dressed today all in blue. As expected he was busily reviewing his notes. Larry Murphy sat in the middle of the conference table, leaning back with his eyes closed, next to his lawyer, Martin Mandel, who appeared to be reading the *Wall Street Journal*, perhaps checking his stocks. The room was noisy, filled with the gabbing, laughing, and telephone speak of the suits.

Gwen focused on Murphy. Yes, he was nice looking in a bland way, but someone beginning to show mid-life wear. He had the start of a stomach bulge on the body of a once upon a time athlete, the beginning of a double chin, and thinning blond hair he combed sideways. And a warm smile. In short, he presented as a 'nice salesman', someone who would appear honest and reassuring in an insurance company ad. Not exactly the personification of evil, but then again Gwen had learned that bad people, like vampires, might look like friendly neighbors.

Moving with difficulty as Gwen was aching most everywhere from Adam's life-saving tackle, Gwen checked out again the two empty chairs next to her. Adam was safely tucked away in his hospital bed. She already missed being able to run legal ideas by him for she'd learned his observations were usually incisive and smart. And his humor helped her handle 'trial' anxiety. As to

Sammy, well worst-case scenario, yesterday's attacks had been too much for him and he'd be a no-show. She thanked her lucky stars she'd already put in his case. Still, she'd thought he might find some solace in watching Larry take his turn under the cross-examination gun, even if only her little peashooter. She glanced one final time at the entry door where the same security guard stood ready to check entrant's bags. Gwen wondered if it was okay to give him a 'thank you' tip for maybe saving her life.

Listening to the happy jabber in the room, Gwen marveled that no one else was experiencing from yesterday's events the harrowing emotions that she was having. For them, it appeared to have been just another work meeting before traveling home to wives and real work. Indeed, several already had stacked their luggage against the wall, prepared to make a quick exit to start their weekend.

At last, Gwen then checkout out the Panel members sitting in their usual order on the dais: the so far silent Elias Pollippi to the left; the Chair, Jay Sawyer, in the middle; and James Grimes on his right, again attired in golf sweater, today it was what Gwen would call salmon colored. All were busy doing paperwork or whatever. Grimes she surmised from his writing in pencil and erasing was trying his hand at the local paper's crossword puzzle. Loretta was at her desk arranging tapes.

Sawyer jostled the microphone and he then called the hearing to order. He expressed relief that the prior day's carnage had been contained and no one present had been harmed. He thanked all for their fortitude, and especially noted the bravery of the guard. Sawyer led a chorus of applause for the 'arbitration hero'. He then thanked Loretta for her quick thinking in protecting her machine and all applauded again. Continuing, he stated that the police had assured him that the attempted assault had no connection to this matter. Still, the Panel had elected to retain the security guard as a precaution.

With the preliminaries done, Sawyer nodded at Loretta and she turned on the recording tape. Despite the absence of the Complainant, the third day of the hearing, August 21, 2003, was now a 'go'.

From her chair Gwen rose and updated the room on Adam's excellent medical condition. Without warning the back door opened and Sammy and his nephew Carlos entered the room. A dour Sammy, wearing golf jacket rather than parka, sheepishly walked to his seat, his eyes down and arms stiff at his side. Gwen observed that his shoulders were already sagging. She suspected that, while he might be happy to see Murphy under attack, he understood as well that it would be difficult today to sit silently and hear Respondents' witnesses present a far different version of his story. She'd warned him such is the nature of a trial – both sides have their say.

Sammy mumbled to her, "Sorry late, car not good."

She reassured him with a pat on his arm. Carlos took a seat in the back, next to the guard. Gwen decided it prudent to confirm with the Panel that he could stay and observe, as he wasn't a witness. She stood and asked, no objections were raised, and Sawyer said 'fine'. With all now in place, Sawyer looked directly at Day. With yellow legal pad in hand, Day walked up to a small wooden podium that had been set up near the Panel's table. He said in his mellifluous baritone, "I call Respondent Lawrence Murphy."

Gwen was surprised that Murphy and not Cavanaugh was the first witness –- and that Day and not Mandel was to handle the initial direct. To appear active from the start, she rose and began the day off with a soft jab, "Mr. Sawyer, I understood that Mr. Cavanaugh was going to be testifying initially. Or is his absence confirmation that Mr. Perez does indeed have limited English fluency?"

Day leaped up like a Rottweiler ready to pounce. The soft vibes of their meeting upstairs had been replaced by the menace of the carnivore. Raising his arm –- and volume, his eyes hooked on

Gwen's, he countered, "Ms. Wilson, it is *my* choice whom and when I call my witnesses." Shifting his gaze to Sawyer, Day continued in a lighter tone, "Mr. Cavanaugh is available should the Panel wish him to testify now based on his in-court observations, but in light of our present time constraints, I am calling Respondent Murphy first. This will help ensure that he has adequate time to state his case and to refute vigorously Mr. Perez's unfounded claims."

"Now wait a minute, ..." began Gwen. Then she shook her head, smiled, shrugged her shoulders and sat down. Day had made it clear that the serious part of the hearing had begun and there were to be, to use a wrestling term, no holds barred going forward. Almost immediately Sawyer supported her assessment. He bellowed at her, "Sit down Ms. Wilson!" adding, "Attorney Day has the right to order the witnesses in his case – as did you, Counsel." Sawyer looked at his watch, then at the apparently standard conference room Big Ben clock.

"To make myself clear, gentlemen and Ms. Wilson. I am expecting we will finish today, even though we've started late. I will not put up with unnecessary or inappropriate colloquy between Counsel. Am I making myself clear? As I have repeatedly said, this is not a jury trial. I assure you the Panel members are conversant, in fact, experts in securities law. While I appreciate the need to make the record, as you know there is no appeal from the Panel's decision – unlike in a trial court. I urge you all to keep that in mind as we proceed. When necessary, the Panel today will move this hearing forward. And, be forewarned, if we don't finish today I am prepared to hold the hearing on Saturday. Enough said. Move on, Attorney Day."

The other Panel members nodded in agreement, although Gwen doubted they had any interest in extending their obligations beyond today. Gwen assumed that Sawyer's outburst represented their decision to exert firmness and bluster in order to get the hearing completed while there was still sunshine. And she wasn't upset with Sawyer's bark, much. Like her, he was probably exhausted from burning the candle at both ends, putting in hours at his law firm while also running the hearing.

Murphy rose and sat down in the extra chair between Day and the Panel. He was dressed in a blue and red checked blazer and open collar plaid sports shirt, as if he were going to a neighborhood barbecue, Gwen thought. Looking up at the Panel he gave them an ingratiating smile showing plenty of teeth. From the podium, Day began asking Murphy background queries. Murphy's initial responses were short and Gwen thought clearly practiced. Before they moved further into less routine areas, Gwen rose and said to the Panel, "I would like to suggest that Mr. Murphy move to a chair closer to this side of the table as I am having trouble hearing his responses." But Sawyer wanted no part of this game of musical chairs and breaking the opponent lawyer's rhythm. He curtly directed Murphy to stay where he was and "... to please keep your voice elevated for the record while speaking into the microphone."

Murphy looked up at the Panel. A sly grin on his face, he commented, "Sorry, but, well, that's an unusual request for me. My wife's always getting on me that I'm talking *too* loud. 'Lower the volume, Larry,' she tells me. 'Even the cows can hear you in Vermont!'"

Laughter filled the room, at least from the men present. Day added his two cents. "Wives. What a surprise, huh?"

More male laughter ensued.

The frivolities over, and Murphy having exuded his charm, Day continued his meticulous review of the evidence. Murphy described his biography: how he decided in college, a small school in Western New Hampshire, that if he couldn't play basketball at the pro level, a likely conclusion as he barely made his school's Division 3 team, his next choice was helping people make money. One of his frat brothers had a connection with a bank's trust department and they were happy to hire him after graduation at a financial sales agent level.

After several years Murphy grabbed an opportunity to join Stanley, Howe as a financial advisor in the firm's small Middleton office. Murphy said he'd moved his family up above the Notch and had learned to love the opportunity to enjoy the outdoors with his three kids and be a force in moving Middleton into economic prosperity. He was active in the Lions club, Moose Lodge, and the local recreation department's men's basketball team. He was passionate, he added, about helping his clients plan for retirement, save for college for their children and grandchildren, in building relationships, and in helping them protect their financial future. And thanks to his hard work, outgoing personality, comfortable way with people, he'd been quite successful. In short, life had been good to Larry Murphy.

As the afternoon progressed, Gwen found no surprises in Murphy's testimony. Day, preferring to use the casual term 'Larry' rather then the honorific Mr. Murphy, ran him through the procedures followed when filling out the required forms, as well as handling Sammy's account. Day introduced documents evidencing Stanley, Howe's customer and compliance regulations. He received Murphy's assurance that, 'yes sir', as far as he knew the company's procedures complied with industry standards and, 'yes sir', he himself fully complied with the firm's requirements. 'Yes, sir', it was incumbent on him to determine from Sammy the degree of risk appropriate to satisfy the suitability of his investments, and,' yes sir', he'd done a quick calculation of Sammy's buying power, age, and money he'd be receiving each year, pay-outs from retirement plans, and the value of this money in different currencies. Sammy, he explained, had told him he'd be moving to the Dominican Republic soon. Once there he was planning on starting again his business manufacturing t-shirts. Then there was also the $400,000 Sammy told him he had in properties in the Dominican Republic, although Larry admitted he hadn't seen any documents supporting this claim.

Day asked, using a more informal tone, "Larry, you've testified you complied with these guidelines by doing due diligence. Can you tell the Panel more explicitly how Mr. Perez's actions misled you...."

Gwen shot up. "Objection. Counsel should not mischaracterize the facts."

Day pirouetted towards Gwen. "I object, Mr. Sawyer. These repetitive interruptions by opposing counsel are improper and unprofessional. They are intentionally offered to confuse my witness. Please instruct Ms. Wilson to stop playing games with this tribunal."

Sawyer, firmly rubbing his forehead as if he had a migraine, sighed, then asked Day to finish his question without testifying as to the facts and also told Gwen to sit down.

Day asked, "Again, Larry, please describe what you did to ensure you complied with your company's guidelines?"

"Sure. I was comfortable Mr. Perez met all these company guidelines. I looked at his company stock; his 401K was rising; income was rising. As I said, he told me he had business interests in the Dominican, a condo and property near the water, he was co-owner in a small manufacturing business, and all this was outside of his work income. He also said he'd traded before although not at a full-service firm like mine. I never had a reason to believe he was an unsophisticated investor. I know this as he would call me three to four times each day, early in the morning, before work, at his break, and he'd tell me *at length* about stocks he'd heard about on CNBC or from colleagues. He knew the lingo; he made recommendations."

"Did at any time you believe he didn't understand the risk?" Day asked.

"No."

Gwen suddenly was distracted as Sammy forcefully grasped her arm and loudly whispered, "Not true. It not true." She whispered back that he needed to be quiet, like Larry had been when he was testifying.

Indeed, Sawyer interrupted Day and said to her client, his words said slowly as if to ensure he was being understood, "Sir, do not speak when Mr. Murphy is talking. If you do, I may have to have the guard remove you from the room. Do you understand?"

Sammy nodded. Gwen already noticed tears forming in her client's eyes. It was going to be a difficult morning for him.

Day paused to exaggerate the impact of her client's misconduct, and then asked Larry, "Did you do what you are required to do based on these documents to satisfy your obligations under the "Know Your Customer" rule and suitability standards?"

Gwen objected. "Leading," she said.

Day erupted at her once again. Facing her he stated, "Come on, Counsel. It is a perfectly appropriate legitimate question in an arbitration proceeding, indeed one you repeatedly used during your direct of your client. And, Mr. Sawyer, if she's interrupting me again for no good reason I ask for sanctions. Her objections are baseless and not made in good faith."

Gwen, her pulse thumping, started to respond when Sawyer interjected, "Sit down Ms. Wilson. You will have an opportunity to cross-examine. We'll move on. Answer the question Mr. Murphy."

Her competitive juices now flowing, Gwen reluctantly sat down on her hands so she wouldn't interrupt. She wasn't sure to be frank whether she was actually helping Sammy with these weak objections, or they served to maintain some control over Josiah's direct. Still, the litigation master, Josiah, had done his share of popping up.

Larry responded yes, that he was familiar with the rule, and, thanks to a checklist he'd developed, he fully complied with it when advising his clients.

"What documents did you make that confirm your compliance?"

"The usual. I note that unlike Ms. Wilson's witness, there aren't enough hours in the day for me to have a file with all those notes, yeah and research, and things like that that she mentioned.

But then again I probably have maybe, I don't know, let's see, um...." Larry reached into his jacket pocket and removed a small pad and pen, then did some calculations. "I'd guess at least three times as many clients as her, and brother, they all want my attention now. I think what likely happened is most of these so-called missing records were kept in the file held by my supervisor, who, as you know unfortunately passed away unexpectedly."

"I see." Day nodded as if that all made perfect sense, then moved on to his next point. "Larry, you've discussed your efforts to determine Mr. Perez's income as well as his liquid assets and that these were considered in your assessment of suitability. Did this

apply as well to your using margin in Mr. Perez's account?"

"Yes, but then again, Sammy was always pushing me to buy, buy, buy. He sure knew about the risks and benefits of margin purchases."

"Did you make any further efforts to verify or check up on the information he told you about his land and all?"

"No."

Gwen sat up. *Is this a good thing?*

Day followed up, "Why not?"

Murphy replied, "It wasn't my duty to investigate what the customer told me. I needed only to take into account what the customer, in this case Mr. Perez, was telling me at its face value. And that was that he had plenty of assets thanks to his company stock, international business and real estate interests, and retirement plans. He was, you know, a bright guy, traded before, I did well for him when he relied on my advice."

"Liar!" The word shattered the air in the room. "You're a fuckin' liar." Gwen realized this was shouted from the back of the room. She saw Carlos, all six feet of him, standing up and spouting a continuing stream of invective in English and Spanish at Murphy. "You son of a bitch ripped off my uncle, cheated him of his money, ruined his life. Now you tell lies, all lies, at his hearing.

All bullshit! Saw a brown man and said it's my day to get rich. You're a fuckin' criminal. *La Madre que te parlô! Vete pa'l carajo!*"

Murphy now rose, his face red. Arm pointing at Carlos as he yelled in return, "You're crazy, twerp. Why don't you shut your stupid mouth. You know nothing, just a wise ass kid shouting crap." With his arms now moving as if pulling in a rope, Murphy added, "Hey, little guy, you want to come closer so I can take you on?"

"You're a big guy, huh? Sure, easy to be big when you're surrounded by other liars." Carlos began moving forward towards Larry before the security guard grabbed his arm and held him in place.

Sawyer quickly pounded his gavel and yelled, "Order, order." It seemed like minutes passed before Carlos shrugged, and both Carlos and Murphy, thanks to Mandel's pulling, sat down. Sawyer advised all that there would be decorum in the room or he'd take action. Gwen sighed, the suits appeared stunned, and Sammy waved at his nephew.

When calm had been restored, warnings given, Day moved on.

Focusing again on Murphy's testimony, Gwen noticed that Day showed no concerns that it contradicted Martha's statement that the 'Know Your Customer Rule' obligated a broker to confirm a client's questionable asset claims. Had she missed something?

Day, seemingly unperturbed by the recent outbreak, continued his cross, mellifluously asking, "Was there anything that changed your attitude about Mr. Perez and his trading objectives?"

Gwen listened intently; this was the moral issue she'd worried could bite Sammy.

"Yes, my reaction to him changed based on my interactions with his wife's divorce attorney."

"When and how did you learn of the couple's divorce?"

"I don't recall the time but it must have been near when Mr. Perez asked me to open a second account in his name, that was as I said I the time I got a call from the wife's lawyer."

Gwen said, "Objection. Relies on information not in evidence."

Sawyer told Day, "Please fill in the blanks as you move forward with your questioning, Attorney Day, much as I allowed Ms. Wilson to do."

Through question and answer, Murphy testified that Olanda's divorce lawyer had told him she'd learned during discovery that Sammy had secretly transferred funds from his account at Stanley, Howe into a second account to hide money from his wife. Gwen squirmed. Sammy had testified under oath the purpose was to protect money he'd borrowed and owed his Aunt Mariah so it wasn't included and divided as marital assets. "This her money," he told Gwen – and the Panel, "not mine, no right to keep." Gwen understood that was in fact the legal rule in the state as this money was a family 'gift' to Sammy, he could show the court it was 'separate property' and so not to be divided as a marital asset. Still, Murphy's testimony that Sammy was trying to cheat his wife left a sour note. She jotted down a reminder to challenge this on cross.

Murphy then denied any churning, saying that the market moved fast and sometimes he needed to make in and out trades. "Doesn't mean high commissions. So no churning." Locking eyes with the Panel he added, "In Mr. Perez's case, I could have made more trading Blue Chip stocks – with less work, and less harassment."

"Larry, you mentioned that Mr. Perez had prior trading experience. What did Mr. Perez tell you about that?"

"Yeah, I was surprised to learn that he'd done some stock trading years before at a discount brokerage firm where Mr. Perez handled his own trading. I remember he said he didn't do a great job which is why he came to a professional like me."

Finally, Day was done and before Gwen could finish taking notes Larry's lawyer, Marty Mandel, stood up and began questioning his client. As she suspected, a neat way of getting two bites. Mandel had Murphy reiterate his testimony that he hadn't done anything wrong and that Sammy had been a difficult client. When he sat down, direct was over. And Murphy looked none the worse for wear. He'd been prepped well, Gwen thought, and told his story like the good salesman that he was. Now she was up to bat. Would she be able to get him off his game? Gwen could feel the tension start in her belly and spread upwards until pressure began weighing down above her eyes. She found acid tablets in her bag and chewed two on the spot.

Sawyer asked if Counsel wanted to take a ten minute break before cross began but all said no, Day and Mandel because their client hadn't been wounded and Gwen because more time wouldn't be much help. Better to get it over and done with. Just looking at the relaxed Panel members, she knew she needed to repair the damage to her case quickly.

How to do that? She'd already relied on Martha and Linda's data they claimed showed illegal conduct when examining Sammy. Now what? Thanks to the limits on discovery, and Respondents' claimed lack of records — both from Murphy's dead supervisor and Murphy and even the company's phone records, she didn't have further damaging documents to introduce –- except the absent stolen hot document. While Gwen was fairly confident the 'missing' records would have strengthened Sammy's case, especially the phone records of Sammy's frequent calls to Murphy, she'd been unable to get copies. All she could do was raise inferences from what hadn't been produced. She needed to pull a Sherlock Holmes trick, inferring guilt from the fact that the dog didn't bark in the night.

After consulting with Sammy – who had nothing to say, Gwen got to her feet and gave Murphy a pleasant and she hoped disarming smile.

She decided to start with some background questions. "Mr. Murphy, I am correct, am I not, that you are actually a *sales* representative at your firm, you have no advanced training in the financial market, just your college business courses, right?"

"Well, I wouldn't say that's correct. Sure, I majored in finance in college, learned some important concepts, but then I had training at both the bank and with Stanley, Howe on being a financial advisor." He sat back with a smile as if he'd won the first round. Then, after a pause, he added, "Oh, and to better serve my clients I also earned my AAMS designation a few years ago."

Gwen nodded, "Yes, I understand that some of the companies offering college SAT type classes also offer Continuing Ed. programs for financial professionals. As far as I know, the AAMS is a designation you can get if you complete a two-to-three-month parttime program that offers an overview of investment management, and is mostly geared towards *new* hires in the field, not those with job experience like you. Isn't that the case?"

"I went nights to a local college and found it very helpful."

"Do you hold Series 7 and Series 66 registrations, Mr. Murphy? Are you CFP Certified?" Gwen knew that the Panel would know what these meant far better than she did so she didn't elaborate.

"No."

"I take that as no to all I mentioned. Did you at any time *sit* for the SIE exam, the Series 7 exam, or the Series 63 exam?"

"Well, you know my clients are happy with what I do, I have no need to take months, years to study for these licenses, these exams are quite complicated and all." "I see. Without any of these professional qualifications, isn't it true, Mr. Murphy, that you are a salesman and not qualified as a financial advisor, a financial consultant?" Gwen continued her attack, "That, in short, Mr. Murphy, you make your living selling Stanley, Howe's services, like a Ford car salesman sells Ford automobiles? Your interest, like the car guy, is to make sales, in your case trades, so you earn fees? And like the car guy, you work for YOU, not the customer? And as we've seen during the past days, in this case that is Sammy Perez."

Day yelled, "Objection," but Larry answered anyways. With his cheeks now blushing, and Gwen thought sweat forming maybe on his brow, he stated, "Look lady, my company calls me *a financial advisor*, and if it's good enough for them, it is good enough for me."

"Except that you are not licensed to give advice, correct? And you are not in a fiduciary relationship with your clients so that *their* interests come first, and not Stanley, Howe's or yours, correct?"

Day jumped up, "Objection, Mr. Murphy is not a lawyer knowledgeable about the complicated and often conflicting classifications of professionals in the financial investment business."

Sawyer nodded and told Gwen to move on.

"Mr. Murphy, you heard the testimony of Mrs. Stoneham, a financial consultant with years of training and experience in this field – and the degrees I've mentioned. She stated clearly that she would have expected to have seen much more trading related documentation in *any* client's files, including Mr. Perez's, do you recall that?"

"Yes."

"Yet as Mrs. Stoneham noted, there were numerous documents missing in Mr. Perez's file that would usually be there – and should be there *by law*, correct?"

Murphy shrugged. "I followed the company's procedures, so I don't know why some things were not there."

"Let's be more specific. Now you are aware I'm sure that pursuant to the Securities Exchange Act of 1934, brokers are required to keep certain records, this Rule is codified at Title 17 Part 240 Section 17a -3, correct?"

"Haven't looked at that law recently, but assume you're right."

"I'm sure the Panel members know I'm right as you say. Isn't it standard industry practice that brokers retain blotters, that is records containing details of all purchases and sales of securities they have made, along with trade confirmations, ledgers for a whole list of items, memorandums for brokerage orders – well a whole list or records, isn't that right?"

"All I know is that I spend lots of time in my day dealing with this paperwork, waste of time but there it is."

"Yet we are left with the mystery of how these records just disappeared. Strike that. Mr. Murphy, you kept for each of your clients additional records in the normal course of business, correct, including, for example, documents in connection with your evaluation and recommendation of stocks, notes of conversations, phone calls, evidence reflecting assets, completed company forms, again lots of documentation of your work-product?"

"As I said, lots of record keeping. But to save time, to be honest, I don't remember what was there or not there as his account traded years ago."

"Of course, Mr. Murphy, you've already testified that you were compliant with company requirements so we should presume all these records I've referred to were indeed completed by you and filed properly, correct? And yet again we have the theme of they have mysteriously disappeared."

Murphy just stared at her, so Gwen moved on, having made her point. "I assume you reviewed your files in preparation for this hearing and that you instructed your firm and your attorney to comply with Complainant's discovery requests?

"My counsel is an experienced litigator; I don't need to instruct him what to do."

"Yes, he is. But you are aware, are you not, that many of these purportedly existing documents were not produced, despite my repeated requests for same, correct?"

"I can't answer that."

"When an expected item is missing, don't we normally infer that it was likely harmful rather than helpful in a dispute...."

"Objection," bellowed Mandel.

"Strike that." Gwen smiled and shrugged her shoulders, implying she hoped that she'd made her point about the missing paperwork.

Moving on to suitability, Gwen said, "Successful stock investing is complicated and generally requires careful analysis of a company's financial data to find out a company's true worth and degree of risk, would you agree with that?"

"You bet."

Gwen then went through the steps brokers generally followed when evaluating stocks –- review of a company's profit and loss account, balance sheet with its Form 10-K, cash flow statement – and established that many of these steps Murphy ignored, claiming they were unnecessary.

Further elaborating on Larry's shoddy or absent research, Gwen asked, "Mr. Murphy, when selecting stock do you look at a company's price-to-earnings ratio, price-to-book ratio, return on equity or other what I believe are called 'value investing techniques' to determine whether a company's stock price is trading above or below what it is worth?"

"To be frank, I rely on the research department of my firm, after all they are one of the best in the world."

"Even if a stock is recommended, doesn't that type of information assist in deciding the price you buy and sell shares at?"

"Like I said, I rely on my firm's advice."

Murphy started to squirm in his chair and began to play with the ballpoint pen he was still holding in his hand. *Click, click, click.*

"Yet you and your firm both failed to take care of Mr. Perez, isn't that so?"

"Not true. We did fine, it was him who caused the loss of money. And all that research, as I say, overrated. You can be overloaded with information in this business, and you need to act sometimes with your gut and well years of knowing how the business works. Lots of times you need to act quickly as the market fluctuates all the time."

Click. Click.

"You are you claim, a qualified financial analyst trained in analyzing stock exchanges?"

"Yeah, lots of training, goes on all the time."

"Yet you are saying you actually just buy and sell what Stanley, Howe, recommends to all its agents, despite the fact that your firm has not identified whether these recommendations are appropriate for the needs of a specific client, such as Mr. Perez, or that these recommendations are consistent with the present market, true?"

"Well, sure I decide what to trade and the price, timing and all that but it's based on my years of experience doing this work along with my company's support, after all that's why I work at a full-service firm. You know, you want heart surgery,..." and here Murphy turned towards the Panel members, "... you hire a heart surgeon, not a GP."

Gwen stopped and let that statement waft through the room. In the silence she heard again, *click, click, click, click.*

"And you charge your clients the fees of a full-service firm I may add, true?"

"My firm sets the fees."

"Doing research yourself on what investments are appropriate for specific clients takes time and effort, correct?"

"Of course."

"So let me get this straight. Mr. Murphy, you have stated that when you made investments in Mr. Perez's account you routinely followed company recommendations – instead of doing your own research and determination of whether the trade was compatible with Mr. Perez's risk level, correct?"

"As I said, ... *click...click...* I have a great company behind me."

"I take that as a yes. So, is this practice of following company suggested buy and sells, the reason why so many of the trades in Mr. Perez's account were in stocks where your firm acted as a 'market maker', and thus earned additional fees for these trades, as I presume did you as well?"

Murphy sat there silently, except for an occasional *click.* Gwen broke into the quiet, "I believe you have answered that."

After returning to her seat and reviewing her notes, she again faced Murphy.

"Mr. Murphy, a crucial process in making investment decisions is identifying and analyzing the amount of *risk* involved in an investment, to determine the risk-return balance, correct?"

"I suppose so."

"Well I would suggest that experts say that is highly significant, especially with a client who can handle very little risk."

"Objection," Mandel yelled from his seat.

Gwen ignored him as she was on a roll. "Mr. Murphy, as you know there are various ways of measuring a stock trade's risk, that is, the probability of a loss. Commonly used metrics I've been advised are determining a stock's standard deviation, value-at-risk, its Beta."

"Yes, there's always lots of data options these days, thanks to all the computer stuff."

"Now you have said that you made money for Mr. Perez, up to a point when his account started on its downward slide, right?"

"Yeah, as long as I controlled the account, Sammy did well."

"And the risk level goal you accepted for Mr. Perez was speculative, correct, a very high level of risk?"

"Yes, we already dealt with that yesterday." "True. And my experts found this goal astonishing. But moving on, isn't it also true that an investment's return at a certain point in time can be artificially high due to the assumption of excess risk – as this gain is often likely only temporary?"

"Well, maybe, I guess." *Click. Click.*

"And wasn't it this higher risk that caused Mr. Perez's valuation in his account to go down and that this decrease in value necessitated numerous margin calls, requiring additional assets to be invested and, well, the avalanche had started and didn't end until the account had no value?"

Starting to rise in his seat, Larry responded, "Hey, all stock has volatility, and turns out he used his stock funds like a bank checking account." Larry then pointed at Sammy and said, "It was not my actions why he lost his money."

Larry sat back down. The room was silent but for the sound of *click, click, click.*

Mandel rose and asked for a five-minute recess, which Sawyer allowed during which Gwen sat at her desk, drank her thermos of hot coffee and doodled to relax.

Twenty minutes later Murphy again took his seat next to Loretta, but without his jacket and apparently his ballpoint pen. He looked pale and drawn, deflated. Gwen thought to herself that's what happens to a bully when you take him on. You can puncture his balloon.

"Just a few more questions Mr. Murphy. I appreciate that it has been a long few days." She handed several documents to Larry, and then walked them to the Panel and Day and Mandel. She said, "Mr. Murphy, I ask you to look at Bates # 1066 and # 1068, copies of pages of the firm's broker operations manual. Do you see in the highlighted portion that if you come by information that causes you to reassess suitability, if that occurs you are to bring the matter to the attention of your supervisor? Do you see that?"

"Yes. Got it."

"Did you ever discuss any such concerns about Mr. Perez's accounts with your manager or supervisor, or for that matter any other person at the firm?"

"No. Other than in the normal course of business that is, and, you know, preparing for this case. I had no reason to."

"Mr. Murphy, is it your testimony that Mr. Perez's limited income from his blue-collar job, initially about $53,000 before he went on disability, which was confirmed by his tax returns that you had, his being near retirement age, his limited education and language issues which you yourself have mentioned made working with him hard for you, the fact that he supported his wife and three young sons, and later divorced which you knew from discussions with his wife's lawyer, and that my client lived in a room with his cousin in Dortman which you knew as letters to him at his prior address were returned undeliverable, and that didn't own a car which you knew as he told you he took the bus to get to your office – all this did not concern you when you determined that the account's stated highly aggressive investment objectives of speculation and growth were *and continued to be* appropriate for this client?

"Um... no." Looking at the Panel, Murphy added, "As I said, I took him at his word, made a decision based on his prior trading experience and apparent financial sophistication. Not my job to do more."

Gwen paused and reviewed her notes. She checked off topics covered and saw a few issues still needed addressing briefly so she stood up and asked, "Mr. Murphy, you have testified that you did not inform Mr. Perez of the account's trading risks or reasons for frequent trades, yet you say you had three to four conversations most every day with Mr. Perez. What did you talk about, the play of the New England Patriots?"

"Objection!" Day and Mandel cried in unison. Sawyer told Murphy he didn't have to answer.

Gwen continued, "You claim you had a change of heart when you learned that Mr. Perez was allegedly hiding money, you say. Did you ever discuss this issue with *your* client's lawyer?"

"No. I'm not sure I knew if he had one."

"With Mr. Perez?"

"No."

"Isn't it true that Mr. Perez told you on several occasions that this money was to pay back his aunt's loan to him? And that you helped him set up this account?"

"Well, you know I don't recall what he said that well. He talked so much, and, you know, I had trouble understanding him 'cause of his accent, limited English. But I do remember discussions with the wife's lawyer."

"Mr. Murphy, based on information provided to me by your firm, it appears that while you have the fewest number of clients of agents in your office, yet you not only are the top commission earner but also your trading results in the most fees for your company, isn't that the case?"

"Hey, I take good care of my clients, so maybe I have a few less than those younger guys who don't have as many family obligations as I do."

"In fact, Mr. Murphy, haven't a dozen or more of your clients, former clients that is, complained to the firm that you pressured them to make trades? I refer you to the copies of such comments contained in the second binder at pp. 8 -15. Isn't that the case?"

"Hey, you do business with the public, there will always be some people no matter how hard you try that you can't make happy."

"Isn't it a fact that you led your region in the number of such customer complaints?"

"I doubt that's the case. My clients generally like me and recommend me to their friends."

Gwen rose and held up an enlargement of a newspaper page, big enough for Murphy and the Panel members to see. "Mr. Murphy, I'm showing you a page from the Middleton local newspaper where your picture is on page one as the winner of a highly prized Stanley, Howe trip to Hawaii. It says you are the only one from your office – and this whole region – to have won this trip, an award it states for quote, "being the highest fee earner for the company in its New Hampshire field offices over the past five years"?

"Yeah, hard work earned me that."

"And sales of company recommended stock, including those where the company acts as a market maker, right?"

"Objection, asked and answered," said Day and Sawyer agreed.

Gwen paused, then decided to break her silence on the hot document in hopes that she might give Respondents some incentive to reach a compromise.

"Mr. Murphy, are you aware of a company program, called I believe Pinehills' Planned Program, 'PPP' for short. It is as I understand it designed to increase high-risk minority business trading?"

Murphy looked puzzled. "Nope."

Gwen looked down the Respondents' table and thought she noticed a few suits inhaling sharply at her question. Maybe.

"One final question Mr. Murphy. You are an experienced professional in your field with all the resources of a large firm behind you. Isn't it true that my client, an Hispanic immigrant who speaks English as a second language, who went to night school for his GED, who has worked a blue-collar job all his life, who barely grasps minimal understanding of computers let alone the complicated financial market, who gave you discretion to manage his account as you were the professional, yet it is this man and not YOU, the Captain of the Team, whom you now claim was the one driving the Perez account bus?"

"That's right."

Gwen perused her note cards, and checked in with Sammy – who remained quiet, fiddling with his coat zipper and pockets. Gwen declared, "I have no more questions of Mr. Murphy."

After a few moments, Respondents' counsel all indicated no redirect and Sawyer said, "Mr. Murphy, you are excused."

As Murphy walked with arms folded back to his seat, Gwen thought at least he looked a little worse for wear. She found herself once again wondering where in the big scheme of things did Larry fit on the moral meter. *Is he an evil man to be hated? Should he have a big E printed on his forehead to warn strangers that this man is a pariah and will eat you alive if need be? Or is he just a small guy who practiced business like many of his industry peers, where a little greed is seen as just part of the package?*

Gwen understood that most field office 'brokers' like Larry didn't make lots of money. That was saved for the higher-ups in the industry. Larry she surmised was basically a middle-aged salesman who worked long hours to pay for his mortgage, nice car, and golf course membership in a community that was far from the glitz and pizzazz of urban life. And far from where he'd hoped to have his career end. He went to work every day to pay for the same type of things Sammy had tried to have, college for the kids, Saturday night dinner at the club, and a car that made him feel good.

Yes, he'd cheated the system to increase his take-home pay. And at Sammy's expense. Still, wasn't he a small cog in the industry that made huge bucks for those at the top, the ones who set the rules and made the big money, who were rewarded even if they took big risks – and lost. Today, is grabbing a larger share of the pie than you are due seen as evil or greedy or even wrong? *Hey, Gwennie, cut out the crap. This man had a choice, comply with the law or steal from your client. He made the wrong choice. Cheating is like pregnancy, even a little cheating makes you a thief.* Gwen shrugged and decided to save further philosophical sophistry for another day – after she'd had two glasses of wine.

What she did expect was that Larry would turn out fine after this arbitration; he was making a profit for the company, had a long list of clients, and likely was viewed as a marketable commodity who could transfer his accounts if need be to another firm.

Sawyer continued, "We probably should take a very brief break. We are about an hour past where we expected to be. So why don't we take another five-minute break. And when we return the Panel would appreciate being informed of Respondents' plan to finish today."

Gwen stood up. Sammy remained seated. Crestfallen, he whimpered, "What they say not true. They lie."

"Sammy, that's what happens at hearings. Both sides get to tell their side. Sometimes, as in this case, it includes 'he said/she said' claims, and, well, that's hard to get a handle on. Hang in there, we're almost finished."

After all the lawyers and their entourage came back from the restroom, or wherever, Sawyer spoke into the microphone, "Back on the record. Next witness."

CHAPTER FORTY-ONE

Gwen, felt exhausted after her cross of Murphy. Knowing that there were more Respondent witnesses to come, she managed to sneak in a piece of Buzz, her caffeinated gum. She tried to chew ladylike.

Murphy's current supervisor, J.B. Bernardo, entered the conference room, was screened by the guard, and then directed to the witness chair. In a suit too large for his small build, balding, and with his thin face framed by a graying goatee, J.B. explained that he was Murphy's current supervisor as the prior one who'd sent Sammy the "churning" letter had died, apparently taking his Perez files with him to the grave. As such, J.B. made clear he couldn't actually testify as to the deceased's previous interactions with Murphy or Sammy. Gwen wondered why this person was testifying at all. She soon learned.

Day began his direct by getting right to the point. "Mr. Bernardo, regarding Claimant's Exhibit 19," Day turned towards the dais to add, "Panel members it is located in Volume 2 at p. 138 of the binders." Now back to J.B., "This is a copy of the letter sent by your predecessor to Mr. Perez that addresses possible high turn-over ratios in his account, what Ms. Wilson has referred to as churning, frequent in and out trades. Do you know why this letter was sent by your firm?"

"It was, I presume, spit out by the computer's algorithms. "

"Objection," offered Gwen. "Hearsay."

Sawyer played with his pen, consulted with Grimes, and then ruled that the Panel would permit this line of questioning, as 'best evidence', and consider the weight to give it later.

"Mr. Bernardo, kindly continue your answer," Day said.

J.B. described how the firm routinely sent such letters to clients as part of account oversight, with copies to supervisors like him to alert them of possible issues and to discuss with their sales people.

"So, let me see if I understand what you are saying. The mere fact that a letter was sent just means the account was flagged, not that there was any *finding* of inappropriate conduct?"

"That's right."

Day then followed up by establishing that there's no record that Sammy complained about his account activity. Gwen wanted to add that, yeah, this didn't happen because, duh, the letter was sent to a dead Post Office box.

Day continued, "Do you know if the prior supervisor talked with Mr. Murphy about this letter?"

J.B. stated, "I believe he did from the initials on the compliance form I reviewed."

Gwen considered objecting again as improper hearsay, but decided that J.B.'s answer likely helped her side as showing that Murphy was on notice.

Sawyer intervened anyhow with a broad follow-up question. "Based on what you know now, did you see anything in Mr. Perez's account that should have been done differently?"

J. B., looking around at Sawyer, and to no one's surprise, answered, "No, sir. In my view, Mr. Murphy complied with industry standards."

Gwen wanted to object to Sawyer that his question was impermissibly broad, but doubted she'd win on that one, so she sat again on her hands.

During Day's direct, which repeated prior testimony, Gwen doodled with her highlighters and wondered about the cost of the proceeding and, again, why no settlement interest. Were the suits so sure of winning? Gwen looked at Sammy, head down, sitting small and aloof beside her, overwhelmed by the case, and life? She wouldn't disagree that his legal battle after almost three days of hearing was facing an uphill fight. And she remembered Adam's odds on the case making victory a distant and unlikely trophy. *So, Gwennie, is there any W as in 'winning' for fighting a just but losing cause – and in the process maybe lose your practice.*

Silence suddenly filled the room. Finally it was her turn to cross. She started by focusing on the firm's poor communications with Sammy. J.B. agreed it apparently ignored the fact that its letters to him were being returned 'undeliverable'. Then she asked J.B. about the pencil jottings on the churning letter. "What's the penciled '8/31' date mean, Mr. Bernardo?"

"I believe that's the date of a prior review."

Gwen knew nothing of this prior review from the documents provided her. *Has the account been flagged for churning twice in the short time it was open?*

"Are you saying that in addition to October, Mr. Perez's account had also been kicked out by the computer for possible churning in August?"

"It appears so. As I said, I wasn't Mr. Murphy's supervisor then."

"Was Mr. Perez contacted in connection with this previous August flagged event?"

"I don't know, as I've said, I wasn't in that office at the time."

"Where are the documents relating to the sending of this August churning letter and the handling of this review? I haven't seen them."

Day interjected, "I don't know that they made it into the binders."

Sawyer's eyebrows rose at this admission. He asked Day, "Do you know where they might be?"

"I understand my client has not been able to locate any such papers."

Sawyer nodded, then wrote down a note on his legal pad and motioned for Gwen to continue.

"Mr. Bernardo, in your time in your present position where you supervise Mr. Murphy along with numerous other brokers, have you seen this happen, two such warning letters kicked out by the computer in this short of a time?"

J. B. rubbed his head, as if combing his missing hair. "I've seen two in quick succession, but a few months apart like this? Actually, now that I think about it, I don't recall that happening. I could be wrong...."

"I take that as a no. And Mr. Bernardo is it possible that there were other similar letters we don't know about, based on the limited records?

"Could be, I guess."

"You also testified that your predecessor talked with Mr. Murphy after the October letter, correct."

"Yes, I saw a note about that."

"So isn't it reasonable to conclude he also spoke with Mr. Murphy just a few months earlier about his excessive in and out trading? And maybe other times as well?"

Mandel stood up before J.B. could answer and called out, "Objection, asks for speculation from the witness."

Sawyer played with his pen while trying to decide what to do, then gave his usual 'he can answer... but...'.

"Yes, I guess so."

"You would have spoken in that situation with your broker, correct, and there'd be a note in the file about this as well?"

"Yes to both. With the death of the person who handled that role, it appears a few files may not be complete or may have been misplaced."

Gwen jumped up and addressed the Panel. "This is just another document not provided that should have been. I move that the Panel take judicial notice of the missing documents, make all reasonable assumptions in favor of Complainant regarding facts not provided, and impose financial sanctions."

Day, Moss and Mandel in unison objected but Sawyer gave them a verbal warning regarding their client's apparent non-compliance with the NASD rules, yet he went no further in terms of a penalty.

With a smile, maybe a crocodile one, Gwen thanked Sawyer for the warning, and then continued with her questioning. "Was there a follow-up compliance action?"

"I don't know."

"And did Mr. Murphy's trading pattern change or stop after this earlier August event?" Gwen perked up and listened for the answer. Such a change was a possible admission of wrongdoing.

"Yes, I did check his trading before this hearing and as I recall it slowed, then shortly after stopped for a brief period. I figured he might have been on vacation."

"But you don't know that, do you?"

"Well, no."

Gwen asked, "The account became very active again, right, as his trading generated another churning letter? Yes or no please."

"Yes."

Concerned there were more undisclosed damning documents, Gwen decided to ask, "Mr. Bernardo, are you aware of any other documents related to the claims in this case that you've seen that you did not find contained in the three binders put together by your firm's Counsel?"

"Objection," yelled voices up and down the table. Before Sawyer could act though, J. B. nodded his head up and down. Sawyer then asked him what he was referring to. "Well the summary of telephone calls done by a company based on Mr. Murphy's phone records."

"Objection," shouted Day. "Client work-product and so not discoverable."

Sawyer nevertheless followed-up. "Do you recall what this summary said?"

J.B. answered that it showed lots of phone calls from Sammy, but real short ones. "You know, like when you call someone's office, the secretary answers, and the person's not there. Short, not like a conversation."

Sawyer asked, "Were there also lengthy phone calls?"

"Not that I recall, some maybe a few minutes longer, you know, like you're in the middle of some task and you speak to your client briefly."

"Attorney Day," asked Sawyer who was clicking his pen very fast, "are you preparing to introduce these into the record?"

"One moment, please, Mr. Sawyer."

Day, Mandel and Moss all got up and consulted together, and then Day spoke. "No, we were not. We did not have confidence that we had obtained complete records from the telephone company for this company to review, Mr. Sawyer. Plus we consider the report to be privileged under the attorney-client work-product rule."

"I see," Sawyer nodded, wrote a note to himself, and then said to Gwen, "Let's move on counsel."

But Gwen was not ready to give up the fight. "Mr. Sawyer, these records should have been produced, at least the underlying telephone documents, as they were maintained it appears in the ordinary course of Stanley, Howe's business. I did request such material and was told there were no such records. These are highly relevant and from what has been described, they affirm the truthfulness of my client's testimony as regards the broker communications. And importantly the ongoing mischaracterizations under oath by Mr. Murphy."

"Ms. Wilson, the Panel agrees that these are attorney-client documents and not subject to discovery. However, should you obtain evidence post-hearing from the telephone company directly on this issue, unlike Respondents' summary prepared in connection with this case, submit that to the NASD and at their direction the Panel is prepared to reconsider them. Please finish your cross of this witness. We are very much behind schedule already."

Gwen stood as if considering her options, made a note, and, with the Panel's attention on her, stated, "No more questions of this witness." But before she sat down she turned back to the witness, saying, "Excuse me, one more question if I may. Mr. Bernardo, are you familiar with a Stanley, Howe program titled I think it is called 'Pinehills Investment Program', 'PIP', or

'Pinehills Investment Plan, LLC'? It has to do with increased trading in minority communities I believe."

A chorus of objections instantly rang out from the other side of the table. Sawyer looked at Day who stammered, "That question is incompetent, irrelevant and immaterial. Moreover, it is improper as it addresses areas not covered on direct."

Sawyer ruled, "Yes, I don't recall that issue being discussed on direct. If this is newly discovered evidence, Ms. Wilson, you may seek to file it with the NASD as I just discussed."

Gwen sat down and didn't say anything further. Better to leave them all in suspense. But the phrase surely seemed to have gotten their attention.

Donald Moss rose. "We have one final witness, Mr. Sawyer, and we expect this to be brief."

"Well that's great. Maybe we should have started with this witness two days ago."

All laughed, even Gwen.

Moss continued, "And to advise the Panel and Attorney Wilson, due to the time constraints we have elected not to call Mr. Cavanaugh to testify. If the Panel wishes, we can provide it and Attorney Wilson with his prepared summary of his findings."

Moss then examined a younger man, Stephen White, who was presented as an expert knowledgeable about investments, and also a lawyer. His role was to address damages. White explained with some complicated numerical analysis that Sammy hadn't really lost all that much. Gwen was soon lost, and she hoped the Panel was as well. Unfortunately, Linda wasn't there to crunch the numbers.

On cross, Gwen decided to have Mr. White, who was presented as a lawyer, help her close Sammy's case. She began by addressing the regulations governing customer stock trading, focusing on the NASD's Rule 2310 that addressed suitability. Day objected on the grounds not covered on direct, but Gwen pointed out that White was introduced as a lawyer and thus able to provide opinions as an expert on legal matters at the core of the case. Sawyer, surprisingly Gwen thought, agreed with her.

As to the imposition of Rule 2310, White stated, as had Martha but not Murphy, that the provision imposed on brokers an ongoing obligation to determine suitability. White then affirmed again Martha's testimony that the SEC's fair practices and anti-fraud standards also require brokers such as Murphy to consider the various indicia asserted by Martha — such as age, assets, employment – when making trading recommendations. Finally, White affirmed once more Martha's position that federal law requires a broker to exercise a 'duty of inquiry' to obtain supporting financial information, and to keep this data current.

Gwen concluded by bolstering Linda's churning testimony. "Now, Mr. White, you're aware of Ms. DeNardi's testimony and her written Affidavit correct?"

"Yes, I am. At least her Affidavit and Exhibit. I wasn't sitting in during her testimony."

"Ms. DeNardi testified that after running the numbers from Mr. Perez's account she found the turnover ratio to be from 5 to almost 7. As a lawyer, you are aware, correct, that courts have applied the '2-4-6 Rule' as a standard for the industry?"

"Yes. That's what the cases say."

"Briefly this Rule provides that for a conservative investor – such as we contend Mr. Perez – an annualized turnover rate of two is suggestive, four is presumptive, and six or more is conclusive of excessive trading, true?"

"The concept of churning depends on the nature of the account and the investment objectives of the client. And here the objectives were aggressive and speculative."

"That's a yes or no question, Attorney White. Do you agree or disagree?"

"I can't answer it that way."

"I have sitting on the table next to me at least three securities practice treatises that state this Rule as the standard approach. Do you want me to take the time to go through them and show you where they discuss the application of the 2-4-6 Rule?"

"You could say that that's the general standard, I would agree."

"Thank you, Attorney White. In fact, you've read decisions haven't you, where courts have also recognized that even for the more aggressive client, a turnover ratio of 6 or more supports a finding of excessive trading, and these courts include the First Circuit where we sit, correct?"

"Yes, I am aware of those decisions. But I suggest that the turnover ratio is just one factor to look at. Trading volatility, for example, might be another."

"Have you conducted a calculation of the turnover ratio in Mr. Perez's account in preparation for this hearing?'

"No, I wasn't asked to do that."

"Ms. DeNardi's calculations of a turnover ratio exceeding 5 have not been challenged. So if we follow the 2-4-6 Rule, Respondents engaged in illegal churning, wouldn't you agree?"

"Um... it is troubling, but I'm not aware of all the factors presented here so I can't definitely state that. As I said, there could be other reasons."

Gwen paused. "Really? Exactly what facts are you missing?

Strike that." Gwen took a sip of water. Looking at Day she said, "Thank you, Attorney White. I have no more questions of this witness."

The table of Counsel representing Respondents affirmed no redirect of White, aware perhaps that he had already hurt their case. And in this way, the testimony stage of the hearing was completed. Not exactly a bang, Gwen thought, but maybe at least a whimper. And after yesterday who wanted more bangs anyhow! The Big Ben clock struck 6:30 p.m. as if to punctuate the end.

Sawyer read from his notes, "The record on tape is closed. All parties have waived making closing statements. I now need each of the parties to affirm on the record that they had a full opportunity to be heard at this proceeding."

"On behalf of Respondents, agree," said the senior suits present. Gwen did as well, failing to add what she was thinking – that the hearing allowed the investment industry to act both like a fox that raided the chicken coop and the overseer of chicken safety.

Sawyer looked out at the parties, consulted with his other two Panel members, and then at 6:50 p.m. said, "With that I conclude the hearing in the matter of Perez v. Stanley, Howe, *et al.* Thank you counsel for your attention and fine presentation of this case."

Before Gwen could pack up her notes and books and transfer them into her rolling bag, as her 'porter' was otherwise occupied in a hospital bed likely watching some game show, the Respondents' side of the table was empty, their suitcases gone. Gwen shook hands with Sammy, made sure he had a ride home with Carlos, and then left the conference room eager to drive back above the notch, happily watch – in her slippers on her home couch – 'Dr. Wheeland, Montana Vet' and learn how to care for dogs that had swallowed too many M & M's when their owners weren't looking. All to be watched with a pint of coffee ice cream and a glass or two of bourbon. It was only then, as she relaxed with anticipation, that she felt the pain in her heart that Adam and his red sox would not be sitting next to her on the couch.

That is until she entered her house and saw a lovely display of early Fall Chrysanthemums with a note. Gwen put her bags down and, with smiling anticipation, read it.

"Dearest Gwen: By the time you get this I will have been discharged from the hospital and left Middleton to deal with pressing matters that require my attention. I can't say more at this point but be assured I will contact you when these matters are settled and I can move on with my life, safely. I will miss you greatly. Stay strong and safe, Adam."

After his signature he'd drawn a big heart. Inside were their initials – connected by a plus sign.

CHAPTER FORTY-TWO

In bathrobe and slippers, Gwen bent down and grabbed the folded-up newspaper on her front steps. She breathed in the nearby forest's brisk pine bouquet that filled her backyard as if she'd planted scented balsam pillows alongside her azaleas. The white birches at the nearby brook swayed in the morning breeze. She laughed, just women drying their hair in the sun.

The scenery surrounding her house, with its 'warm maple syrup with pancakes' memories, reminded Gwen that several weeks had already passed since the arbitration hearing ended.

During this time, without fanfare, the warm days and chilly nights of late summer had rolled over into fall, her favorite season with its leaf piles and pumpkins and apples picked off the tree, still warm from the sun. Already she'd noticed signs of nature's metamorphosis. The days were shorter. Canada's colorful fingers had already marched down from the north, and begun painting the distant mountain peaks gold, ruby red, brazen orange. The maple leaves were teasing, like Vegas strippers, unveiling beneath the green a hidden layer of crimson. Mornings brought the shrill call of flocks of birds, congregating together before starting their long journey south. Much had happened, except for a decision in Sammy's case.

Gwen had spent the days after the hearing at home doing basically nothing – other than napping lots and trying to overcome the pain of Adam's absence. She expected he'd already left for some unknown location, presumably stateside but maybe not. Once Gwen returned to her work routine she struggled to hold on. Even basic tasks seemed overwhelming. *Is there a medical disease called 'post- trial PTSD'?* Getting up and out in the morning became harder and harder as the days progressed. But, being the 'big boss', she pushed herself to get to the office to keep her team busy, and paid. Yet once there she accomplished little. She'd even missed several filing deadlines, a dangerous practice for any lawyer.

"Hey Judy, is there a pill I can take to cure this debilitating malaise?"

Judy suggested either a trip to Paris or once-a-day multi-vitamins. Gwen settled for the pills, along with a walking lunch. She also began looking at want ads in the local newspaper. *Would I be happier in a job that focuses on brawn rather than brain? Could I enjoy being an auto mechanic where I fix cars so they run good?*

She had no good answers to her own questions.

During this melancholy time where she felt a certain rapport with Picasso's Blue Period, her pals Judy and Mary had been saviors. Each juggled their jobs and her practice demands to cover for her. They even offered to hold off on their salaries until the bottom line was better. Gwen was thankful for such friends. And John had offered to help with her cases. Still, she couldn't get out of her funk. She'd had times before after a hard-fought emotionally draining case when, even if she'd won, there followed a period of restlessness, languor. Almost like a marathoner who having crossed the finish line, becomes afterward lost at sea. Gwen assured herself she just needed time to recover, to recharge her batteries, to rekindle her mojo. Maybe the answer was that affordable vacation she'd been searching for, something slow and sleepy, or better yet demanding and dangerous, like white water rafting in the Arctic, or square-dancing classes at the nearby Y. She tickled her day calendar for the last day of September: 'check for cheap, dicey vacation'. Then, after looking at the trees swaying in the whipping wind, she revised her memo, squeezing in the word 'warm' before 'vacation'.

A week later, arriving early at her office, Gwen began sifting through the yellow mountain of messages on her desk. Halfway through she noticed next to the pile an opened letter with a cover note from Judy that read, 'Gwen, delivered certified mail/' Gwen's pulse quickened and she started to feel dizzy. *Has the Perez decision arrived?* Despite her anxiety to read the verdict, her first response was to procrastinate so as to avoid any bad news. She replaced her sneakers with her office shoes, played with the blinds until the sun's rays landed on the client chair and not her desk, and organized her pens in a neat row and by color. Finally, holding the letter away from her in case it bit, she looked more closely at it – and then let out a deep sigh. *Relax Gwen, no NASD logo.* Sitting down, her feet hanging over her desk as her pulse recovered, she read the typed missive.

Darling Gwennie:

I'm writing to let you know I am fine. Pretty much recovered. Settled into a new place that's acceptable, for now. Except, you know, you aren't here. I miss you. As for school, the Dean was nice and I took my exams on-line so at least finished the summer semester.

I'm working on settling with my ghosts from my prior life that somehow found me. I am lucky to be here to do that and, like Bill Murray in the movie Groundhog Day, I want to get this take right. Did I say I miss you? Your touch, your smell, your smarts ... YOU!

I hope you are in a good place. And your team, whom I miss.

Enough.

Enclosed is an affidavit I drafted, signed and had notarized. I hope it's not too late in helping Sammy's case. To catch you up, after the hospital I moved West to deal with the aforesaid old but resilient specters. (Sorry for the legalese, see what you've done to me!) During the past month off and on I've helped the FBI with the shooting case – as I need to know more what was going on if I can move forward in my life. As a favor, my FBI new friend Harvey Gladstone sent me a box of stuff that I'd left in my apartment, including papers I'd kept safe in a hidden box. These, Gwennie, included an extra copy I'd made of 'the Judy letter'. Sorry I kept this hidden from you, but it was awkward to discuss. I shall reveal all when we meet. I hope you will be able to use it to get relief for Sammy. It is attached to my affidavit.

My affidavit I hope does the job. I explain that I obtained the letter as part of background on a different matter I'd been dealing for an unnamed company that involved Stanley, Howe. This is almost true and as I said, I will explain it all when I see you in person. I tried to make clear that you were not in any way involved, nor responsible. Fudging maybe, but true enough.

I do this with love. And for Sammy. And because I want to say I'm sorry for not being open, trusting, with you.

Gwennie, on my honor, I will never willingly put you in harms way. Or be less than honest on whom I am in my heart.

As I promised, I'm working hard on resolving my situation. Have high hopes. Fingers crossed. I'll get closure on this mess. Give me time. This is NOT our end.

The note was signed "Always, Adam."

Gwen held the letter up to her cheeks and pressed it against her skin. She smelled the musk scent. Rocking up and down in her executive chair, she explored in her mind how to use Adam's gift without endangering her career. *What are my options? What's the right thing to do?* Thank goodness, the NASD was being so slow in issuing its decision, so there still might be time to pull the victory sword from the rock.

On the fingers of her right hand, Gwen ticked off reasons to go ahead and use the letter:

1) it could be Sammy's 'get out of jail' card leading to at least a small settlement and a better life;

2) it showed that Stanley, Howe's big honchos probably ran, at least approved, an illegal program to make extra money at the

expense of persons of color, and low-income working-class folks like Sammy – and so the company and its brokers were not only cheaters but blatantly immoral cheaters and should be sanctioned;

3) her agreement with Anna limiting access didn't apply, not clean hands, and in any case wasn't binding, no legal contract;

4) she surely could use the money she might receive.

Now she held up her left hand and raised fingers for reasons not to use it:

1) Because she had Adam make secret copies of the letter despite Anna's conditions that she'd accepted, so she'd not only known about the Pinehills' program but used this info during the hearing, and maybe that was unethical, just a little; and

2) She was fighting big law firms that had the resources to ruin her career.

After this demanding calculation, where the score stood four to two, Gwen concluded that using the letter as leverage in some fashion had the upper hand, or at least the most fingers. It was then that she noticed attached to the envelope a flattened paper ring – made from a sticky note and scotch tape – with a drawing of what appeared to be a ruby colored pear-shaped stone. Clipped to the ring was a small yellow sticky note. In Adam's scratchy handwriting, it read, "Not able to give you nicer one, yet. Know, babe, when you look at it, you're in my heart."

Letting out a cleansing breath, Gwen put the documents including her new jewelry in her desk drawer, next to her small bottle of Basil- Hayden bourbon.

That night, Gwen racked her brain for a plan on how to use the 'hot letter' to help get Sammy a good and fair settlement, all while not placing her career at risk, to the extent protecting it was still important to her. And she tussled with her decision to put the paper ring safely in her underwear drawer, for now. But, she told herself, she'd made no promise to keep it there.

A few days later, back at the grind of lawyering, Gwen looked once more at her watch. It was already mid-morning and she'd made little progress on her 'Plaintiff's Motion for Discovery' that needed to be mailed this week. At least she was feeling more herself and had decided that the multi-vitamins were working. She'd discovered it was fun to choose a different color pill each day, like creating a weekly rainbow. (The daily lunch walk seemed to have faded into oblivion.) As she was adding a paragraph demanding copies of all tax returns in the past five years, Judy knocked, then entered.

"Gwen, there's a phone call for you. Someone from the FBI named Harvey. Said you were expecting to hear from him. Do you know a Harvey?"

"Not sure, name is familiar. All was such a jumble when the shooting happened. But I better take it before they start to look at me as a co-conspirator. Not a good idea to decline some calls, like those of Mother Nature – and the FBI."

Picking up her desk phone, she said in her friendly 'how can I help you' voice, "Hello, this is Attorney Gwen Wilson."

She was greeted by a high voice with a distinctive Brooklyn accent. "Hi Attorney Wilson. My name's Harvey Gladstone and I'm calling to see if we can set up some time when we can meet to talk about the incident at the arbitration hearing. We're trying to finish our investigation."

"Sure, Harvey. Would you like to come to my office?"

"I'd prefer if you came to my place. I'll be in my office tomorrow in the federal office building in Concord, a little closer to you. Just in case I need to ask questions about any physical evidence we have, and such."

Gwen agreed and tickled in her Red Diary, "Meet FBI, Harvey" for the following afternoon. *Should I consult counsel?* Nah. Nothing to worry about, she assured herself, ignoring the adage that a lawyer representing herself has a fool for a client.

The next afternoon Gwen grabbed her take-home workbag and prepared to meet a suave, handsome FBI agent who wore a gun in his shoulder holster and always got his man – and now woman. As she'd already done the routine with agents after the shooting spree, she wasn't too nervous to meet with 'the Feds'. Still, her mouth felt so dry that she couldn't salivate even if a luscious piece of chocolate cake were placed in front of her. As she was leaving her office, she grabbed a few cough drops and a bottle of water from her desk drawer, just in case.

"Judy, I'm leaving now for my appointment with, can you believe I'm saying this, the FBI."

"Call me if they arrest you and you need a change of clothes."

"Very funny. Maybe I'll dock your pay this week for 'not so funny work-product'.

Both women laughed. A nice feeling Gwen thought.

Gwen drove the hour to the state's Capital still feeling some trepidation. As usual, she admired the shiny golden dome you could see from all around the city, even from Rte. 93, the multi-lane US highway. She parked across from the Federal District Court. Getting off at the 17th floor in the adjacent office building she approached the receptionist, was directed to take a seat in the sparsely furnished waiting room, and before she could get comfortable – or admire all those framed pictures of FBI hunks (excepting J. Edgar) – better than English landscapes she decided, Harvey Gladstone walked in and escorted her to his office.

The small room was bright, thanks to the large windows behind Harvey's desk. Instead of pictures of FBI heroes on the wall or of fleeing foxes, Harvey's credenza showed off his two cute children laughing on a swing and his smiling button-nosed blond wife pushing them. The remainder of the credenza was devoted to overflowing accordion files and used paper coffee cups. And Gwen noticed a law degree on Harvey's wall. Not too threatening.

Reaching out his hand, Harvey said, "Hi, may I call you Gwen? Thanks for coming."

After the formalities were over, he got to the purpose of the meeting. Gwen initially had a little trouble keeping up since he spoke very quickly, as if he didn't have enough time to get a word out before the next one tumbled forth. Still, coupled with his somewhat Brooklyn accent, Gwen felt like she was back at home in the Big Apple. She sat in the empty wood chair – no college name engraved – and looked at this mythic person, 'the FBI agent'. Harvey in his white shirt with rolled up sleeves, absent tie and empty gun holster, appeared generally normal. In fact, he looked a lot like her insurance agent – a little mousy with his wire spectacles, beginning of a waist bulge, hair thinning on top, and no-nonsense smarts.

"Yes, of course Harvey. Gwen it is. But I'm not sure how I can help you as I gave several interviews to the FBI agents after the...um, the shooting." Gwen stopped, alarmed that she felt she might actually break down and cry at just the mention of the traumatic event. *Can talking about the shooting bring me such intense sadness and stress weeks later? Am I that vulnerable?* She took out a tissue from her bag and blew her nose.

"Sorry, not sure where that came from."

"It's not uncommon, Gwen, to carry the trauma of the event for a considerable time after it's over. It is still a fresh and frightening wound. It happens to most of us. I still remember in my early days at the Bureau when I was on an assignment to arrest a purported drug suspect at a motel in Miami. My partner was behind me at the main door to the room and we had agents as well in the back in case the suspect decided to flee through a back window. We all had our guns drawn although we'd been assured he was sleeping. Sure enough, before we were set to begin the raid, he began shooting through the door. Thankfully we were approaching low to the ground and the bullets went over our heads. Our guys in the back jumped through the window at the same time that we burst through the door and this perp was on his back before he could present more threat. So no one was hurt, yet I still visualize the scene – and find it hard to swallow when I do." Chuckling to himself, Harvey continued, "After that, and my wife's input, I decided to accept any management promotions that came my way.

Anyhow, enough about the life of an FBI agent, purpose of my asking you to come in today is that I'd like to review with you your statements, and update you on the state of our investigation. I thought that might be of interest."

Gwen shifted from crying to smiling as if she were flipping pancakes. "Yes, Harvey, it very much is. Thank you for being so considerate."

They proceeded to spend the next hour reviewing the facts, Gwen's observations, her actions, and her memory of events. Gwen soon realized that Harvey was very good at what he did – which was not too different from what she did when deposing witnesses. If her practice went bust, perhaps she'd check out the FBI's employment offerings. She was pretty sure she could learn to fire a gun with some aplomb. After all, as a kid she'd won several junior riflery awards at summer camp.

Harvey commented, "Your statement seems all in order and consistent with our findings. Anything else come to mind since then that may be helpful?"

"No. Can you share with me your findings?"

"Sorry, Gwen, no official Bureau report yet and case is still open. But you pretty much know the gist from our talk today. Without being specific, I guess I can give you the general outline, your being a lawyer and all. Our investigation's shown a low-level hit job based on an unfortunate confluence of facts. Some Vegas Casino consortium, actually an LLC like probably the insurance company you use for your homeowner's policy, anyhow the big stockholder at this one company hotel, had had a past dispute with Adam about a gambling debt."

Gwen nodded. "Yes, he told me that after his fiancée died he'd had a bad period where he'd done things he regretted."

"I can't of course provide you with confidential information about the underlying issues, but somehow an assistant – as yet unidentified – to this owner found out about Adam's location. A fluke. Seems someone in New Hampshire with connections to this assistant had seen Adam's picture in the local newspaper. In fact, as I recall, he was with you in the picture. Then a chain of events happened. Just bad luck for Adam, and well I guess also for the perp. Adam had been on our radar in connection with some help in a gambling investigation on the West coast, perhaps related to what you were saying. There was some conflict that presented concerns about whether the matter had been successfully resolved. I thought it had with the involvement of some third party, a financial entity of some kind. Our agents out there believed he was safe so we didn't follow up.

But, well, as you know that apparently wasn't the case. Anyhow, the shooter we've learned was a known thug who'd worked in the past as an enforcer for this Casino organization. I've been told that our experts think that it many have been your shiny necklace that made the guy miss initially. Your jewelry it seems reflected and magnified the light from both the window and off the chandeliers so it was hard for this guy to see. And of course there was the protection from those law books." Smiling, Harvey added, "I look at my legal library, especially the thick books like Wechsler's *Treatise on Federal Civil Procedure*, with much more appreciation these days."

Gwen and Harvey chuckled at this.

Harvey continued, "Thankfully, the security guard reacted quickly and prevented more damage. To finish up, Gwen, we caught the shooter's accomplice without much effort. With a little persuasion, he volunteered to assist us but it seems that we can't connect the big boss in Vegas to the event. I understand that Adam has gone to assure himself that the mistake has been corrected and all is well."

"Thank you for sharing this Harvey." Gwen fiddled with her necklace, this time a simple hanging gold chain, and tried to understand the impact of Harvey's information. There seemed to be much said, but much also held back.

She asked, "But exactly how was Adam involved? Why was he a target?"

"Sorry, due to confidentiality rules about ongoing investigations, I can't say anymore, Gwen, other then that we think this was a mess- up."

Gwen sat quietly, trying to sit on her hands so she didn't object and ask questions. Like, she thought: *What in hell was Adam doing to even be on a hit list?* Gwen knew he'd surely seemed scared when they biked, and then his nasty reaction when Sarah took his picture. *Is this why? Was this about some old gambling debt – or something else? What is the connection to his coming here, to Middleton, a small town in the middle of not much? Does it have to do with the 'hot letter'? A financial firm that's apparently in the picture? And, yeah, is there more to his 'seeing me' and working in my office, maybe too coincidental? Damn it, what should I believe about this guy?*

Gwen moved on to the logistics of the event, an area she thought not *verboten*. "Harvey, if this guy was a pro, why did he try all this at a public place like the hearing? Couldn't he have found Adam and done him in so to speak at a place where the risks were less apparent?"

"You know, I've asked myself that as well. But, remember, some of these guys, well, they're not the brightest bulb in the chandelier. And they're small townies. He's dead so I can't ask him. But his buddy implied that they didn't like driving through the Notch, foreign territory to them. Like you and me, both imports from the City; rural country with its moose and bears are not their natural turf. Plus, you know, all those green trees and mountains. Wilderness. Scary stuff to them, unlike guns. They figured it was a straightforward job, in and out – or so they thought – and they'd be gone before anyone was the wiser. As I said, maybe not the best plan."

"I've been wondering also if there's any connection between the break-ins at my home and office and this event. I can't figure out why anyone would want to take my home safe and leave the cash behind?"

"None we could find."

"And the attack on my client, Mr. Perez?"

"Again, none we're aware of."

A long silence followed as Gwen weighed whether to ask again about Adam, why he was living here, what he'd done. She decided not to. Harvey likely wasn't going to give her more, and the more she knew, ... the harder it might be to trust her judgment the next time she met a super great guy.

Gwen stood up getting ready to leave when Harvey, on his own initiative, raised the issue of Adam. She sat down, as it appeared there was more to discuss. Looking down at his desk, his lips inverted inwards, he fiddled with his pen, and did the manly FBI thing of playing with his paper clips, un-joining them, then joining them again. He then said in a less formal tone, "Gwen, on a more personal note, I have been in contact with Adam. He has recuperated almost fully, after a few initial setbacks. I wanted to meet you in person, not just to explore the case and your memory, but, ...well, to pass on a message from Adam."

Gwen immediately tensed, her hands gripping the chair's arms. With her brain cells suddenly swimming in heavy liquid, the best she could offer was a fake smile. She muttered, "I'm glad he's better." Catching her breath, she added with more force, "Um... please wish him a happy life from me." Gwen sank into the chair and pushed her hair back behind her ears. Neither she nor Harvey spoke.

After she'd crunched her knuckles some, Gwen added, "What's the message Harvey?"

"Ha, almost forgot. See, to be clear, I say this as a friend of his as we've gotten to get close, not as an agent, Adam asked me to tell you... you know, let me look at my notes here so I don't mess it up." Harvey picked up an index lined note card on his credenza. "He said that he's trying hard to be his own fixer and when things work out he has plans to finish law school." Looking up from the note Harvey added, "And I can tell you, he can be a pain in the butt when he's determined." Then, moving his paper clips he added, "He's even joked that once he gets his law degree he might apply for a job with our agency. But don't worry, we both understood he was just joshing. He tells me you guys are going to practice law together protecting our environment, leaving, he said, 'the gun stuff' to me." Checking his note card again, Harvey continued, "He also said that when I think it safe, he'd like you to think about taking a hiatus from your practice and to join him on the West Coast while he gets things resolved."

Now facing Gwen again, he said, "Anyhow, Gwen, that's pretty much it. Message given. I can pass on your wishes if you like as I have ongoing contact with Adam. Actually, as I said, he's become pretty much of a friend. I promised him when he returns, I'll take him on the basketball court."

Gwen sat glued to the chair, frozen in place, like a thirty-something ice sculpture. Finally able to move her mouth, she answered truthfully, "I don't know what to say."

Harvey rolled down his sleeves, sat up in his chair, and nodded. After waiting for Gwen to say more, he reached into his desk and then handed Gwen one of his private business cards. "If you'd like down the road, Gwen, any time, here's my direct line. Give me a call and I'll update you on events and on Adam's progress as I learn it. And you can use me to contact him if you like."

Using her arms to push herself up from the chair, Gwen placed the card in her suit pocket. She thanked Harvey for reaching out to her, turned, and left. If her life depended on it, she realized as she descended on the elevator, she couldn't remember what color shirt Harvey had been wearing. Or even if he'd worn one. Or whether it had been snowing in his office. All had turned fuzzy.

Gwen stopped for a take-out coffee and drove slowly back to Middleton. It had been hard being without Adam in her life. But his proposition asked her basically to give up her professional life, her friends, her family, her house – everything important that comprised 'her', for at least the near future. Sure, she looked forward to a two-week vacation, but to drop all that she'd built up and build her life on Adam's shoulders... or is it ribs, that was a really big ask. She would be in a way like her mother, a person with a present but without the backbone of past history. That price was too high.

Gwen left a message for Harvey that night – thanks for his help but would he please let Adam know that she would not be joining him in the Adam hinterland. And to herself she added, *Adam, good luck with your fix, but so many questions and concerns remain that even though we found a special connection, now that we're apart, I'm aiming to move forward with my life – as if you had jumped off the Earth.*

CHAPTER FORTY-THREE

Time to act. Now, Gwennie.

Gwen knew she needed to take the bull by the horn and make her move. She was pretty confident that the Respondents believed the case was in the bag for them, so they had no pressure to settle. She needed to create some pressure of her own to skew the playing field towards her end, and now she had ammunition. For days she'd been tossing and turning over what to do with Adam's 'gift'. But it came with an expiration date. Once the Panel issued its Ruling, the game likely would be over. *No more procrastination, Gwennie. This plane needs to take off.*

Closing her door and instructing Judy to hold all calls, Gwen got out her sample motion book and drafted an Emergency Motion directed to the NASD. She explained in the Motion that: 1. There'd been no decision issued yet in the case. 2. As Mr. Perez's counsel, post-hearing she has received highly relevant document setting out the plans of Stanley, Howe to operate a marketing program, The Pinehills Investment Program ('PIP'). This program, on its face, presents evidence of a marketing scheme that promotes unsuitable and excessive trades. Of most concern it is directed at low-income persons like Claimant, Mr. Perez. This scheme, as designed, impacts negatively on persons of color (such as Mr. Perez) and raises substantial issue of racial discrimination. 3. Gwen added a paragraph that a third party had provided this information to her, attaching Adam's notarized Affidavit. 4. She pointed out that Respondents had failed to comply with the NASD's discovery rules by not providing this highly relevant information, and that its employees' denials under oath and the firm's non-disclosures further raise issues of perjury and conspiracy.

Gwen ended her pleading by requesting that the NASD issue Judgment for Sammy as requested in his Statement of Claims, and award sanctions against Respondents, including paying Sammy's attorney's fees and expenses.

In bold letters Gwen labeled her Motion a 'Draft' and added "Confidential" at the top. She placed a copy in an envelope addressed to Day and included a cover letter explaining she was prepared to file her Motion with the NASD, with an information copy to the Securities and Exchange Commission, the federal regulator of the securities industry, as well as the U.S. Department of Justice and local media. She suggested, however, that, alternatively, as there had been no decision issued yet, the parties together reach a fair and reasonable resolution. Gwen inserted a timeline for negotiations of 5:00 p.m., and listed her office's fax number.

She then had Mary drive down to Day's office and hand-deliver the missive. She'd fax a copy to Mandel later, as Day, being the big honcho, would be the lawyer controlling a settlement.

"Judy, hope that does it. Now the wait begins."

The rest of the afternoon Gwen and Judy tried to keep busy while having one ear alert to the fax machine waking up.

And so the office's grandfather clock counted off the minutes, and then chimed the hours. When it sang three times, Judy began pacing the floor. Gwen assured her they were still in the game, as Day needed to consult with Moss and then Moss's boss, going on up the corporate ladder.

By 4:30 p.m., with Mary joining in the vigil after her drive, the trio sat huddled next to the black fax box. Judy brought out the stale tea biscuits left over from last month's tea break, and they munched in unison, waiting.

Five o'clock arrived and no fireworks. Mary said, "The watched pot never boils. Maybe we should just play some cards or something."

"Too nervous," Judy said.

By 5:30, depression was beginning to set in. Silently, the three listened as the minutes passed, one by one. Gwen, looking grim with her lips compressed, finally at

5:50 p.m. said, "Looks like, ladies, our gravy boat won't be docking at shore today."

Judy and Mary moaned. Gwen, being captain of the sinking ship, did the captain thing and thanked the crew for their help 'above and beyond'. Then, with a shrug, she ended, "We persevered and that's a plus. Time to pack up and go home."

"Wait," Judy said. "I think it's alive."

'Beep... beep, ...beep. Silence.

As Gwen was grabbing her coat the magical fax machine again began doing its thing, but this time with zest. The sound of beeping, gurgling and shaking filled the room.

"It's like Frankenstein," Mary said, "waking up from the dead."

Soon the device was spewing out paper from Day's office. All three watched as the fax paper came through, line by line. After page one, the machine spit out a second, then a third-- and a fourth page then appeared. Gwen worried her machine didn't have sufficient paper if Day's response was much longer. Finally, the machine groaned, then emitted a final beep and stopped.

For Gwen, it was lovely watching the box slowly spitting out the equivalent of justice and dollar bills, almost as magical as finding a 'hot document.'

Judy pulled the sheets from the machine and set them out on the conference table. All three women crowded around the pages. Mary, her voice tremulous with anxiety, started reading out Page one.

Gwen, I'm in receipt of your draft Motion and cover letter. In light of the Panel's unexpected delay in issuing its decision, like you, I have been considering possible alternative resolutions. Gwen, the old proverb says 'great minds think alike'. I don't know if that's true but just this morning I too reached out to my clients and co-counsel to discuss the status of this matter.

Before Mary read further, Judy yelled, arms floating in the air,

"It's a win!"

Gwen cautioned them that victory was not yet in their grasp and to wait to hear the rest, although she was feeling more confident thanks to the cordial and casual tone of the response so far. She piped up, "You hear that crew, '*great* minds' he says. Ha-ha. And, yeah, if you believe the readiness timing is a coincidence, I have a bridge to sell you." Pushing up her sleeves, as if readying for a stock ticker's verdict, Gwen added, "So, Mary, read on."

Mary continued, but her voice was now more self-assured, "I am pleased to say that my client appreciates the complexities of this matter and the apparent unfortunate misunderstandings by all parties that impacted Mr. Perez's account."

At this point, Judy began dancing in circles while yelling, "We won, oh Lordie, we won."

Mary was more restrained and merely hooted while waiving her pen in the air. But Gwen wasn't at ease yet, not until the settlement terms were presented.

Mary stopped her hooting and read to the group the rest of the fax message.

> While we are confident that we presented a winning case should the matter proceed to decision, nevertheless, as you suggest, in light of the risks attendant with any litigation, and the concern that there may have been some minor miscommunications in the handling of Mr. Perez's account that were perhaps attributable to or magnified by the unexpected passing of the supervising manager....

Gwen stopped and took a deep breath, crossing her fingers on both hands — and her feet.

Mary nodded 'yes', then read on:

> ... therefore, to avoid further time and the expense of fighting over re-opening the case, Respondents are prepared to make a one time offer to settle this matter,

which offer is subject to confidentiality by all parties.

All three women let out the Middleton version of a Bronx cheer. They waited in suspense for the 'tell', but Day's letter ended with the notice that he would be faxing over shortly the terms of 'the Offer'. Day had added that he believed it to be 'quite reasonable' in light of the strength of their client's case. Day closed with the admonition that the settlement proposal would be 'take-it-or-leave-it', no further negotiations were to be held. As had Gwen, he set a quick deadline for a response – yes or no – by noon tomorrow. For the first time that Gwen could recall, she was pleased to have a drop-dead date that was sooner rather than later.

Smiling, with cheeks pleasantly rosy, Gwen at last crowed, "Yes." In a more sedate, lawyerly voice, she added, "Our push worked, ladies. Day's legalese says, 'you got us, we want to put this baby to sleep, along with all the documents involving PIP'." Now all that was required was to wait a few minutes for 'the envelope please' that announced what Sammy won.

And so the women sat around the large conference table and waited for the ka-chunk and beep of the fax machine. Minutes passed and only silence. Judy got up and began traipsing around the table, arms chugging.

"Gets the tension out," she called as she walked by Gwen one more time. Mary gobbled the remaining stale cookies, chewing while drumming her fingers on the wood table. Gwen closed her eyes and thought about warm beaches.

At last, after 22 minutes, but Gwen thought who was counting, they heard the honeyed hum of the machine. The women took turns reading the additional pages. After each term was digested, Gwen translated the legalese into English. The Respondents had agreed to pay a total of, wow, $225,504.85.

At this information, Judy and Mary stood up and loudly applauded. Gwen explained that from this amount under her fee agreement with Sammy would be deducted his obligation to pay the NASD's fees, out-of-pocket expenses including the money owed to Martha and Linda, a bonus for her office staff for overtime work, and of course her fee. Plus likely taxes down the road. Gwen added she wanted to pay John a reasonable sum for his assistance, despite his almost fuck-up of the case.

Mary took out a legal pad and began to do the calculations. The three women discussed the terms of the Offer, and whether it should be accepted – for about ten seconds.

"Do we need to run it by Sammy?" Mary asked.

Gwen shook her head no. "He signed a Power of Attorney so I can act on his behalf as I was concerned I wouldn't be able to reach him in case a development required immediate action. And, by gosh, it has."

Summarizing their discussion, Gwen said, "Okay team, we are a united YES! I'll let Day know before there is any risk the fax machine suddenly goes on the brink, or the NASD decision arrives via FedEx tonight, or Middleton's hit by a tsunami and we lose connection with South of the Notch."

After waiting a half hour for face-saving purposes, Gwen faxed Day that her client accepted the Offer as is. She included a signed copy of the settlement plus a copy of Sammy's POA authorizing her to sign on his behalf. Worried about last minute obstacles, or second thoughts, Gwen added that the settlement process needed to be completed within the next two days – as she would be going out-of-state. Before Judy turned off the lights, the Gwen 'family' hugged, high-fived, and even danced a little jig to the tune of 'Mary Had a Little Lamb'. They understood that this settlement should enable them to work together at least into the near future. All that was missing was a fortyish cute guy in sneakers.

And, Gwen thought, maybe also her desire to still be in general practice down the road. While happy now, and feeling great relief the case was over, Gwen understood that all her sweat, blood (she remembered her staple cut), and tears helping Sammy likely would have at best marginal impact on the practices of Stanley, Howe and

Larry. And negligible if any impact on the securities industry's trading practices. Thanks to the confidentiality of the process, there'd likely be no Dortman parade for the winners.

Still, Gwen patted her own shoulder and sent a virtual hug to Sammy. David had --with help-- defeated Goliath and that was something to cheer about. And there was the minor victory as well; Gwen doubted that Stanley, Howe would operate its PIP program as the business and legal risks of doing so, as Sammy had shown, were probably significant.

Late that night Gwen decided she should attempt to notify Adam of the ending of the Perez case as he had worked hard on helping her with the suit, and surely helped bring about the settlement. Not sure how to reach him directly, she sent a brief email message to Harvey Gladstone asking him to please send a note to Adam that said, without breaching NASD confidentiality, "Thought you'd like to know that Sammy's case has been settled, good money. Thanks for your help. Gwen."

CHAPTER FORTY-FOUR

Like a mosquito smelling blood, Gwen zeroed in on the large neon light that blasted 'Good Food' to highway travelers. Arms loaded with gifts, she entered the diner.

Tonight her office was officially celebrating Sammy's win. ("A win's a win," Judy had announced, "whether by settlement or verdict, or blackmail, and it deserves a party.") Gwen had selected for the occasion that they meet at yet another restaurant owned by a former client. Thanks to Gwen's legal acumen, the restaurant had stayed 'in the family' rather than the hands of greedy out-of-state developers. Since then Gwen had become a filial member of the close-nit Greek clan. She even knew the secret handshake (a hug followed by kisses on both cheeks). The family's matriarch, Lucinda, a large woman with warm motherly eyes, greeted Gwen at the entrance with a big, enveloping hug and then the 'handshake' routine. Gwen was barely able to remain standing, let alone hold on to her packages.

Surviving the greeting, Gwen while walking by the busy tables,sneaked a lingering peak at the enticing mile-high desserts displayed along the back wall. Gwen also noticed that flying from the ceiling were Halloween witches with brooms, happy goblins, and even plump vampires, all in the spirit of the upcoming candy holiday.

Suddenly, at the thought of Halloween Gwen experienced a 'Brian' flashback. They were wearing not-too-scary masks, they'd gone trick or treating after work along Lexington Avenue. Filling their backpacks with goodies from the bodegas and neighborhood stores lining the street, they giggled together at their *chutzpah*, as the passersby stared and smiled at the young couple, clearly in love. Gwen, wondering what triggered that memory, realized that she was still feeling happy. *Gwennie, a good omen that maybe facing your anger issues with Adam has helped free you to remember times with Brian fondly yet still able to move on in this life.*

Smiling, Gwen approached the back corner of the restaurant where she could see her team – her best friends in the world. They were already busy drinking and gabbing. John stood up and beckoned her over. She was pleased that her payment to John from Sammy's settlement had assuaged any remaining ill feelings that might have been left over from the Perez case.

Mary shouted over the diner's roar, "Hey Gwen, come on over boss. Join the party. We've already started celebrating with booze." Martha raised her cocktail with umbrella to prove the point.

Gwen looked around the table, pleased that the entire extended office gang, some with spouses in tow, had shown up. Mary came with her on-again, off-again, Ralph Lauren-dressed boyfriend. They seemed cozy. Judy sat across from hubby Jim who appeared more ready to nap than to party. Gwen wondered if one of their kids were sick until Jim explained that he'd been up most of the previous night with their bitch who was expecting puppies.

Jim added, "Can't believe I'm more anxious about this birth than I was with my actual human children."

Laughing, Gwen replied, "Bitches, always making demands on men." Jim chuckled, his warm smile lighting up his tired face.

Gwen felt sad that Sammy hadn't been able to make it over from the islands to join in the fray. His most recent postcard had read, "Too busy with T-shirt business, going good. See you soon, Sammy."

After more drink orders were taken and food choices made, Gwen surveyed the scene. *Am I wrong, but are my friends more confident, more assured, since the Sammy case? Did we all grow a little in ourselves, maybe, even me?* She knew some important decisions had been made in the several months since the end of the arbitration hearing. Judy had started evening classes in paralegal studies offered this term at the town's high school. At the same time, Mary was hard at work studying for the law school entrance exam scheduled for later next month. Linda had fancied herself up as appropriate for the firm's newly named CPA partner, with a visit to Martha's hair stylist and eye glasses befitting the executive. Sitting up tall, Gwen thought she also appeared more assertive, maybe having adopted that part of Martha's lifestyle as well. As for Martha.... Well, Martha remained 'Martha', a confident, competent, and collected professional. But at the recent Big Brother Big Sister luncheon that Gwen and Martha had attended, Martha had let out a non-investment advisor belly laugh at the speaker's lame joke. And she'd given Gwen friendly hugs when they'd parted.

And how have I changed? Professionally, she was better able to 'go with the flow', less a perfectionist. She'd always been her hardest critic, so this was good, maybe meant less Pepto-Bismol down the road. And she found herself speaking out more with her attorney colleagues, sharing with these mostly men the woman's voice on issues. Perhaps she was taking on the 'yes, I'm good at what I do' law firm Partner mystique. Good growth, she thought, patting her back with the arm not holding the beer. Yet, at the same time her cynicism towards the legal system had grown. She'd spent much of her life fertilizing the historic soil where lay her heroes, Justices Marshall (John and Thurgood); Brandeis; Douglas; Brennan, but instead of a growing thriving Morning Glory vine, the soil lately had put forth wilted flora. She was aware that the once pitter-patter of her younger idealistic heart when approaching 'The 'Law', had these days often remained sluggish and silent. Was she still drawn to the law's flame? Or had the long hours, demanding stress, and tilted playing field tarnished her lady with the scales?

So, Gwennie, is a life change in line for me? Lately at night while struggling to sleep, Gwen explored in her mind the appeal of academia, maybe teaching at Adam's law school. She'd loved it when she'd subbed for John and taught several of his classes. Now that she had a small nest egg, she could financially pursue a course change, provided she was very, very frugal. Should she set sail? But where in the world did she want to go?

"Gwen, Gwen, are you there?" Mary shouted into her ear. "I've been trying to get your attention – it seems forever. Were you on another planet? Come on Counselor and Captain of our ship, we have wine and *hummus, slouvaki, baked feta.* We're waiting for your toast."

"You bet, Mares." Gwen looked around the table. Shoulders back, head rotating to take in all her friends, she raised her beer glass and said, "Here's to best friends who are the purest golden olive oil of life – and who gift to me so generously every day, come what may. Sammy, sorry you're not here. I thank you all from my heart for your help these past many, many months. While the big firms hand out engraved Lucite cubes to be displayed in your office as a trophy for a win, I've improvised and with Sammy's help are giving you far more practical gifts– t-shirts. Great for jogging, painting, sleeping." Gwen added silently, even bike-riding. Gwen then handed out her gifts: specially designed t-shirts sent from Sammy that were made on his machine. They read on the back, *"Lawyer (noun): A person who writes a 10,000-word document and calls it a 'brief'.* On the front was the blindfolded lady with her scale. Below was written, "A Woman's Place is in the Courtroom." All laughed at the design as they tried them on.

Judy jumped up, beer bottle raised, and added, "And congrats to Sammy, who's wowing the women in the Caribbean, or so I expect, and making great t-shirts."

All raised their glasses and clanked them together. Gwen missed the glass filled with orange juice, but it was time to be happy. That's when she ordered eight big pieces of seven-layer chocolate cake – that she shared with her extended family.

✳✳✳✳ ✳✳✳✳ ✳✳✳✳

Who said there wasn't going to be a victory parade? By the

time Gwen recovered from her chocolate overdose weeks later she received in the mail another postcard from Sammy, but this one was a printed invite to his Dortman 'party' to celebrate his victory with family and friends. At the bottom of the invite was printed in pencil. "Please Attorney, bring team, better team than Mr. Murphy."

And Gwen did just that, inviting Martha, and Linda, and John, and Mary and Judy and she decided on a lark even Adam via FBI agent Gladstone to join her for Sammy's party in Dortman on the second Friday night in November. All (except the sneaker guy) sent a 'yes' RSVP, well actually Martha had answered, "Hell, yes."

The party night was cold and crisp, with the hint of the smell of early snow in the air. Olanda's white house looked inviting thanks to the colorful mums and pumpkins on the porch. Gwen had picked up Mary and Judy and they found they had to park blocks away, thanks to the numerous cars on the streets near the house. Once again Gwen decided that most all of Dortman's residents must be Sammy's extended relatives. The brassy rhythm of Latino music blasting from outside speakers greeted the trio when they arrived and filled the block with festivity. Gwen chuckled to herself, surmising that the music likely could be heard at the nearby Chinese restaurant with its swimming fish, the place where she had first convinced Martha and Linda to join in her Sammy escapade. Oh, and yeah, where she'd gotten that cookie with its paper fortune.

Gwen pushed through the throng of visitors and entered the living room. Not much had changed since her visit many months ago when she'd reminisced about family connections and their importance in life. Looking up she saw Sammy in the kitchen waving at her. Wearing another floral shirt, he was surrounded by women, all it seemed offering him food. His nephew Carlos came over to the women to make sure, after getting a big hug from 'the Attorney', that Gwen and her friends had all had a supply of beer and chips. Gwen had been having Carlos work for her one afternoon a week when he didn't have classes so he could earn extra money to pay for textbooks, and maybe get a glimpse of a future career path. With drink in hand, Gwen found herself marveling at the warmth and energy she could feel all around her.

As the trio settled in on the living room couch, the partygoers started exiting the house and walking down the street. This parade was headed for Sammy's uncle's café, the very place where Gwen had prepped Sammy for his direct exam some months before. Gwen, Judy and Mary, arm-in-arm, along with her fellow office team, joined in the parade, watching with awe the younger relatives who were dancing their way to the café.

As the gang began entering the front door a blaze of lights suddenly lit up along the side of the entryway. Gwen wondered if this was a part of the parade celebration – or the central office of the electric company.

The crowd stopped, then stared as Sarah, the Middleton journalist, former interviewer of Adam, accompanied by a small video crew – well, actually one photographer – stepped into the lights and spoke into a microphone. Before Gwen knew it, Sarah was interviewing the exuberant, smiling Sammy. Her now former client pointed to Gwen and waived her over, his relatives dutifully pushing her forward until she too was in the limelight being interviewed by Sarah. Gwen boringly explained that she was unable to comment on Sammy's case as arbitration matters are confidential. But when Sarah pushed for more, Gwen tried to find a twist within what she thought was acceptable. She came up with a statement that her personal view is that in America the Rule of Law is the foundation of our democracy. Venturing further out on the low limb she added that this law is to be applied the same to all persons, no matter their color, gender, or financial position. This appeared to do the trick as the crowd applauded. Then Sammy added something in Spanish and gave her a hug, which was followed by the group now giving Gwen a Dortman cheer in Spanish, or so she thought.

And as quickly as it began, the show was over. Sarah and her one-man crew packed up their gear. As she was leaving, Sarah whispered to Gwen, "Hey Gwen, thank your friend for the package and legal tip. This will be a big feel-good story, wait and see." Startled, Gwen jerked back on her heels, then started to respond ... but Sarah had already slipped away. *What the hell is she talking about?* But Gwen had no time to investigate further for she was now inside the restaurant. And watching Mary, Judy, Martha, Linda, and John already eating and singing with the relatives at their large table. Gwen promptly grabbed a spot at the table and joined in. A good time was had by all.

When Gwen got home later than expected, before collapsing into bed she jotted down two notes to herself on the small pad on her night-table: 1) Send email to Artie, family matters, call her; and 2) What was Sarah talking about? What 'big feel-good story'? Am I in trouble?

Gwen turned from stomach to side to back and back again during the night, worrying that if there was a breach of the settlement agreement's confidentiality provision, could Stanley, Howe or Murphy have a leg to stand on if they demanded their money back....

Will this case never end?

CHAPTER FORTY-FIVE

February's powerful winds swept across Concord's Downtown Crossing, whipping the parade of flags in front of the capital building. Gwen tightly pulled Judy's handmade knitted pink and green scarf with raised red roses across her face in an effort to keep her cheeks from turning into frozen popsicles. The day was overcast with the special feel of a New England storm brewing over the distant mountains. A sudden breeze caught on Gwen's long coat and, like a fish in a casting net, she was swept through the revolving doors into the haven of the building's heated lobby. Once inside Gwen rubbed her face, generating a semblance of warmth. Removing her protective sunglasses, she checked the Capital building's directory for the 'Office of State Senator Charles Starlight'.

Gwen had received a telephone call the week before from the Senator's office asking for a meeting. Gwen had no idea what would bring on such an invitation from her local state senator, as she hadn't even supported his right-wing candidacy. In fact, other than exchanging a few sentences at a state bar meeting, she'd had little interaction with her elected official. Finding his office listing, she entered the lobby's ornate gold -filigreed elevators and pressed eight. Exiting the car she walked down the hall until she saw Room 809A, its glass front door declaring in large gold letters, 'Office of State Senator Charles W. Starlight, 6th Congressional District'. On entering, she approached the older woman behind the receptionist's desk and explained she was there for a 10:30 meeting with the Senator.

In a cheery welcoming, very British voice the woman said, "Hello, dear. Why, you must be Attorney Wilson. So glad you could make it in this bloody weather. The Senator just stepped out for a moment but he's expecting you. Please give me your coat and help yourself to a cup of tea dear while you wait."

Smiling back and wondering if she'd mistakenly entered the offices of PBS's *Masterpiece Theatre*, Gwen answered, "Tea would be lovely. Even mud season is looking good with this weather." After depositing her wet parker, Gwen picked up one of the many copies of the *Wall Street Journal*. She sipped her tea and read about the Fed's recent actions on lending rates. Then she moved on to the more fun legal gossip column, 'Whose making news'. Perusing down the page, a name jumped out at her – Jay Sawyer. Gwen held the paper closer and read, 'Esteemed Securities Law Attorney, Jay Sawyer, senior partner at a leading Wall Street firm, has been selected as lead counsel by a large investment house to represent the firm in a major securities industry action filed by the SEC. Kudus to a future Cabinet selection?'

Gwen's hair on her arms bristled. *Nice to see he's moved up in his career, and so quickly. No wonder he hasn't found time to write a decision in the Perez case.* While Gwen thought Jay ran a fair hearing considering the NASD's pro-industry rules, she understood nonetheless that no such approach would be expected to govern the Panel's decision. It was highly unlikely that an ambitious lawyer would stomp on his industry's interests. And clearly Jay had higher aims in his sight.

Gwen was up to p. 15 of the newspaper when Senator Starlight strode into view.

"Hi Gwen. Thanks for coming on such a lousy morning. Whatever happened to global warming?" He gave her a charming smile. It was as if they were old friends from college days who were getting together for an afternoon catch up at the local pub over a pint.

"I thought, Senator, you did not believe global warming to be real?"

Starlight smiled. "Ah, yes, well, let's say I have an open mind on such environmental matters." Another charming smile followed by, "Come on into my office so we can talk in private."

Gwen was dutifully impressed with this room that featured

oriental rugs, walnut inlaid desk and with matching credenza, and expansive views of the Merrimack River. Pictures of smiling celebrities covered one wall. Most of the famous people Gwen could recognize had their arms thrown around the Senator's shoulders against backgrounds featuring sailboats, ski runs, red clay tennis courts, and panoramic skylines of world cities. *Such a multi-faceted person is our Charlie.*

The Senator offered Gwen a fifteen- minute monologue that she had difficulty following, although she noticed he kept returning to the theme of the sad turmoil of the state's judiciary. Charlie's closing to this monologue finally arrived at the purpose of the visit.

"Gwen, you know we have had our political differences over the years, but even from a distance I have always admired your legal skill, your acumen. And there's your connection to your community. Who didn't feel a warmth in their heart when they saw on what seemed like all the state's major news channels a few weeks ago that interview in Dortman with you and your client, a person of color I readily noticed, all to celebrate your legal victory? Truly, it was like the whole Hispanic community came out to tell you they loved you. Most inspiring. But you know, for me – someone who admires a person's reputation for honesty above all, I find it even more impressive that you've retained your integrity in what I know can be a tough business. Yup, your integrity is something people respect, Gwen." The Senator stopped and then, placing his hand on his chest, added, "Something I respect."

At this point in his monologue the Senator paused and Gwen realized it was her time to say 'thank you' with modesty, which she did. Charlie then got to the bottom line. "Anyhow, as I mentioned, the last few months have seen some media attacks on...um... several members of our judicial branch, attacks that I think are, you know, overly aggressive, but the damn regional press is picking up on them with gusto. Now, last week I was informed that Justice Brenzanni of our Middleton Superior Court is undergoing chemotherapy for recently diagnosed bladder cancer – I trust you will keep this in confidence – and she has notified the Chief Justice that she will be resigning her seat. So I, I mean the Senate Judicial Committee on behalf of the Governor and Executive Counsel – which as you know is elected, needs to find a lawyer to replace her. Preferably, the word is out, a woman lawyer in a locale not now represented – and that includes your area above the notch. The appointment will be to fill her vacancy 'till her term ends, another few years. And, my dear, your name was recommended to me by several people as the person for the job."

"My name? Who would have suggested my name?" Gwen almost fell over backwards in surprise.

"Gwennie, I understand your friends call you that, hope you'll allow me the honor. I've closely watched your practice since you moved to our state. As you know, Chris and I were friends. Anyhow, as I was saying, you are held in high regard not only by fellow esquires of the bar but also by members of both political parties."

Gwen said, "But, Charlie, I haven't been active in the state bar or political committees." \

"Gwen, let's not be overly modest. I know how bright you are, seen it myself. You went to an Ivy League law school – as did I, you know, you did your dues at a big New York City firm – all qualifications respected by the bar, and by judges. Be assured, your proven capabilities, trial experience, well they make you more than qualified. Just the other day, a friend of mine, Josiah Day – of course you know him. Why he mentioned to me how he recently was involved with you in that Dortman case and on the sly he mentioned how impressed he was with your...now let me remember...yes he said your ardent handling of the case. And integrity, he added."

Gwen stood silent, wondering whether Day had a vested interest in the appointment. *Did they worry she'd somehow pursue the PIP program and other Sammy issues on a grander scale? Did the recent Dortman publicity raise concerns that his clients would be seen as racists if the truth got out? Or his role in covering that up? Would her being on the bench ensure she wouldn't actively play on the field?*

Gwen shook her head. She reminded herself that more likely Day just thought she was a good lawyer and wanted to help her out, after all they were both outsiders in the legal old-boy insider game.

The Senator held up his hands. "Okay, I get it, there's also the political thing. Not wanting to be coy, but I – and the Governor – recognize the advantages of, shall we say, a more diverse viewpoint on the state bench. With a liberal leaning Justice being forced to resign, and a woman at that, there is strong pressure on both parties to appoint to *her* seat another experienced female lawyer. One – how should I put this – with a similar progressive viewpoint of the law. My dear, you clearly fit this bill better than anyone I can think of. So, in short, on behalf of the Governor and Executive Counsel I've been authorized to offer you the opportunity to be the newest member of the state's bench. Do you want it?"

Is this a dream? Have I actually been offered a judgeship? Gwen told herself: you're merely a small-town lawyer with mostly blue- collar and small business clients. You've not given much more than lunch money to the local political gurus. You've no prosecution experience, the general route to the bench. *Why Me? Is it as innocent as a confluence of factors favoring her appointment?*

"Gwen, I know this maybe is a little sudden, but the situation requires that I act quick. I'm confident you will be an excellent choice." Walking over to his chair, Charlie sat down and swiveled back and forth, then, offering another of his best pal smiles, he went in for the closure, "You can do much good on the bench, you know. And, as a further incentive, because I understand your career concerns, let me tell you in confidence another plus factor to compensate for any pay-cut you're likely to have. Between us, my committee is seriously considering creating another specialized court like the Housing Court, but this time setting up a state 'consumer court' for consumer protection matters. On the quiet, a number of fellow members hinted that you'd be strong candidate for this job, once you got your feet wet, that is. Not promising anything, of course, but it may be a juicy plum for you to tackle."

Gwen smiled back at the Senator while her mind raced ahead. *I am qualified, have a nicer temperament then most judges I've encountered, and, yeah, I am woman – hear me roar. So, stupid, don't look a gift horse in the mouth. Even if that horse is a gift offered by the slimy Senator from my district. So what if maybe Josiah Day's calculating praise had been the generator of my appointment.* For an instant there was a squawking in her subconscious that this didn't smell right. She sighed and then instructed the cautionary voice to go fly a kite. She could do good, bring about some justice on the bench. *Time to be bold, lady. Time to lean-in, to learn from Jay and all the other males that don't hesitate to toot their horns. It's time I think of me, my needs, my happiness, how I may want to make my mark in life. I've done my bit for the little guy, planted lots of little petunias in my garden, now maybe I'm ready to leap forward to, well, arboretums.*

Gwen managed to state firmly, and this time with some spoon-fed political savvy, "Senator, I am pleasantly taken aback, I admit. I appreciate sincerely your kindness along with your committee's support in considering me for Judge Brenzanni's seat. While I am deeply sad that the Justice is having to deal with her serious health issues, I realize that her condition will likely place great demands on her time and energy." Gwen paused.

"And, Gwennie?"

"Senator, I would be very pleased to accept this honor. But I would like to sleep on your offer. Such a career shift would seriously make changes not only to my life but impact on my staff and clients."

"Of course, Gwennie, I understand, and there you go, showing the integrity I talked about. However, I need your answer by tomorrow afternoon. We plan to get this announcement released to the media before the Friday press-drop. And if you say no – which I hope is not the case – well, I need time to pursue this matter elsewhere. As I deeply hope your answer will be 'yes', just so you know, I will make every effort to accommodate your starting time frame."

"Thank you for that, Senator."

"Charlie, please, as I'm hoping we are likely to have lots of contact going forward. No need for formalities."

"Yes. I'll give you a call by tomorrow noon, Charlie."

"Fine. Here's my card, Gwennie, the one with my private line. I hope you will accept this opportunity. Your service, and that's what it is, will be good for New Hampshire."

With a smile and heavy pat on her back, Charlie led Gwen out of his office through his personal door, and gave a faint waive as she stood and waited for the elevator. Then he returned to doing the people's business.

In little over half an hour had her world turned around. *A judge. Am I ready for this?* Being a judge was most every lawyer's secret ambition, at least in theory. To make new law. To issue rulings that would shape her state. To have the position and power to help people live a better life. To spend her time with issues addressing fairness, right and wrong, life choices. While musing about a future life in robes, Gwen decided a visit to the ladies' room at the end of the floor made sense before her long commute home in the sleet. On her way down the corridor she passed on the right the Northeast regional office of the Federal Securities and Exchange Commission, i.e., the SEC. Printed in gold letters on *this* glass door were the words, "Acting Director, Josiah P. Day, Esq.." Her pulse thumped.

By the time she got to her office Gwen had decided to apply her finger analysis to this decision. On the positive side: 1. I've followed the legal rules in pursuing the Perez case. 2. And in settling it. 3. I've maintained the level of confidentiality I had agreed to. 4. I've just been offered a judgeship for which I am fully qualified on merit, 5. I'll have a chance to practice the kind of law I've always wanted – where the law, not money, politics, nor connections governs.

Now she calculated the cons: 1. I'll continue to practice law and not make enough money to pay my bills, 2. I'll struggle to find justice in the current state of trial court practice where overwhelming criminal cases and inadequate funding make getting a decision, let alone justice, too often wishful thinking.

Gwen compared the two lists, then consulted with Judy and Mary.

That night, with her team's blessings, she decided to do the honorable thing. She would accept being designated "her honor" – and work as hard as she could to make good law.

Before going to bed, Gwen left a message for the Senator on his private line. "Thank you, Charlie, my answer is yes, I'll be delighted. Tell me what I need to do."

CHAPTER FORTY-SIX

Middleton overnight had been transformed into a glorious white winter wonderland. Gwen's Prius moved slowly as the March snowstorm covered Main Street in a wrapping of soft down. Driving behind the lead plow, Gwen marveled again at Middleton's road-clearing assembly line. It almost was as awe inspiring as the Old Man had been when he served as sentinel for the Notch. First a row of three plows cleared the snow, pushing it in stages to the trailing plows, then eventually to the side of the road. The cute, smaller sidewalk plow then took over and in a swift, upward motion, which brought to mind the Celtic's great Larry Bird's lay-ups, thrust the white confetti into the trailing truck. The accumulated frozen water was finally dumped into an artificial pond behind the town's offices, to be used when needed later on the town's playing fields. Modern New Hampshire recycling, Gwen thought, transforming Mother Nature from frozen crystals to frog water to soccer turf – with minimal fanfare.

Waiting at a stoplight, Gwen reached into her pocket for sugarless gum to help keep her alert. No caffeine version though as she was off that chemical pollutant. Only healthy fare for her now that she was about to take on the robe. Her appointment to the Superior Court had gone through smoothly, but the start date had been delayed to accommodate Judge Brenzanni's docket. As of now, while the announcement had been made, she was still working on client cases and making plans to transfer those she wouldn't be completing in time. Arrangements had been made for her to start 'Judge School' in a few weeks to prepare her to take on her new position, especially the handling of criminal matters. And there was one interesting change she'd noted since the word was out – other lawyers were treating her so much nicer.

The traffic light turned green. Gwen rounded the corner and saw that her office's parking lot hadn't yet been plowed. Annoyed, she backed up, made a right turn, and was able to park in Peaches' lot down the street. After buying a takeout decaf coffee and muffin – the kind filled with fibers and nuts, Gwen stopped on the slightly icy sidewalk leading to her office. Sticking out her tongue, arms akimbo, she chased the falling frozen flakes, each one having a one- in-the-universe geometrical pattern. Her mouth tingled delightedly as they melted away, almost as much fun as eating chocolate –- but without the calories. Gwen's pulse beat happily.

On today's agenda was a meeting with tax counsel helping her with a client's estate plan, followed by lunch with "the lovely Lola', her massage friend in the office upstairs who had a legal question, and the afternoon presented the likelihood of a nasty 'husband' deposition, thanks to the aggressive antics of his divorce counsel. It seemed that, despite the implementation of no-fault divorce, most all divorce cases now were mean-spirited affairs, challenging her belief in the institution of marriage. Maybe being single – as half the nation was – seemed the best place to be, as she told friends trying to fix her up (mainly Judy). She still didn't understand how partners who'd been intimate could so quickly turn into vituperative vipers.

But then again, as she'd learned from her brother Artie and from Adam, broken trust can be cruelly painful, a hurt that lingers. Even these many months later she woke some mornings smiling, expecting Adam to pass her a cup of morning coffee. Or the Times' art section, or tickle her out of dreamland. And she'd be angry at his mess-ups, until she remembered the price he paid, and kept on paying. But one thing she knew, whoever and wherever he was, he'd missed the chance to get a thank you morning kiss for shoveling her walkway. Still, he had come through for Sammy. She continued to suspect in spare moments that it was also Adam who was Sarah's whistleblower 'friend', remembering that she'd given him her business card, and if so, what other 'nefarious perhaps' things had he been up to during his time in Middleton.

The good news, however, was that Artie had responded to her

overture, and he was planning a trip her way in the next few months so they could 'touch base and chill out together.' And visit with their mom.

Picking up her mail from Judy's inbox — as usual Gwen was the first one in the building – her eyes panned in on a letter bearing the engraved calligraphy 'NASD'. The ruling had finally arrived, thankfully a product of the law's renowned glacial speed. Gwen procrastinated as best she could to delay confronting the verdict. Placing her coffee cup on her desk, her breakfast muffin on the restaurant's napkin, she used the plastic knife in her top drawer to carefully measure and slice the muffin into eight even pieces – better to extend its life. When there were no more crumbs to devour, holding in her breath, she removed the six- page decision.

After a deep cleansing breath, Gwen scanned the decision's summary. Then she put the cover letter and opinion down.

Sammy had lost. The arbitration panel found unanimously -- on all counts – for the brokerage firm and for Murphy. Adding insult to injury it further ordered that Sammy pay over $40,000 dollars to compensate the agency and opposing counsel for the arbitration's expenses.

Gwen's heart sank until it crunched down on her eaten muffin. It was like opening a much- awaited birthday present, one in a big box with fancy wrapping, only to discover inside a box of lima beans. *Dickensonian!* With no Sawyer body present to punch, Gwen pounded her fist on her desk until her hand hurt too much to continue. Then she crumpled up each page of the decision into a paper ball. She walked around her office shooting them into her wastebasket, yelling "Gotcha" each time one went in. Once the veins in her wrists no longer noticeably pulsed, she sat down and contemplated the morning sun rising over the mountains. As she watched the scene, she couldn't help but laugh out-loud and wish to the agency and its minions, *'Good luck, assholes, in finding Sammy's whereabouts, and in recovering a dime from him. Did you forget, he has no money – as you and your money-grubbing greedy accomplices stole it all!'*

After her last client left that afternoon, Gwen recovered the pages of the decision from her trash and reviewed them again. She'd been right. Sawyer had essentially copied verbatim his decision written years ago concerning the middle-class investor's similar claims, the ruling she'd discovered only after filing Sammy's complaint and having accepted the Panel members. Sawyer must have been happy when he found that the template was still on his computer.

The opinion stated that Sammy either controlled his account or he provided financial information to Murphy that made the trading suitable. They rejected Martha's position that the law required Murphy to do more, avoiding the 'know your customer' precedents. The Panel further stated that if Sammy were unhappy with Murphy's conduct, especially after being contacted by the firm's compliance office, he should have complained. *Seems they were asleep when I showed that Sammy never got these contacts as they sent them to an old P.O. box and not his current address. And, anyhow, the guy who sent them died and so was unreachable, at least in this world.*

Finally, the Panel found both Martha and Linda's testimony "failed to demonstrate any violation of industry standards that led to Mr. Perez's losses." The *chutzpah* in ordering Sammy to pay all that money just confirmed the Panel's disregard of the hearing's facts, including that Sammy was disabled, receiving SSDI, and had no savings left!

In short, the Panel's opinion relied on their disbelief of Sammy's story and that they were not persuaded by Gwen's case: the firm's churning letters, phone records, Linda's statistical computations, the lengthy record of highly risky and market maker trades. Day and Mandel were right, after all. The case had been about whether they liked Sammy, found him believable. The clear answer was no. Reading on, Gwen almost laughed when coming to the decision's off-hand comment, after ruling substantively for Respondents that, well, the firm and Murphy should be chided for poor recordkeeping and inadequate communications with Sammy. *You think that was their worst fault?* No penalties, though, were imposed for this lax management.

Gwen wondered once more what influence the allegation that Sammy hid funds from his wife had played in contributing to the Panel's position. And his late tax payment to the IRS. She'd seen their interest perk when these issues came up. If only Sammy had clued her in before the hearing, she might have been able to show better these claims were nonsense. But Sammy had not taken her into his trust.

There it is, that word again – trust. And what can happen when one fails to do so. Did we all fail at that – Sammy, Adam, and me? Somehow, dogs don't seem to have so much difficulty with trust. Maybe that's why they are superior beings.

Gwen twiddled her thumbs and thought back on the case and what did she really believe, outside of the conference room. While she'd mostly believed the gist of Sammy's story, she knew from experience that the truth most often lies in-between the white and black versions of reality. Sure, there had been claims during the case that caused a little bird in her head to chirp a warning. There was Olanda's reluctance to meet with her, Sammy's daily phone calls to Murphy and his pushing stocks he'd heard about, his co-incidental transfer of funds into Mariah's account during his divorce, his prior stock experience. Maybe even Sammy's ambition to be a "rich" guy who could afford like his work pals, of all things, a new car and to pay for his children's college. And yet, at bottom, Gwen was convinced Sammy had been wronged, an unsophisticated family man, a religious man, who spoke Spanish and lived in a white house surrounded by asphalt and who'd been bulldozed by corporate greed in his quest to be an American success.

Gwen sipped her coffee, looking out at the white sky, and reminded herself not to be disappointed in the process's outcome. Winning at trial was always a long shot.

A face-saving 'settlement' turned out to have been a reach, for unlike her clients, the Carpenters who'd reached an easy resolution on far less damaging evidence, Sammy was not a wealthy investor who a firm like Stanley, Howe would want to cultivate and make happy. And, maybe, the industry followed different settlement standards for working class clients of color.

After considering all this, Gwen decided she'd walk away from the case taking comfort in that she'd done her best, been there when no one else would take the case, and neither she nor her women team had given up when the odds of success seemed desperate.

Except, thanks to Adam and the settlement, she and Sammy had won!

Before she left for the day, Gwen typed up a quick note to the NASD that as regards Perez v. Stanley, Howe *et al.,* their records were incorrect and should have stated that all the parties had settled the matter several months ago by agreement, and she, and the other parties she understood as well, had timely notified the Association of this case's final resolution. She put this notice in an envelope and placed it on Judy's chair to send by certified mail, return receipt.

Then she walked back into her empty office and stood in the open area behind her client chairs. Slowly, moving her feet to the old tune 'Old McDonald Had a Farm', Gwen raised her chin, flapped her arms, and performed her family's famous "chicken dance" – all while chanting repeatedly in line with the music, "Tough luck Panel. Too late bozos. We have the money! We have the money."

CHAPTER FORTY-SEVEN

"Your honor, there's a post card for you I thought you might find of interest." Judy stood underneath the ceiling fan that pushed warm summer air around the old, wood paneled, book lined room called the funny word, chambers. The three tall windows offered no relief from the unseasonal late September heat – as their rope pulleys no longer lifted them even an inch. But the windows served an important purpose; they let sunshine in to the judge's chamber.

Gwen sat behind a pile of briefs, all demanding relief in a complicated criminal conspiracy case. Criminal law continued to be a mysterious language to her. Still she thanked her many years of watching 'Law and Order' so she could at least converse with the lawyers standing before her. She was surprised to discover how much crime there was in and around Middleton, where she was assigned to sit on the bench for the present. Who knew how many bicycle thefts there were in the town? Curled up on her large red leather chair, she twirled around every so often, just to give her stomach muscles and quadriceps some exercise. In the process, she glanced at the framed pictures on her credenza: Artie and Brian attired in ski gear, her mother prettily combed and garbed at the nursing home. Her picture of Adam lying on her couch, law book on chest and big grin with dimples had for the moment been stored in her credenza's bottom drawer.

Gwen smiled at Judy, her now Law Clerk responsible for her calendar and secretarial matters, and, of course, also her Chief Knitter. "First, cut the crap with this 'your honor' stuff in chambers. After all these months I'll wring your neck if I have to tell you again." Gwen chuckled as she added, "Which of course would make me a criminal appearing in my court. Not a good look. As to the postcard, I hope it has a picture of a cute puppy, or a glass of cold white Chardonnay. I sure could use either as a pick-me-up after reading these soporific mind-numbing memoranda.

Almost makes me want to give up my sobriety and switch to caffeinated coffee again. Did I write such tripe, Judy, when the shoe was on the other foot?"

"Of course. All billable hours."

"So what's this postcard?" Gwen said as she pushed the papers off her desk pad.

Judy placed a colorful card on Gwen's desk — which was a cheap government issue, unlike the second- hand bankers mahogany work of art she'd used when in private practice. Gwen studied the picture.

"Nice looking beach. Um... withdrawn." Gwen was working on using, when possible, the litigation lingo heard in her courtroom. "A great looking beach with some hunk swimming in the turquoise water and a few women lying on towels wearing quite limited beach attire. Not bad. So what is this? An ad for a luxury cruise you hope I go on?"

"Look at it more carefully, Gwennie," Judy said softly, her eyes moist and her grin wide.

Gwen turned the card over and saw that it was addressed to 'Best lawyer Attorney Wilson'.

Raising an eyebrow, Gwen commented, "Guess the sender didn't learn of my ascension to the bench." Then she read the card.

In scratchy handwriting, with several words crossed out, it said:

Dear Attorney: Want thank you big as ocean for what you done to help me. My life now good. I happy on island. Fish with cousins, play at beach. Dance with nice looking ladies. They like me so I do lots dancing. That good cause I eat too much my sisters and cousins island food. Almost good as Olanda cook. Boys come visit when not in school. We swim, play soccer, lots video games. They now beat me, I no win no more. But that good. I learn use skype.

You come visit. Be guest. I pray on Bible every day that Lord's angels keep you safe, happy like me. My sister and Mariah say *hola*. Also, Mariah has store. I help her. I good at sales. Say thank you to 'my sue Team', they in my heart.

Your client and island *bróder*, Sammy Perez

Gwen studied the ceiling and watched the fan's blades turn slowly. Fighting unexpected tears, she wondered if there were indeed angels floating around above her. Having a group...a flock ...whatever, having angels on your side isn't a bad thing in life.

It had been many months since Gwen had elected to become an Honorable, instead of a possible illegal whistle-blower lawyer. Her copy of the 'hot' document continued to cool in her home safe. Maybe it was time to throw it out. Had the bench been the right choice? If personal happiness were the standard to apply, her answer was a confident YES. One sign of her happiness was that she was no longer looking at want ads for auto mechanic positions. The law had again become an ethical standard for human conduct, one that she could commit to and work to protect. She hoped her decision had been a good choice for New Hampshire's citizens as well.

Gwen had already found career contentment in her new role. Even more, she was enjoying judging. While initially feeling great trepidation at being 'the Decider', she'd grown to appreciate not only her competence, but also her opportunity to have impact, to make change for what she saw as the better choice.

One unexpected bonus had been that she had now more free time in her day, thanks to cutting out the administrative paperwork and the time-consuming billing that for years had accounted for every fifteen minutes of her workday. This had allowed her to participate more directly in the community. And so she was volunteering at the nearby domestic abuse center. Plus walking dogs at the local animal shelter. In fact, she'd given a forever home to one of these dogs, a black and white Springer Spaniel/lab mix. While she was going to name the pup after her childhood pet parakeet, Justice, she decided upon reflection that might be a heavy moniker for a little pooch to have, so instead she named the frisky pup after her grandma 'Molly'. So far Molly seemed happy with her choice and was thriving, in fact, the star of puppy kindergarten. And when she ran after squirrels with her long ears flapping straight out like airplane wings, Gwen found herself laughing, grounded nicely in the moment. Thankfully, so far, the squirrels had always been faster. At home, Molly reigned as boss over much in her domain, despite Gwen's ongoing efforts at being 'alpha' —as she was used to being in her courtroom. With her cute sappy puppy eyes, she even became a welcome presence when Gwen occasionally brought her to work. (As she was in charge, no one complained.) Indeed, lawyers attending her court had started to bring little dog treats to hearings. Gwen worried that some might view this as a form of bribery, but as yet she hadn't had the heart to stop the practice.

"Thanks, Judy, for the postcard. Good to see that all's worked out for Sammy. We done good I think, after many twists and turns."

Both women wiped their teary eyes; Gwen also inhaled deeply. Smiling, she sat up in her grand swivel chair and consciously changed her tone to that befitting a 'your honor'. "Okay, Jude, let me know when Plaintiff's attorney calls to set a date for the pre-hearing conference."

"Sure thing, Judge. You have some time next week we can look at."

Gwen watched Judy leave her chambers. On reflection, it had been a busy time since she was sworn in, finished Judge 'Uni', and began the court circuit routine, sitting in different counties in the state every few months. After starting, she'd quickly hired Judy to fill in as her most important aide until Judy was ready to move on in her personal life. On Friday afternoons when court was closed, Gwen continued to visit with her mother whose disease continued to progress, despite all the love Gwen could give. Gwen still felt pain that her mom wasn't able to be there at her swearing in ceremony.

But Artie flew out – on a plane he actually owned and piloted. She was proud they'd reconnected again and both now committed to making this family bond continue. Most of her fellow Middleton lawyers also attended her big day, as had Senator Starlight and, she was astounded, Josiah Day and Bradford Foster, and Anna who was in line to make Junior Partner.

Yet, despite all the attention she'd had, she was finding herself feeling lonelier. As a judge who must operate with care to maintain the appearance of neutrality, she didn't feel comfortable chatting with lawyer friends, nor conferring about cases with former colleagues. This meant that her time shooting the breeze with John no longer happened. At least for now. Still, most days were so busy she barely made it to bed before finding herself in nod land.

Gwen's gaze shifted to the black robe hanging on the umbrella stand, the only piece of furniture, new or used, that she'd taken from her old office – which she'd recently learned had been rented to a podiatrist, that is, a woman podiatrist. Now the old office, she thought, was moving up in stature as it had two medical professionals, this new doctor along with her friend, Lola, the massage therapist.

Gwen was surprised that she still felt awe when checking out the hanging black symbol of the law's power; she found it difficult remembering that this was her gown to wear, at least for the present. Thankfully, unlike her prom gown, it was nice and loose and comfortable, and getting more comfortable with time.

Yup, Gwen decided, maybe she'd been too quick to dismiss the Rule of Law as an historical force. After all, looking back over time, powerful documents, whether on stone like the Hammurabi Code, paper like England's Magna Carta or the Pilgrim's Mayflower Compact, or the stories and directives told by mouth and then written down in the Bible, these had helped humans live together and their societies prosper. As she looked at the state's statute books filling two shelves in her bookcase, Gwen felt privileged she could now be part of implementing these governing rules to promote social good.

Picking up her red editing pen, Gwen sighed contentedly, and then went back to work.

****** **** ******

"Hear ye, hear ye, hear ye! All persons having any business before the Honorable Justices of the Plymouth Consumer Court, draw near. Give your attendance and you shall be heard. God save the State of New Hampshire. Live Free or Die."

At this cue, Gwen walked in, attired in her black robe – which covered up jeans and a warm sweater to fight December's chill. Quickly taking her seat at the Judge's raised bench, she leaned down and asked her clerk, Bobby, what the next case was on the docket. While she missed Judy, she'd hired as her new Law Clerk someone who lived closer to the Plymouth courthouse, Bobby Barry, a law school grad, former history teacher, father of two, and Latino who gave her the gift of Spanish should she need it.

Bobby handed up a pile of papers and whispered, "A suit by a woman, a senior, against an appliance company she claims hasn't refunded her money and she says they do this to all the old people."

Gwen sat back, waiting for the attorneys and or parties to move forward to the tables inside the gated area. The past few months had been unsettling, exciting, scary, and challenging. After an initial stint in Superior Court, as hinted by Charlie, the state legislature had approved earlier than expected in its term a new consumer specialty court – a trial court on a trial basis. The Chief Justice, upon learning that Gwen had handled consumer cases in private practice, and with Charlie's recommendation, promptly assigned her to be this court's first judge, even though she was still a rookie. Gwen saw it as an exciting opportunity, and quickly informed the Chief, "Thank you, Robert. It will be my pleasure to serve."

The new court sat in Plymouth, a college town just below the

Notch and so about halfway between Middleton and Concord. As Plymouth was a tad too far to commute, Gwen had sold her beloved ranch house with its wonderful vistas for a small once-upon-a-time working farm a few miles out of town with plenty of space for Molly to explore. She'd moved her mother to a nearby nursing home, and quickly settled into her challenging job, starting a court from scratch.

Life had moved on, as it tends to do, for her Sammy team as well. Judy was quilting beautiful show stopping creations out of her house – when not continuing her paralegal studies, walking her dogs, or parenting. She'd sent Gwennie a picture of her latest award winner – a quilt that could have fooled you for thinking it was a stained- glass window. Mary also had shifted her world. With Gwen's recommendation, and excellent LSAT scores, she'd applied for and been accepted at an excellent law school in an adjacent state. Every few months, when not studying, Mary drove North up U.S. 93 for periodic reunions with the Wilson team. Gwen was looking forward to her visit over January break when they both would hit the ski mountain nearby. Gwen had finally decided to take ski lessons –- and was now practicing on the bunny run – with all the five-year olds.

Martha had been in touch with Gwen on occasion, and they'd enjoyed a few dinners together, though they now avoided Chinese food – Gwen had decided that fortune cookies were too dangerous. After the Perez case she'd written a well-received article that dealt with securities practice and ethics, and the ongoing obligations of registered representatives and financial advisors when handling clients' accounts. Now a hot business topic, she found herself in demand, making speeches to large brokerage firms who paid her well. She'd even squeezed in a presentation before Congress. All good for the small investor, Gwen thought – as well as for Martha's career.

And Linda. Maybe she'd made the most growth. After the case she'd been made the first female partner in her CPA firm and continued her growth by writing an article that was accepted by a national CPA magazine. It discussed the industry standards for churning and how to improve them, with lots of computations that were indecipherable to Gwen. The article was in demand and Linda was busy speaking at meetings and getting regional prominence on her new area of expertise. Linda promised she'd come by some Saturday when not in tax season and they'd catch up.

Gwen was enjoying her new puppy. Molly was providing Gwen what puppies do best, giving her sloppy greetings and unconditional love. And forever trust. Gwen figured her very active pooch had another eight years or so of puppyhood, so she was set for a while. And next semester Gwen looked forward to teaching as an adjunct at Adam's former law school. She was already preparing her course material.

Life was full, and then some. Yet, at times she found herself thinking back on her days with Adam. The longing would overtake her without warning. She wondered about his new life and whether she'd have fit in. She missed him –– in body and soul. So, despite the fulfillment that life now brought her, she still mourned the past, just a little. She measured it as a low-grade fever that appeared at times, but she realized, now less often.

Maybe, that was because all was not bleak on the social scene. Being the new professional in Plymouth, a college town, she'd been invited to student and faculty events. She'd reached out to community groups to introduce the new court. Some dinner dates and movies had followed, even though there'd been no spark yet. Except, *maybe there had.*

Several weeks ago at a college symposium – on law and the genome –– she had met Benjamin Dracut. He was tenured and taught biology at the college. They'd had several fun dinners together – and she enjoyed his company. Older than her, he'd spent the past four years dealing with his wife's cancer. Her death two years earlier had left him alone with two teen-age boys. He was just finding the courage to interact with the world again, so they were taking their relationship slowly. But Ben was cute, in a distinguished professor sort of way, with a trimmed goatee turning gray, and dark eyebrows that flew off his face, when not partially hidden by his ever-present spectacles. From their limited encounters, Gwen already knew Ben was smart, gentle, had a New York ironic wit, and he focused on her when she talked. He liked animals, enjoyed photography, and relaxed by going fly-fishing. Gwen was thinking of inviting him over to dinner, now that she had unpacked her mother's dishes so she didn't have to use paper plates. She smiled when thinking of him. *Fly-fishing? Maybe he'll take me fly-fishing on the Mad River -- when the river melts, that is. As long as I don't have to actually catch anything living.*

Gwen heard the clerk call the first case and a young woman lawyer stood up and started to explain her client's claim against the store.

CHAPTER FORTY-EIGHT

"Kick, glide, kick glide." Gwen repeated these instructions out loud until she came to a stop at the turn, and decided to take a much- needed breather. Inhaling, she filled her lungs with the cool, crisp, cleanness of country air. Yes, it was a beautiful New England winter day. Magical. Looking up at the deep blue sky, she watched as puffy white clouds floated by, pushed gently ahead by the morning's breeze. She watched as elephants, camels, rhinos — a whole animal parade marched past her viewing stand. The purple of morning's shadows slowly disappeared into the dark woods, replaced by a pale blue blanket awaiting a winter picnic.

Except, instead of reclining on the ground with wine and grapes, she was sliding on it, thanks to the long sticks attached to the front clasp of her funny shaped leather shoes. And, not to forget the two bamboo sticks hanging from her gloved hands, thankfully now firmly planted in the snow to help her retain her vertical position. Behind her she heard Ben approaching. "Kick, glide, kick, glide," he'd been shouting to her to help get her in rhythm. So far, she'd stayed upright in the two narrow grooves and had successfully, albeit at glacial speed, swooshed across a portion of the meadow, kicking forward followed by a brief glide, focus on balance, and then kicking forward again with the opposite leg.

Gwen couldn't remember how many years it had been since she'd gone cross-country skiing. She knew it was more than never, but not much more. When Ben had asked her to join him and his boys on a Saturday morning ski, she'd casually, in fact almost jokingly, said, "Sure, would love to, but that means getting my old skis out of their current 'rest in peace' place, wherever that is."

He'd laughed, thankfully unawares that she was also cringing. Ben advised Gwen that they'd "... want to get on the trails soon, before warmer weather conditions make sloshing along on semi-frozen water not much fun."

Gwen assumed 'soon' was far ahead somehow. Alas, the appointed day had secretly, quietly crept up on her calendar. So here she was, swishing along on the soft white crystals. At least, thankfully according to Ben, she wasn't sloshing on slush.

The day began early when Ben picked her and Molly up in his Volvo. His two teen-age sons and the family's two dogs filled up the back seats and storage area with just enough space left over for Molly. Ben drove to a small farm a mile or so off the main two-lane road that led up to the nearby downhill skiing complex – the scene that captured most all of the skiing crowd. Ben explained to her that the farm served as a cross-country ski center in winter and, with the help of a little mowing, a golf driving range in summer. To make it a four-season venture, the farm owners made maple syrup from their maple trees' sap in the spring, inviting guests to watch the 'sugaring off', and in the Fall, from a truck parked along the highway, they sold bottles of this magical sweet elixir to tourists visiting to see the changing leaves. Very enterprising, Gwen thought. But that was the way of New Hampshire farms, above and below the Notch, as they tried to make a living out of rocky soil.

After parking in the dirt lot – the only car there – all four ventured into the cold and put on their skis, clicking each boot's toe clasp into the ski's metal binders. Gwen had dressed for the occasion in a pair of slightly tight old woolen ski knickers she'd found buried in a clothing box. Still she was pleased she could still zipper them up. Long woolen socks and five layers on top completed her outfit. The plus was the red hat with moving pompom, a reminder of Sammy's winter attire, for warmth and visibility – in case she disappeared when falling into a snow mountain. Ben and his boys were in dungarees, polar jackets, and headbands. Their dogs wore red kerchiefs around their necks. Molly wore her fur. Gwen appreciated that no one made fun of her old-fashioned get up, or Molly's lack of one.

Ben suggested the boys and four-legged creatures ski ahead. That way, he explained, he and Gwen wouldn't be in any rush as she tried out her skis. Gleefully the boys, trailed by the dogs including Molly, raced across the meadows and were soon out of sight in the woods. Gwen was pleased that Molly had joined in, already comfortable with Ben's animals. Slowly, Ben and Gwen traversed back and forth in the flat beginner area. After almost falling a number of times, but for her bamboo sticks, Gwen at last got skiing, moving opposite arms and legs in motion as her skis gripped the parallel horizontal ruts. "Hey, Ben, I think it's coming back." Then she started moving faster. This raised the issue of how to stop. All she could recall were the words 'gravity' and 'butt'. She figured that would have to do when the need arose.

"Hey there, Gwen," Ben yelled from behind, "you look pretty comfortable. Having fun?"

Gwen wasn't prepared yet to turn around so she yelled back, "Starting to come back, but not sure I'm feel...." Gwen's right ski jutted outside the prepared trail, soon to be followed by her behind and poles. Gravity and butt did work, she realized. *Not so bad!* Gwen checked her body parts, those still in the snow and those not. All seemed fine. "Not sure that's exactly the way it's supposed to happen," she yelled.

"Need help?" Ben asked.

Feigning the confidence of an athlete, Gwen responded nonchalantly, "No, should be fine." With effort she managed to align her skis so they both faced forward. Then, joining her two poles together, she leaned forward and pushed against them while she slowly raised her body back into a vertical position. Soon she was back in the groove, kick, glide, kick, and glide.

"Good job, Gwen! Falling's part of the fun. Here, watch me." Ben proceeded to land on his rear end while raising his poles to the sky and letting his skis dangle in the air. Then he too put all appendages in place and rose to his vertical height. Except, unlike Gwen, he was laughing.

"Nicely done, Professor," Gwen said, and she too began to laugh.

They spent the next hour going in large circles around the meadow, sloshing in the ruts, smoothly gliding on the trail at times, and mostly staying upright. The boys, pink cheeks and all, returned from the woods, all three dogs in tow. At Gwen's insistence, Ben joined his sons and the three pooches in skiing one more time around the meadow, all racing to the end. Ben trailed sufficiently behind that his boys pretended to be asleep by the time he finally reached the starting point. But Gwen had noticed how athletically graceful Ben was as he skied around the field. He reminded her of Brian, so graceful on skis, well until one fateful run. And she was pleased that Molly held her own.

After Ben caught his breath, and lightheartedly dealt with his sons' ribbing for being so slow by sharing some snowballs with them, Gwen and gang took off their wood sticks and walked back to the car — which was now accompanied by at least a dozen vehicles. Gwen's legs felt so shaky she wasn't sure she'd make it, but she did. After providing a drink of water in bowls, Ben loaded the dogs up into the back seat and gave them treats. He assured her they'd all soon be snoring. Gwen still could feel her feet tingling and her ankles complaining — a present that lasted the rest of the afternoon. But otherwise, she had energy to burn, and an appetite that required attention.

All four humans traipsed into the log cabin restaurant adjacent to the parking lot, their leather boots leaving a wet trail on the wood floor. The sweet smell of burning hickory and maple wood filled the air. They were led to a wooden table covered in red-checkered vinyl near the fireplace. To Gwen's surprise, the other tables were crowded with 'locals.' The young waitress took their order for pancakes — Gwen ordered the banana and walnut version — and when they arrived the server set out a sampling of the farm's own maple syrup in its various grades – light, amber, dark. Before Gwen knew it her plate was empty and the syrup had managed to walk over and cover her fingers. She handled the problem by just licking them until all was mostly white and smooth, like the snow.

On the ride home, her cheeks a healthy red, she enjoyed talking and laughing and guffawing about everything under the sun with Ben and his kids. The dogs in the meantime, as Ben had predicted, were fast asleep, their soft snoring serving as soothing background noise during the drive home.

Gwen thought about the morning as they covered the miles to her farmhouse. No worries about strange men with binoculars, just casual family time outdoors, sharing time together, the adults watching that all were safe, and allowing each the freedom to do their own thing at their pace, with Ben showing a patience and calmness that Gwen found enviable. He'd pushed her enough to get her going but then supported her fully as she'd stumbled and fallen and gotten up. And he was giving, content to allow her to crawl along even if it meant he wasn't swooshing along at his pace. Maybe some competition between father and sons, but all good, especially as Dad was pleased to be third over the finish line. Nice time, Gwen thought, super boys, and their dad, well he seemed pretty special too. As to the dogs, well Molly had given her approval, glad for a chance to not be alpha perhaps. Next time, though – and she hoped there'd be a next time – she'd buy her pup a red kerchief so she'd feel part of the pack.

CHAPTER FORTY-NINE

Who would have thunk she'd be back to school at her age.

Thanks to a surprise April storm, Gwen squeezed her car into a cleared space between the snowbanks sculpted overnight by the plows. She pulled her large litigator bag out from the back seat, the very bag she'd used at Sammy's hearing, and wheeled it down the walking paths across the yard to the brick three-story building. Before entering she took a moment to savor the quiet serenity that had settled over the sprawling law school campus as the school day came to a close. In the fading light she could still see the blue and purple lupines planted on the snow by the setting sun's long rays. Soon, for a magical moment, noctilucent light would paint the clouds pink, orange and crimson. But then the Earth would swirl on its axis and as the sun descended behind the horizon the glowing sky would turn gray, then dark as night took its hold.

Although still early in the semester, Gwen knew she loved teaching: the sharing of information; the discourse with students; the challenge each case presented to define legal boundaries; and watching her students learn the skill of thinking logically. Each class to her was a treasure hunt where she and her students followed judicial reasoning in the assigned cases, leading them to the pirate's chest and its rule of law.

After checking her mailbox in the faculty lounge, Gwen walked down the empty corridor and was the first to enter her classroom. She was greeted by stark white walls, a long row of windows, chairs arranged around a large conference table, and a large green blackboard covering the wall behind her seat. After writing with chalk key parts of her lesson outline and case citations, Gwen sat back in her chair to review her notes. Surreptitiously she watched her students trickle in, greeting each other gregariously as they took their seats. Already Gwen felt motherly towards them. While maybe not a prestigious law school, she'd found her students smart with common sense. Many had overcome challenges she wasn't sure she'd have done just to be at the school: mothers squeezing in a career between parenting demands; first in the family to pursue post- college; older students seeking a way to improve their career prospects. Some juggled a regular job with school. Sitting in their dungarees, suits, nurses' uniforms, they exuded grit and perseverance. And hope. All reminiscent, she thought, of the students that had comprised Sammy's discovery 'associates.'

When the minute hand touched twelve, Gwen rose and began the lesson. "Should goldfish have different legal rights depending on the context in which they are presented? For example, whether a goldfish is a charity fair's prize, swimming in a plastic bag; or it is part of a museum's art display swimming in a blender; or it is someone's pet swimming in a glass bowl. Should the context determine how humans can – or should – legally treat them? Where is the line between ownership rights and illegal cruel and abusive action? And what is the governing law on which you base your opinion? Please open your casebooks to page 132."

Gwen called on a young woman still wearing her waitress work uniform to begin the discussion. "Charlotte, I think you were assigned the 1956 Knox case. Please start us off by summarizing the facts set out in the court's decision and the legal issue presented to the court."

For the next half hour the students discussed the meaning of the phrase "live animal" as used in a one-hundred-year-old state statute and whether and when it covers goldfish. Gwen walked around the room, asking a series of hypothetical questions using different fact scenarios to help define the legal principle. "So, if a museum visitor could turn on the blender and kill the goldfish, the display showing human 'control over life and death', is this art — or cruelty, and is the goldfish a 'live animal' protected by the statute? What if there was a cute white mouse with a pink nose in the blender? A cat in a really big blender? A dog in a microwave?"

While the class eagerly offered their views, Gwen noticed the door to the classroom open and a likely new student enter. He took a seat at the far end of the circle from her. Gwen was puzzled, briefly wondering if she'd missed the Dean's notice of an 'add' to her class list. But she focused on her lesson, moving the class on to the next set of cases.

At a pause in the discussion, the visitor stood up and, in a deep male voice that caused Gwen to stop, frozen in place, softly said, "I'm sorry to interrupt, Professor Wilson, but I've just joined the second-year class and signed up for your course. Is it all right if I sit in today even though I haven't yet read the material?"

Remaining frozen, Gwen's body somehow continued to pump air into her lungs and blood into her heart. Despite his added ten pounds, slightly graying black hair, designer glasses, and beginning beard, she knew this student – how could she not? Adam smiled now like a Cheshire cat, his grin curling upwards, showing not only lovely white teeth but also a mischievous twinkle in his eyes. Casually, sitting with his legs spread out and arms resting on the table, he looked confident and relaxed. Almost as if they were sitting together on lounge chairs under the Caribbean sun, chatting away about dinner plans while holding frozen coladas with straws -– and with no worries on the horizon. Even without her glasses she recognized his adorable dimples, the slight creases around his eyes, the way he tilted his head when he was happy and excited.

The class became quiet. All her students' eyes were focused on her. Gwen tried to speak, but the noise she made, even to her, sounded more like a high-pitched croak from a pond frog. She grabbed her water bottle under her desk and took a swig, clearing her throat. Finally, she said, "Adam, correct? It is Adam?"

He nodded, laughing a little as if she'd read out loud a funny quip. "Yes. Adam, Adam Revere."

The other students looked on, oblivious to the meaning of the question. Gwen paused. After playing with the clicker on her pen and cracking a few knuckles under the table, she said with more control, "Welcome Adam." She added, after another pause, "Of course we're pleased to have you join us. Would you see me in my office after class?" As he nodded, Gwen added, "And I have an extra copy of our casebook so you can follow along with our discussion." Gwen handed the book – colored blue not red --to the student on her left and asked her to pass it back towards Adam. "Mr. Revere, we're up to p. 159." Shaking her shoulders, more of a sort of shimmy to break her body's rigid tension, Gwen turned the pages in her casebook and moved on to the next decision – a case that addressed competing ownership rights in a lost dog.

After the two-hour class, Gwen as usual felt weak and fatigued – but also exhilarated. Teaching this one class she'd found was physically and intellectually exhausting. She assumed that was the reason the dean's office put out an unending supply of sugary chocolate candy next to the faculty mailboxes. Wheeling her books, she walked up the stairs to her office. She was aware, in fact all senses were on maximum alert, that Adam trailed behind. He sat down, silent, in the extra chair in her office and waited. After changing into her boots, bundling up in her coat, picking up a stack of papers the office secretary had copied for Gwen's next class, Gwen turned off the lights. Then she turned and suggested to Adam that they stop for a coffee.

Reaching out to wheel her bag, he offered, "You're the Professor, Gwennie, so whatever you want. I'm ready to follow you to the stars and beyond if you like." This was offered with another one of his ear-to-ear grins.

As Gwen slid into her car and pulled out, Adam walked over to his silver sporty Lexus and followed her to the 'Circle Diner Two' in downtown Plymouth. A reconditioned old railroad car, this local landmark sat on old train tracks once used for shipping woolen goods. But the car was now squeezed between two stores, one selling 'Plymouth Huskies' athletic gear, and the other anything that dealt with music.

When the waitress came to their booth, both ordered coffee,

decaf for Gwen. Adam, his eyes open wide, ordered a slice of homemade "decadent" chocolate cake, 'to share' he proposed. They sat silently looking at the other customers, and then as the tension rose, each turned and focused on the other. Gwen, who'd thought she'd never see him again, was wondering if perhaps this were a dream, or maybe, depending on their conversation, a bad dream. What she did know was that her life had changed lots since Adam had ventured elsewhere.

Adam broke the quiet. "My darling Gwen, you look marvelous. I can't take my eyes off of you — you'll see, even when my chocolate cake comes, and you know how much I love chocolate! *Professor* Wilson, is it, or I understand, *Judge* Wilson? Ha, makes me a little nervous, that."

Gwen smiled back at him, as if from habit. To her amazement, she even started to relax, the tension in her airways and aorta having lessened. *I'm just having another bite out with Adam, Gwennie.*

Playing with her empty bag of fake sweetener, she stayed on safe ground, her work. "Come on, Adam, don't be silly. My friends are under threat of torture if they call me Judge, or any variation thereof. Although, now, um... Professor does have a nice resonance to it."

"Gwen, if you like I can say Professor Gwen..." "Sorry, just kidding. We've never been formal with each other, not the time to try, I think."

"Yes, I agree," he whispered, tears forming in his eyes — a fact that Gwen decided made them warmer and inviting, and, yes, sexy. But then again, her body felt hot and tingly already.

The coffees and cake came. Adam poured milk into her cup, "You like it light, right?" He put four creamers in his. Locking eyes with hers he said, "I know it's a surprise to see me. For me too, I mean, that I'm actually here and with you. Although I've wished it so often."

"Is this just a visit then?"

"No, Gwennie, this is a *stay*. It's a 'put your roots down' stay. All the time I was away I couldn't stop thinking about us. But I was, well... I didn't see how I could make it happen for a while. I promised you I wouldn't come back until I was sure it was safe and things were settled."

She waited.

Adam began to play with the table's accoutrements, first the ketchup bottle, then he sashayed the salt and pepper shakers back and forth. "I worked at resolving my issues. The whole thing was just all tangled with various parties involved, each one controlling part, well, chunks of me. Lots of miscues, misdirection, miserable days. And in the process, babe, I discovered something special about me. I want nothing more than to settle down, you know, have a normal life. Be an adult with responsibilities and a future that would give life some meaning, satisfaction. Above all, I've come to know that I want *you*, my darling Gwennie, as my life partner; you make me a nicer person, one I like better. I think we fit together well, like puzzle pieces." Adam moved his hands closer to hers and then gently ran a finger across her closed lips. "Then surprisingly I realized it was time to, you know, to think about adding to my team – to our team – maybe kids, dogs, turtles."

"No snakes."

"Yeah, no snakes."

Gwen listened. *What am I feeling? Has there been too much in the way to still care – time and distance, unanswered questions, trust issues?* "I hear you, Adam. I am so sorry; it sounds like it's all been hard." Gwen reflexively grabbed one of his hands. It was hard, strong, nice and familiar. A warmth rose up from her chest to her neck, then her cheeks, then it hit the part of her brain that controlled emotions. *Is sympathy for his situation drowning out my anger and hurt? Am I suffering simply from empathy weakness?* But, Adam, we have both crossed bridges since you disappeared on me. Do we want to retrace where we were? Is that possible? I do know that I need more than just the simple tale you've told me. I need the truth, I need to be able to feel trust, fill up our trust bank account again. Sorry, but as you can see there's lots of 'me' in my message. As there was 'I' in yours. Can we get to 'we'?"

"Damn it," Adam paused. Taking out a tissue from his pants pocket, he blew his nose. "I ask for mercy, Professor. Let me try to get this out. I've been able to cap the bottle so no more need for deception or hiding or inability to commit. No more false life. That's no way for either of us to live. I want to be the guy who takes life seriously, not the guy who treats it like a game, a crap shoot, and who messed up bad." Adam stirred the remaining coffee in his cup. "Finally, I've come to grips with what is important – to me, and I think to us. You know how that can happen?"

Gwen nodded.

"I think we're a lot alike, Gwen. You know, I want to live near nature; I've come to love New England's mountains, the changing shape of life each season. Like you. No more gallivanting around the world on larks."

"Nice to see you love this area of the country, Adam." Gwen laughed. "Hey, but don't forget the bitter cold nights, the unexpected snowstorms, and the mud."

"No, that's not it. I'm not talking about a geography lesson. Sorry I didn't say this right. First off, I want to do all this with *you*. Gwennie, what I love most is you. I want that other part, sure, but even more I want to share it with you. Like we did."

Gwen sat quietly, not sure what she was feeling. Here was the scene she had run in her head for so many months coming to life. Had some phantom turned on the movie reel? "But what about the danger? Can you come back?"

"I'm really confident I'll be left alone." Adam sat silent for minutes, rubbing his eyes and wringing his hands.

Gwen waited again.

"I know it is time for me to come clean, Gwen, to build that trust you were talking about. I know there are lots of unanswered questions you likely have, some stories I've told you in the past that weren't all exactly the truth. I'm ready to make amends and start a clean slate."

"That's at least a start, Adam. Now tell me more."

"Okay. Much of what I said was true, some of it was borrowed from friends, and maybe, okay, action movies. And some was what I'd hoped was the case to make you accept me more. At least when we first met."

Gwen sighed. "I'm not sure I understand."

"Please be patient, this is so hard for me, but I know it needs to happen. To start with, I did make lots of money as a young man, the computer company and all. And I did lose my way after that, gambling, drinking, a foolish kid partying with the rich. I did tell you the truth about Kila, okay maybe several versions, but the essence of it was true. She did die in that bicycle accident. I did have a fall off the cliff, got into trouble finally in Vegas where I gambled away most of my fortune, and then couldn't pay off my losses. Not smart, but then again, at the time I was addicted to self-destruction.

So, tried to work out a deal with the corporation that owned my debt, the dark side of Vegas, the side you shouldn't be messing with. I finally was able to take out a loan thanks to a friend with a lender; he'd helped me with my funds when I had my business and then hit the jackpot. I was able to pay off most of what I owed – and I thought the company had forgiven the difference as part of the deal. Turns out I was mistaken. Who'd think I'd need that in writing.... Anyhow, I believed there was no longer any danger, physical that is. I'd gotten an assurance of that, but somehow the message hadn't reached all those enforcers in the hinterland, including the pizza guy whose 'family' buddy had seen my picture in that damn newspaper. Really, a confluence of bad luck for me. Anyhow, the gunslinger just wanted what he thought was an open bounty – which as I said I'd been told had been cancelled. And anyways, I'd been assured the word out was only to pressure me, not to, you know, shoot me. See, once you're in trouble with these guys, no certainties you're safe. Why I found myself always looking over my shoulder, despite the deal."

"Like in the movies," Gwen said.

"Yup, the bad "B" ones anyhow. As I said, to do this, pay off the remainder owed, I got help from my friend's bank, which was my former business bank. But the deal included another provision, one that would get me off the hook of paying back some of what I now owed them. Something to do with taxes and the full loan not being disclosed on the books.

This is where it gets tough to explain. Turns out my new friendly bank that paid off my debt is owned by a big international investment firm that also has some kind of relationship with Stanley, Howe. The deal was that instead of putting up assets to secure the loan, I would do some work for them. Seemed reasonable, an opportunity even. Way to get out from under immediately. All the pressures, see, were crashing in on me, and so I said yes."

"Adam, what a sad tale. But I'm not sure I understand where you're going?"

"Gwennie, how can I say this? I'm so ashamed, you see, and I didn't know then what I learned later...."

Gwen began to be alarmed. "Adam, just say it."

"Gotcha. Yes. Say it directly. To your face. But it is pretty complicated, and not sure I actually know all the pieces, just relying on what I heard from others and maybe some surmise. As I said, the lender's parent company also is affiliated with Stanley, Howe. Whose executives, I think you knew some of the names, were becoming, or so they claim, concerned about the PIP program's trial results – which showed a trail of bad trading results. I was told the program was intended to be a way for the firm to engage in trading services in communities of brown and black people, you know, to diversify their customer base more, but that it had gotten out of hand. The execs were worried as a result of the trial run and its unexpected losses; there might be regulatory or legislative repercussions, especially as there was a trail of not very well written communications. Well, we know that for sure.

And that's when Sammy's small case came to their attention. Seems that Stanley, Howe's executives were confident they'd win in arbitration and the case would be forgotten, thanks to all being confidential. They decided that was a better option than a settlement as they believed Sammy to be a bad apple, you were a small-town lawyer, and they figured you'd never find out about the PIP program anyhow. As you know Stanley, Howe had private investigators do background checks on you and Sammy, sort of I understand typical tactics for these big firms. Well, they asked me to see if I could be part of that pre-trial prep, to ingratiate myself and figure out what you were doing with the case, and generally keep the Stanley, Howe executives apprised of the case activity and if there was any reason to worry about PIP. I thought foolishly at the time, no big deal, easy way to free myself. In fact I liked the idea of going to law school at their expense, I thought would give me some structure to my life as I was flailing dealing with all the financial crap. They..."

Gwen sat up and loudly said "What? What are you telling me Adam?" Her face began to turn red as she considered his story.

"I know this is hard to hear, Gwen, it is a devil for me to tell you. But listen to it all, please, babe, don't reject me yet. Promise?"

Gwen nodded, but barely.

"That's how I became involved, it was easy once I helped during that discovery day, just a bit of luck that. Except it did enable me to meet you for which I'll always be grateful. You know the rest." Adam sat without explaining further, as if to get a second wind before sailing the difficult shoals ahead.

Gwen sat there nonplussed, waiting for more.

"Yup, I've been a dunce and a jerk. But you see, that was *before* I knew you, understood Sammy's case. They told me the case was frivolous, brought by an angry man with a gambling problem, they told me he was a gambler who'd traded before with another company and then went after them, and who now was trying to do it again, using his race as a way of bleeding the company for money he'd lost. And I believed them. Until I learned differently when I was helping *you*. That's when I stopped really helping *them*. Instead I pretended to play their game without actually doing so. See, I couldn't fess up to you as they still had me over the barrel, thanks to my contract with them. But they didn't need to know things. Once I was fully on board, I really did my best, Gwennie, to help you and Sammy."

What am I to think? Adam's saying he's been a spy? He's spilled all my legal plans to the securities company from the beginning? He's been a worm who infested my case form the start? And what of us? Was anything real between us? Gwen drummed her fingers on the table, thinking hard about what she'd heard. And whether she should just get up and leave.

"Let me get this straight, Adam, when we did the hot document copy, that was all a fake, the pretending to be nervous and all? Did you let Anna know about the steal?"

Adam, head hung down, blew his nose again. "No, Anna didn't know. As I said, I didn't deal with the law firm. And I was nervous about pulling it off without a hitch. As you know, thankfully I made an extra copy of the document for me, just for protection."

"And the robbery of my house and office, did you do that?"

"Well, not actually. But I did let them know you kept two copies of the document. But I didn't say exactly where, although maybe they didn't need more. You weren't exactly creative in hiding them. I had no idea, babe, that they would hire someone to steal them, believe me."

Gwen was taken aback; she'd thought her apple picture over the coffee pot had been a pretty secure place. She promised to cross off the security field from her list of possible careers. Focusing on Adam, she asked, "And the attack on Sammy?" "Not my doing. My understanding is some PI they hired went overboard

– and has since been fired thanks to Attorney Day. You should know that Day, I've been told, was working to have some compensation paid to Sammy for this before the settlement was reached."

"At least that's good to know. What of the hearing, did you squeal to them then?"

"I pretended to, just generic stuff I thought would be true in any case, nothing specific. When asked for more, I blamed ignorance of the law. Honest Gwen, I was doing everything I could to help you win the case. Gwen, remember this all happened because they misled me, made me think I was helping them win a case where they were in the right. Justice they told me was on their side."

"And in the park, when we saw those two men, and you seemed scared, what was that about? And with Sarah?"

"Unexpected, that's all. By that point my friend with the lender had told me there'd been some mix-up with the Vegas settlement deal. Enough to make me nervous, and he suggested I try to lay low if possible. But let me be clear. My friend said he'd been taking care of the miscommunication and that I should be safe. He told me also that he'd alerted the FBI here to the possibility, and Harvey contacted me and assured me there'd been nothing on their radar to worry them. They believed there was no risk. I would have left if there were any likelihood of danger, for sure. All just lousy communication."

"That's how you know Harvey?" "Yes, he's a good guy."

"Yes."

"Gwen, I won't stay if I there's the slightest risk of harm to you. I swear. All tell me – and after the unintended mess here I've gotten assurances *in person* and in writing sort of from the big guys – that they consider it over and done with. And, well, after the shooting and all, the last thing these Vegas guys want is to get the FBI interested. So I should be safe as ... I guess gold in Fort Knox.

"Good news is that while I was away, babe, I pushed myself to reach out to old friends. I thought I'd lost my tech genius label, thanks to my not very secret problems, and, yeah, past abuses of their good will. But they were kind and forgiving, so I ended up helping them deal with computer matters. Thankfully I still have some tech skills and am a good salesman. Result is, and maybe only good thing out of this, thanks to really lucky timing and my input in closing a big merger, I no longer have financial pressures going forward. In fact, I can use my resources now to build the environmental law office we've dreamed about starting." Adam reached out and placed his palms on the table. "So, Gwennie, I expect you probably need time to digest all this." Counting on his fingers, a little like Gwen did when making a decision, Adam continued, "Please remember: one, you can trust me, I am trustworthy; two, I want to share my life with you; and three, we can do great things together, we make a good team."

Gwen sat and played with her knife – trying to absorb all that he'd said into her brain, but she was having trouble focusing, thanks to the sudden lack of oxygen in the diner. After a pause, she said, "I see, Adam. Lots to digest. About your time away, anyhow. But I'm not hearing much about your time here, living we me. Adam, I need to know more about us. I opened my heart to you. How much was fake and how much real? Tell me the truth."

Adam sighed, and pressed his lips together. "You are right to ask that. And maybe, when we first spent time together, until I learned what utter rubbish I'd been sold about Sammy and you and the case, I was working on being, you know, flirting with you, trying to get close as part of my job. But that changed for sure once I got to know you. One thing I know is true Gwen, at least for me. We were real. Honest. On Kila's memory, I pledge to you that my feelings have been true, genuine, something to build trust on. These are not just words, they live, my wonderful Gwennie, in my heart."

Gwen shifted in her seat and contemplated the ceiling with its stained tiles. *Am I a fool to believe him? Or is this what loves about, trust, to accept his word, no matter how wild and fantastic?* "Adam, I don't know what to say. I've missed you, oh my God, every day. But Adam, you certainly sensed that, you knew that when you left. Then you left me lingering, no word, no note, no...."

"Gwen, I didn't think I had to right to connect until I was a free man, so to speak. I did what I could with the Sammy document, sending it to you, and I also sent it to Sarah, that crazy journalist, with some conditions of course."

Gwen nodded, then turned away. "How do I put this? To me you were gone — and I believed never coming back. I've worked hard to move my life forward. *Without you.* I have a new job, new house, new puppy, new responsibilities. You can't just pop in and out of my life at your convenience."

"Yes, I love that about you. You are an independent strong woman with your own demands and needs that I must respect. But inside, my dearest Gwennie, where it counts," here Adam pounded hard on his heart, "in your innermost heart, where *your* soul shines, aren't we the same people as before? Didn't we find a special connection, a completeness that makes each of us better? I think we are good together, fantastic together!" Adam paused. Then, rubbing his hands, he spoke very quietly, "But I can't speak for you."

Gwen stayed silent.

"Am I wrong?" Adam asked, his voice rising up the music scale.

Pushing her hair behind her ears and then aligning the saltshaker with the pepper shaker, Gwen looked into Adam's eyes and said, "Please, let's go more slowly, all right? This has just been a shock for me."

"If that will make you happy, of course it is all right with me. Can I see you for dinner tomorrow night? Or is that too soon?"

Gwen smiled, to her surprise. "Friday night is okay. I have a commitment tomorrow." *Molly and I have plans to watch a movie and share popcorn with Ben and his boys. Should I tell Adam this?*

"Great. Super." Adam continued, "I want you to understand, and I mean this from my core, I am *here*, I will make a life for myself *here*. I will finish school and maybe set up my own business or practice law, or do what I think I always wanted to do, work on behalf of the environment. Here. I want you to be a part of that life. To share that life with me. I can be patient if you want. I will wait until you are ready or if you ask, until the moon turns blue. So, Professor, I will email you tomorrow about Friday dinner, is that good?"

"Yes. Adam. Yes."

Adam got up, put a $20 bill on the table, blew her a kiss, and then walked out of the restaurant. He hadn't even touched his chocolate cake. She watched him until the outside door had closed shut.

Gwen sat, rubbing her cheeks, combing her hair with her fingers, trying to resist pulling on her knuckles again. She sipped her cool coffee. *What am I feeling? A lot of "I" focus in that speech. But then again, Adam has a life plan which is good, a plan he says he wants to share with me.* Yet, the thought kept popping up, *Gwennie, what is it that you want? What will make you happy?* She knew she was finding she liked Ben more and more, but they'd just started to know each other, and Ben was still recovering from his loss. And she'd loved Adam, maybe still did. But he came with history, some wonderful, some not so much. Gwen did know as she sat there in the diner, with a ferocity that caused her hands to form two tight fists, that her answer to Adam's question would be on her terms and in her time.

During the next few weeks her busy life proceeded at its fast pace both professionally and socially. While she felt alone at times, she also felt fulfilled inside and generally happy. Adam did as she had asked, and went slowly and Ben continued to reach out and get closer. In addition to her judging demands, she spent time with her friends and continued being involved in the community and seeing her mom. Regularly she spoke with Artie and enjoyed their newly found closeness.

And then one morning as she prepared to make her 'judge entrance', she received a phone call on her private line.

"Hello, Judge Wilson here." "Morning Judge, this is Brad Foster of Stearns, Foster. I was wondering if this might be a good time to talk, trying to catch you before court begins."

"Hello, Brad. Nice to hear your voice." Gwen tried to catch her breath as she shifted gears and speculated why this call out of the blue. Was there some lingering issue in Sammy's case she didn't know about? Or maybe he wants to invite me to speak at some bar dinner about the new consumer court? Gwen quickly told Brad she had a few minutes to spare and how could she help him.

"Well, Judge..."

"Gwen, please, I save the formalities for court time."

"Sure, Gwen. you'll find it welcome. My firm has been considering beefing up our securities department, in particular, to expand it to address more *investor* litigation claims so we represent both sides of the equation. As you know, in the Perez matter our client elected to farm out the trial part of the case to another firm, partly we were advised, because they thought we were a little thin in that area. With more and more clients needing legal advice and support in this field, we've committed to adding a full partner position, one who would focus primarily at the moment on representing investors, including small investors.

"To get to the point, not surprisingly your name came up during our discussions, both based on your and my experience together and opinions of other parties practicing in this specialty. So this is an exploratory phone call to see if you might have any interest in joining us. I'm sure we can work out details as to compensation, benefits, and such. But I want to assure you that this is an important senior level partner position and that you will essentially be building your staff once on board. And if things go well down the road, we'll be offering an equity interest. Gwen, also, to let you know, we are committed to bringing in more diversity at our firm and excited at the prospect of having our first female partner."

Gwen sat stunned. Was she being offered a partnership with Stearns, Foster, one with potential for an equity interest? This was a major coup in any New Hampshire lawyer's career. It would bring her not only enough money to buy her dreamed of house on the lake, and yes take a luxury vacation in the sun, but the prestige to influence the development of the law in this area. And help many more Sammy's. She'd be leaving much of the grudge lawyering – depositions, document production, billing, to her firm's associates, the 'Anna's'.

"Gwen, are you still there? I can call back later if you prefer."

"No, Brad, sorry. This is just so unexpected. But as you know I have a somewhat newly found passion for this field of the law. I find it both exciting and challenging, and it may be rapidly developing. At the same time, I am quite content at the moment with establishing this new consumer court and making it a success."

"Yes, Gwen, and the word amongst the brethren at the bar is that you are doing a commendable job in Plymouth. And we would, of course, work out timing to limit any negative effect on 'your' court. Don't want to influence you any, but on the QT, I've been told via intimations from the political powers that be, in particular one State Senator who apparently has been bowled over by you, that there will be an opening in two years on the Appeals Court for a new Justice and that they'll be looking to add a woman lawyer who has both Plaintiff and Defendant business *and* consumer experience. Especially someone who can relate to the legal issues North of the Notch. He further implied that a position as a partner with one of the state's large firms would be an excellent credential for any appointee, gives the candidate some extra gravitas. Of course, I can't promise anything but such an appointment would be strongly supported by my partners."

"Yes, I see. Oh, sorry, Brad just looked at my watch and I need to go. Brad, sounds like a marvelous career opportunity but I'll need some time to consider it properly."

"Of course, Gwen. Not urgent, but we do want to act reasonably soon. Once again, please know that you have my strong support in all this. I look forward to speaking again in maybe a week or two? Perhaps we can invite you down and you can meet some of my partners, get to know our firm, a sense of our commitment to the legal profession. Maybe even arrange a round of golf at my club, if you play. Please give me a call on my private line when you think you're ready to move forward with this discussion and if you'd like to attend such a meeting."

"Great, speak with you in a few weeks. Have a great day."

And with that Gwen hung up as her clerk knocked on the door and entered. "Judge, we're about to begin."

Gwen thought about this one more unexpected possible shift in her career, her life. She'd found a happy place here in Plymouth. She would be fine if the music stopped here. She loved helping to bring closure – and fair resolutions – to the cases before her. And she loved teaching students who cared more about their future as 'officers of the court' than the grade on their papers. Yet, for sure, she knew there'd come a time when her 'honeymoon' with her trial court life would start to fade. Even brief conversations with other judges warned her that all was not perfect for practitioners on the bench. Still, she didn't need perfect. At the same time, she could feel the excitement of being a partner at a large Concord firm. But she was aware that such a job also meant more of the exhaustion and long hours she'd encountered with her own little firm. Would she be able to control some balance in her life?

Gwen knew that she'd changed as a lawyer. No longer was she the young advocate willing to take on the world to bring about justice, the idealistic caretaker of the Rule of Law. The woman lawyer who'd fought for fairness, even when no financial reward was assured. Had she had too many years experiencing financial pressure, gender bias, difficulties with overburdened courts, the list went on... to do that anymore? Gwen thought the answer was yes, that what she wanted now was to find a better balance in life, a happier place that offered rewards for her talent and also time for her. Maybe she wasn't that better person anymore; instead she was ready to pass on the do-gooder banner to the crop of new lawyers she was helping to train. *Gwennie, is there shame in this change? Defeat? Wisdom? Or is it like knowing when you're skiing too fast and it's time to slow down – being smart.* Whatever her decision, she'd make it with eyes open, and ten fingers ready to count the pros and cons.

Putting on her robe, she smiled as she thought of getting home tonight and giving Molly a cuddle and squeezing in a quick walk together before wine and bedtime. Tomorrow she'd see Ben, and Adam had kindly offered to go with her to visit her mother on Friday. Maybe on Sunday, after catching up on writing her case decisions, she'd make time to assess the appeal of a partnership at an esteemed law firm.

She did know that, for now, life is good. *Carpe Diem.*

www.ingramcontent.com/pod-product-compliance
Lightning Source LLC
Chambersburg PA
CBHW071918150726
47999CB00001B/20